D0030268

Praise for #1 *New York Times* bestselling author

LISA JACKSON

"Bestselling Jackson cranks up the suspense to almost unbearable heights in her latest tautly written thriller."
—*Booklist* on *Malice*

"When it comes to providing gritty and sexy stories, Ms. Jackson certainly knows how to deliver."
—*RT Book Reviews* on *Unspoken*

"Provocative prose, an irresistible plot and finely crafted characters make up Jackson's latest contemporary sizzler."
—*Publishers Weekly* on *Wishes*

"Lisa Jackson takes my breath away."
—#1 *New York Times* bestselling author Linda Lael Miller

LISA JACKSON

SUSPICIONS

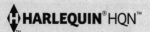HARLEQUIN® HQN™

Recycling programs
for this product may
not exist in your area.

ISBN-13: 978-0-373-77805-8

SUSPICIONS

Copyright © 2013 by Harlequin Books S.A.

The publisher acknowledges the copyright holder of the individual works as follows:

A TWIST OF FATE
Copyright © 1983 by Lisa Jackson

TEARS OF PRIDE
Copyright © 1984 by Lisa Jackson

This edition published by arrangement with Harlequin Books S.A.

For questions and comments about the quality of this book, please contact us at CustomerService@Harlequin.com.

Printed in U.S.A.

CONTENTS

Book One:
A TWIST OF FATE

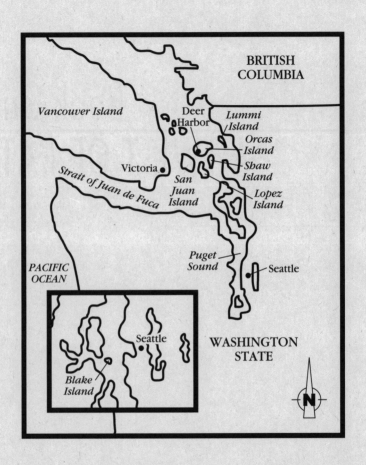

Chapter 1

The telephone receiver was slammed back into its cradle with such force that the paperweight sitting next to the phone slipped off the desk. Two framed pictures of a round-eyed, blond-haired girl rattled and then dropped onto the corner of the desk. The tall man who had slammed the telephone so violently righted the portraits with care, clasped his hands behind his back and resumed his pacing. *Would it ever be possible to communicate with Krista again,* he wondered. His shoulders were slightly slumped, and there was a pained darkness just beneath the anger in his eyes. He swore an oath, aimed for the most part at himself, and continued pacing in front of the wide plate-glass window.

For a moment he paused to look out the window and try and control his rage. A fading California sun was dispersing the final rays of daylight inland as it settled peacefully into the tranquil Pacific Ocean. Long lavender shadows had begun to deepen against the white sand of the beach, and the first cool hint of autumn hung crisply on the air. Kane closed his eyes tightly, as if to shut out the serene view. Turbulent emotions stormed through his body. He kept telling himself that he couldn't change the past, that he couldn't blame a dead woman for his daughter's condition, and yet he did.

A solid rap on the door interrupted his black thoughts, and automatically Kane called out a terse acknowledgment. A moment later Jim Haney marched through the door carrying an ungainly sheaf of papers and a long manila envelope. Jim's tired face held a genuine smile, although he also noted the severe lines of stress that contorted Kane's body. Kane's normally impeccable wool suit was wrinkled and his expensive silk tie askew. Harsh creases webbed from the corners of Kane's deep-set gray eyes and there was a cold, hard determination in the set of his jaw. It wasn't hard for Jim to surmise the reason for Kane's obvious annoyance. Jim knew Kane well enough to recognize that Kane was angry and concerned over his eleven-year-old daughter. The guilt that Kane bore silently was beginning to show. Kane needed to think about something else—anything else—and Jim hoped that he had found the solution to Kane's studious disinterest in anything other than the near-fatal accident that had left his daughter disabled.

Jim's smile remained intact as he met Kane's annoyed gaze. "I guess this about wraps it up," Jim announced, fanning the air with a smooth sheaf of computer printouts. Kane's cool eyes followed the green and white pages with only feeble interest while Jim continued. "The Seattle sale—it's final—and all of the loose ends are tied up…except for one."

"So quickly?" Kane asked skeptically as he settled into the worn leather chair behind his desk and began scanning the printout.

"For once it looks like we may have gotten lucky."

"Good!" There was a note of finality to Kane's words. He looked up at Jim with a grim smile. "Then there's really no reason for me to wait, is there?"

Jim coughed nervously before meeting Kane's unwavering gray stare. "Are you sure that you're making the right decision?"

Involuntarily a muscle in Kane's jaw tightened. "Let's just say that I'm making the only decision possible."

"But to just pack up and leave all of this…" Jim's voice trailed off as he waved expansively. The gesture encompassed the entire gray concrete office building of Consolidated Finances, the understated but costly furnishings and the calm ocean view.

Kane's eyes swept the office, noting the leather furniture, the thick plush carpet, the book-lined cherrywood walls, and then fell back on his friend. "Think of it as a prolonged leave of absence, if you like."

"Then you will be back?" Jim asked guardedly.

"When I have to be," Kane agreed, with an expression of distaste. "No doubt the board of directors will insist that I come back and oversee the operation from time to time." Kane returned his attention to the computer sheets before him. Quickly shuffling through the smooth, flat pages, he located the report that he sought. A dark furrow etched its way across his forehead as he reread the printout. "Still losing money in the legal department?" he asked, almost to himself. "I thought that we had cleared up that embezzling scam last week and had gotten rid of Cameron—or whatever his name was. Didn't we?" He turned his sharp eyes on Jim.

"That's the one loose end that's still dangling. It looks as if Cameron has an accomplice."

"*What?*"

"I had a hunch from the beginning that someone was working with him, but I couldn't prove it until I made sure that Cameron was out of commission. I'm not sure who the culprit is—haven't been able to dig up any tangible proof—but

I've narrowed it down to a few possibilities." Jim handed Kane the manila envelope. "Here's some personnel information on some of the suspects."

Kane reached for the envelope. "Well, whoever he is, he must be a damned fool! You would think that with all of the hubbub about Cameron, anyone else involved would be busy covering his tracks rather than taking any further risks. This guy must get his kicks by flirting with danger."

"It may not be a man," Jim suggested.

Kane cocked an interested black eyebrow. "A woman?" A satisfied, almost wicked smile crept over his lips.

"Like I said before, I'm not sure, but it looks as if Cameron has always been…fond of the ladies. He's had a reputation for promoting women."

"Whether they're qualified or not?"

Jim shrugged. He didn't like the glint of inquisitive interest that had stolen over Kane's features. "I haven't had Cameron arrested as yet, but he's being watched. Hopefully his colleague will surface soon."

"So you're telling me that Cameron is still on the payroll and that although you're sure he hasn't taken any more funds, someone near to him has." Kane Webster was beginning to show his anger.

Jim squirmed only slightly as he went on to explain. "That's about the size of it. We're watching Cameron round the clock, night and day. We know that he hasn't pocketed the funds himself, because we've kept him tied up with auditors and the like ever since it became apparent that he was embezzling trust funds. So far he hasn't become suspicious."

Kane wasn't convinced. "And his *friend?*"

"Somehow she's still manipulating the accounts and taking money." Jim shook his head and grimaced. "I haven't been able to trace it to her as yet. She's very clever."

Kane sat thoughtfully in his chair and pulled out the personnel files that Jim had handed him. He didn't doubt Jim's assumption that Cameron had a woman accomplice. He'd worked with Jim too many years not to respect the younger man's opinion. Jim's suspicions had always paid off in the end for Consolidated Finances.

The names on the personnel reports meant nothing to Kane, and at first glance, all of the files seemed to hold nothing out of the ordinary. "You're sure that the thief is one of these people?"

Jim nodded his head in affirmation. "No one else has the authority to move bank funds so freely."

"But couldn't someone else forge a superior's order?"

"I thought about that too. I had it checked out, but the auditing system of the bank is too complete. No, our misguided embezzler is sitting right there in that envelope. All we have to do is figure out who she is."

Kane puzzled over Jim's recent discoveries in what had appeared to be a sleepy little Seattle bank. His eyes narrowed as he thought about the trap that he would set for Cameron and his accomplice. The fact that it was a woman interested Kane. He had learned several years ago that women could be a devious lot, and it only reinforced his bitter opinion of the opposite sex to learn of the female embezzler.

Jim Haney watched the play of emotions that traversed Kane's dark features. He had worked with Kane for over ten years and had come to know his boss as well as anyone. Kane was a fair employer, but Jim knew from past experience that Kane could be ruthless if crossed. Right now, as Kane's lips thinned, Jim was thankful that his name wasn't Mitchell Cameron. And he couldn't help but feel pity for the unfortunate woman who had gotten tangled up with Cameron. Jim had his own opinion about the accomplice's identity, and he had met the woman. It was damned hard to believe that such an intelligent, sophisticated woman would be involved with the likes of Cameron. Oh, well—that was Kane's problem. "Did you want me to have the police go to work on Cameron?" he asked.

"No." Kane shook his head, still immersed in his thoughts. "I'll see to it personally. I'm leaving for Seattle tonight." A satisfied grin moved over Kane's features.

"You're really going to enjoy throwing the book at Cameron, aren't you?"

"And the woman! I don't like any thief—especially when she's got her hands in my pockets!" Kane retorted. "This just gives me one more reason to head north as soon as possible."

"That's something I don't understand at all," Jim admitted. "Why you bought that miserable excuse of a bank—it's been losing money for years—just so you can freeze your tail off in Seattle."

"California lost its sparkle for me quite a while ago," Kane muttered tersely, then softened his tone as he caught the wounded look in Jim's eyes. "You know of course about Krista. The doctor thinks a change of climate would be good for her. As soon as I have a permanent residence, I'll send for her."

A personal question died on Jim's lips as he noticed the sober tone of Kane's final words. He hadn't gotten to be vice president of Consolidated Finances by asking questions that were none of his business. He'd heard the rumors associated with Kane: a glamorous ex-wife, a sticky divorce and an unfortunate accident. But Jim had never pried. He was too interested in self-preservation to open doors that Kane preferred locked.

Kane pushed the manila envelope into his briefcase along with a small portrait of his daughter. He paused for a minute and looked at the eager young face before tucking the picture into a side pocket in the leather case. That accomplished, he snapped the briefcase closed.

"The moving company will take care of the rest of this litter," Kane observed, looking around his office for one last time. "If you need to get in touch with me, Carla has the number of my hotel in Seattle."

"Good luck," Jim said, clasping Kane's hand warmly.

"Let's hope I don't have to rely on luck!" With a smile that didn't reach his eyes, Kane walked out of his office for the last time.

The early-model Volkswagen Rabbit skidded to an abrupt halt, splashing dirty rainwater from the street up onto the sidewalk. The driver of the little yellow car was a slim, striking woman who pulled the emergency brake, slung her purse over her shoulder and slammed the car door shut without taking the time to lock it. She hastened through the damp September evening toward the cozy Irish bar.

There was a determined and slightly mysterious gleam in her large eyes as she hiked her raincoat up and clutched the collar tightly to her throat. Sidestepping a puddle of water as if it were second nature, she pushed her way through the stained-glass door of the restaurant.

The familiar interior was dark, but Erin's eyes became quickly accustomed to the dim lighting and the air thick with cigarette smoke. Loud, tinny music was coming from a rather bedraggled-looking band reminiscent of the late fifties.

Unconsciously Erin wiped away a few drops of rain that still lingered on her cheeks, while she moved her gaze over the Friday night throng of customers that was heralding the beginning of what promised to be another rainy Seattle weekend.

Appreciative glances and admiring smiles followed her movements, but she ignored everyone other than the distinguished man of about fifty sitting before the polished bottles and the mirrored backdrop of the bar. Erin's eyes met his in the reflection, and for a moment a dark, guarded look crossed over his distracted blue eyes. Finally he smiled tightly and motioned for her to take the vacant stool at his side.

"Mitch," Erin sighed almost gratefully. "What on earth are you doing here?"

He hesitated, and in that instant, any warmth in his eyes faded. "How did you know where to find me?"

"Olivia Parsons thought you might be here," Erin replied. Her smile disappeared at the thought of the leggy brunette.

"Oh, I see. Dear old Livvie," Mitch mumbled sarcastically. "Your friend and mine! Here's to friendship." He waved his glass theatrically in the air and signaled to the bartender for another drink. "What can I get you, Erin?"

"Nothing," Erin whispered, trying to keep the conversation as quiet as possible and yet be heard over the din of the band.

"Nothing?" he echoed, mimicking her. "Not going to join me for old times' sake?"

"What are you talking about and why are you here?" she asked, confused by his cynical attitude. Where was the kind man with the soft voice and the dry sense of humor whom she had known for over eight years? Mitch didn't bother to answer her questions. He seemed intent on evading the issue, but she persisted. "Mitch, what are you doing here?"

"What does it look like?"

"It looks suspiciously like you're getting smashed," she replied honestly.

"Very astute, young lady. I always did say that you were a smart girl, Erin." Mitch drained his old drink and reached for the new one. "Are you sure you won't join me? The Scotch is excellent!" Erin shook her head, but Mitch accosted the bartender. "Bring the lady a glass of Chablis," he commanded over Erin's protests.

Erin was having trouble hiding her annoyance with her boss

and his unpredictable mood swings, but she kept her temper in check and tried a more subtle approach with him. "Why did you leave the bank early today?" A glass of chilled white wine appeared on the bar before her.

"You haven't heard?"

"Heard what?" Erin asked uneasily. There was a menacing quality about Mitch that she wasn't accustomed to and didn't like.

Mitch shrugged and Erin noticed that his shoulders drooped. "Why don't you ask Kane Webster, if you're so interested."

"Webster? The new president of the bank? What does he have to do with the fact that you left the office and your clients in order to promote a hangover?" she inquired. Mitch had changed dramatically in the last several months. His behavior had become erratic, almost secretive, and his work had suffered. However, until today Erin had never had to cover for him with a client or track him down in some bar. Erin counted Mitch as one of the few close friends she had in the world, and it pained her to witness his deterioration.

She couldn't forget that Mitch had helped her through an agonizing period in her life by offering her a challenging job and a chance to bury herself in her work. He had encouraged her to do postgraduate work in law and keep busy in order to forget about Lee and the embarrassment and heartache she had suffered while she was married to him. Mitch had helped Erin realize that when Lee had left her eight years before, it hadn't been the end of the world. When she had needed a friend, Mitchell Cameron had been there. And now, if Mitch had a problem, Erin vowed to return the favor.

"Mrs. Anderson was in today," Erin stated, and took the glass of wine from the bar. "She was very disappointed that you weren't able to meet with her yourself. Somehow she didn't really think that I was a suitable replacement for the head of the legal department, and I can't say that I blame her. I certainly wasn't very knowledgeable about her grandfather's will or the estate…"

"That's her problem," Mitch stated blandly and again focused his attention on the bottom of his glass.

"It's not Mrs. Anderson's problem," Erin corrected.

"Well, it certainly isn't mine!"

"But the bank…"

"To hell with the bank," Mitch spat out and slammed his glass on the polished counter. Several of the patrons close by turned interested eyes on Erin and Mitch. Erin felt herself shrink. The last thing she wanted to do was cause a scene.

"I don't understand what's gotten into you lately," Erin began in a low whisper. "And I don't know what Kane Webster has to do with you coming down here to drown your sorrows, but if there's anything I can do—or if there's something you want to talk about…"

"I don't want to talk about anything! You're the one who came looking for me," he reminded her crossly. "I didn't invite you!"

"I was worried about you."

"Well, don't worry over me. I can take care of myself!" Mitch's voice was bitter.

"Mitch, what in the world is going on?" she asked. Erin was stung by his acrid words, but compassion held back the sharp retort that had entered her mind as she watched Mitch order another drink. It was apparent that something was eating him, and because of the kindness he had shown her in the past, she held her tongue. She reached for his sleeve and in a quieter voice asked, "Won't you please tell me what's wrong?"

"Wrong?" The word ricocheted back at her followed by Mitch's mirthless laugh. "What could possibly be wrong?" His blue eyes glittered like ice. "Unless, of course, you think that being fired from a bank that you've given twenty years of your life to is a problem."

The meaning of his words struck her like an arctic blast. "Fired? Webster fired you? But why?"

"Like I said, ask him—if you've still got a job. Who knows, you could be next!"

"But he hasn't even come up from California yet."

"Oh, he's here all right, and mark my words, all of the employees at First Puget—oh, excuse me—Consolidated First Bank better be ready!" he pointed out sarcastically.

Erin sat for a moment in numbed silence. The thought of Mitch being fired was absurd, ludicrous. Mitch had been prominent in building the legal department of First Puget to one of the most prestigious in the city. It was true that for the first time in over a decade the legal department had lost money, but certainly the new president wouldn't hold Mitch solely responsible, would he? Nothing made any sense to her anymore. Mitch caught the look of confusion and pity in her eyes. His attitude softened momentarily.

"Look, Erin. Don't waste your sympathy on me. And it's really not a good idea for you to be seen with me. Believe me, it would be in your best interests to just leave me alone."

"You look like you could use a friend," Erin suggested.

"What I need now is a good attorney, not a friend."

"But you are an attorney," Erin replied, still completely perplexed.

Mitch looked her squarely in the eyes. "I'm a lawyer, yes, but I specialize in civil law. What I need now is a criminal lawyer."

"I don't understand…."

"You don't have to," Mitch answered abruptly and stood up. "I told you before, I don't need your sympathy or any of your self-righteous friendship!" He turned his back on Erin, fumbled in his pocket for a moment and threw a wad of crumpled bills onto the bar. "See ya around," he called over his shoulder, but Erin didn't think he directed his words at her.

"Mitch...wait," she began, but his long uneven strides carried him out of the door and into the night. As she watched him leave she was still recovering from the shock of his dismissal. Why would he have been fired? It was hard to believe that she wouldn't see him on Monday morning, sitting behind his large oak desk, puffing on a slim cigar and perusing the *Wall Street Journal*.

"Looks like you've been stranded," a smooth male voice suggested intimately. "How about a drink with me?"

Erin turned in the direction of the voice and murmured a firm "No, thanks" to the young man with the clipped mustache. He shrugged his shoulders at her denial, as if it was her loss, and manipulated his attention to a lanky blonde sitting near the dance floor.

Erin made her way back to the car. The drizzle had turned into a downpour and the late afternoon sky had blackened. The drive home was automatic, and as the windshield wipers slapped the rain off the glass, Erin thought about Mitch and what it would be like without his presence in the bank.

She had suspected for several months that Mitch was in the throes of some personal problem. At least it had appeared that way. He had seemed tired and worried—no, more than that—tense, tightly coiled. The closer the final date for the imminent bank sale had drawn, the more tightly wound Mitch had become. Erin had told herself at the time that it was only her imagination, that all of the employees of First Puget were bound to be a little anxious about the new management. But now, as she drove through the dark, slick side streets, she chided herself for not seeing and acknowledging what had been so transparent: Mitchell Cameron was in deep trouble.

Its exact nature she couldn't guess, but it was serious enough to have cost him his job.

Without thinking, she killed the motor of the car as she pulled up in front of the Victorian apartment house. Closing her eyes and rotating her head, Erin tried to relieve the tension in her neck and shoulders. She wondered about Kane Webster. What kind of a man was he? What did she really know about the man, other than the few neatly typed memos with the bold signature that had crossed her desk?

She hadn't heard much about his personal life. Apparently he preferred his privacy. Occasionally Erin had seen his name in print—in the financial pages. If she had read anything about him in the social pages, it usually had to do with his ex-wife, a gorgeous model who had made an unsuccessful attempt at becoming an actress. But that was several years ago, before an accident that had killed Jana and left the daughter crippled, or so it was rumored.

Erin frowned to herself as she thought about her new employer. One thing was certain: Kane Webster had made his fortune on his own, spending the last decade purchasing failing financial institutions and transforming them from operating in the red to operating in the black. He had gained a reputation in financial circles for being something of a rogue because of his unorthodox methods of operation. But if results were the measure of success, Kane Webster was prosperous. It was as if King Midas had reached out and touched the ailing banks himself.

Wearily Erin got out of the car and locked the door. She started up the short shrub-lined walk to her home and smiled at the elegant old house. It was a lovely Victorian manor, perched on a hill overlooking the city. The front porch was comfortable and trimmed in ornate gingerbread. The turn-of-the-century home had been fashioned into apartments twenty years before, and the contractor had taken care to accentuate the nineteenth-century charm of the house. Erin had fallen in love with it the first time she had laid eyes on it. Ignoring opposing arguments from just about everyone she knew, she had used her small inheritance as a down payment and purchased the building two years ago. Or to be more precise, she and First Puget Bank had purchased it; there was still a sizeable mortgage against it.

Even in the drizzle of early twilight the old manor looked warm and inviting. The white three-story building with its gently sloping roof and deep gables had a picturesque aura that was distinctly "Old Seattle." Upon close inspection it was obvious that the house was in sad need of many repairs, but tonight Erin overlooked the chipped paint and the rusty drainpipes. She had applied for an employee loan with the bank to make the needed improvements, but she knew as well as anyone that her loan would be a very low priority to Kane Webster. With a bank that was already losing money, how could he possibly make any low-interest employee loans?

Erin's own apartment, located on the uppermost floor of the stately house, was an attic converted into a cozy loft with a bird's-eye view of the city. She climbed the stairs slowly, sifting through the various pieces of junk mail and complaints from her tenants. Her mind was only half on the stack of mail in her hands, when she heard the telephone ringing. Racing up the final steps, she hurriedly unlocked the door, threw the mail on the table and grabbed the phone.

"Hello?" she inquired, breathless from her dash up the stairs.

"Erin, honey, it's good to hear your voice. Where have you been? I've been calling for hours," a friendly male voice said.

"Lee?" Erin asked hesitantly.

A good-natured laugh bellowed from the other end. "Hi! How've you been?"

"Fine, Lee," she managed, wondering why he persisted in calling her. After the last call two weeks ago, she thought he understood that she didn't want to see him again.

"What do you say we get together? You know, have a couple of drinks and a few laughs. I'll come by and pick you up in a half hour," he suggested.

Erin was tempted. There had always been something seductive about Lee, not in the sexual sense, but in the fact that he was such an outgoing, likable kind of guy. The same qualities that made him great fun at a party made him an immature husband. Erin could almost picture Lee's college-boy good looks—thick blond hair with just the right amount of wave and laughing blue eyes.

"I don't think so," she replied, trying to take a firm stand with him and failing.

"Why not? Don't tell me you've got other plans?"

"No…" Erin responded, and wondered why she hadn't lied and just gotten rid of him. After all these years and all of the heartache, why couldn't she just slam the receiver down and end the conversation?

"Then, let's have a night on the town…"

"I can't, Lee. I'm sorry. I've got a pile of work to catch up on before Monday."

"But it's the weekend," he coaxed in a honeyed voice. "You know what they say, 'All work and no play makes Erin a dull girl.'"

Lee chuckled, but something in his words brought Erin crashing back to reality. Suddenly she remembered just how little she had in common with a boy who refused to grow up. She recalled the shame and humiliation she had suffered while playing the role of dutiful wife.

"No, Lee. That's not what *they* say at all. That's what you said eight years ago."

"Hey, baby, that's all water under the bridge. Come on, what would a drink hurt?"

Erin sighed audibly. "Look, Lee, I'm not in the mood. Not tonight—not ever. I thought I made that clear to you a couple of weeks ago."

There was a pause in the conversation and Erin could almost hear the wheels turning in Lee's mind.

"Just what is it that you want from me?" she asked.

"I told you—we could have a few laughs."

"Why not just turn on the television and catch reruns of *Gilligan's Island*," she suggested and immediately regretted the sarcasm in her words. Nervously she began tapping her fingernails on the tabletop.

"I have to see you," he pleaded.

"Why? It didn't matter eight years ago. Why the sudden interest?" Erin's voice had begun to shake. Memories began to wash over her.

"You really want to do this the hard way, don't you?" Lee accused.

"I don't even know what you're talking about," Erin sputtered, but an uneasy feeling was growing in the pit of her stomach. This wasn't just a friendly call. He wanted money from her—again. Suddenly Erin felt a deep pang of pity for the man who was once her husband.

"Look, honey," Lee cajoled with only a trace of uncertainty in his voice. "You know I lost the job in Spokane, and well, since I've been back here, my luck hasn't been all that great. I thought that…you could loan me a few bucks, just until I get back on my feet."

Erin swallowed hard before answering. "You haven't paid me back from the last time that I helped you 'get back on your feet.'" Erin's voice was flat. She hoped she sounded unshakable.

"Things just didn't turn out in Spokane. You know how it

is, what with the lousy economy and all. It's just hard to get started."

"Oh, Lee," Erin sighed, and felt herself wavering.

He sensed the change in her voice. "I just need a few hundred to get started…"

"Spare me the sad story, Lee," Erin interrupted. "I can't loan you any money right now. I just don't have it."

"Don't have it—or won't lend it?" Lee asked desperately.

"I'm sorry, Lee."

"I doubt it!"

"I don't think that you and I have anything more to discuss. You were the one who made that decision several years ago. Good night."

Erin hung up and noticed that her hands were trembling. Why did he always affect her this way? It was as if she was reliving those last few months before the divorce had become final all over again. Why didn't Lee just disappear from her life completely? Was it her fault? Did he notice her hesitation and somehow construe it as an invitation? While they were married, he had wanted his freedom so desperately. And yet, since the divorce had become final, he kept showing up, trying to rekindle the dead flames. When he finally moved to Spokane, Erin had breathed a sigh of relief. She thought that finally he would make a life away from her.

That was why she had made the mistake of loaning him fifteen hundred dollars, hoping that he would establish himself in Spokane. But his plans had backfired, and he was back in Seattle. It hadn't lasted six months.

Erin shook off her raincoat and started taking the pins from her hair. She couldn't worry about Lee right now. She had too many other pressing problems, the first of which was to get up early in the morning and straighten out the mess that Mitch had made of the Anderson will. That meant that she would have to go back to the bank on a Saturday, but she saw no other solution. With the new boss in town, it wouldn't do to have him walk in on Monday morning and face an angry beneficiary.

Erin shook her hair down to her shoulders and made her way to the bathroom for a long hot bath. It had been a tiring and disturbing day.

Chapter 2

In the silent city, the stark marble building knifed upward through the early morning fog. Workmen were already removing the old lettering to announce formally that First Puget Bank had become one more cog in the banking machine known as Consolidated Finances. Erin felt a surge of sadness as the final gold letter was lifted off its marble support. It was disheartening to realize that an institution with eighty-year-old roots on the banks of Puget Sound could be so easily transformed into a new, slick piece of financial machinery. Erin couldn't help but feel that some of the personality of the bank would be lost in the transition. Quietly she let herself into the building with her own key and waved to the security guard near the door.

The large foyer of the bank was conspicuously quiet without the usual din of customers, tellers and ringing telephones. It was an eerie, tomblike feeling, and usually gave Erin a feeling of peaceful tranquillity, but today she felt somber.

The elevator was waiting for her, and with a vibrating groan, it whirred into motion and lifted her to the twenty-third floor and the maze of offices that comprised the legal department. She walked in the glow of the security lights, not bothering to turn on the bright iridescence of the outer office fixtures. As she passed Mitch's office she lingered for a moment, experiencing a stab of regret and bitterness. Why couldn't things have worked out better for him? Why did Webster let him go? She wondered about the circumstances surrounding his departure. Was Kane Webster really on a witch hunt of sorts, or was there more to the story? She touched the brass doorknob but released it quickly. What good would it do to go snooping in Mitch's office—it would only stir up unwelcome feelings. The best idea would be to do her work and leave the building before depression really did settle on her shoulders.

Erin's office was dark, but she clicked on the brass desk lamp rather than the overhead fluorescent fixture. The lamp bathed the desk area in a gentle warm glow and gave the room a more intimate and less businesslike atmosphere. She adjusted her reading glasses and pulled out Mitch's dog-eared copy of the Anderson will. As she began to read the verbose and tangled document, Erin became totally consumed by her work. She pulled out several large volumes and unconsciously began humming to the airy notes of the piped-in music. Within minutes she settled herself comfortably on the carpeted floor of her office and became oblivious to anything other than the interesting terms of the document.

Kane stepped out of the cab and handed the driver a healthy tip. He stood for a moment on the curb and squinted up at the tall building he had purchased. With stern satisfaction he watched while the new sign for Consolidated Finances was put into place. He couldn't help but wonder if, as Jim had suggested, he had made a mistake in purchasing this particular bank. It had lost money for nearly two years through terrible mismanagement and was teetering on the brink of bankruptcy. It would take a great deal of finesse on his part to avoid the collapse of the entire organization. Perhaps he had been rash in his decision to acquire the bank. In his eagerness to get away from a glittery lifestyle in California, and in hopes of favorably relocating his daughter, it was possible that he had been too hasty in his decision.

It was too late to start second-guessing himself at this point. With a determined grimace he let himself into the newest in a series of West Coast branches of Consolidated Finances.

As the elevator took him upward he reflected on the position of the bank. Certainly it was salvageable. The first order of business was to plug the embezzling leak. Kane smiled to himself. Nothing would give him greater satisfaction than to deal with the woman who was attempting to steal money from the account holders of the bank. He'd already dealt with Cameron, just yesterday, and fired the bastard. Unfortunately Cameron hadn't given Kane any clues as to the identity of his accomplice. Kane had underestimated the man. He had expected Cameron to crumble into a thousand pieces and give him any information he required in return for immunity from prosecution. But Cameron was made of sturdier stuff, it seemed.

Cameron's attitude had reinforced Jim's opinion—the accomplice had to be a woman, someone Cameron cared enough about to try and protect. Kane hoped that there might be a clue in Mitch's office, just one tiny shred of evidence as to the identity of the woman.

The steel doors opened and Kane stepped into the dimly lit reception area of the legal department. As he was about to snap on the lights, he paused. Was it his imagination or was someone actually humming? His eyes swept the reception area and the adjoining offices until he saw the golden glow of a desk lamp illuminating a partially opened door. The humming continued, a soft womanly quality in its melodic tones. Kane's mind speculated about the woman. Who would be here alone on a Saturday, early in the morning, when the bank was closed? Security personnel? A custodian? Unlikely.

Kane smiled almost evilly to himself and left the hallway in darkness. Maybe for once he had gotten lucky. It was about time for his luck to change. Perhaps the job of finding Cameron's accomplice was going to be much easier than he had first supposed. Stealthily he strode onward toward the beckoning doorway. His jaw tightened and he cautioned himself to be wary. It would be easy for a thief to cover her tracks if she was smart enough to realize that he could be suspicious of her. He would have to tread lightly. Silently he made his way to the door, unprepared for the scene that met his eyes.

A small woman with thick black hair brushed loosely over her shoulders was sitting on the floor of the office. She sat cross-legged with her back to the door, and she was pouring over an enormous pile of open-faced legal documents and books. The office itself was an incredible tangle of notes, books and loose papers. The object of his inspection wasn't what he had imagined. Wearing tight-fitting jeans and a bulky violet sweater that hid none of her soft curves, she was so absorbed in her work that she didn't hear his entrance. A pair of reading glasses perched tentatively on the end of an upturned nose and a pencil caught behind one ear kept her hair from falling in her face. Absently, to herself, she continued humming. To Kane she appeared more like a college student preparing for final exams than a businesswoman, and she hardly looked the type who stole. There was a tranquil but nevertheless faintly disturbing beauty about the young woman.

Kane's reflexes hardened. No matter who this woman was, he had to force himself to keep his objectivity about her. Right now she had unwittingly assumed position number one on the list of embezzling suspects, and Kane couldn't forget that fact. No matter how innocent or vulnerable she seemed, she was most likely to be the snag in the legal department. It didn't matter that the elegant curve of her jaw conformed to her regal bearing, or that her obsidian hair shimmered with streaks of indigo…. Before he let his thoughts wander any further, he caught himself. The last thing he could afford at this point was to feel any interest in her whatsoever.

He coughed to get her attention, and immediately she swung her startled head in his direction. Her eyes met his, and just for a moment he felt as if he was slipping into their lilac depths. Even over the top of her reading glasses, he could see that there was a tremor of fear in those luminous eyes, and involuntarily he wanted to reach out and comfort her. But he forced himself to remain standing, unwavering.

Erin had been completely oblivious to anything other than her work, but a soft cough interrupted her thoughts. She whirled to face the intruding noise, half expecting to see a familiar face.

"Mitch?" she called from habit.

The man standing in the doorway was a stranger and a ripple of alarm broke over her. Her surprise was revealed by the barely concealed gasp. Whoever the tall man was, he had evidently been standing in the doorway for several minutes. He had been right over her, silently appraising her. The thought of his eyes traveling unrestricted over her made her uneasy, tense.

"Were you expecting someone?" he asked.

"Yes…no…you surprised me."

He cocked an eyebrow and leaned against the doorjamb, still watching her intently. He was a tall man, and even in his casual clothes Erin could tell that he was well-proportioned and lean. Strong, broad shoulders supported the expensive weave of his open sport coat. As he stood somewhat insolently, his supple legs strained against the light weight of his tan corduroy slacks. His hair was thick, burnished auburn, laced with traces of gold that gleamed in the warm light of the room. His face was tanned and angular to the point of being harsh, and his gray eyes held hers in a severe gaze that spoke of power and hinted at arrogance. For a moment neither spoke, and Erin felt the spark of electricity in the air.

"May I help you?" Erin inquired in her most coolly professional voice. She guessed at the identity of the intruder and tried to present a calm and efficient demeanor to her new superior. It wasn't an easy task, considering the fact that she was sitting cross-legged in a semicircle of legal documents. She rose as gracefully as possible, without letting her eyes waver from the calculating face of the man who just last night had fired Mitch.

"You're Miss O'Toole?" he continued his inquiry, not answering her question, and only breaking the power of his gaze by a glance at the carved nameplate on her desk.

"That's correct," she agreed, for some reason unable to smile. "I assume you're…Mr. Webster?"

"Kane," he suggested. His silvery eyes drove more deeply into hers and she could feel that he was watching her response, almost anticipating her reaction. "You were expecting me?"

"No, of course not."

"Then…you were waiting for Mitchell Cameron?"

"I told you before, no."

"Then what exactly are you doing here?"

She paused for a moment. It had to be evident that she was busy with legal work, didn't it? Perhaps it was the way that he asked the question that made her feel a need for caution. "I was working."

"I can see that," he scoffed, and for a minute a smile threatened to creep over his face. "But I guess my question should be more specific. Why are you working—" his eyes scanned the office "—seemingly alone, on a Saturday?"

"I am alone!" Was he relieved? "And the reason that I'm here is that there has been a tremendous increase in my work-load with the conversion to Consolidated," she replied, but he didn't seem to be listening. To her consternation he came into the room and casually hooked one leg over the desk corner, as if to remind her that he owned the place—literally.

She felt a need to back away from him—to put a little space between his body and hers, but she ignored the temptation. Intuitively she knew that she couldn't show him the least sign of vulnerability or weakness. The harshness in his attitude and his tight-lipped questions made her stiffen and become increasingly wary.

"I see," he mused as if he really didn't. He tented his hands under his chin in a thoughtful and, in Erin's opinion, overly dramatic pose. "Then you're saying that you're overworked?"

"No…"

"No?" He smiled broadly, but the grin didn't light the cold depths of his eyes. "Then you must be inefficient," he suggested.

"I beg your pardon!" Erin blurted, the color draining from her face. What was he doing to her with all of these insane questions and inaccurate accusations?

"Well, it has to be one or the other, doesn't it?"

"Of course not!" she rifled back at him, and suddenly felt as if she had just swallowed a well-placed morsel of bait. He was toying with her for some reason, and it frightened her. To hide her nervousness she began stacking the legal volumes back on the shelf and tidying the scattered papers. She started to arrange her desk in brisk, sure movements, all the while aware that his eyes touched her face, her hands, her neck, her breasts.…

She pulled her attention back to him. "I explained that I had a little extra work to finish up. For some reason, that apparently irritates you. I had no intention of offending you so…."

"You haven't offended me." His voice was softer.

"Then what is it with you? I'm just trying to do a decent job, for your bank, I might add, and you march in here unannounced and start an interrogation!"

"Have I been interrogating you?" he asked gently, and reached for her wrist.

"You still are!" she retorted as his hand captured hers. His fingers were a warm, soothing manacle and her pulse began to heat with his touch. Her eyes flew to her wrist, to his eyes, to his fingers and back to his eyes. Then, as abruptly as he had reached for her, he let the hand drop. The intimate gesture had startled Erin, but the release was a disappointment. Unconsciously she drew away from him. He was too commanding, too powerful, and her response to him was too violent.

"I'm sorry," he apologized, and his dark brows drew together. "I didn't mean to make our first meeting an inquisition. I didn't expect to find anyone here today."

"Neither did I," she breathed. "And that's precisely why I came in—to work without interruption—from the telephone or…anything else." Her breathing was still uneven; the man made her nervous. She tried to control herself and avoid overreacting.

"Do you come in after hours often, Miss O'Toole?" Another question!

"Only when I feel it's necessary!" she responded cuttingly, and then feeling immediately contrite, added, "Please call me Erin. Everyone else does."

"Fair enough. I like to keep things on a personal level."

Erin's black eyebrows shot skyward with his last remark, but she decided it would be wiser not to comment. She had only to remember his grip on her wrist and the storm of emotions that had seized her with his touch. She didn't understand why she was overreacting to him, but she knew that it would be best to put distance between them.

He rose to leave, and Erin felt the air slowly escape from her lungs. She needed time to collect herself, to be alone. However, before reaching the door he paused.

"What was your relationship with Mitchell Cameron?" he asked.

Erin swallowed hard and met the chill in Kane's eyes. "He was my boss," she replied curtly.

"That's all?" Kane's angular face was tense, his jawline firm.

Erin narrowed her eyes. "No…that isn't all!" she said defiantly, watching his gray eyes grow a shade more calculating.

"Somehow I didn't think so."

"Mitchell Cameron is my friend. That fact won't change, even if you did fire him!"

"So you know about that," he thought aloud. "Did Cameron tell you?"

"That's right."

"Did he explain why?"

"I thought maybe you could answer that one." Now she goaded him.

Kane slammed the door closed, reversed his stride and came back to Erin's desk. He planted his hands firmly on the polished surface and pushed his face to within inches of hers.

"What exactly did he tell you, and when?"

"I don't really know if it's any of your business," she shot back at him. Why was he so angry with her? She didn't understand it, but she felt her temper rise with his.

As quickly as a cat springing, he reached out for her and pulled her face near to his. "Anything about this bank is my business!"

"But Mitch doesn't have anything to do with the bank anymore, does he?" she asked rhetorically. "You took care of that!"

She felt his closeness, the warmth of his hand against her chin, the light pulse in the tip of his fingers, the heat and magnetism that seemed to radiate from him.

"Why don't you tell me about 'your friend,' Mitch," he coaxed, and suddenly the fingers that had been rough became gentle. His thumb persuaded her to relax as it moved sensually along the line of her chin and jaw, stopping just short of her throat.

"There's nothing to tell," she whispered, trying to think coherently and disregard the intimate persuasion of his hand.

His eyes, flooded with passion, cooled. "Just how good friends are you?"

"Good friends—just that," she managed, and seeing the clinical hardness on his face, pushed his hand away, adding, "Nothing more. And I resent the implication."

"Implication?" he mocked.

"That I sleep with him. That is what you were getting at, isn't it?" she asked with a bitterness she couldn't conceal. "Not all successful women sleep their way to the top!"

"I didn't mean to imply..."

"You certainly did! I really don't understand what all of these suggestive questions are about. I came in here to get some work done!" Erin began gathering the loose papers on her desk as she attempted to stem her anger. She knew it wouldn't do anyone any good to let her temper surface, but she couldn't help but feel a deep-seated resentment toward the man who had fired Mitch. She wondered fleetingly about her conflicting reactions to the man—his touch, his words—but she pushed those provocative thoughts aside as she snapped the desk drawer shut, locked it and retrieved her car keys from her purse.

"I'm only trying to find out firsthand how the staff of this bank works," he explained.

"So that you can fire us all?" she rifled back at him.

A twinkle lighted his steel-colored eyes. "Is that what you're so upset over? You're angry because I let Cameron go?"

How could she explain that everything about him upset her, threw her off balance. "It's really none of my business," she admitted, her poise and professionalism back in place.

"If it makes any difference to you, I have no immediate plans for—how shall I phrase it—restructuring the personnel of the bank. At least not until I see firsthand exactly how efficiently each department runs."

"Except in Mitch's case," Erin prodded, still confused.

"Cameron was different, and as you so aptly stated, 'it's none of your business.'"

Kane pressed his hands together and his lips thinned. "Do you make a practice of working here alone?"

He prepared to analyze her response, but it seemed innocent. "Not usually. But as you must realize, Mitch had been wrapped up with your auditors and computer people."

"And you had to assume his duties alone?" Kane guessed.

"Not entirely," Erin conceded. "Olivia took over a few of Mitch's clients..."

"Olivia? Parsons? The executive secretary?"

"She's more than that. Actually an assistant officer," Erin explained, thinking about the sultry woman who had once so openly flaunted her affair with Lee before the divorce was final.

Kane's eyes never left Erin's face. He noticed the embarrassed burn on her cheeks, the furrowed brows and the slight droop of her shoulders. Something was definitely bothering Miss O'Toole, and he meant to find out exactly what it was.

He noticed that she picked up her purse, a gesture that indicated that she intended to leave. She couldn't, not yet.

"If you'll excuse me, Mr....Kane," she requested. She started to walk past him, but his hand reached for her arm.

"You're leaving?"

"That's right," she agreed but remained standing still, conscious only of the warm touch of his hand on her arm.

He grimaced. "I was looking forward to having someone here while I set up my desk."

"But you didn't expect anyone, did you?" she reminded him.

"No, I didn't. But since you're here, you might as well give me a rundown on exactly how this department functions—or at least the way it did in the past."

"Sorry—I've got plans this afternoon," she lied. He was still touching her and the feeling was delicious, warm, inviting. The dimly lit room was beginning to close in on her, and she knew that she had to get away from him and clear her head.

"What about tonight?" he persisted.

"Still busy." She smiled up at him but felt her lips begin to tremble. He eyed her curiously and she wanted to shrink away from him and melt into him all in the same motion. As if he understood her feelings, he pulled her a little more closely and asked his final invitation in a whisper, his breath fanning lightly across her face. "What about tomorrow?"

Her eyes reached for his and she found it impossible to lie. "I...I don't know."

"Come on," he persuaded. "I'm new in town. You can show me the sights."

"I thought you wanted to discuss business...."

"We will."

"I don't date anyone I work with." His eyes touched her forehead, her cheeks, her chin, her throat.

"Don't think of it as a date," he murmured enigmatically. "Consider it…an orientation meeting."

"But…"

"I won't take no for an answer. I'll pick you up at ten."

"No!"

Kane released her. "I'll see you in the morning," he stated as if it were already a fact.

She didn't answer. Couldn't. But she found the strength to tear herself away from the imprisonment of his stare and walk out of the office with as much pride as she could muster. She wasn't thinking clearly; her thoughts were tangled in a web of emotions. Her mind was as ragged as her breathing, and there was an impulse and yearning that she had never experienced in her lifetime.

Once outside the building she hurried to her car and only paused to take in full, mind-clearing breaths of fresh air. Her fingers trembled as she fumbled with her keys. She kept telling herself that her reactions were bordering on insanity. She had met a man, a very attractive and charismatic man, under tense circumstances. The feelings that had flooded through her were merely a release of that tension—that was all.

But the more she tried to convince herself that she was once again in command of her feelings, the more helpless and vulnerable she felt. Not since her marriage to Lee had she let any man come so close to her, and the powerful magnetism and raw energy that she felt when she met Kane frightened her. She couldn't, wouldn't, let her emotions get so out of hand. She had to avoid being alone with him, for she couldn't trust herself around him. In the past she had always scoffed at the kind of chemical attraction that had received so much public acceptance. Now she wasn't so sure.

She started the engine and roared out of the parking lot, all the while mumbling to herself that she was acting irrationally.

★ ★ ★

Kane sat at his desk long after Erin had made her hasty departure. He had waited by the window until he had seen her actually leave the building and drive away. Now that she was safely gone, he lifted the long manila envelope from his briefcase.

The ordinary printouts that had seemed so dull yesterday had taken on a new luster and significance today. The desk chair groaned as he settled into it and pulled out the neatly typed report marked O'TOOLE, ERIN. He reread the information on its pages, slowly turning the facts over in his mind.

One piece of information leaped out at him. It seemed that Miss O'Toole had for a while been Mrs. Lee Sinclair before reassuming her maiden name after her divorce. Kane frowned deeply and inexplicably to himself. Erin had been employed by the bank for over ten years. In the past eight, with the aid of Mitchell Cameron, she had been rapidly promoted until she had reached her present position as second in command of the legal department. Quite an accomplishment for a thirty-two-year-old woman.

Kane rubbed his chin thoughtfully as he continued to study the file on Erin. It seemed that she had purchased a building a couple of years ago—with the help of an employee loan granted, of course, by Cameron. And just recently she had again applied for more funds, to renovate the building.

Several items didn't add up in Kane's mind. Erin seemed forever in need of money, but she had loaned her ex-husband a tidy sum about a year ago. A copy of the canceled check made payable to Lee Sinclair had been included in her file; Jim Haney had done his research well. The fact that she seemed always in debt was a bad sign. Also, for such a young woman, she had been promoted rapidly—too rapidly. Bad sign number two. And, from Cameron's comments on her personnel evaluation reports, Mitchell Cameron had trusted her completely. Bad sign number three.

And what about today? She had called out Mitch's name when Kane had entered her office. Was she expecting him, or had she merely been sent by Cameron to continue his dirty work? She had obviously spoken to Cameron last night; she admitted it herself. Just how deep was she in with Cameron and how much did she know? The suspicious questions rattled around in Kane's head until he scowled to himself and threw the report on the desk.

It was difficult to imagine Erin O'Toole Sinclair as an embezzler. Although the evidence was stacking up against her, he couldn't forget her delicate features and surprisingly innocent eyes.

Thoughtfully he rubbed the weariness from the back of his neck. Somehow the satisfaction that he had expected to feel while tracking Cameron's accomplice was missing. He chided himself and accused himself of being a fool. He was beginning to soften where Erin was concerned, and he couldn't let that happen, especially since she was probably robbing him blind at this very moment.

He slanted another severe glance at the file. The name that seemed to leap from the page at him was Sinclair. His lips drew into a thin, hard line. It was ludicrous, but the piece of information that bothered him the most wasn't the incriminating evidence against Erin, but rather the fact that she had been married at one time. It was infuriating for him to imagine another man making love to the dark-haired woman with the wide eyes and provocatively defiant tilt to her chin, even if it had been years ago. He chuckled to himself humorlessly. What did he expect, anyway? That any woman that attracted him be a virgin?

It was the word that his own mind had used that jarred

him back to reality. He was *attracted* to Erin, and he couldn't allow himself that luxury. He couldn't let her get under his skin, especially if she was indeed what he suspected her to be.

With a disgruntled shove, Kane pushed the file back into the drawer and slammed it shut. Then, after shaking himself mentally, he locked his desk, somehow wishing he could throw away the key.

Chapter 3

It was late afternoon by the time Erin arrived home. She had spent the day window-shopping and walking through the heart of the city, mindlessly watching the crowds of shoppers and breathing the salty air from the sound. She had avoided going home, content to wander among the tourists as she attempted to sort out her confused feelings. She didn't want to deal with anything or anyone until she had set her uneven emotions back in balance. But try as she would, she was unable to push Kane Webster out of her thoughts.

Erin was angry and resentful of the way Kane had so high-handedly dismissed Mitch. She was offended by his insinuations that she had compromised her morals for career advancement by sleeping with Mitch. And, perhaps more than anything else, she was afraid of and uncertain about the feelings that he could stir in her with only a look or a touch of his fingertips. It was as if he were attracting her and repelling her at the same time. What was it about him that caused such warring emotions to battle in her weary mind? Something about him excited her, fascinated her, and she felt as helpless as a moth compelled to an irresistible flame. It was a flame that would surely burn her with a molten passion until she was consumed by heat and fire.

Even the old Victorian apartment house didn't seem as comforting as usual. As Erin was about to mount the stairs to the loft, Mrs. Cavenaugh, oldest of the tenants, opened the door of her apartment and called to Erin before she could escape.

"Erin, honey," Mrs. Cavenaugh cajoled sweetly while leaning heavily on her cane. "It's already getting dreadfully cold in here. I thought you were going to do something about that insulation. The floor is just like ice, and it's starting to bother my arthritis again." The kindly, bespectacled old woman smiled at Erin.

"Yes, Mrs. Cavenaugh, I know," Erin sighed as she paused on the lowest step. "And I promise that I'll get some bids on the insulation this week. There...uh, have been a few changes at the office. I've been pretty busy and I guess I've been neglecting my duties around here. But that's no excuse. I'll take care of it."

Wise, faded blue eyes scanned Erin's face, and Mrs. Cavenaugh shook a slightly crooked finger at the younger woman. "I could tell that something was bothering you from the moment you dragged yourself through the door. It's not that ex-husband of yours again, is it?"

"Oh, no! This has nothing to do with Lee..."

"Humph! Always said that boy would come to no good."

Erin began to protest again, but Mrs. Cavenaugh would have none of it. "You know what you need, don't you? A cup of my chamomile tea. A good strong one." She gave Erin a knowing wink. "You're in luck—I have a pot brewing this very minute." A crafty look came over the wrinkled face, and she turned to lead Erin into her apartment.

"Oh, no, Mrs. Cavenaugh, I couldn't..."

"Nonsense!" Mrs. Cavenaugh sputtered. "Now, you come in here and tell me what's really bothering you!"

Erin stopped protesting to smile and follow the bent figure into her apartment. The poor dear woman wasn't really looking for Erin to complain about the cold floors at all, Erin realized. Mrs. Cavenaugh just wanted some company to brighten the long afternoon and evening. Erin decided the least she could do was enjoy a cup of tea with her elderly tenant, even if it was the foulest concoction ever to be poured from a silver teapot.

As Erin expected, the long, lace-covered coffee table was already set for two. A service of shining silver teapot and fragile porcelain cups adorned the table, and the air was scented with the strong aroma of chamomile.

Erin sat graciously in the floral side chair while, with slightly shaking hands, Mrs. Cavenaugh poured the pale ochre liquid into one of the cups. "Sugar?" she suggested, and without waiting for an answer, dropped two lumps into the light-colored brew.

Erin took the cup and sipped at the tea while Mrs. Cavenaugh settled herself into her favorite worn rocker. "So now, Erin, tell me about your problems at work." Light blue eyes sparkled with interest as Erin briefly sketched out her morning at the bank. Erin glossed over a few of the details, carefully omitting any references to the bevy of emotions that her new boss had aroused in her. But Mrs. Cavenaugh's knowing eyes saw more than Erin had hoped to divulge.

"So this new boss of yours…what's-his-name…" Mrs. Cavenaugh began.

"Mr. Webster." Erin supplied the missing words.

"Yes…what's he like?" Eyes, crinkled at the corners, stared earnestly at Erin over the rim of the tiny cup.

"Oh, I don't know," Erin said with a shrug, hoping that she

appeared aloof. "He's…all business, I suppose. You know, the typical banker type."

"I wonder…" The old woman paused dramatically, but Erin refused to rise to the bait and defend her position. "You say that he let Mitchell Cameron go? Why?"

Erin frowned into her teacup. "I don't know," she replied earnestly. "But I intend to find out!"

Mrs. Cavenaugh's laughter crackled through the apartment. "And I don't doubt that you will." Why did Mrs. Cavenaugh seem so pleased? "Do you expect to corner Mr. Webster at work on Monday and get to the bottom of this?"

"I hadn't really thought about it. He wants me to meet him tomorrow—show him the city, let him know firsthand about the bank. But I don't think it would be a good idea. You know how I feel about my free time…"

"Oh, nonsense!" The sweet, wrinkled woman smiled and waved her hand, dismissing Erin's argument as if it were a bothersome insect. "Yes, I know all about your need for privacy, and I know why. But, Erin, it's been eight long years since that louse of a husband walked out on you, and you can't hide away forever. Why not have some fun with this Mr. Webster? How could it hurt?"

"I have no intention of 'having fun' with Kane!" Erin exclaimed, bristling. Mrs. Cavenaugh's eyes seemed to dance at Erin's familiar use of her employer's first name. "*If* I were to go, it would be strictly as a business meeting!"

"Call it whatever you will, it doesn't matter. But for goodness' sake, honey, *go!*" Mrs. Cavenaugh seemed to sense that Erin was wavering, and she added one final incentive. "How else do you plan to find out about Mitchell Cameron, unless you confront this Webster? I would think that you would prefer to do it while you were alone with the man." She seemed thoughtful for a minute, letting her teacup rest in her hand.

"This isn't the kind of thing that you would want to start a scene over—now, is it? It just wouldn't do to let on to all of the employees. It's too scandalous, don't you think? What would it do to employee morale?"

Erin laughed at the thinly veiled attempts of the kind but conniving old woman to persuade her. "Why is it that I feel manipulated?"

Mrs. Cavenaugh spread her palms upward in a helpless motion, suggesting that she didn't have the faintest idea what Erin was implying, but a devilish twinkle remained in her eyes.

"Look, Mrs. Cavenaugh, I just may go with Kane tomorrow. But don't make anything more of it than what it is—a business meeting. I've seen that look in your eyes before, so don't go playing matchmaker for me," Erin warned with a pleasant smile as she set her empty cup on the table.

Mrs. Cavenaugh chose to ignore Erin's bit of advice. "More?" she asked, holding the teapot in midair over Erin's cup.

"No, thank you. I'm sorry, but I really do have to get upstairs. But you're right," she added, placing her palm on the hardwood planks of the floor, shiny with patina. "I think there's a draft coming from the bay window." She walked over to the window in question and ran her fingers around the sill. The cold air made her frown. "I'll see to it that somehow we warm this place up before winter really sets in." Erin dusted her hands off against her jeans. "Thanks for the tea."

"Don't mention it," the elderly woman responded with a wave of her hand. "You know you're welcome here anytime." She was smiling smugly to herself, seeming quite pleased.

Erin let herself out of the quaint little apartment and headed up the stairs. She glanced at her watch and realized that it was too late in the day to get anyone out to weatherize Mrs. Cavenaugh's apartment this weekend. She jingled the keys in the lock and gave a hefty shove to her own sticky front door. There were so many things that needed to be done to the apartment house and so little time and money to do them with.

With a sigh she took off her jacket and headed for the kitchen. As she made herself a quick sandwich she thought about Mrs. Cavenaugh. She was right, of course. The only logical way that she would find out the circumstances surrounding Mitch's dismissal would be to confront Kane directly, especially since Mitch was so mysterious and cynical about the situation. However misguided Mrs. Cavenaugh's motives were, Erin had to admit that the little old woman made sense. And, no matter what, she couldn't run away from private discussions with her boss forever, could she? Any emotions that had started to entangle her would just have to be straightened out and dealt with in a professional manner.

The pastrami sandwich that she created tasted like mustard-covered cardboard, and after a few nibbles she put it back into the refrigerator. Mrs. Cavenaugh's biting words came into her mind. "It's been eight long years since that louse of a husband walked out on you. You can't go on hiding forever!"

Is that what I'm doing? Erin wondered as she flopped down on the soft cushions on the couch. *Am I hiding? From what—or whom?* Ever since her personal life had been thrown open to the public, and she had become the object of speculative gossip, Erin had vowed to keep her privacy securely guarded. Lee's open affair with Olivia had scarred Erin so badly that even today, eight years afterward, she refused dates with coworkers in an almost paranoid way. With the exception of a few close friends no one at the office had any ideas about her love life.

Some love life! She had to laugh at herself at the thought. Except for a couple of men who had interested her only slightly, she had hardly dated since the divorce. It was easier, and she preferred to keep her feelings under tight rein, thus avoiding any further conjecture about her personal life.

Eight years ago Lee had seen to it that Erin was the topic of conversation in the bank cafeteria. Whether he had intended that she discover his affair with Olivia, Erin couldn't guess. But it hadn't taken long to find out about his clandestine meetings with one of the most seductively beautiful women in the bank. When she had discovered the affair, Erin had crumbled. But Lee had seemed to blossom and feed upon her humiliation. Even during the first confrontation he hadn't been upset or contrite but rather smugly proud. Erin and Lee had separated, and Lee's fascination with Olivia continued to thrive. He was forever throwing the affair in Erin's face as if, somehow, she was to blame for the failure of their marriage. For a while she had tortured herself with the same thoughts.

But as Lee's attraction for uncomfortable confrontations with Erin increased, Erin realized that he drew a malicious satisfaction from taunting her. He saw to it that he and Olivia were everywhere that Erin went. During working hours he would come into the bank and meet Olivia for coffee. At office parties he would escort the sultry Olivia, never missing a chance to display his affection for her with a gentle kiss or a whispered endearment—always within eye- and earshot of his former wife. At the time Erin told herself that it shouldn't bother her, and during the day she kept up a seemingly unconcerned and professional appearance. But at night, after long lonely hours working toward a law degree, she would find herself alone in the bed that she had once shared with Lee and she would cry bitter tears of frustration.

That was years ago, and somehow the pain had lessened. Now, looking back on the past, Erin wondered if she had ever really loved Lee. She had cared about him, yes, and her pride had been severely bruised by his betrayal. But she doubted that she had ever loved him, and certainly not with the passion that she knew he had found with Olivia.

After the liaison with Olivia had cooled, Lee had come back, hoping to rekindle the ashes of their broken marriage. Erin had waited for that day, falsely thinking that she would feel a vengeful satisfaction from slamming the door in his face. But when he had actually arrived on the doorstep, he looked tired and ragged. He was unshaven and had large purple circles under his eyes. His clothes were disheveled, and even his perfect blond hair had seemed to lack its usual luster. It had taken all of her strength to close the door on him in his embarrassed and confused state. She had turned him away, and instead of feeling the grim satisfaction of sweet revenge, she could only feel empty, dry and sad for her ex-husband. After locking the door, she had run into the bathroom and been sick for the rest of the afternoon, retching until her stomach had emptied and her body shook from the ordeal.

Erin stretched out on the couch and shook her head, trying to dislodge those vivid and melancholy memories of the past. She ran her fingers through the thick tangle of her black hair. The long evening stretched ahead of her as she clicked on the television to clear her head. The selection of sitcoms and variety shows was dismal, so she picked up a mystery novel that was guaranteed to interest her and curled up again on the antique sofa. But the spy thriller that should have held her attention, didn't. She found her thoughts traveling backward in time to her marriage only to jump forward again to this afternoon and to Kane Webster. With a disgusted sigh she tossed the book onto the coffee table and stared into the dusk. She let her mind wander at will until late in the night.

The doorbell chimed precisely at ten o'clock the next morning. Erin paused for a moment as her defenses wavered at the thought of facing Kane alone. Impatiently the doorbell sounded again, and she forcibly steeled herself before opening it.

"I thought that just maybe you had run out on me," Kane joked. He seemed affable, yet there was still that underlying hardness about him, a doubt that she had felt yesterday.

"I wouldn't think of it," she quipped back lightly, but felt her stomach tighten as she realized just how many times last night she had thought of avoiding meeting him.

"Good. Now, how about a cup of coffee?" he asked as he walked into the apartment and rubbed the chill out of his hands.

"Are you offering me one, or asking for one?"

Hearing the sarcastic tone of her voice, he cocked his head in her direction. "Are you angry with me already?"

Erin hadn't realized until then that she *was* angry with him for setting her life off balance. "No...of course not. I didn't mean to snap at you," she apologized.

"Then you won't mind if I use your phone?" he inquired. "I promised to call my daughter this morning, but I didn't want to disturb her earlier."

"The phone is in the bedroom," she replied, and smiled at him for the first time that morning.

He excused himself and threw his jacket over the hall tree before he set off in the direction that she had indicated. Not wanting to intrude, she went into the kitchen and began brewing the coffee. The apartment was small, and it was impossible for her not to overhear part of his conversation, although she purposefully turned up the volume of the radio. The last thing she wanted to know about was Kane's personal life. She had to try to keep things on a business level with him. Unfortunately even the classical music couldn't drown out Kane's voice as it rose in volume and unsuppressed anger.

"Krista! Don't even suggest such a thing! I'll be back in two weeks, and then we'll move you up here…" There was a long pause, and then Kane's voice softened. "I know how you feel, honey, honestly I do. But Dr. Richards thinks…" Another long pause. The conversation was extremely one-sided. "Look, Krista, I know that Aunt Sharon would like to have you stay until Christmas…. But the doctor and I think it would be best to get you into school here as soon as possible." Silence. "We'll talk about it later. Goodbye, honey."

It was several minutes before Kane came out of the bedroom, and in that time the lines around his eyes had seemed to deepen. Although he managed a smile, Erin could see that it was forced. He was preoccupied and tense. Through the soft folds of the fabric of his lightweight sport shirt, Erin could see the contours of his muscles, and they were tight. He walked into the living room and stared out of the window without seeing.

There was something in the droop of his shoulders that made her want to reach out and place a comforting hand against his cheek. He was having problems with his adolescent daughter—that much was evident—and Erin wanted to soothe away some of the mental pain he was experiencing. But she hesitated and remained in the kitchen, dawdling over coffee that was already brewed. It was safer somehow, watching him from a distance, wishing that any pain that he might be feeling would disappear.

When at last he turned back to face her, some of the strain had left his face. He ran his gaze over the apartment, appearing to study its contents. At that moment Erin sensed that her life was laid bare to him. The dusty rose couch, her weathered volumes of Shakespeare, an array of slightly disheveled plants, the antique rocker—everything was explored by Kane's cold gray eyes. It was as if, from the objects in the room, he could understand her and penetrate her soul. A part of her wanted to be examined by his eyes and touched by his mind, but another, more suspicious side of her objected to his appraisal.

Thoughtfully he picked up the discarded paperback mystery novel from the coffee table along with a worn volume of poetry by Keats. He opened the poetry book slowly and settled himself uncomfortably on the couch, with his long legs cramped under the coffee table. "You read this?" he asked, half to himself.

Erin poured the coffee but remained in the kitchen, still unsure of how to handle the conflicting emotions that surfaced each time she was alone with him. To answer his question she explained, "I read a variety of things, depending upon my mood."

"So I see," he agreed, eyeing the paperback spy thriller.

Suddenly she knew that she had made a mistake by seeing him in the intimacy of her own home. She felt too vulnerable, too transparent, too visible. Kane was alone with her, looking into the secret corners of her life, and unexpectedly she felt threatened. She had overheard part of his disagreement with his daughter, and she felt a desire to comfort him, and yet a need to turn her back on him and his problems. She couldn't let his life get tangled with her own; hers was too complicated and too precarious. She had to work with him as an employee; she couldn't let her emotions carry her away. She braced herself as she carried the two steaming mugs of coffee into the living room. "Kane," she began, placing a cup near him, "I don't think that it would be a good idea to go out today."

"You want to stay in?" he asked, deliberately misinterpreting her. "That would be fine with me.... Thanks." He reached for the cup and took an experimental sip while still watching her.

"No...I don't want to stay here. What I mean is I don't think that you and I should see each other..."

"Why not?"

"Because, for one thing, I make it a practice not to date anyone I work with."

He smiled to himself. "Then obviously, you're not as insecure about your job as you pretended to be yesterday. Wasn't it just yesterday morning that you accused me of plotting to fire you, along with all the other employees of the bank?"

"You're avoiding the issue," she challenged, a feeling of exasperation beginning to wash over her. "I'm not up to playing word games this morning!"

"Then let's be honest with each other, shall we? Why is it that you won't go out with me?" he asked, his silvery eyes capturing hers.

How could she tell him what she herself really didn't understand? Was it possible to explain that she felt a desire to be with him and an urge to run from him?

"Are you afraid of me?" His voice broke into her thoughts.

"No!"

"Well?"

"I just don't think it's a good idea to mix business with pleasure."

"Then," he seemed to agree, "let me assure you that you'll have a very unpleasant afternoon!" He placed his cup down and smiled at her in a perfectly sickening and victorious manner.

"Be serious...."

"I am! So far, you haven't given me any viable excuse for not spending a quiet afternoon together."

"But I thought..."

"It doesn't matter what you thought." Kane reached for her hand across the table, stifling her protests. "I just want a chance to get to know you better. Is that such a crime?" His angled face was earnest and open. Any doubts she had conceived earlier were quickly cast aside with the touch of his hand on her palm and the peaceful serenity of his gaze.

"No…"

"Good! Then let's go, shall we?"

She pulled her hand away from his and reached for her jacket. He pulled his legs from their bent position under the table, stood up and let his eyes roam over the apartment. His perusal was slow, steady and deliberate. Erin felt herself once again becoming more uncomfortable as the silent minutes passed.

"Do you like living here?" Kane finally asked, all of his attention drawn to the features of her face.

"Why do you ask?"

"I guess because this apartment house isn't exactly what I expected." He lifted his shoulders and shrugged into his jacket.

"Just what did you expect?" Erin was intrigued by the conversation. Perhaps if she could draw him out, he would explain his feelings about her and wash away those last traces of doubt that nagged at Erin's mind. She could sense that there was something he wasn't telling her. It was as if he was purposely being wary with her.

"Oh, I don't know," he began in answer to her question. "But this place—it seems a little out of character," he remarked, looking at the faded Persian rug and running his fingers over the antique craftsmanship of the lead-glass windows.

"Out of character?"

"You're a career woman, right?" he asked, and Erin nodded her head in agreement, all the while wondering what he was leading up to and somehow not wanting to know. "This apartment—for that matter, the entire building—just doesn't fit with my interpretation of today's liberated woman…"

"Why not?"

"Truthfully," he chuckled, "because it looks like the set

for one of those black-and-white slice-of-life movies of the forties."

Erin arched an inquisitive black eyebrow. "And you expected smoked glass, chrome fixtures and black vinyl upholstery?"

"Something like that."

"Sorry to disappoint you," she quipped, leaning against the door.

"You haven't disappointed me—not at all." His eyes found hers for an instant, and then his gaze swept the loft. "I knew when I met you that there was a darker, more private side of you. A side that you prefer to keep hidden away. Am I right?" His hands came up to the door, pressing on the wood and creating an imprisoning barrier near her head.

Erin met his questioning gaze with defiance. He was too close to the truth, too close to her. She drew in a deep, trembling breath. "You're right. I am a very private person, and I like it that way. What I don't like is anyone coming into my home and attempting to psychoanalyze me!"

A smile tugged at the corners of his mouth, but his eyes revealed only arctic cold. His breath whispered across her face. "Is that what I'm doing?"

"I hope not," she breathed, trying to still her racing heartbeat. Surely he could hear it—he was so near.

His finger reached out and stroked her cheek and his eyes covered her face and throat. "Maybe it would be a better idea to stay here today," he suggested silkily, but abruptly changed his mind. "On second thought it might be too dangerous to stay here…come on. I don't like being late."

"Late? For what?"

"You'll see…" There was just a hint of intimacy in his tone. Erin pulled her jacket tightly around her shoulders, as if she were experiencing a sudden chill. "What have you got planned for today? Where are we going?" she demanded.

"You really don't want to know!" He moved one of his hands and helped her with the light calfskin jacket. His fingers brushed against her arm and lingered. Or did they? She pulled abruptly away from him and cinched the belt securely over her waist.

"Of course I want to know! Where are you taking me?"

"Just come along. And don't try to kid me. I haven't known you very long, but believe me, I know you well enough to realize that you like surprises and mystery in your life."

"I'd just like to know what makes you such an expert on me," she muttered and reached for the door angrily. She was angry because he was correct in his assumption about her, but she hated to admit it. Before she could open the door, he grabbed her forearm and whirled her around to face him.

His eyes reached into the depths of hers. "You can't hide from me, Erin," he whispered. "I won't let you." She could feel herself trembling at his touch. Her lips parted, but the denial that was forming in her mind died.

He lowered his head slowly, and his lips melted into hers in a kiss that was soft, beckoning and full of promise. She found herself yearning to respond to the warmth and tenderness of the embrace, but she forced herself to pull away. If he had any questions about her reaction to him, he didn't ask them. Instead he pulled her tightly against him and led her down the steep steps of the apartment building.

There were many thoughts that crossed her mind, and just as many questions that didn't have answers. She ignored the flood of emotions that carried her out of the house and into the sleek black sports car. Kane helped her into the car and then slid into the driver's seat. He started the engine and the sporty machine roared to life. Neither Erin nor Kane spoke, and the silence was as heavy as the gray Seattle fog, but Erin discovered an inner warmth that she didn't know existed.

Chapter 4

Kane drove steadily toward the heart of the city, carefully maneuvering the sporty little car down the steep inclines of the hills in order to save the muffler on the roller-coasterlike grade. Through the fog the gray waters of Elliott Bay lapped lazily against the waterfront. As they crested a final hill Erin was able to see the wharf and the bustle of activity along the crowded and colorful piers.

After parking the car, Erin and Kane strolled on the boardwalk that flanked the water's edge. Kane's hands were pushed deep into his pockets and his gaze slid over the water. Salt spray brushed against Erin's cheeks in a chilling embrace. Seagulls marauded the shore, calling out their lonesome cries. White, gleaming ferryboats plowed their way through the water, leaving only a frothy wake on the gray-blue waters as they disappeared into the fog.

Kane led Erin into a tiny bistro on the wharf. The warmth of the cozy restaurant was a welcome relief from the chill of the seawater and fog. They were seated at an intimate table near the window where they could watch the activities along the piers from the shelter of the bistro.

As the waiter brought the fresh seafood omelettes, Kane studied his empty coffee cup before looking into Erin's eyes.

"I suppose that you overheard my conversation with Krista." It was more of a statement than a question.

"Part of it."

"Why didn't you ask me about her?"

Erin met his gaze unwaveringly and noticed the rigid line of his jaw. Was he always so tense when he thought about his child, she wondered to herself. Aloud she responded, "I didn't want to pry."

Kane took a deep breath and looked out over the waters. He seemed to be wrestling with a weighty decision. Finally he turned his head back toward Erin. "Krista's handicapped."

A startled look threatened to possess Erin's features, but she managed to make her voice steady. "I'm sorry," she whispered.

"So am I," he groaned and threw his napkin on his empty plate.

"Do you want to talk about it?"

"Do you want to listen?" His face was a mask of indifference, as if he suddenly regretted his outward display of emotion. *No,* she wanted to scream. *I don't want to know anything more about you. I'm attracted to you and I'm afraid of the attraction. I can't learn anything more about you that might bind me more tightly to you. I have to push away from you...I have to.*

"Of course I'll listen," she murmured, quieting the voice of suspicion that nagged at her.

"Krista is eleven. She was ten when the accident occurred." A dark, faraway look crossed his features. As he continued, his voice was flat, betraying no emotion. It was almost as if the words were part of a well-rehearsed speech, devoid of feeling or life. "She was riding in the car with her mother, my ex-wife.

They were going to some 'retreat' or 'support group' meeting for the weekend. I really don't know much about it except it was the latest self-improvement seminar to be offered. Jana, my ex-wife, was forever following the latest self-improvement craze. It was one encounter group after another. Maybe I'm in part to blame for that too."

Kane shook his head, as if clearing out unpleasant memories. Erin waited in silence as he continued.

"Anyway, it doesn't matter what new kick she was on. It just so happened that she had called and told me where she was going. I was angry. I didn't think that Krista needed to be exposed to all of that pseudopsychiatric garbage, and I told her so. We got into a helluva fight and she hung up on me. Two hours later I got a phone call from the police telling me that Jana was dead and Krista was in the hospital. To make a long story short, Krista's been in and out of the hospital ever since. She's still unable to walk unassisted."

"She's paralyzed?" Erin asked cautiously.

"Not exactly." Kane's eyes clouded for a minute. "It seems that she was lucky—nothing was actually broken in the accident. Jana was thrown out of the car and killed instantly, but Krista remained in the car, and other than a few cuts and bruises and a sprained left wrist, the doctors can find nothing physically wrong with her."

"But…"

"I know." Kane nodded his head. "It seems as if the cause of her paralysis is mental."

"I don't understand." Erin's brows knit in concern. What was Kane actually saying?

"I don't either. But what I can gather from the doctors is that she blames herself, or perhaps me, for the accident."

"No! That's not fair!"

Kane shrugged his shoulders. "Why not? Maybe if Jana and

I hadn't fought, she would be alive today. Maybe the argument was the catalyst for her reckless driving."

"You can't blame yourself," Erin argued.

"Then who can I blame?"

"No one. It was just an unfortunate accident..."

"Try explaining that to a ten-year-old girl who has just lost her mother."

"Oh, Kane," Erin sighed, and reached for his hand.

Her hand was warm and comforting, and for a moment Kane forgot that he suspected Erin O'Toole of thievery. What was it about her that had made him open up to her and tell her the story of Krista's paralysis? Why was it so necessary that she know about him, that she care?

The waiter came to remove the dishes and bring the check. Kane helped Erin out of her chair and smiled disarmingly down on her. "I'm sorry," he apologized. "I didn't meant to bore you with my problems."

"You didn't bore me," Erin admitted.

"Well, let's push all those black thoughts aside for the day, shall we?" he asked, and took her hand powerfully in his. "I'm sure that when Krista gets up here and settles in, she'll be fine." Convincing as his words were, he didn't seem to believe them himself.

It was nearly afternoon, and they hurried down the boardwalk to catch the Blake Island ferry to visit the Tillicum Indian Village. Once on the island, they were entertained by the folklore and art objects of the native inhabitants. Erin was fascinated by the blending of the modern and ancient cultures. The fog had lifted and the day was cool, but pleasant.

They spent the day hiking over the island and watching the everyday rituals of life in a tribal Indian village. Late in the evening Erin and Kane, along with the other tourists, were guests of the tribe and feasted on Indian baked salmon cooked in hot coals, as they had been for centuries. As twilight descended, the torches were lit, and Kane wrapped his arms possessively around Erin's waist. They sat on the hand-carved stone steps of the amphitheater and watched the colorful display of folk culture as enacted by the inhabitants of the island. In the flickering light of the stars and the torches, Kane's features looked stronger, more masculine. The scent of his cologne wafted over Erin, and involuntarily she pressed closer to him.

Darkness covered the island as the entertainment faded. Erin and Kane made their way back to the waiting ferry. The warm lights inside the vessel winked at them, but Kane led Erin onto the deck. The wind had become stronger, sending a salty spray into their faces as they stood on the deck of the boat and watched the sparkling lights of Seattle call to them across the narrow stretch of water.

Kane held Erin tightly, the power and warmth of his body molding to hers. During the day all of her defenses had melted. Ever since he had opened up to her and explained about his daughter, she had felt a kinship and warmth toward him. And the doubts that she had experienced were withering.

He stood behind her with the strength of his arms wrapped securely over her waist. They were silent as they watched the distance and felt the giant boat move through the black water. The engine of the large vessel whirred noisily and rhythmically and the darkened waters churned white as the ferry headed inland.

A light drizzle had begun, but Erin didn't move, afraid to break the spell of the evening. Although the September nip in the air was cool, Erin was warm, pressed firmly against the heat of Kane's body. It was as if they had made an unspoken pact that neither wanted to violate by speaking.

The drizzle increased into raindrops, and even the hardiest

of the tourists shuffled into the interior of the ferry. Erin and Kane remained outside alone, content to feel the salty breeze against their faces and the heated promise of each other's body. Kane nuzzled the back of her neck, letting the wind whip her hair over his face. She could feel her skin become alive with his touch, her blood begin to warm with his caress. Unconsciously she leaned closer to him.

He murmured her name, seeming to give it a special and intimate quality as it caught on the wind. She pivoted to face him and he cupped her chin in his hand before pressing the moist tenderness of his lips firmly over hers. She parted her lips involuntarily, letting his tongue trace a silken path over her mouth tentatively before slowly and sensuously exploring the moist recess and enticing her to do the same. He wrapped himself more closely around her as his tongue stroked and danced with hers.

The rain came down in silvery droplets, sliding over Kane's face and past Erin's cheek to her throat and finally to hide below the collar of her blouse. Kane's kiss deepened and his hand moved gently but persistently against her back. His lips roved over her face and neck, kissing and licking the drops of rain from her eyes, cheeks and throat. An urgent moan escaped from his lips, and he finally pulled his face away from hers. His eyes slid over her body, seeming to probe every inch of her being. They had darkened to misty gray, and a pulsating passion was blazing in their dark depths.

A raindrop passed over Erin's neck, and Kane stooped to kiss it away, his lips brushing over the hollow of her throat. She shuddered, more from his delicate kiss than from the cool night air. Her knees buckled and he pulled her to him, but a blast from the ferry's horn announced that they were docking. All too soon the jewellike lights of the city had blossomed into streetlamps, and the intimate water journey was over.

They walked back to the car in silence, each absorbed in private thoughts. Erin wondered how she could possibly work for a man she needed so passionately as a woman. And what about his daughter, who blamed him for his wife's death? And Mitch—could she bring up the subject of Mitch's dismissal with Kane, or would it be the wedge that would come between them? For, as unlikely as it seemed, Erin was unwittingly beginning to look upon herself and Kane as a man and woman with a deep understanding of each other. *But that's crazy,* the realistic side of her mind argued. *You don't even know the man.*

And Kane wondered about Erin. Could this enigmatic and beautiful woman really be a viable suspect in the embezzling scheme? She seemed so…innocent, if that was the right word. It was so easy to talk with her; he had already confided in her concerning Krista. That was probably a mistake, he thought now. But for the moment he didn't want to believe anything about Erin other than what he felt. She was bewitching and he meant to find out all he could about her—tomorrow. Tonight he just didn't give a damn whether she was embezzling or not.

The black sports car whipped through the quiet streets, sending sprays of water as its tires slashed pools of standing water. The windshield wipers moved in tempo, pushing the raindrops off the glass. Night closed in on Erin as the black interior of the car seemed to melt into the darkness of the evening.

Erin's senses were heightened. In the warmth of the enclosed sports car, she could smell the tangy scent of Kane's cologne and the masculine essence of his rain-drenched body. For the entire short ride Erin was aware of the man next to her. As he shifted gears, she could see the long hard lines of his fingers and the athletic slant of his legs straining against the fabric of his pants. She had trouble concentrating on anything other than his potent masculinity.

As they approached the apartment house, he killed the engine and sat motionless, his hands still gripping the steering wheel. He glanced toward the windows of Erin's third-floor apartment.

Erin cleared her throat. "Would you like to come in? For a drink—or a cup of coffee?"

He rotated to face her, and even in the darkness she imagined flames of smoldering passion burning in his eyes. "I'd like it very much."

He opened the door for her and they walked up the long staircase noiselessly. Although they didn't touch, Erin felt a bond between them bridging the inches of open air that separated their bodies. She licked her arid lips as she reached into her purse for her keys. Many emotions had come and gone since he had hurried her out of the apartment this morning. God, was it only twelve hours ago? Erin had hesitated only slightly when she thought about asking him up to her apartment. She knew how precarious it was for her to be alone with him, but she couldn't resist extending the invitation and the evening. Mrs. Cavenaugh had been right; she had hidden herself away from the world of men for much too long.

Her fingers shook as she tried to unlock the door, and Kane took the keys from her hand. He escorted her through the doorway and into the small apartment. Erin went through the motions of taking off her jacket, but her mind was on Kane and the intimacy of the apartment. There was no place to hide. "Could—I offer you a drink?"

He took off his jacket and let it fall casually across the arm of the couch. "Sure."

Erin moved into the kitchen and opened the liquor cabinet, but her thoughts didn't leave Kane. Although he was in the living room, the air was charged with electricity and anticipation. It was difficult to think, to move. Why had she asked him up to her loft, and why had he accepted?

She managed to put together some Irish coffee, and the cups were steaming as she carried them into the living room. Kane was standing at the window, looking into the night as if he could penetrate the darkness. His shirt was moist and clung to his body, and the ripple of his muscles was evident through the fabric.

When she entered the room, he turned to face her. His face was ragged, torn with emotion, and she knew that he was as tense as she. "Anything wrong?" she asked.

"Nothing," he whispered, but the besieged look on his face didn't disappear. "Thanks," he said with a tight-lipped smile and sampled the hot drink.

"There is something wrong," she challenged. "I can feel it. It's something about me, isn't it?"

"You're imagining things," he retorted, and took a long swallow of his drink.

"No...I'm not. It all started yesterday, at the office."

His gray eyes bored into her, daring her to continue. "I don't know what you mean."

"I think that you do. You were angry that I was at the of-fice—don't deny it. And all of those ridiculous questions about Mitch. It has something to do with him, doesn't it?"

"Why don't you tell me," he suggested huskily. "What do you know about Mitchell Cameron?"

"Nothing—except that you fired him, and I don't know why!"

He set his cup down on the table and strode quietly over to where she was standing. His voice was barely audible, but he pinned her with his gaze. "You can't even hazard a guess?" he coaxed.

"No!"

"Why don't you try?" His fingers reached upward and found the nape of her neck. He lifted her hair from her shoulders and clasped both of his hands gently around her neck, massaging her shoulders through the light rain-washed fabric of her blouse.

"I have no idea. I only know that the legal department wasn't profitable…" His gray eyes snapped.

"Is that it? Would you let him go because of one bad year?"

"What do you think?"

"I don't know. I don't know how you work…"

"Sure you do," he suggested smoothly, and Erin felt that she had known him all of her life.

"Aren't you going to finish your drink?" she asked, not able to concentrate on anything other than the warm enticement of his hands. His thumbs traced lazy patterns of seduction along her throat, gently persuading her mind to think of nothing other than his overpowering maleness.

His eyes looked over at the half-full cup of Irish coffee. "Is that my cue to leave?"

Erin braced herself, trying to ignore the dizzying sensations that seemed to build up from within her and explode at his touch. "It's…it's getting late."

"And you'd like to go to bed?" he cajoled, his dark eyes alive.

"I…you…we have to work in the morning," she stammered, her senses reeling from his closeness.

"That we do," he agreed.

Erin's pulse was beginning to dance wildly as Kane's hands coaxed her to newer heights of sensuality. She could feel his breath, smell his clean masculine scent, and she knew that he was going to kiss her.

His arms moved to her waist and coiled possessively around her as his mouth brushed velvet-soft kisses down her cheek and throat. Her head fell backward, and he rained kisses up and down the length of her exposed neck. Erin's chest grew tight, and her breath began to whisper in short, shaky breaths.

His hands toyed at the hem of her blouse, at first tentatively, and finally with determination as he tugged the blouse out of the waistband of her slacks. His fingers explored the soft, supple muscles of her back, warming her skin to a rosy glow. Her knees began to give way, and he caught her, pushing his lips over hers in silent union. She moaned, and at the invitation of her parted lips, his tongue found hers, flicking and dancing with moist sparks of unfettered passion.

Moving steadily upward, his hands inched up her spine in a delicious spiraling motion. Her skin heated and caught fire. All her nerve endings ignited in hot boiling passion. His fingertips slowly and sensuously moved forward until he was kneading the tight muscles of her abdomen.

Her breasts ached against the confinement of her bra, and when at last his fingertips played with the lacy garment, she sighed. He pushed her gently and persuasively to the floor, and she felt the cool floorboards press against her fevered flesh. Slowly he let his hands slide to the buttons of her blouse, slipping each button easily through the buttonholes. As the blouse parted he unleashed her breasts from the lacy bra. "God, but you're beautiful," he moaned, looking directly at the full white curves of her soft breasts.

She felt her fingers working at the buttons of his shirt. When at last it was opened, and the expanse of golden bronze skin was visible, she moaned with pure animal pleasure. "So are you," she said huskily, watching his firm muscles flex under her admiring gaze.

His thumbs idled over her nipples as he fondled her breasts. Masterfully, he enticed her nipples to erection, and a smile of triumph lighted his eyes as he noticed them harden. He looked once into her eyes, the smoky gray of his gaze blending into the lilac-blue passion of hers.

It was as if she were drugged; all she could concentrate on was taking and giving pleasure. Her female body was overshadowing her mind. As Kane loved her, explored her, exulted in her, she, too, took satisfaction from touching and enticing him. Body was controlling mind in the sweet dreamlike mist of lovemaking.

They rolled together on the floor, and he rained kisses upon her face, her neck, her breasts. His tongue licked paths of fire over her body and kindled an aching need in her innermost core.

Endearingly his mouth descended on her breasts, and he suckled as if a babe, kneading the sensitive tissue with his hands as his lips lured love from her nipples. His body was upon hers and she felt the bittersweet pain of his weight over her. The cold floorboards touched her back, and his warm, naked torso inflamed her soul, causing boiling currents of lava to course through her veins.

"Oh, Erin," he called against her, and her pounding heart was triggered to a more passionate rhythm. He tore himself away from her and saw the disappointment in her eyes.

"I want to go to bed with you," he breathed, "and I want to make love to you."

"Are…are you asking me?" she gasped, drawing much needed air into her lungs.

"I've been asking you all night." He levered himself over her and leaned on one elbow while one hand still massaged her breasts.

"I want to…" she murmured, closing her eyes and trying to think rationally. Would the ache subside? Would she really be able to make love to him? Would she be able to stop?

"But…" he prodded, his breath ghosting over her hair.

"But…" She breathed heavily. "But…I'm afraid."

"Of what? Me?"

"No…"

"Then it must be that you're afraid of your husband," he guessed.

"Lee? How did you know about him?"

"A small surname discrepancy in your personnel file."

"Oh," she murmured, pulling her blouse over her breasts. Suddenly she felt conspicuously naked.

"He is the problem, isn't he," Kane asked gently, but there was a cold and calculating edge to his voice.

"No…Lee has nothing to do with us," she managed, but her mercurial temperature had cooled.

"You're still in love with him, aren't you?" His eyes regarded her gently, and he pulled her closer to his body and rocked her.

"No…you're wrong. You've got it all wrong. I'm not in love with Lee. Sometimes I wonder if I ever really was." His eyes followed hers to look out the window. "Oh, I thought I loved him, once, but some of the things that he did…that he said…" She still couldn't talk about it without getting a catch in her throat.

"Erin, honey. It's been a long time, and still he affects you. Are you sure that you're not still emotionally involved with him?"

Tears began to flow from her eyes, and he brushed them away. She tried to look away from him, but he forced her head in his direction, softly cupping her chin in his fingers. His movements were gentle, but his thoughts were grim. Lee Sinclair, whoever the hell he was, had scarred Erin, and Kane meant to know all about him.

"Have you seen him recently?"

"No...he moved to Spokane about a year ago." For some reason Erin couldn't tell Kane about the phone calls and the fact that Lee was back in Seattle.

Kane continued to rock her in silence, only the thin line of his lips belying his calm and comforting actions. Slowly Erin composed herself. She wondered how she had ever let things get so out of hand. She felt an embarrassed burn on her cheeks as she realized that she was sitting half-naked on the floor of her apartment with her new boss, weeping like a teenager, nearly jumping into bed with him. It was frightening and confusing, completely out of character.

"I'm sorry," she sniffed, managing a feeble smile. "I really don't know why I fell apart."

"It's all right. Here." He pulled the afghan from the couch and wrapped her in its rainbow-colored tiered folds. "Are you sure that you're okay?" She nodded, and he rose from the floor, pulling her with him. "Why don't you go in and get in bed? I'll bring you some tea."

"No! Oh, no...I'm fine, honestly." She was embarrassed by her emotional outburst, and the last thing she wanted was that her boss should wait on her. She hiked the awkward blanket over her shoulders, but it seemed determined to slide to the floor.

"You're sure?" he asked, cocking a suspicious eyebrow in her direction and buttoning his shirt.

"I'm sure." Her voice was still husky, but the firm quality and tone that he recognized as control were back in her words.

She could tell that he was reluctant to leave, but after a final kiss to her forehead, and his hastily scribbled hotel phone number, he left her alone.

After he closed the door, she listened to the sound of his shoes clicking down the steps. Silently she counted them. Finally she heard the front door open and close with a thud. A sporty engine roared to life and faded into the night. Erin felt more alone than she had in years.

Chapter 5

The morning newspaper was spread before her as Erin sat down to a light breakfast of toast and jam. Her eyes wandered aimlessly over the headlines on the front page, but her mind refused to budge from the intimate moments she had shared with Kane. What had seemed a natural and beautiful lovemaking experience in the darkness had somehow lost its enchantment in the morning light. It wasn't that she regretted getting to know Kane, not at all. But he was her boss, and she couldn't let her body control her mind where he was concerned. Professionally it just wasn't sound judgment to get emotionally involved with an employer. And, although she could still conjure up the enigmatic image of his tanned masculine body and mirthless gray eyes, she wouldn't let it control her.

She applied a healthy spoonful of raspberry jam to her toast as she turned to the financial section. As her eyes met the black-and-white photograph of Mitchell Cameron, she let the knife fall to the table. The picture was several years old, and Mitch was smiling with his pleasant self-assured grin, but the caption in black boldface print captured her attention.

FINANCIAL LAWYER ALLEGED THIEF—and in smaller print—Mitchell Cameron Accused of Embezzling Bank Funds.

"Oh, no!" Erin gasped, and her eyes read and reread the newspaper article several times. "There must be some mistake," she murmured to herself. "There has to be!" According to the article Mitch had been manipulating bank funds for the better part of two years. When the bank was sold, an audit found him out, and the new president, Kane Webster, had fired Mitch. The police were summoned and Mitch would be arraigned for indictment within the week.

Erin raced to the telephone and dialed Mitch's number. A busy signal beeped flatly in her ear. Either Mitch had taken the receiver off the hook, or he was already being plied by inquisitive friends and reporters.

As quickly as possible she scooped up the paper, grabbed her purse and slipped on her coat. She took the steps two at a time and nearly ran over Mrs. Cavenaugh on her way out the door. On the run, she apologized to the startled old woman and hurried out to the car. She turned the ignition, the little car sparked to life and Erin proceeded on a mad dash to the bank, hampered only by the early-morning rush-hour traffic.

When she got to the bank, it was already crawling with employees. Although it was still early, it seemed that everyone had arrived with time to spare on this first day of new bank ownership. Erin pushed herself into the crowded elevator and wedged herself between two women.

"Have you seen the paper today?" a middle-aged woman with a faddish, curly hairstyle asked her friend.

"Not yet—I usually wait until coffee break. There's just not enough time in the morning, what with getting the kids off to school, you know," the shorter woman in a pink raincoat replied.

The elevator started its upward motion. "Then you haven't

heard about Mitchell Cameron?" the curly-haired woman asked.

"Cameron? The head of the legal department?"

"That's right. Seems that the new president—that Mr. Webster—had him fired."

"No!"

"That's right," the taller woman said with a firm shake of her head. Her voice lowered, and she looked over her shoulder as she continued. "They suspect that Mr. Cameron was involved in some embezzling scheme…"

"The head of the legal department? Are you sure?"

Erin pretended not to hear the conversation. The elevator stopped on the seventeenth floor and the two women continued their conversation as they disembarked. Erin closed her eyes for a minute. By this time the entire bank staff had heard about Mitch. Could it possibly be true? She fervently hoped that Kane was wrong about Mitch.

The elevator stopped with a jolt, and Erin walked into the legal department. She was early, and only a few of the more aggressive young employees had made it to their desks. There were a few new faces in the crowd, probably some of Kane's imported troubleshooters from California, Erin guessed as she passed by the reception area and picked up her telephone messages. The most compelling of the notes was a handwritten memo from Kane indicating that he wanted to see her in his office immediately.

After taking off her coat, she armed herself with the newspaper and marched into his office. An eerie, nostalgic feeling gripped her when she discovered that the familiar brass nameplate of Mitchell Cameron had been torn from the door. Only two fine drill holes remained in the wood panels to remind Erin that just last week Mitch had occupied this office.

Kane was sitting behind the desk when she entered. He motioned her to be seated in one of the side chairs as he finished scribbling some notes on a legal pad. But instead, she remained standing with her arms folded against her chest. The rolled newspaper was clamped firmly under her left arm.

"Have you seen the paper?" she asked him, echoing the conversation she had overhead in the elevator.

"Yes," he replied, looking up from his work.

"And you read the article on Mitch?" she accused.

"I've read several, starting last evening," he replied evenly. His eyes searched her face and he studied her intensely.

"Is it true?" she asked, her incredulity registering on her face. "Did Mitch really embezzle? How do you know—and why did you let the press find out about it? Do you know what you've done? You've ruined his career. He worked for this bank for over twenty years, and in one clean sweep you destroyed him!"

Her voice had risen with her emotion. She flung the paper onto his desk and turned her head away, biting on her fingernail and trying to piece together her shattered poise. Kane rose from the desk and crossed the room to close the door. He came back beside her and placed his hands on her shoulders. Gently he rubbed the tension out of her neck and shoulders.

"Don't," she implored. "Don't touch me—just give me answers, preferably straight ones!"

His fingers stopped their comforting motion but remained against the back of her neck. Her hair was pinned into a businesslike knot, twisted behind one ear, and Kane rested his hands on her exposed neck. Her head was bent, and she pressed a hand to her forehead as she waited for his explanation.

His voice was low and soft as he began to speak. "You've met my associate, Jim Haney?" His fingers felt the barest of movements as she nodded. "During the conversion, while Jim was still working here in Seattle, he…discovered that funds were being funneled out of some of the larger trust accounts. It took Jim quite a while, but finally he tracked down the culprit."

"Mitch?" she asked in a voice that was barely audible.

"Yes."

"But…how can you be sure?" She pivoted her head upward to find his face, and there was an unhidden pain in the depths of her eyes.

"Erin. We caught him red-handed. There's no doubt." The words were spoken softly, but there was an almost cruel hardness in his features.

Tears threatened to spill from her eyes, but she forced them backward and vainly attempted to keep her voice from shaking. "I…I just can't believe it." She averted her face from his intent study.

Kane propped her chin between his fingers and let his thumb rub it caressingly while tracing the line of her jaw. "You were very close to him?" he asked gently.

Erin shook her head faintly and bit her lip. "He's been a good friend to me." Her eyes were shining with unshed tears when she looked up at Kane's face once more. "He…he helped me through a very difficult time in my life…" she explained, and gave in to the urge to lean against him. His arm wrapped securely around her, and for a moment Erin forgot everything other than Kane's comforting presence. This couldn't be the same coldhearted man who had fired Mitch, could it? Had Mitch really stooped to thievery?

"The difficult time," he whispered. "The divorce?"

She nodded mutely against the smooth fabric of his jacket.

A knock resounded on the thick mahogany door, and before Kane could respond, the door swung open. Olivia Parsons, with all of her self-assurance and poise in place, breezed into the room with only a brief apology.

"Excuse me, Mr. Webster…Erin." She included Erin out of courtesy. Her cool green eyes swept over the intimate scene before her, and although they reflected a glimmer of interest, her professional aplomb never wavered. Erin moved away from Kane with as much grace as was possible, but she was sure that Olivia hadn't missed the tender embrace between employer and employee. "I didn't mean to disturb you, but your secretary indicated that you needed these financial statements before the board meeting this afternoon." The tall brunette with the svelte figure and sleek Halston original dress handed Kane the stack of papers that she was carrying. The confident smile that she was wearing never left her face.

"You must be Miss Parsons," Kane surmised, his eyes traveling appreciatively over the neatly typed pages.

"Please call me Olivia," she responded. She gave Erin a fleeting head-to-toe appraisal, as if seeing her for the first time. Turning back to Kane, she continued. "I really didn't know that you were busy," she apologized again, and Erin felt a tide of crimson creep steadily up her neck.

"No problem," Kane assured Olivia, and escorted her out of the room. "Thank you for taking the time to bring the reports by."

"Anytime," Olivia suggested in a voice so throaty that Erin barely heard it.

Once Olivia had made her exit, Kane closed the door and deliberately turned to face Erin. His back was pressed firmly against the polished wood grain of the door, as if he were using his own body as a barricade against another intrusion. His body had stiffened, and all of the familiar fondness had escaped from his features. His face had become a mask devoid of emotion, and his words were no longer tender or caring. They were brittle in the air.

"I don't think that my office is the place to continue this discussion," he said tersely.

"I think it's a perfect place to discuss Mitch—right in the middle of his office!"

"Is that how you still think of it, as Mitch's office? If so, you had better change your mind. Mitchell Cameron is gone. He was an embezzler—a thief—and he's no longer with Consolidated Finances. I hope that fact doesn't hamper your work." He strode across the room to the desk. "We can discuss this later...tonight if you like. But right now I'm very busy." He sat at the desk and started reading the reports that he had received from Olivia.

Erin watched him with disbelieving eyes. How could he change so rapidly? It was as if he were a kind, considerate gentleman one moment and a heartless bastard the next. He looked up at her and flashed a perfectly condescending smile at her, but she knew it was an act. She had been with him enough to recognize the cool distance in his gray eyes.

"You're the one who called me in here," she reminded him, and waved the green personal memo in the air. "Just what was it that you wanted to discuss?"

The petrified smile fell from his face and a darker, more volatile expression took over. "I wanted to ask you to dinner tonight."

"You've got to be kidding! First you call me in here. Then you nearly throw me out. And now you expect me to go out with you?" Sarcasm dripped from her words. "Not a chance!"

"Why not?"

Erin sighed wearily, tired of the argument. "For the same reasons that I spelled out to you yesterday."

There was a pool of darkness in his eyes. "You're afraid of me, aren't you?" he suggested, and then continued. "Or is it yourself who scares you?"

"It has nothing to do with fear, and you should know it! It's just that I don't think it would be good for either of us, professionally that is, to be the subject of office gossip or speculation."

"Don't you think that you're putting the cart before the horse?"

"I don't know what you mean," she sighed.

"In order for there to be any gossip, there's got to be a glimmer of truth. Someone has to start the rumors, and since I'm not one to 'kiss and tell,' I've got to assume that you are. Otherwise, there would be no cause for concern, would there?"

"You don't understand," she accused with a vehemence that interested Kane. "Gossip…it can be vicious—ugly! It can ruin your life!"

"Only if you let it—the same as anything else. Now, why don't you be honest with me—no, make that honest with yourself—and tell me what's really bothering you. I can't believe that a little innocent speculation about what you do after-hours is all that traumatic. For God's sake, Erin, you're a thirty-year-old divorcée, not a whimpering virgin! What kind of lily-white reputation are you trying to create?"

Her eyes narrowed and she planted her hands firmly against her hips. "The point is that I like to keep my personal life just that—private! And even though you and I won't go around telling anyone that we're seeing each other, believe me, the word will get out."

"And everyone will just naturally assume that because we're dating we're sleeping together, right?" he surmised, elaborating on her logic. He threw the neatly stacked reports down into an unruly pile on his desk and covered the floor space that separated them in long, swift strides. He didn't touch her, but he was close enough that she could feel the delicious warmth of his breath as it fanned against her hair. She stood her ground, not moving an inch, but every nerve ending of her body was rigidly aware of him and his nearness. "And even if some of the people around here think that we sleep together"—his fingers touched the silken skin of her cheek softly—"what's so bad about that? What do you care what other people think?"

Erin's lips thinned into a white line. She tried to control her temper and ignore the warm feelings that Kane was commanding from her. She pushed herself away from him in order to think clearly and avoid the compelling magnetism that seemed to surround him. "I've worked very hard to get where I am with this bank, and I don't need the frustration of knowing that coworkers think that I sleep with the boss to promote my career."

"Would you mind it if they thought you slept with the boss because you wanted to and not for career reasons?"

"You can't possibly understand!" she whispered, and turned on her heel to leave.

As she pushed open the door to make her exit, she heard Kane's parting words. "You, Miss O'Toole, are paranoid! And I'll pick you up at seven-thirty!"

Kane's voice boomed through the open door. Several of the secretaries looked up from their typewriters to stare openly at Erin. She tried to ignore their curiosity and continued toward her office. She could feel their speculative glances boring holes into her back, but she managed to return to the security of her office with a modicum of poise.

Outwardly she controlled her ragged Irish temper, but once in the sanctity of her own office, she could feel the fumes of anger rising steadily within her. No doubt half of the legal department had already sized up her situation with the new boss, and it wasn't even ten o'clock yet! She tried to concentrate on her work, and she told herself not to be childish, but she couldn't help but feel that Kane had betrayed her trust by announcing that he planned to see her after work. To make matters worse, he had brushed off the subject of Mitch's dismissal with an arrogant wave of his hand and very little explanation.

During the remainder of the day Erin saw little of Kane. All of his contact with her came via his secretary in the form of interdepartmental memorandums. They had no personal contact. She had seen him only in passing, and he had smiled at her with the same polite but less than enthusiastic smile that he rained upon all of his employees. He showed her no special attention, which was exactly what she had wanted. And yet, a small and very feminine part of her yearned for the vaguest sign of emotion from him. Affection, endearment, friendship—anything that demonstrated that he cared for her in a more intimate way.

For most of the afternoon she attempted to bury herself in her work to avoid any further confrontations with Kane. It also helped her ignore the whispers about Mitch and the speculations about the embezzlement.

It was long after five o'clock when she rose and tucked away the paperwork that was still spread unfinished on her desk. Although she had worked diligently, she had accomplished very little because of her preoccupation with Kane. He had asked her out early that morning, and she had refused, but her mind had wandered relentlessly back to the invitation. *What would it hurt?* her persuasive mind taunted.

But what good would it do, her more rational nature inquired. Yes, Kane was an interesting man, and yes, she would like to spend some time alone with him, and perhaps she would, if circumstances were different. But as things stood, she couldn't reconcile herself to live a double life of daytime employee and nighttime lover. No matter how she would try to convince herself otherwise, she was attracted to Kane as she never had been to any other man. Given an alternative set of circumstances, she knew that she could fall deeply in love with him. But, as fate would have it, she couldn't allow herself the pleasure of falling in love with a man for whom she worked.

It had taken her all day to come to the decision that she would have to explain her position to Kane once and for all. She threw her coat over her arm and clicked off the lights to her office. Most of the staff had left the building, but she knew that Kane was still working. She could hear his voice through the door. Rather than disturb him, she continued past his office toward the elevator.

Before the elevator doors parted, the door to Kane's office opened. Erin quickly resolved to herself that this would be as good a time as any to have it out with him. She turned to face him and discovered that he wasn't alone. Olivia Parsons was with him, looking as if she was hanging on his every word. Rather than intrude, Erin whirled and faced the elevator. Just as the doors were opening, Erin heard Kane call out to her.

"Erin, wait!" Kane hurried to Erin's side. "I'm glad I caught up with you. Do you need a ride home?"

"I've got my car," Erin replied, a little tartly. Why did Olivia always seem to be a part of the conversation? She looked cautiously at Olivia, but the calm expression on the brunette's face didn't appear to hold the slightest hint of interest.

"Then I'll see you at seven-thirty," Kane rejoined.

Erin looked from Kane to Olivia and back to Kane. "I... don't think so...not tonight." Olivia's eyebrows raised just a fraction of an inch. The gesture was almost unnoticeable, but Erin caught the movement and the silent gleam of fascination in Olivia's perfect green eyes.

"Going out?" Olivia asked casually. "I don't blame you. Who wants to cook after a full day at the office?"

Erin couldn't resist the temptation of disagreeing with Olivia. "Oh, I don't know. I've always enjoyed cooking."

Olivia's face registered disbelief, but it was Kane who answered. "Good!" he interjected. "I haven't had a home-cooked meal in ages. We'll eat at your place."

Erin was about to reject Kane's suggestion, but Olivia stilled Erin's tongue. "That's terrible!" she sang out sweetly to Kane. "I tell you what. Why don't you come over to my house for a special dinner? We'll have fresh seafood from Puget Sound…"

"Thanks, Olivia. I appreciate the hospitality." Kane seemed to agree, and Erin could feel her heart beginning to shred. Kane shot Erin a questioning look and continued, "But I've got other plans." His response was gentle but firm.

"Some other time…" Olivia persisted, only slightly dejected.

"Some other time," Kane agreed evasively.

There was a slight pause in the conversation, and finally Olivia broke the silence. "I guess I'd better be running along. I'll see you in the morning." Although the farewell was meant for both Erin and Kane, Olivia's warm green eyes looked directly into the cool gray depths of Kane's gaze. Erin could almost see the invitation in those emerald pools.

Olivia slipped into the elevator, and it started its descent before Erin began. "Look, Kane. I've made a decision. You can't come over tonight…and I can't go out with you. It's as simple as that!"

She pressed the elevator call button and waited for Kane's reaction. She expected that he would be violent, but when he spoke it was with quiet deliberation.

"You…would deny me a home-cooked meal?" he asked, and there was a mischievous smile in his eyes.

"Of course not, but you've got to understand…"

"It's settled then. I'll bring the wine." He slipped his hand beneath her elbow and guided her into the elevator. As the doors shut he wrapped his arms tightly around her and kissed her feverishly on the lips. All of the warmth and intimacy that had been denied during the day was surfacing again in his passionate embrace.

Before Erin could respond, the elevator stopped on the fifth floor, and Kane released her to smile at two of his new employees. Erin was sure that even in the slightly dimmed elevator light, the two young women could see her swollen lips and the trace of passion still lingering in Kane's eyes. When she stepped out of the building she hurried to her car, and Kane didn't follow. How was she going to deal with him and the web of emotions that was entangling her more tightly each day?

It was crazy and she knew it, but she felt that she was beginning to fall in love with Kane Webster. The thought made her shudder as she reached for the headlights and the windshield wipers. *You're a damn fool, Erin O'Toole,* she chided herself. She couldn't be, wouldn't be, in love with her boss. It was an impossible and ridiculous situation, but nonetheless, it existed.

She was still arguing with herself as she stopped the car in her familiar spot in front of the apartment house. She bent her head against the wind and slight drizzle of the evening. A welcome light came from Mrs. Cavenaugh's window and Erin stopped at the doorway to the little old lady's apartment. She waited several minutes before Mrs. Cavenaugh's voice called through the door.

"Who's there?"

"It's me, Mrs. Cavenaugh...Erin," she responded, and immediately heard the click of locks as Mrs. Cavenaugh opened the door. The old woman peeked timidly through the crack in the door before removing the final chain and opening the door widely.

"Come in...come in," Mrs. Cavenaugh welcomed her.

"I can't...I'm having company tonight."

"Oh?" Mrs. Cavenaugh didn't even have the decency to hide her interest. "Mr. Webster?"

Erin eyed the half-bent old woman with loving suspicion. "How did you know?" she asked.

"Lucky guess," the old woman murmured, her blue eyes dancing with pleasure. "Don't you have just a minute to tell me all about it?"

"No, I'm sorry, truly I am." Erin's face was earnest, and Mrs. Cavenaugh didn't doubt her sincerity. "I just dropped by to tell you that I got hold of someone to install the insulation. They'll be here by the end of the week."

"Good!"

"Look, I've really got to run."

"I understand," was the kindly reply. "Oh, by the way, Erin, did you know that Mr. Jefferies is planning to move out by the end of the month?"

"Oh, no," Erin sighed, and then quickly hid her disappointment. "I knew that he had been thinking of moving in with his daughter and her husband, but I didn't think that he had made up his mind."

"Seems they made it up for him," Mrs. Cavenaugh asserted. "I'm sure he left his notice in your mailbox."

"Oh, thanks for reminding me." Erin crossed the hallway and opened her mailbox. Among the various bills was Mr. Jefferies's notice of vacancy. The last thing she needed right now was one more empty apartment. She needed the rental income just to keep up the mortgage, let alone the repairs and upkeep. But she couldn't show her worries to Mrs. Cavenaugh. She called out to the friendly elderly woman as she mounted the stairs, "I'll let you know exactly when the repairmen will be here."

"Thanks, honey," Mrs. Cavenaugh responded before closing the door to her apartment. Erin raced up the remaining stairs, anxious to get into the familiar and secure surroundings of her own apartment.

Kane pulled the small black sports car to the curb and snapped off the motor. He sat in the darkness for a minute, staring at the apartment house that Erin called home. He was angry and he was tense, but he tried to control his emotions so that Erin wouldn't become suspicious.

Erin was already home. The lights in her apartment glowed in the night, and the Volkswagen Rabbit was sitting where she had parked it in front of the house. Kane's eyes moved from the car back to the building. Even in the unearthly glow of the streetlamp he could see the signs of age and disrepair in the large old home. Was this apartment house the cause of Erin's financial woes? Could she possibly be moving funds out of the bank for the upkeep on the costly old house?

He had thought he would feel a deep satisfaction in catching Cameron's accomplice in crime, but as he came closer to the truth, the satisfaction had soured in his stomach to a feeling of sickening disgust. He knew now that Erin was lying to him, and somehow he had to find a way to prove his theories about her, as much as he despised the idea.

He took in a long breath as he thought about Lee Sinclair. Erin's ex-husband was supposedly in Spokane, but with a little checking, Kane had discovered that Lee had moved back to Seattle over six weeks ago—about the same time that Erin had applied for her employee loan. Could she still be involved with him, and was he the drain on her money? Perhaps he was the catalyst in the partnership with Cameron.

Kane's hands tightened on the steering wheel until his knuckles whitened. He could only hope that he was wrong and that someone else was the embezzler. God, how he hoped so. There were still a few more possibilities, but unfortunately, right now the evidence was stacking up very heavily against Erin O'Toole.

Angrily Kane pushed his disturbing thoughts aside and got out of the car. He was furious at himself, at Erin and particularly at Lee Sinclair, whoever the hell he was.

Erin had just placed the pan of lasagna in the oven when the doorbell rang. Before she could cross the room, the door swung open and thudded against the wall. Kane strode into the room and closed the door just as angrily as he had opened it. Erin had begun to smile, but when her eyes met his, her face froze. His gray eyes were guarded, a stormy fog clouding their depths. His casual clothes, the same ones he had been wearing earlier, were disheveled and his tie was loosened rather haphazardly. "Don't you ever lock your door?" he muttered.

"Of course I do…but I was in a hurry…"

"That's no excuse!" he rifled back at her.

Erin was confused by his only slightly suppressed anger, and she felt her temper rise to meet his. "Look, Kane, thanks for your concern, but it's really not your problem."

"It is my problem, when it concerns your safety."

"I'm all right. I just forgot to latch the door. That's not such a crime."

A more contrite look softened his features. "I suppose you're right," he sighed, raking strong fingers through his coarse brown hair. "I didn't mean to jump down your throat." He walked over to her and brushed a light kiss across her forehead. "But I do wish that you would be more careful."

"I'll try," she agreed in order to ease the tension that was building between them. She could see that he was beginning to relax, but the lines near the edges of his eyes looked deeper than they had this morning. She tried to tell herself that it was probably just the first day at the bank that had taken its toll on him, or possibly that he was concerned about Krista. But she couldn't help feeling that there was a larger problem storming through his mind—a problem that concerned her.

"Would you like a drink?" Erin suggested.

"Oh." He slapped a palm against his forehead. "I forgot the wine—something came up at the bank. Forgive me?"

He was teasing, Erin knew, but she could sense an inner turbulence below his light attempt at humor. "Consider yourself forgiven," she agreed, "but my liquor cabinet isn't all that great."

Kane walked over to the cupboard that she indicated and searched through the bottles. "Saying that is being kind. It's downright pathetic."

"I don't see that you have much room to complain, since you were the one who forgot the wine in the first place," she reminded him, trying to suppress a smile.

"Touché, Miss O'Toole. Now let's see what we have in here." His voice was muffled as he pushed aside partially filled bottles of liquor and finally pulled out an unopened bottle of brandy. With a triumphant flourish, he held out the bottle for Erin's inspection. "Look at this. Maybe the evening won't be a total loss after all!"

"A loss? You practically insisted on inviting yourself over to a home-cooked dinner, and already you're insinuating that the evening will be wasted?" She could feel him looking at her, but she didn't turn around and started slicing the greens for a salad. She was only kidding, of course, but he deserved a shot after barging in that way.

In a moment his arms were encircling her waist and his breath moved her hair as he whispered in her ear. His voice was low and full of promise as he spoke. "I don't think that any time would ever be wasted if I could share it with you."

She let the knife slip to the counter. His touch was warming her abdomen, and the feel of his hot breath against her neck made her heart race. She tried to keep her head and recapture the light mood of the minute before. "That sounds like a line if I ever heard one."

"A line? Oh, Erin, don't you think I'm a little too old for lines? Don't you know what you mean to me?" There was a torture in his words as if he was admitting something that he himself didn't want to hear.

His hands persuaded her body to rotate and face him, and when her eyes found his, she saw that his gaze had darkened with a smoky passion. Smoldering embers lit his eyes as he bent his head slowly downward to capture her trembling lips with his. The warm, seductive pressure of his mouth roving passionately over hers made her dizzy. She tried to blink and restore some sanity to her emotions, but she couldn't. It was as if her entire body began and ended where her lips met his. Her knees began to give way and melt beneath her. And as he tasted her, an aching need began to consume her.

Her response was complete. Her blood warmed in a swirling moist heat. She began to return his kiss, hesitantly at first. But as he kindled the fires of desire within her body, she responded in kind. Her kisses became anxious pleas for a more intense lovemaking. Boldly her fingers crept up his chest until her arms encircled his neck. She felt the thick muscular cords near his spine and unconsciously began to massage away the tension that seemed to devour him tonight.

Kane groaned with pleasure, his voice an echo of hers as she gasped for air. His tongue met hers and danced hungrily in a torrid fever, first flicking light touches to hers and finally molding it with a moist and fevered need. "Erin," he breathed, letting her name whisper against her. "I need you...tonight."

Erin's mind continued to remind her that she should stop him now, while she still had the chance, but she found herself resisting common sense and embracing temptation. Never had she felt so ignited, so completely female.

His lips scorched a trail of featherlight kisses from her eyes to her throat and on to her tender ear. His delicious breath tingled her inner ear, sending shock waves of passion resounding through her mind. She let her head fall away from him, hoping to somehow make her neck and earlobe more available to him. His thumb traced the hollow of her throat, gently at first, but with increased pressure in tight little circles…around and around, until she thought that she wouldn't be able to breathe.

Erin sighed briefly and resigned herself to the fact that her mind wanted him as much as her body did. "Oh, Kane," she murmured, "I need you too." She succumbed body and soul to her desires and arched her hips against his. His breath ruffled her hair and he smiled down at her before lifting her off her feet and carrying her into the bedroom.

"I know that you need me, Erin. I thought that you would never realize that we were meant to be together."

"Together?" she breathed.

"As man and woman. I knew it from the first time I saw you, sitting amid that ridiculous pile of books in your office."

Together as man and woman, she thought, *but for how long? For an hour, a day, a week?* Her mind raced forward, but her body wouldn't let go, not tonight. She felt him pressed hotly against her, smelled his warm clean scent and saw a stormy passion in his face that she had to capture. She needed him every bit as much as he needed her, and perhaps much, much more.

Erin let herself follow the path of her emotions. The magic of his kiss had aroused her to the point of no return, and she was heedless of anything save his sensitive touch. She couldn't deny herself any of the pleasures that he could spark in her. Since that first moment in her dimly lit office, she, too, had been aware of him first and foremost as a man. His sensuality couldn't be ignored, not for a second. His dark eyes, well-muscled body and virile self-assurance had enticed and beckoned to the center of her femininity, and she was tempted beyond reason to respond.

Erin's body seemed to warm from the inside out, melting in fevered washes of heat and desire. Any reservations that might still have lingered in her mind were slowly and unconsciously stripped away from her as he rained liquid kisses over her skin.

The bedroom was bathed in moonlight. Kane laid Erin on the bed, and she felt the cool satin of the comforter through the sheer silk of her blouse. She was still dressed, although as he stood over her, she felt naked. Naked to the pain of needing him. Naked in the knowledge that she loved him. And naked in the recognition that her love was unreturned. His heavy-lidded eyes were unreadable, but Erin was very certain that although there was a smoke of passion in his gaze there was no flame of love.

Regardless of that fact, she couldn't and wouldn't deny the urges of her body. She loved him, despite his lack of love for her. The bed sagged beneath Kane's weight, and Erin felt herself tremble. His finger traced the length of her arm, but his eyes never left hers. He was watching her, almost studying her, seeming content to let his gaze caress her.

"Tell me no if you want me to stop," he commanded in a hoarse voice. His lips brushed tentatively over hers.

Her response was a grateful moan. Their lips met in a hot embrace, and she let her arms wind around his neck in a display of total abandon. She wanted all of him with a burning need that she had never before felt.

He let his hands stroke her face and throat in moth-soft caresses, until at last they reached her collar and finally the buttons of her blouse. He opened the blouse slowly, letting the fine silky fabric part of its own accord. And then gently he raised her shoulders to let the blouse slip to the floor. His eyes watched her torso as her breasts rose and fell with each of her gasping breaths.

"Erin…God, but you're beautiful," he sighed, fingering the lacy bra that was still a seductive barrier between his flesh and hers. His fingers teased and finally unclasped the skimpy piece of lingerie, until at last her aching breasts were unrestrained.

A groan escaped from his lips as he slowly massaged each dark-nippled breast to arousal. When he could feel the hardness of her breasts, he cuddled them softly and buried his head between the two feminine peaks. Erin arched against him, unable to control the hot urges that were firing her. She reached for his shirt, and as quickly as possible, removed it from his body, until her anxious fingers found the thick soft mat of fur that covered his chest and the male nipples beneath it.

As he enticed her, so did she him. She let her fingers touch and caress the firm muscles that flared rigidly over his body. Her hands traveled up his spine, vertebra by vertebra, feeling the hardness of his back through the moisture of his sweat.

The room was dark; only the soft glow from the partially opened door mingled with the moon glow to add a shimmering pallor to the night. But Erin could see Kane as clearly as if it were a bright summer day. All of her senses were alive to him. His touch fired her, his scent encouraged her and his salt-sweet taste lingered on her lips and tongue.

His hands traveled to her skirt and panty hose, quickly discarding a portion of the clothing that separated them. He cast off his pants as rapidly, never for a moment leaving Erin alone. Always one part of him was pressed warmly and possessively over her.

Her blood was boiling through her veins, spiraling upward from the deep mercurial well that was vibrating from the essence of her femininity. His lips traveled over her breasts, teasing and tasting each one while his hands slowly and rhythmically rubbed soft patterns against her abdomen, dipping deliciously below the elastic of her panties, and then letting the fabric snap tantalizingly against her skin.

Kane toyed with her last article of clothing until she thought she would go mad with the urgency of her need for him. When the agonizing last flimsy barrier was finally freed from her body, she groaned in pure animal pleasure and desire. He let his lips graze the muscles of her abdomen to circle her navel. His tongue warmed her flesh and she pulled him more closely to her.

All thoughts of anything but the mastery of his lovemaking were torn from her mind, pushed aside as quickly as her clothing. She was conscious of only one thing: the bruising, pulsating desire that dominated her mind and body. Time had ceased. Doubts had fled. All that she cared about was Kane: the skillful play of his fingers on her thighs and buttocks, the searing brand of his kiss over her breasts and abdomen, the enticing lure of his strong body.

She could feel the granitelike touch of his naked leg against hers, the soft hair tickling her cleanly shaven skin. She could also tell that he was holding back his physical needs to give her the utmost pleasure. In the half light of the moon she could see his arousal and feel the warm length of him brushing against her.

Just as she felt that she would surely melt with need of him, he came to her, fusing the fine muscles of his body with hers in a hot, rhythmic blend of passion. She felt him push her over the delicate edge of desire to fulfillment, and in the warm wash of exploded passion, he came with her in a burning torchlike shudder of surrender.

Erin felt a sigh flow from her lips as she held him tightly and securely, holding on to him as if her life depended on him. It had been many, many years since she had made love to a man, and never had she felt the wonder or the magic that Kane had aroused and satisfied in her tonight. Although she felt an incredible bliss, her torn emotions got the better of her, and she began to feel the hot sear of tears burn at the back of her eyes.

Embarrassed at herself, she tried to move away from Kane and blink back the unwanted tears. But as she slid against the satin comforter, his arms locked over her, imprisoning her.

"Where do you think you're going?" he whispered silkily, his voice still holding the satisfaction of afterglow.

Erin's voice caught in her throat and she couldn't force herself to answer him.

"Erin?" Kane's voice was more aware than it had been. "Is something wrong?"

She shook her head negatively, but when she did, she felt his strong fingers reach up and stroke her face. His hands stopped their movement as his fingertips encountered the first tear that had slid unrequested down her cheek. "Oh, no," he murmured.

"It's not…what you think," she managed to sigh.

"Did I hurt you?" His voice was uneven in the night.

"No…no…Kane…"

"Then why? I don't understand." His words were raw with concern.

"Neither do I," she admitted as the tears began to flow freely past the web of her lashes and down her cheeks. She shook her head in self-deprecation, letting the ebony curtain of her hair fall loosely around her face. How could she do such a thing to him, she asked herself silently. And how, when she was so deliriously happy, could she feel so confused and torn?

"Erin." His voice had lowered an octave, and he brushed her hair away from her face so as to kiss the tears from her cheeks. "Is something wrong?" He held her gently to him, letting her skin press tightly to his, while he covered them both with the comforter. In the quiet room, he rocked her in the cradle of his arms.

"No…nothing…nothing's wrong…" Her voice wavered.

"What is it? You're not ashamed of making love to me, are you?"

"No…no…never." She felt his breath feathering the back of her head as he sighed with relief. "It's nothing I can explain," she continued. "The last few weeks have been hard…." Could she tell him about the badly needed repairs to the building, the confusion she felt about Mitch or the taxing telephone calls from Lee? "…I guess I've been tired." She wanted to explain how she felt, but there were so many conflicting and unsettling emotions warring within her that she didn't want to think about them. Not tonight. She just needed to feel the peaceful security of Kane's arms around her.

Kane clutched her more urgently to him in a protective embrace. He could feel the beating of her heart, a warm pulse fluttering lightly under his fingertips and vibrating against the velvet smoothness of her breasts. He wanted her to speak—to confess. He needed to assure her that he could make everything right. He would find a way to help her out of the mess that Mitchell Cameron had created.

Kane's voice rumbled against his chest, and she could feel the deep manly tones pulsing against her naked back. "I want you to know that if you do have a problem—any problem whatsoever—you can come to me." His last words sounded like a confession. "I'm on your side."

"Oh, Kane," she breathed, wanting to confide her innermost thoughts and share everything with him, yet unable to bare her soul any more than she already had. "There's really nothing to tell. I'm…just a little keyed up. That's all…." She could feel herself smiling at him through her tears.

Outside a cloud crossed the moon, giving a misty aura to

the light that passed into the bedroom. She turned to face Kane, and his eyes looked all the more omniscient in the unnatural moon glow.

"I hope you realize that if you ever need a friend, you can count on me," Kane murmured, before lowering his head to hers and kissing away the final tears that stained her cheeks.

As his lips found hers, she tasted the salt of her own tears, mingled seductively with the uniquely male taste of Kane. She parted her lips, and in a moment the kisses deepened to rekindle the fires of passion that possessed them.

With a gentleness that belied the tension that pushed against him, Kane caressed Erin and together they discovered the secrets of inflamed desire and glorious love. Erin fell dreamlessly to sleep in the warm strength of Kane's arms. But Kane didn't sleep. Too many uneasy thoughts about Erin strained against his mind. He looked at her asleep and brushed an unruly wisp of raven hair off the perfect alabaster sheen of her face. Sleeping in the moonlight, she seemed so childlike, innocent and vulnerable.

But his mind continued in its ugly pursuit of the truth. Why had she lied to him? And why did he care so much?

Chapter 6

Erin felt comfortably warm and drowsy as she stretched lengthwise in the bed and tucked the silken comforter more cozily around her neck. She sighed softly to herself in pleasure as she slowly awakened. All the tension that had been gathering in her body over the last six months had somehow ebbed gently away from her. She smiled to herself contentedly before realizing that she felt so dreamily happy because she had made love to Kane Webster—her new boss!

Her dark lashes flew open as the reality of the situation dawned upon her. The bedroom was dark and the bed was empty. Kane must have left her and disappeared into the night as she slept. A feeling akin to desperation cascaded over her, and the bed, once warm and comforting, seemed cruelly cold and empty. She wondered silently to herself how she could have been so foolishly naive to expect him to stay with her. She was achingly aware that she loved him, and although she didn't want to care for him so deeply, she accepted the naked truth of her love. But she wasn't so foolish as to expect that he could possibly reciprocate her feelings of the heart.

Erin mentally chided herself for her thoughts of love. For all she knew, Kane might consider her just another easy conquest. The infuriating phrase "one night stand" crept into her mind. For all her bold talk of not mixing business with pleasure, she had invited Kane all too easily into her heart and into her bed.

You're an idiot, she swore at herself as she decided to get dressed. She reached for her teal blue skirt that was still lying in the discarded heap of wrinkled clothing at the side of the bed. After pulling her panty hose on furiously, she began to step into the skirt.

"Don't get dressed on my account," Kane's voice whispered across the darkness to her. Her disappointed heart leapt at the sound of his voice, and she whirled toward the doorway to find Kane leaning casually against the doorjamb, his gaze wandering recklessly over her body. Involuntarily she crossed her free arm over her breasts, while with the other she tugged vainly at the skirt.

"I…I thought that you'd gone," Erin murmured, and feeling somewhat embarrassed by her partial nudity, she hastily grabbed the sheet from the bed and pulled it togalike around her body. Kane watched her swathe herself with the white sheet, and in his mind he likened her to a Greek goddess.

"Now, why would I want to leave?" he drawled huskily as his eyes traveled lazily over her one exposed slim leg and up to her eyes. Her fingers tightened around the sheet and yet she felt naked.

"I don't know," she admitted, "but when I woke up, you were gone and I didn't hear any noise. I thought that you must have…." Her words died as she interpreted the expression in his clear gray eyes.

He stood still in the doorway watching her. One well-muscled shoulder rested against the doorjamb. The light from the living room was behind him, and his silhouette in the darkness seemed to intensify the broad strength of his shoulders and the powerful play of muscles on his chest. His shirt was still unbuttoned as if he were just in the process of getting dressed when he heard her awaken. Erin found it hard to concentrate on anything but his tanned skin and the invitation of his open shirt. Unconsciously she gripped the sheet a little more tightly.

"I'm not going to leave you," he replied seriously, and then wondered at the promise he heard echoing in his words. He could see Erin's face in the cloud-shadowed moon glow—a delicate, regal oval placed in relief by the tangled mass of black hair that cascaded down to rest against the marble texture of her bare shoulder. The hollow of her throat beckoned him, but he resisted reaching for her. She was beautiful, almost an inspiration, and Kane had difficulty reining in his emotions. Her lilac eyes shimmered in the half light, and Kane was sorely tempted to go back to the bed and crush her passionately against him. How could he ache so much for one woman? he asked himself. And how could any woman who appeared so innocent and vulnerable be mixed up with something as gut-wrenchingly dishonest as embezzling? The onerous thoughts that battled in his mind must have been evident on his face because Erin's expression changed from innocence to wariness. God, why did he want her so badly?

Kane cleared his throat, and in an attempt to break the heady silence that was entrapping him, tried to lighten the suddenly tense moment. He cocked one black eyebrow in mock suspicion and effectively changed the subject.

"So you thought that I had left you, did you? Wishful thinking on your part, wasn't it?"

"Wishful thinking? What do you mean?"

"You've been trying to weasel out of fixing dinner for me all day, but it won't work. I'm here and I'm famished!"

"The lasagna! Oh, no! I forgot all about it!" Erin wailed.

She started to hike her skirt upward over her hips, while still grasping the sheet.

Kane stood, unmoving and bemused, in the doorway. His silvery eyes never left her body. Erin sucked in a deep breath. Although she was uncomfortable about dressing in front of him, intuitively she knew it would be useless to try and dissuade him from watching her. She gave him an irritated glare that only seemed to amuse him further as she tried to squirm into the tight blue skirt and attempted to keep the sheet positioned modestly. Her efforts were in vain, and a deep chuckle erupted in his throat as he unabashedly studied her dismal efforts at privacy. Finally, when she slipped the skirt up to her waist and tried to tug at the zipper, it got caught in the sheet and Erin gave up. After the passionate intimacy of only an hour before, Erin realized that her modesty must appear slightly neurotic. With a burning flush of scarlet on her cheeks, she untangled the sheet from the zipper and let the sheet fall to the floor.

"Damn!" she swore under her breath when the skirt was in place at last. She raised her deep round eyes to him and met his gaze unwaveringly. Her breasts, two white soft mounds, were unshielded, and she moved slowly as she finished dressing. "You're not making this easy, you know," she accused, her eyes never leaving his. He met her challenging gaze with an amused twinkle in his eyes. "The least you could do," she continued, "is take the dinner out of the oven so it doesn't burn!"

A condescending smile touched the corners of his lips. "You expect me to help with the cooking?"

"Why not? You obviously intend to help with the eating," she bantered back at him, and attempted to hurry through the doorway. Just as she tried to pass him, he placed a strong arm across her path. The action effectively barred her passage and barricaded her into the bedroom.

"Not so fast," he murmured seductively. Erin felt her throat tighten.

"But the meal—the lasagna. It's probably cremated!"

"It'll keep," he breathed, his eyes holding hers. His head dipped downward, and before she could utter any further protest, he kissed her softly. His lips lingered over hers for only an instant before he dropped the imprisoning arm and pulled his head away from hers. "I just wanted to thank you."

"For what?" she asked breathlessly.

"For just being you." His words warmed her, and she felt more than a little light-headed and dizzy, but the steady pressure of his warm hand against the small of her back forced her into the living area of the apartment. She couldn't help but smile as she noticed that he had set the table for two and pulled the slightly overcooked casserole from the oven. Candles graced the intimate table. The wine was poured. The meal was already served.

"You did this?" she asked, surveying the table that he had set with enviable care. "And I slept through it?" Amazement was evident in her voice.

"Surprising, isn't it?"

"That's putting it mildly." She shook her head in concentrated thought. "I'm normally a light sleeper," she murmured as she walked into the kitchen.

"That's because you haven't been keeping the right company."

"And just what is that supposed to mean?" she inquired cautiously as she put the finishing touches on the meal and placed the salad on the table next to the lasagna and warm bread.

"Just that you'd probably sleep more soundly with me."

Her eyes jumped to his face as she took the chair opposite his at the table. She took a deep breath and decided that it was time to set him straight about her. Perhaps he had gotten the wrong impression and thought that she was somewhat promiscuous.

She began slowly and deliberately. "Kane, I want you to understand something about me," she requested.

"Such as?"

"Contrary to what you might think…" She struggled with her next words as they caught in her throat. "I don't normally…I mean…" She shook her dark curls in frustration. "What I'm trying to say is that I don't make a habit of sleeping with a man whom I barely know." She watched for his reaction.

"Oh?" His voice was interested, and he pushed his plate aside to give her his full attention. She saw no criticism in his misty eyes, only concern.

"I hope that I haven't given you the wrong impression about me…."

"You mean because you slept with me?"

Two dark scarlet points of color brightened her cheeks, but she bravely continued. "That's exactly what I mean." Her words were hushed, and for a moment she was forced to look away from him. When she brought her eyes back to his, she held his gaze steadily and her voice became coolly even. "I don't really understand why I think that you have to know this, but for the sake of my own somewhat Victorian morals, I want you to realize that I don't have casual affairs. In fact, other than my ex-husband, there has been no one. Until you."

"I know that," he assured her in a voice as grave as the night.

She fingered her wineglass and took a long swallow of the rosé. She studied the pale pink liquid and swirled it in the long-stemmed glass before continuing the conversation. "Then why did you ask me all of those insulting questions about Mitch?"

At the mention of Mitchell Cameron's name, a scowl darkened Kane's features. Once again his face was guarded and his eyes became two silver shields. "I didn't know you then," was the terse reply.

"And in just three days you know me well enough to evaluate my love life?" she returned, and heard the sarcasm in her voice.

"I probably know a lot more about you than you think."

Her lilac eyes fastened on his, and a rush of indignation that she couldn't conceal colored her words. "You haven't been checking up on me, have you?"

"No more than I have any other employee of the bank." It was a lie and he knew it, but he couldn't let her think any differently at this point. He hated himself for the lie, but he was trapped by the web of suspicions that plagued him and by the storm of emotions that captured him every time he looked into her eyes.

"Then why all the insinuations about Mitch? Can't you believe that a woman can make it on her own without sleeping with the boss?"

He arched an expressive black eyebrow, and she felt immediately contrite. The question that was unspoken hung between them on a charged electric current. Unashamedly Erin answered it. "You know that I didn't make love to you because of my job."

"Then tell me, why *did* you sleep with me?" he coaxed.

"For the same reason that *you* slept with *me*," she responded, lifting her chin proudly. "Because I wanted to." His tight frown seemed to relax, and he took a sip of his wine as he surveyed her over the rim of the wineglass. His gray eyes concentrated on her. She seemed so honest. It was impossible to think that her beautiful face would lie. Why hadn't she been truthful about her ex-husband? Erin O'Toole was an enigma, a ravishing, seductive enigma.

Erin struggled with her meal. Why did she feel such an

uncontrollable urge to explain everything to Kane? And why did she feel the need for caution? As she put aside her fork, she spread her hands outward on the table, her fingers reaching up in a supplicating gesture. "Mitch was my boss, and he was and is a very dear friend. No matter what he's done, nothing will change that. But there was never anything more between us than personal friendship and professional respect for each other. Can't you believe me?"

"Of course I do—now," Kane replied. "But you can't blame me for my suspicions. Until I met you in the bank last Saturday, I didn't know anything about you other than what was in your personnel file. I knew that you had been promoted rapidly—perhaps too quickly—and I wanted to know why. You have to understand that no matter how close you are to Mitch, he is a thief!" Kane's cold gray eyes grew dark. "It's my responsibility to the bank, the stockholders, the savings customers, everyone, to know everything I can about each employee. It would be ridiculous to think that I would rely on Mitchell Cameron's judgment."

Kane's words hit Erin like a splash of cold water. She was stunned, and her voice was brittle as she asked the question that was uppermost in her mind. "Are you trying to tell me that you don't think I'm qualified for my position, that the only reason you could see that I would get the job was because I might have slept with Mitch?" she challenged, stricken at the thought.

His voice was strangely devoid of emotion. "I'm saying that it's difficult for me to believe that a thirty-two-year-old woman is second in command of the legal department of a major Seattle bank...."

"And if I were a man?" she fired back at him, her eyes deepening to the color of a midnight storm.

"Sex has nothing to do with this!"

"Sex has everything to do with this," she argued, slapping her palm against the table and rattling the silverware. "You seem to overlook the fact that I spent the last six years of my life in night school, for the most part doing postgraduate work in corporate law! If it weren't for the fact that you bought First Puget Bank, I would probably be a practicing attorney today!"

It was Kane's turn to be angry and his words sliced through the air. "I don't see how I could have possibly hindered your legal career! What does my ownership of the bank have to do with it?"

Erin swallowed with difficulty and licked her arid lips. She tried to think calmly and took a long swallow of wine to quench her parched throat. Getting angry wouldn't solve anything, she told herself, and giving in to her sometimes volatile temper would only hinder the situation. Carefully she explained her position. "There are several reasons that I haven't been able to take the bar exam."

"And somehow they are all my fault," he surmised.

"I'm not blaming you," she insisted, and began toying with her napkin. "First Puget was paying my way through school. Any class I took that pertained to my job was paid for by the bank. Other classes I paid for myself. That is—until the bank sale."

"You mean, until Consolidated Finances bought out First Puget?"

She nodded.

"Lack of money prevented you from taking the exam?" His jawline hardened and a tiny muscle began to work in his jaw as he clenched his teeth together. One more reason Erin needed money, as he saw it. Just how desperate was she?

"Money isn't the only problem," she sighed, wishing there were some way to avoid this particular discussion. "You see, in the past six months, there have been several departmental changes…and Mitch wasn't around a good deal of the time. I had to spend a lot of my free time at the bank, working."

"And you didn't have time to study for the examination?" Was there a slight undercurrent of sarcasm to his question?

"It's not as simple as going out and getting a driver's license, you know!" she snapped back at him, her strained temper unleashed at last. Viciously she speared a portion of the lasagna and forced the bite into her mouth.

For a few seconds neither she nor Kane spoke, and they finished the remainder of the meal in silent battle. When she hazarded a surreptitious glance in his direction, she felt her anger flow out of her. Perhaps it was the deep concentration of his knit brows, or the play of light on his gold-streaked chestnut hair. Or maybe it was the seductive way his mouth curved, or his bronzed chest as it peeked out from beneath his shirt. Whatever the reason, she felt her temper cool as she watched him. Her heart was torn and she ached to understand the man whom she loved so urgently.

Why, she wondered, did she feel that he was holding something back from her? Why did there always seem to be a dark, unasked question in his eyes? Was he like she was, insecure about a commitment to a fellow employee? Was it possible that he had a girlfriend, or perhaps a fiancée, waiting for him in California? Or was it a brooding concern for his daughter that made him seem so remote at times? How could she love a man so desperately and still feel that he wasn't being completely honest with her?

She finished her meal, excused herself and began brewing some coffee in the kitchen. Despite the uncomfortable conversation, Kane ate hungrily and Erin was pleased. What was it about preparing a meal for the man she loved that made her feel so satisfied? Some age-old maternal instinct, she supposed and smiled to herself. She had experienced the same satisfied sensation with Lee in the first few months of her marriage. It hadn't lasted long! she reminded herself.

At a time like this why would she remember her ex-husband and the few good times that they had shared? She tried to dispel her mood of melancholy remembrance by pouring the coffee and carrying it into the living room.

Kane had risen from the table and was standing at the window, staring out across the darkened Puget Sound. From his position, he could see the jeweled lights of Seattle winking on the quiet black waters. A deep blanket of fog was beginning to roll into the sound.

"Even at night this is a spectacular view of the city," he thought aloud, accepting the coffee that Erin offered. She, too, looked into the misty night.

"That's one of the reasons that I had to have this place," she agreed, and then laughed. "Along with a very long list of other things."

"Such as?"

"The charm of this old house. Everything about it speaks of a different time, a more romantic period in history." She ran a caressing finger across the cool wood of the windowsill. "The craftsmanship is exquisitely ornate, and I doubt that it could be duplicated today. This house was built with love. Look at the woodwork, the carved stairs, the beveled windows, everything! Even the builder who separated it into apartments and added all the modern conveniences took enough care to keep the flavor and the grandeur of the house in mind. I fell in love with it the minute I saw it," she admitted, and was surprised at how easily she had opened up to Kane about her feelings for the old mansion.

"Didn't anyone warn you about the expensive upkeep of such an old building?" he asked cautiously as he sat down on the couch. She took a seat next to him and shook her head thoughtfully.

"Everyone I knew tried to talk me out of it. Even my parents, who live on the East Coast, flew out here to try and dissuade me. They all told me that I was throwing money away. How does the expression go? 'Good money after bad'? They swore that the upkeep of the place would ruin me financially." She shrugged her slim shoulders and looked out the window again. "But the more people tried to talk me out of it, the more I absolutely had to have it!"

"Watch out," he cautioned with a smile. "Your rebellious side is beginning to show."

"Is it?" she asked, turning her attention back to him. She had considered herself many things, but never rebellious.

"That dark, private side of you that I told you about yesterday. It's surfacing," he suggested.

Once again the conversation was becoming too intimate for Erin. She was beginning to feel claustrophobic, as if he were closing in on her. Something made her draw away; she tried to change the subject. "In any event I bought this place and haven't lived to regret it yet."

"And were all those people who gave you advice correct?"

"What do you mean?"

He took a long, experimental sip of his coffee and studied her intently. "I mean, has this house become a financial burden to you?"

Erin swallowed before answering. Just how much did she want him to know about her, and how much did he already guess? "It hasn't been easy," she admitted reluctantly.

"Tenant problems?"

She shook her head negatively. "Not really. Most of the people who rent here have been with me for years, and they are very nice people who take pride in their homes. Once in a while I have a vacancy problem, but the primary difficulty with this place is the repairs. You see, I'm not exactly handy with a hammer or a saw."

"I wouldn't worry too much about that," he teased and lightly touched her shoulder. "You have talents in other fields." His whispered words were tender and comforting, and she felt that she had known him all her life. His fingers touched her hair. He felt himself drawn to the ebony sheen of her curls. They were as black and inviting as the night itself. He caught himself and struggled to maintain his objectivity where Erin was concerned, but found it difficult to put his feelings for her in their proper perspective. She had lied to him and he knew it. Whether she admitted it or not, Lee Sinclair was back in Seattle. Kane felt that he had to press Erin tonight, before he became all the more entangled in her mysterious womanly charms. He couldn't let himself forget that it was imperative that he understand what devious thoughts were being spun in that regal head of hers.

"What about your ex-husband?" Kane prodded.

"Lee?" she asked, perplexed. "What does Lee have to do with anything?" Nervously she pushed an errant strand of hair back in place. Why did Kane continue to bring up the subject of a man whom Erin would rather forget?

"What did he have to say about this place and your purchasing it?"

"He couldn't say much. We were divorced at the time," she responded with a finality that she hoped would effectively close the subject. But still he persisted.

"Tell me about the divorce," he coaxed.

"Why?"

A smile toyed with the corners of his mouth. "Because I want to know all about you…." he suggested silkily.

"I don't like to talk about Lee."

"Why?"

"Are you interrogating me again?" she asked, promptly regretting the acidity in her words. She got up from the couch and shrugged her shoulders. "It bothers me...to talk about Lee."

"Did he hurt you so badly?" he asked, his voice gentle.

Her eyes glazed over with the shame that she had borne. How could she explain the embarrassment of Lee's affair and the messy divorce? "Yes," she whispered, "I suppose that he did hurt me, but only because I let him."

"By loving him too much?" he asked severely.

"No, by being so young and naive. At the time I thought that all marriages were made in heaven, and I didn't think that I would fail, or that he would *use* me...." She found that she was trembling. The cup of coffee shook in her fingers, and she was forced to set it on the bookcase in order to hide her reaction from Kane.

"There was another woman?" he guessed, and Erin, with her back to him, let her shoulders droop as she nodded.

"My pride was wounded very deeply." She pulled her lips into a thin line of self-deprecation and squared her sagging shoulders. "I just never thought that I would end up as a divorce court statistic!"

"You didn't want the marriage to end?"

She turned and faced him. "You don't understand. I didn't want to fail, but I *had* to get out of the marriage to Lee. I couldn't bear the hypocrisy!"

Quickly Kane moved off the couch and reached for her. He pressed her quietly against the strength of his chest. Although she was still shaking, she could hear the steady beat of his heart, and his silent support helped calm her.

"Erin," Kane breathed, sharing in the agony that had embittered her.

"It's all right," she murmured against him. "I don't know why it still bothers me...at times. The pain has been gone for a long while."

She felt his arm tighten around her, and his voice was barely a whisper when he asked the question. "Do you ever see him?" Kane asked with an urgency she couldn't understand.

"I haven't seen him for over a year, since he moved to Spokane." The pressure of his hands against her back increased and she felt compelled to continue. "But he has moved back to Seattle, and he has called me."

His grip slackened, but the deep lines of concern that etched his forehead remained. "He wants to see you again?" Kane asked, and his eyes narrowed a fraction.

"I don't want to see him," she sighed. "So I haven't."

"Is he being overly persistent?" There was a thread of steel in Kane's voice.

"Yes...no...no, not really..." She rubbed her temple in confusion. "Couldn't we talk about something else? I really don't like to be reminded of that period in my life. What about you?" she asked, her lilac eyes searching his. "What was your marriage like?"

Kane released her and scowled. His lips formed a thin line that was neither a smile or frown. "I suppose that's a fair question, since you bared your soul to me."

He strode purposely back to the couch and raked his fingers through the thick waves of his hair, before picking up his lukewarm coffee and staring into the black liquid.

"My marriage to Jana was a mistake from the beginning," he admitted with a frown. "I guess I probably knew it at the time, but I was much younger then, and it took me quite a few years to finally admit to myself that we had made an error that was destroying us."

He looked vacantly out the window into the fog before continuing. His dark brows pulled together in concentration and carefully Erin came closer to him and perched on the arm of the sofa as he began to speak.

"In the beginning I was attracted to her because she was an incredibly beautiful and famous woman. You know, the glamorous model. I was just getting started in my business at the time, and I was flattered that she would even give me the time of day. I convinced myself that I loved her, when actually there was never any love between us. I was young enough to think that beneath all the glitter was a beautiful person hidden in that gorgeous body. A typical male mistake. And of course I was wrong.

"We had a whirlwind romance, I guess you might say. Lusty affair would be more exact. In any event just as I was beginning to suspect that we were too different ever to get along, it was too late—she was pregnant. I talked her out of the abortion and into marriage."

His lips thinned and he shook his head derisively. "I guess that I was a damned fool to think that a baby would change things between us, that our differences would work themselves out. And as it turned out, Jana and I had very different impressions about family life. She resented having to give up her figure and her career for the sake of her pregnancy, and she resented being a mother and a housewife. After five years of battling with her I agreed to the divorce that she wanted so desperately. As I said before, the marriage was a mistake from the beginning, and I knew it. But no matter what, it was worth every minute of the arguments—because of Krista."

He cleared his throat as he thought about his daughter and a sadness stole across his features. Erin felt an urge to brush away the signs of strain that seemed to age his face. The line of his jaw tensed as he spoke. "The biggest error in judgment I made was that at the time I didn't fight for custody. I subscribed to the same myth as the rest of the world: A young girl needs to be with her mother, regardless of the weaknesses or the frame of mind of the woman." A tortured look came into his steely eyes. "And then, to compound the mistake, I threw myself into my work, trying to erase the memories that had become painful. My attitude—it wasn't fair to Krista. To put it bluntly, I neglected my child. Not because I wanted to, but because I wanted to hide from the memories." He closed his eyes for a moment and rubbed the back of his neck to ease the tension that had knotted at the base of his head as he thought about the divorce and his child. He seemed tired and weary; Erin felt the burn of tears threatening to spill from her eyes.

His voice was a muted whisper when he continued. "I saw Krista occasionally of course, but not nearly as much as I wanted to or should have…it was just too difficult, too much of a struggle." A black eyebrow cocked sardonically. "A selfish attitude, wouldn't you say?" he asked her rhetorically. His next sentence was one of self-condemnation. "I was a bastard of a father!"

He hesitated only slightly, and that was to wave his arm emphatically, stilling the protest that was forming in Erin's throat.

"Within a year Jana was trying to rebuild her career. It was difficult for her because she was six years older and slightly out of shape. Modeling, for the most part, is for the very young woman with an almost boyishly slim figure. No one in the New York or Los Angeles agencies was interested in Jana. As far as they were concerned, Jana was yesterday's news.

"Then this Hollywood actress obsession took hold of her, and unfortunately she failed, dismally trying to remember her lines as the cameras rolled." He rubbed his chin thoughtfully. "It was at about that point that she began making the self-help and group therapy rounds. She went through periods of fad diets, deep depression, sensitivity groups—you name it and she was into it. I suggested that she go to a respected local psychiatrist, but she ignored my advice as usual and preferred to stick with the most faddish encounter group of the day.

"That's when I decided to do something about Krista. As poor a father as I had been, even I knew that all Jana's neuroses couldn't be good for an impressionable nine-year-old girl. Damn!" He swore at himself and bit his lower lip in annoyed remembrance. "I should have seen it earlier. Maybe I could have prevented all of Krista's problems. Perhaps if I had been paying a little more attention to my kid rather than my business interests, Jana would be alive today and Krista would be walking like a normal and healthy eleven-year-old!"

"You can't blame yourself," Erin objected. "You tried to help."

Steely gray eyes flashed fire at her. "'Too little, too late,' as the saying goes."

Erin had trouble keeping her silence. She saw the emotions that were ripping him apart as he thought about his past. His fist clenched tightly before he thrust it into the pocket of his pants.

"There's really not all that much more to tell," Kane admitted in a softer, more controlled voice. "I was concerned, and I suggested that Krista come and live with me, at least for a while, until Jana could—how did she phrase it—get her head together. But she wouldn't have anything to do with it. Krista was a burden to her, and both she and I knew it, yet she wouldn't allow my own daughter to come and live with me! Sometimes I felt that Jana was using Krista as a weapon against me." An almost evil look stole over his lips. "And it worked! Not only did it bother me, but Krista became steadily more introverted. She always had been a somewhat shy, quiet child, but it seemed that she was withdrawing too deeply into herself, becoming sullen." There was a long pause while Kane drew in a steadying breath. "And then, of course, there was the accident. Up until that time, at least I could talk to Krista." His eyes darkened with a quiet rage at the circumstances that had led to the isolation from his only child. "But since the accident and her paralysis, I have trouble communicating with her about anything. It's as if she's punishing me for what happened to Jana...." He shifted his weight uncomfortably on the couch before murmuring, in a barely audible voice, his own self-condemnation. "I suppose that I deserve it!"

"No!" Erin challenged.

"For God's sake, Erin. Krista watched her mother die!"

"Oh, Kane, don't go on blaming yourself for something that no one could prevent," she begged.

"Easier said than done," he muttered.

Telling the story had been an ordeal that Kane hadn't prepared himself for. He was nervous and amazed at his own confessions to Erin. It was never his intention to divulge so much of himself to her. He didn't want her to be able to see into his mind, and yet he had just given her the chance.

Kane had told himself that he needed to get to know Erin to find out more about the embezzling scheme at the bank, but the pleading look of innocence in her eyes, the soft, petulant curve of her lips, and her clear-sighted, intelligent mind all trapped him into admitting things that he had hidden from the rest of the world. Why was it so damn easy to talk to her, to confide his most introspective thoughts to her?

Erin was obviously moved by his story; he could see that in the caring look of pain she directed toward him and the unshed tears in her eyes. God, he reminded himself, he had to get away from her while he still could.

He cleared his throat and put his empty coffee cup on the table. Avoiding her eyes, he reached for his jacket and slipped the sport coat over his shoulders. "I guess that we had better call it a night," he declared with a touch of tenderness in his voice. He fought the urge to draw her into his arms and kiss away the tears she was trying courageously to hide.

"You're leaving?" Was it a surprise or disappointment that made her touch her lips provocatively?

"I think it would be best."

"Why?"

"I thought you were the one who wanted to keep our relationship strictly business...."

"It's too late for that now," she whispered, and her wide violet eyes touched his.

"Convince me," he coaxed huskily, and mentally cursed himself for his own weakness.

"What would it take to convince you?" she teased, still blinking back the tears that pooled in her eyes.

"Use your imagination...."

A slow seductive smile lit her eyes. "You're wicked," she accused. "You know that, don't you?" She crossed the living room and let her fingers slide inside his jacket to press warmly against the light cotton fabric of his shirt. Powerful muscles tensed under the sensitive touch of her fingertips.

A slow groan of agonized pleasure escaped from his throat before he lowered his head to hers and captured her lips with his. "Oh, Erin," he whispered as he swept her off her feet and carried her toward the bedroom, "why is it that I can't resist you?"

Chapter 7

The bed creaked and shifted in the darkness.

"What are you doing?" Groggily she asked the question. Erin's eyes fluttered open as she felt Kane stir and move out of bed.

"I have to get up—I have work to do today," Kane replied and rubbed her tousled head fondly. In the inky blackness of the predawn hours, he could see her. Even after a passionate night of lovemaking, she looked serenely enchanting against the stark whiteness of the bedsheets.

She groaned and rolled over. "But, oh, God, it's only"— Erin reached for the alarm clock and pulled the luminescent dial within inches of her face and sleepy eyes—"four-thirty in the morning." There was another agonized groan as she pushed the clock back on the nightstand. "No one in his right mind gets up at this time of day," she moaned, and stuffed her face back into the downy softness of her pillow.

The bed sagged under Kane's weight and he pressed a warm kiss against her forehead. "Do you want me to stay until dawn?" he asked quietly. "What about your tenants, not to mentioned our fellow bankers? You were the one who didn't want our relationship open for public viewing," he reminded her. "Besides all of that nonsense, I need a shower, shave and a change of clothing."

Even to Erin's cobweb-filled mind, Kane's reasoning seemed logical and clear. She propped up her head with her hand and tugged at the quilt close to the base of her throat. An autumn chill stung the morning air.

It took a little time, but slowly she began to awaken, and with interested eyes, she watched him get dressed. It was strange how comfortable she felt just being with him, how natural and right it all seemed. But he was correct. The fewer people who knew of their relationship, the better.

Kane left just as dawn was stretching its golden rays through her bedroom window. She listened as his car roared off down the hill and faded in the distance. It was a faraway, lonely sound that retreated into the misty morning air.

It was impossible to fall back into the heavy slumber that had come to her in Kane's arms. And so, with one final assessing and dubious glance at the clock, she got up, showered and dressed for the day.

Surprisingly, with only a few hours sleep, Erin felt wonderfully refreshed after the hot needlelike spray of the shower pulsated against her skin. She toweled herself dry, applied a thin sheen of makeup, twisted the ebony strands of her hair into her businesslike chignon and stepped into her favorite burgundy suedelike suit. As she tied the broad white bow of her silk blouse she glanced in the mirror, and the woman in the reflection smiled back in genuine fondness. Erin felt good about herself this morning.

Fingers of fog still held the city, but the bright morning sun sent prisms of colorful light streaming heavenward in what promised to be a gorgeous fall day.

Unwittingly Erin smiled as she pushed her way through the large plate-glass doors of the bank building. The dismal feeling of trepidation that had been with her during the transition of ownership of the bank seemed to have disappeared. Even as she brushed by Kane's office, she felt only a tinge of regret for Mitch. She still had a fondness in her heart for her ex-employer, but she realized that there was nothing that she or anyone else could do to help him. He had never returned any of her calls, although she had left several messages on the mechanical answering device that Mitch had installed. She had tried her best. Now, surely, if he needed to get in touch with her, he would.

As she passed by the outer reception area, she reached, by habit, for her messages stacked neatly on the main reception desk. She smiled inwardly as she read the bold scrawl that she recognized immediately as Kane's handwriting. It was concise and stated only "Tonight, eight o'clock." Erin couldn't restrain the blush that slowly climbed up her neck nor the look of satisfaction that touched the corners of her eyes. She wondered how transparent she must appear.

The secretary who had compiled the messages for her was a professional woman of about sixty, who neither commented nor indicated in any manner that she had read or interpreted the intimate message in Ms. O'Toole's slot. Relief washed over Erin as she read the look of total disinterest in the gray-haired woman's smile and the professional "Good morning" that was her usual greeting. Nothing appeared out of the ordinary. Even before Erin began to move toward her office, the secretary resumed the quick staccato rhythm of her lithe fingers on the keyboard of the typewriter.

It was midafternoon before Erin actually saw Kane again. He was conferring in the hallway with a man whom Erin recognized as a vice president of the loan department. For a quick instant Erin's mind traveled to the employee loan that she had requested and wondered fleetingly if it was the topic of conversation. From Kane's reaction she doubted that he was discussing her need for funds.

As she passed the two bankers Kane gave Erin a perfunctory nod of his head to indicate that he had seen her, but there was nothing the least bit intimate in his gesture. It was an act of courtesy to acknowledge an associate. For a moment Erin's temper began to rise, and she felt angry until she understood the reasons for his discretion and feigned lack of interest in her. It was what she had requested, insisted upon—that their relationship remain secret, clandestine—and he was adhering to her request to the letter.

As she closed the door to her office she found herself still thinking of Kane and the tenuous relationship that existed between them. How could something so wonderful as falling in love with Kane seem so wrong? Why did she feel two conflicting urges warring within her mind? One feminine part of her wanted to share the happiness she had found with him with the world. The other more cautious and rational side of her nature urged her to silence. After all he was still her boss, the man who signed her paychecks, and it would be easy for anyone to misconstrue her feelings and relationship with him. She had been the target of curious and malicious gossip before, and she had vowed never to let herself be put in such an emotional and compromising position again. She knew how devastated she had been eight years ago, and she steeled herself against any intrusions into her private life. She hadn't wanted to fall in love with Kane; it had just happened. Perhaps, together, they could avoid the speculation and gossip. Surely it couldn't be that difficult to keep things on a professional level at the office, could it?

Erin lulled herself into a sense of serenity. It was a brilliant autumn afternoon, and other than the slight snub from Kane, the day had gone well. It wasn't until late afternoon that her tranquil mood was destroyed.

Contrary to what she had expected, Erin had accomplished more work this day than she had in weeks. Kane Webster had seemed to more than amply fill Mitchell Cameron's shoes, and all the disturbing telephone calls and interruptions that Erin had become used to had vanished. For the first time in over six months she could devote all her attention to the piles of probate work that had accumulated in her "Incoming" basket.

Erin was actually giving herself a mental commendation as she surveyed the clean desktop and slipped into the burgundy jacket before leaving the building. Just as she reached into the open desk drawer for her purse, there was a sharp rap on the door, and Olivia Parsons, not waiting for an invitation, glided into the room.

At the sultry brunette's entrance, Erin felt a cold tingle of apprehension at the back of her neck. Olivia was holding a clipboard pressed firmly to her breasts and jangled something metallic in the air.

"New keys!" Olivia announced, and dropped a ring of keys with a jingle onto the desktop. The green shimmer of Olivia's street-length designer dress matched the emerald essence of her eyes. "I'll need all your old keys," she stated flatly, and waited, somewhat impatiently, with her long fingers resting against her hip. The action emphasized the long, seductive curve of her leg.

"My keys? Why?"

"Standard procedure, after something like this embezzling thing with Mitch. Who can guess just how many sets of keys he's had made for any door in this building?"

"Of course," Erin agreed, and found herself relaxing a little as she realized that Olivia was just doing her job. Erin understood the liability of the bank. Even if Mitch had turned in his set of keys, he could have a dozen copies hidden away. The bank couldn't take the chance that he might sneak back into the building or the vaults.

"Here they are," Erin stated, producing the keys from the side pocket of her purse. She handed them to Olivia and the dark-haired girl frowned as she counted them. "Where's the other one?" Olivia asked, a puzzled expression crowding her neatly arched brows.

"I don't have any others. Just the key to the front door, the probate file cabinet, and Mitch's office—unless you want my desk key."

"No," Olivia answered, checking the corresponding numbers on the keys against her chart. "What about the key to the securities cart?" she asked, her green eyes reassessing Erin.

"I haven't had the key to that cart in years," Erin said, thinking aloud. Absently she rubbed her temple. "It had to have been over seven years ago." Again a chilly feeling of apprehension swept over her and her stomach began to knot.

"But the ledger here indicates that you should have a key to that cart," Olivia maintained. Laying the white formal sheet of paper on Erin's desk, she pointed to a line showing that Erin did, in fact, receive the key in question within the last year.

"It's a mistake…" Erin sighed. "I never had that key!"

"But aren't those your initials next to Mitch's signature?" Olivia pressed.

"Yes…it looks like I signed out for the key. But I didn't. There must be some mistake.…" Her voice trailed off. She knew that she had never had that key. The whole situation was absurd. And a little frightening. Anyone with that key could withdraw negotiable stocks and bonds from the cart if given the right opportunity. A perfect plan for embezzlement. The thought sickened her.

Olivia studied the report for a few seconds more and then, with an elegant wave of her hand, dismissed the subject. "I guess it really doesn't matter since all of the new locks have already been installed. Just sign here for the new keys and I'll see that this securities key matter is cleared up." Erin scribbled her initials next to Olivia's, relinquished the old set of keys to the leggy brunette and snapped the new ring of keys into her purse.

Just as she was about to leave Olivia paused at the door. She thought for a moment before turning to face Erin once again. Her voice was low as she asked, "What do you think about Mitch?" Her normally lively green eyes had deadened. "Isn't it awful...."

Erin slowly shook her head and rubbed her chin nervously. "I don't like to think about it—or even talk about it. It's something that I don't understand at all," she confessed, and hoped that the conversation with Olivia had ended. Something about the brunette always made Erin uneasy. But Olivia wouldn't let the subject die.

"I know what you mean." Olivia seemed to agree. "I would never have guessed—not in a million years." She paused once again, her gaze flicking up the length of Erin's figure as if something else were on her mind. A flame of life leapt into her eyes. "It must be especially hard for you," Olivia intimated.

"It's been hard for all of us," Erin agreed cautiously.

"Yes, but with you it's a little different, wouldn't you say?"

"I don't know what you're getting at."

"Oh, sure you do," Olivia replied as she brushed back an errant wave of thick copper hair. "You don't have to play naive with me. I know how close you were to Mitch."

Erin's patience, which had been thinning ever since the lanky girl had entered her office, snapped. She pulled the strap of her purse over her shoulder and said with a coolly professional voice that suggested the subject was closed, "Mitch is a good friend of mine—nothing more!"

"Oh?" The question seemed innocent enough, but the curl of Olivia's petulant lips suggested disbelief. "The same way that Kane Webster is your good friend?" The color drained from Erin's face, confirming Olivia's vicious accusation. "Well, honey," she continued with an exaggerated wink, "no one can accuse you of not knowing which side of the bread the butter's on!" After her final invective, and with a self-satisfied smile, Olivia slipped out of the office.

Erin stood in stunned silence in the aftermath of Olivia's remarks. Although she was alone, she felt a storm of scarlet embarrassment climb up her neck. It was happening again! Already! The gossip had started, and who better to start it than Olivia. Erin swallowed hard, and sagged against the desk. Why had she been so foolish—she should have seen it coming. All the gossip, the knowing glances, the snickering laughter behind her back, all over again!

She let her forehead rest on the palm of her hand as she slowly tried to recompose herself. It had been a good day, she reasoned, and she shouldn't let Olivia ruin it. But that was the trouble, Olivia had ruined it. Why, after all the years that had passed since the divorce from Lee, did any little biting comment from Olivia still wound her? Eight years had passed since Olivia's tempestuous affair with Lee. Although at the time, Erin had blamed the slim brunette for the breakup of her marriage with Lee, she knew now that she had been grossly unfair. If Lee hadn't taken up with Olivia, another pretty face would have caught his wandering eye and lured him away from the bounds of the marriage. Lee was only too willing. It was just unfortunate that Lee had been reckless enough to choose to have an affair with someone whom Erin saw on a daily basis. It seemed to compound the pain.

The problem with the marriage had not really been Olivia, but rather the differences between Erin and Lee. Although Erin recognized that now, she still found it hard to accept Olivia for what she seemed to be: a very knowledgeable and efficient assistant officer of the bank. Although the problems of the past were long dead, Olivia's presence at the bank and her vicious tongue continued to plague Erin. She never felt that she could completely trust Olivia.

Was she being unfair? Erin asked herself as she once again gathered her purse over her shoulder, straightened her skirt and headed out the door. Perhaps Olivia's attempt to communicate with Erin about Mitch was only natural. Both Olivia and Erin had cared very much for Mitch, and each had worked for him for nearly a decade. Perhaps Olivia felt the need to lash out because of Erin's cool attitude toward her. It was just possible that Erin was holding too much of a grudge against the sultry woman who wore the designer dresses and tailored suits with such seductive bearing. Erin sighed heavily to herself. Maybe she had never given Olivia a chance.

But the knot in Erin's stomach continued to tighten. She just intuitively didn't trust Olivia. It wasn't so much what Olivia said that managed to get under Erin's sensitive thin skin, but the way the words came out. Double entendres, sly winks, suggestive innuendos—all at Erin's expense.

As Erin found her way downstairs and out to the parking lot, she tried to dismiss the anxious feeling that had seized her with Olivia's interruption. But as she unthinkingly put the key into the ignition switch of the car, she hesitated and watched, nearly hypnotized, as the other keys jangled and swung near the steering column. How had her name gotten on the list of people who had keys to the securities cart? Try as she would to remember otherwise, she knew that she had never, in the last few months, signed out for that key!

And yet the presence of her own initials negated her perception. Would someone within the bank use her good name for his own purposes? Could someone have forged her initials? Mitch, perhaps? Would Mitchell Cameron stoop so low? With a disgusted grunt to herself and a firm shake of her head, she started the car and dismissed her traitorous thoughts. Where had her loyalty gone? Mitchell Cameron had been kind to her, a friend when she needed one most. She wouldn't turn her back on him now—nor would she imagine that he would use her name for his own advantage. But then, how could she explain about the key? Could it be, as Olivia said, just a mistake? Probably. And yet...

There were still slight traces of fog along the waterfront and in the downtown area of Seattle, but as Erin's yellow VW climbed the hill that supported the apartment house, the mist thinned and by the time she was home the evening was cool but clear. Only a trace of fog could be seen in the wisps that clung to the dark waters of the distant sound.

It was nearly seven, and Erin wanted to dash up the stairs to get ready for Kane, but propriety stopped her. She set her purse and briefcase on the lowest step of the staircase and knocked softly on Mrs. Cavenaugh's door.

A curious blue eye peeked at her through the peephole. Then quickly the door opened, and the slightly bent figure of Milly Cavenaugh greeted Erin with a warm smile.

"Good evening, Erin. I didn't expect to see you tonight," Mrs. Cavenaugh said cheerily, and winked broadly at her young landlady.

Erin's face creased with anxiety. "Why not? Didn't the repairmen show up?"

"Did they ever...." Mrs. Cavenaugh replied with a disapproving purse of her lips. Disgust darkened her eyes and she shook her head as she remembered. "They were here...an entire battalion of them…tracking in mud and heaven-knows-what-else into the house!" Erin's eyes followed the sweep of Mrs. Cavenaugh's hand as it included the front porch, entry hall and stairway. The oaken planks of the hallway were, indeed, imprinted with scrambled tracks of mud-laden, booted feet.

"Did they finish the job?" Erin asked, dragging her eyes away from the mess on the floor and back to her elderly tenant.

"Partially, I think. It seems that it's going to take more work than the original estimate showed," Mrs. Cavenaugh announced, thinking carefully.

"More work? Why?" Dollar signs flashed in Erin's mind.

"Something about dry rot in the floorboards, I think," Mrs. Cavenaugh explained with a shrug of her bent shoulders. "I'm sorry, dear, I really didn't pay too much attention—I was too busy trying to get them to wipe the dirt off their boots."

Erin felt her heart sink. Dry rot? What was that exactly? Something to do with the condition of the subfloor and support beams, she thought. It sounded like it would cost money—lots of it.

"Is something wrong, Erin?" Mrs. Cavenaugh asked, assessing the worried look that had appeared on Erin's face. "Would you like to come in and sit for a moment? I could brew a pot of tea…."

Forcing herself to smile, Erin shook her head. "Nothing's wrong, Mrs. Cavenaugh. I was just a little surprised to find out about the dry rot."

"Oh, it's probably nothing to be concerned about anyway," the elderly lady thought aloud, dismissing the subject with an expansive wave of her hand. Her pale blue eyes took in the concerned look on Erin's features before asking the question that had been entering her head ever since she had seen Erin through the peephole.

"How did things go at work today?"

Erin was still concentrating on the bad news of the dry rot, wondering how extensive the damage was and just how many hundreds or thousands of dollars it would take to correct the problem. Mrs. Cavenaugh's question startled her.

"Pardon me?"

"Work. The new boss. How're you two getting along?" Thinly veiled interest sparked in her kindly blue eyes.

Erin pulled out of her reverie at the mention of Kane. "Everything's going just fine, I guess. Mr. Webster seems to be quite capable."

"And Mr. Cameron?" the old lady coaxed inquisitively.

Once again concern clouded Erin's violet eyes. "I don't know," she replied honestly. "I haven't been able to reach him."

Mrs. Cavenaugh played with the strand of pearls at her neck and clucked her tongue. She wagged her head in disbelief. "I read about it in the papers. Embezzlement—it's a nasty business."

'I just wish that I could talk to him," Erin sighed, and leaned heavily against the banister of the staircase. "It's all so hard for me to accept."

"But your Mr. Webster…"

"He's *not my* Mr. Webster," Erin interrupted, her cheeks coloring in indignation. Mrs. Cavenaugh's blue eyes sparkled more brightly.

"Whatever," she replied with a dismissive shrug. "What does he think?"

"Oh, he's convinced that Mitch is guilty," Erin murmured, her slim fingers running along the clean cool lines of the wooden railing. Talking about Mitch and the embezzlement drained Erin, and she realized that she shouldn't be discussing bank business with her neighbor. She straightened her shoulders and changed the subject to a less personal issue. "Have you seen Mr. Jefferies?" she asked Mrs. Cavenaugh, and motioned toward the apartment on the other side of the staircase. "He hasn't changed his mind about vacating his apartment, has he?"

"As a matter of fact, I saw him this morning when I was getting my mail," the gray-haired woman replied importantly. "No, his daughter insists that George will be better off closer to his family." With a catty wink the wrinkled woman continued, "He is getting on in years, you know."

Erin suppressed the smile that tugged at the corners of her mouth. She knew for a fact that Mr. Jefferies was a good ten years younger than Mrs. Cavenaugh, although the sprightly little old lady would be loathe to admit it.

Erin lifted her shoulders in a dismissive gesture. "Oh, well, you win some and you lose some. I guess I'd better put an advertisement in the *Times* and put the Vacancy sign back up. It seems that I just took it down!"

"Has anyone ever told you that you worry too much?" Mrs. Cavenaugh asked, shaking a knowing and gnarled finger in Erin's surprised face.

Erin laughed in spite of herself. "Everybody and anybody. Or so it seems."

"Well, they're right! And what does all that worry get you? Nothing but stomach ulcers and trouble! Now, you take my advice, and—what is it they say these days—you loosen up!"

Erin grinned and impulsively gave the little old woman a bear hug. "You're right," she murmured, and patted the elderly woman's frail shoulder.

"Of course I am! You should do yourself a favor and listen to me more often," Mrs. Cavenaugh rejoined with a proud lift of her chin. "And…if you're as smart as I think you are, you'll put your hooks into that Webster fellow in a big hurry!"

"Mrs. Cavenaugh! Have you been spying on me?" Erin inquired with mock dismay.

The older woman shook her gray head savagely. "Just look-ing out for your best interests, honey. That's all!" Then, with a dismissive shrug of her thin shoulders, she added, "Call it spying, if you will. But somebody's got to take care of you. I saw the way that ex-husband of yours treated you—and I want to make sure that you don't get hurt again…"

Erin tried to protest, but the severity of Mrs. Cavenaugh's wizened blue eyes held her tongue.

"Now…this Webster fellow, I've seen the way he looks at you."

"And?"

"Unless I miss my guess, which isn't very often, I'd say he's fallen head over heels for you!"

"You can't be serious!"

But the knowing and pleased look on Mrs. Cavenaugh's weathered face added silent conviction to the little old lady's words.

"I…I had better be running along," Erin said a little breath-lessly as she thought about Mrs. Cavenaugh's words. Could she possibly be right? Erin picked up her purse and her briefcase and called over her shoulder, "Don't worry about the mess in the hallway, Mrs. Cavenaugh. I'll have the janitor clean it in the morning…."

"Oh, Erin," the lady at the bottom of the stairs beckoned.

"Yes." Erin turned to look back down at her, and she could tell that the woman was struggling with some sort of decision.

"I thought that maybe you'd want to know—Lee was here today, asking about you."

"What?"

"He left you a note, I think." Her blue eyes beseeched Erin. "Everything's okay, isn't it?"

Erin hesitated only slightly. "Of course," she managed, but she heard the hollow sound of her own words. As she mounted the final stairs to her apartment, she heard Mrs. Cavenaugh's door close and the sharp sound of a bolt being turned in the lock. All of the airy feeling that had cascaded over her from Mrs. Cavenaugh's suspicions about Kane's feelings for her had vanished at the mention of Lee. As she thought about it Erin wondered how the little old lady had even seen Kane, but there was something in Mrs. Cavenaugh's pale blue eyes that bothered Erin. The dear little woman really believed that Kane was falling in love with her. But how would Mrs. Cavenaugh even suspect?

Erin shook her head and pulled the pins from her hair as she closed the door to her loft. If only she could believe that Kane could love her or at least learn to love her. Erin's vivid imagination began to run wild.

But just as her heart began to race in anticipation of Kane's love, her rational mind cooled her response. What about the wariness she had sensed in the steely depths of Kane's gray eyes? Why did she always feel that he was studying her—trying to read her mind? Why did she feel that he didn't completely trust her? Her blood cooled and a shudder raced up her spine. The situation was impossible.

It was then that she noticed the white envelope that had been shoved under her door. The note from Lee.

Chapter 8

It had been nearly two weeks since Erin had found the note thrust intrusively into her apartment. The message was a simple request, "Please call," and a number that she recognized as a suburban Seattle telephone listing. She had tried to call Lee once, but was relieved when no one answered. Several other times she had been tempted to try and reach him once more, but before she had found the nerve to dial the number, she had changed her mind and left well enough alone. If he really needed her, she reasoned, he would get in touch with her again. A few times she had wadded up the note in an effort to throw it away, but she hadn't. This morning the note was once again before her as she leaned against the kitchen counter, studiously stirring a bit of honey into her tea. It sat menacingly on the counter, inviting her to make a call that she knew would only bring her more heartache. Was she a coward? Why did she let him linger near her to remind her of the past and the pain.

She took an experimental sip of the warm amber liquid. As the hot tea slid down her throat, Erin thought about the past two weeks of her life. The days had gone fairly well. On the surface it seemed as if everything in the office was running efficiently, just as a well-oiled banking machine should. For the first time in months Erin had cleaned out her pending probate file along with a series of other nagging paperwork problems that had been building on the corner of her desk for several weeks. Her fear over gossip or rumors spreading concerning her relationship with Kane had been unfounded, other than the one unfortunate and vicious incident with Olivia. Kane proved himself to be a capable and fair employer, and outwardly Erin appeared to enjoy working for him. It had even been possible for her to work professionally with Kane by forcing her personal feelings for him into the background and never letting her emotions color her objectivity or judgment. It had been excruciatingly difficult at times not to reach out and touch him or smooth the worried look from his brow. But she had managed to look the part of a disinterested employee. At least she hoped so.

It was the nights that disturbed her, she realized now as she moved restlessly from the kitchen, taking the teacup and the crumpled note from Lee with her. Then, after carefully setting the teacup on the coffee table, she spread out the crushed piece of paper and smoothed its creases against the arm of the sofa. The seven digits of Lee's home phone leaped out at her, and in a moment of sudden decisiveness, she shredded the note into tiny pieces and tossed them disgustedly away in the wastebasket, something she should have done two weeks ago!

Erin sunk into the soft rose-colored cushions of the couch and continued to reflect on the changes in her life. When she was alone with Kane, she felt a freedom and a rapture that were hard to describe, an enthusiasm and exhilaration that she thought had been lost with her teens. Just the light touch of his hand on her shoulder or his throaty whispered voice could send her spiraling into an emotional bliss that was both wonderful and frightening. Never had she given her heart so willingly or so easily. She knew that a part of Kane wanted to love her; she could feel it as they made love. But for some unknown reason, he wouldn't let himself enjoy the pleasure of loving her. At first she had thought that the failure of his marriage had hardened him against a commitment to the future, but lately she had sensed that it was a more personal problem that made him withdraw. A problem somehow directly relating to her.

She shook her tangled curls and looked into the teacup as if she might find the answer to her dilemma in its amber-colored depths. Why the restlessness? Why did she feel like an aerialist carefully balancing her life on a flimsy tightrope and knowing that sometime, although she couldn't be quite sure exactly when, the tense, frail wire would snap and send her catapulting downward into an empty black emotional abyss? The conflicting roles of daytime employee and nighttime lover were constantly at war in her mind.

Erin sighed deeply and ran her fingernails in deep grooves along the overstuffed arm of the antique sofa. There were times when she was alone with Kane that the stone wall of wariness in his eyes would weaken, and she would feel an exquisite happiness, the blush of love. But on other occasions, when she lay alone in her bed, listening as he drove off into the night, she discovered a sense of desperation and loneliness that caused feverish nightmares to disturb her sleep.

Why the torment? Where was the relationship leading them? Why couldn't she come to grips with and accept the affair for what it was—a pleasant, sensuous experience? Why did she insist on coloring her feelings with love?

A key turned in the lock. Kane had returned. Erin could feel herself beginning to coil in tension. Nervously she waited for him to enter—just as he had every night for the past two weeks. But tonight would be different, she vowed to herself. Tonight she would insist upon answers. Why was there always a darkness in his eyes?

Kane entered the room and shut the door behind him. The stern look on his face only made Erin's heart hammer more wildly. He was dressed casually in jeans and a tan pullover sweater. His chestnut hair was slightly messy as if he had forgotten about it over the last few hours. It was obvious that he had hurriedly stopped by his hotel before coming to see her. Unusual. The pattern of their life together had been established over the last two weeks, but this Friday night was obviously different to Kane as well as Erin. Even under the intensity of his gaze she reminded herself that she had to know, tonight, what it was that held him away from her.

"Pack your bags," Kane commanded without even a smile as a greeting. She jumped at his abrupt command, and for a moment his arctic gray eyes collided with hers. She felt a chill of dread pass over her body. His mouth was a tight, grim line that was neither a smile nor a frown. The grooves across his forehead seemed deeper tonight, as if he, too, had been wrestling with a troublesome and weighty decision.

"Do what?" she asked incredulously. Surprise and indignation registered in the startled expression that crossed her face. She was still sitting on the couch with her legs curled up and tucked underneath her. She almost dropped her teacup at his abrasive command.

Kane ignored her question. Preoccupied, he paced distractedly in front of the couch, his fists balled deeply in the pockets of his jeans. As he passed in front of her, Erin couldn't help but notice that his jeans, slung low in the waist, strained against his thighs and buttocks with each of his long strides. As he paced she was reminded of a caged animal, and she could almost visualize his tightly controlled muscles rippling beneath the fabric of his clothing. Forcefully she pulled her attention away from his virile male anatomy and tried to read the expression on his face.

"Didn't you hear me?" he growled, and stopped his absent pacing. "I asked you to go and pack."

"No, you didn't," she corrected, her eyes locking with his. "You *ordered* me to pack without so much as a greeting or explanation!"

Anger snapped in his eyes, but his reply was strangely soothing. The rage that was burning quietly within him was controlled. "You're right," he expelled in a long breath, "and I'm sorry. I...I'm a little distracted this evening," he offered as an apology.

"I noticed!" she retorted, and then seeing the worried creases that pulled his thick dark brows together in concern, she amended her hot retort. "I guess it's my turn to apologize," she admitted wearily. "I didn't mean to snap. I've been a little distracted myself."

"Oh?"

"Nothing to be concerned about," she averred with a wan smile, and wondered why she didn't have the strength of character to lay her cards on the table and confront him with her unanswered questions about their relationship and the future. Instead she chose to sidestep the issue. "Now." She smiled feebly, luminous lilac eyes looking pleadingly up at him. "What's been bothering you?"

"Oh, God, Erin," he moaned and let his forehead drop to his hand in a gesture of total defeat. He raked long tense fingers through the wheat-colored highlights of his burnished hair. How could he explain that he was only a hairbreadth away from confirming his suspicions about her? Could she imagine how close he was coming to finding all of the pieces of the puzzle that would tie her into the embezzling scandal?

Although everything was still circumstantial, it was stacking together so neatly that it was actually beginning to scare Kane. Although no more money had been taken from the bank, the most damning piece of evidence that he had found so far—a discrepancy in the securities cart key registration—proved as well as anything that Erin had been lying to him. How long did she expect the charade to work? How could he help her and get her out of this mess? What could he do? It would all be so much easier if he just didn't give a damn!

"Kane," Erin said unsteadily, still sitting, looking both childlike and wise at the same moment. Oh, God, he thought, was she going to confess? Could he bear it? His muscles tensed, and he could feel the pressure as his jaws tightened together in a viselike grip. "Is there anything I can do?" she offered in a whisper.

Erin had noticed Kane stiffen at the sound of her voice, and she was aware that the wall between them was rigidly back in place, but she felt a strangling need to climb the invisible barrier and reach out to him. Why was he suffering so?

"There's nothing you can do," he stated flatly. "There's nothing anyone can do."

She twisted her fingers together. "Is it Krista?" she asked with a shaky breath.

His gray eyes smoldered with indecision. "That's part of it," he conceded, and hated himself for his duplicity. Dropping his body down on the couch next to her, he let his head fall backward as if it were too heavy to support. He sat staring ahead, with only inches separating him from her. Her senses were alive to him, her nerve endings stretched taut. Erin could feel the heat of his body, smell the inviting scent of his aftershave, see the darkening shadow of his beard. But he still didn't touch her. His hands rubbed thoughtfully against his knees, and he looked straight ahead through the window into the late afternoon sky. "I talked with Krista again today," he said in a voice that seemed remote.

"And?" Erin prodded, not knowing why she should be concerned with Kane's reclusive daughter.

"She doesn't want to move to Seattle," he sighed, and drummed his fingers against his thigh. "Absolutely refuses!"

He turned his head to look in her direction and their eyes met in a chilly embrace. "I'm going to California next week to get her and move her up to Seattle with me."

"And you're worried about her and the adjustment," Erin guessed.

"Wouldn't you be?"

"That goes without saying. Is…there anything I can do to make it easier on you?"

"Would you come to California with me?"

"To get Krista?" At Kane's cursory nod, Erin expelled a long breath and shook her head firmly and negatively. "I don't think that would be a very good idea. She's going to have to adjust to a whole new city. I think you should be alone with her. She doesn't need the intrusion of a virtual stranger."

She could see in his eyes that she had convinced him and she continued, "But if there's anything else that I can do…."

"There is something," he suggested, and for a moment the tension seemed to vanish.

"What?"

"Pack your bags for the weekend" was the brief reply, but the passion that had been lurking in his eyes came alive. His silvery eyes embraced hers, and he reached for her hand. His thumb drew slow, lazy circles on the inside of her wrist, and heat began to climb up her body. "Oh, Erin," he breathed, and his lips found hers in a feverish kiss that seemed to pulsate with need and urgency. When he dragged his mouth away from the supple curve of her lips, he looked savagely into her eyes, asking questions that she couldn't understand. Then a softness stole over his features as he took a handful of her hair in his palm and pressed her head against the protection of his chest. In a ragged breath he asked, "Do you know how hard it's been for me, forcing myself to keep my hands off you at the office?" He growled deep in his throat. "There were times when I thought I would actually go insane, having you so close and not being able to touch you...."

Her arms circled his waist, and she kissed the swell of his cheek. "I know..."

"No, I don't think that you can imagine what it's like—seeing you every day and not being able to touch what is mine."

"Yours? Possessive, aren't you?" she quipped sarcastically.

"Absolutely!" His grip on her tightened, and when she tilted her face to meet his, the warmth of his lips captured hers in a passion that spread fire through her veins. With great difficulty she pulled her head away from his.

"What did you say about packing my bags?" she inquired, trying to ignore the warm intimacy of his breath as it tickled her face.

"You and I are getting away for the weekend," he stated, and with apparent effort he released her from his tenacious embrace. "Hurry up," he ordered. "We don't have all day. I want to get moving before we run out of daylight!"

"Kane!" Erin said with mild irritation. "What are you talking about? Where are we going? Why do I need to pack?"

His smile twisted grimly and Erin saw the weariness and cynicism deep in his crystal gray eyes. "You and I are leaving this city, the bank—" his eyes swept the homey apartment "—this house, everything! We're going to get lost in the wild for a couple of days!"

"The wild?"

"That's right!" Half dragging her into the bedroom, he

opened the closet, against her protests, and found her suitcase. "I'm tired of sneaking out of your bed in the middle of the night like some…gigolo!" He ignored Erin's gasp of indignation and began opening her bureau drawers. She caught his reflection in the mirror and saw that a hard, tense mask had come over his angular features. He looked up, his gray eyes held hers and he said with disgust, "And I'm tired of not being able to touch you in the light of day!" His hands were pressed firmly on the dresser top, and he pinioned her with his gaze, cold and distant, in the looking glass. Tense fingers slowly rubbed the wooden surface of the dresser. "Damn it, woman!" His fist pounded against the cool wood. "I'm sick of hiding, and I won't do it anymore! So, beginning tonight, we are not going to keep this affair in the dark, as if we're ashamed of it! You and your paranoia over rumors can go to blazes!" He spit the words out as if they were a bad taste in his mouth. His anger was burning in the darkness of his gaze.

"Kane," Erin implored. "Why are you so upset? What…"

"Look, Erin. We've played the game your way for nearly two weeks, and it's tearing me apart!" His entire body tensed for a second before he took in a long steadying breath and controlled the note of rage that had entered his speech. In a softer voice he continued, "Let's have an entire weekend alone together—what do you say?"

"I don't understand…"

"Let's go somewhere where we can walk in the sunlight together—where we can be seen kissing…."

"Is this what's been bothering you?" she asked, as she put a staying hand on his sleeve.

"Oh, Erin," he sighed, holding her at arm's length and letting his eyes search her face. "There are so many things that are bothering me," he admitted, and a tortured look twisted his features.

"Can we talk about them?" she asked quietly.

"That's exactly what I have in mind. But I thought a change of scenery might do us both some good."

"You know that I can't leave at the drop of a hat."

"Why not?"

"My tenants…I've got an advertisement in the paper to rent the apartment downstairs."

"The apartment on the first floor, across the hall from Milly?" he asked.

"That's the one—how did you get on a first-name basis with Mrs. Cavenaugh?" Erin asked, a suspicious black eyebrow arching heavenward.

"That little old lady has excellent taste," he laughed. "She likes me."

"And she told you about the vacant apartment?" Erin guessed.

"That's right," he agreed with a smile that any Cheshire cat would envy.

"Then you understand why I have to stay here…"

"Don't worry about the apartment," he said dismissively. "I'll rent it until I find a more permanent residence. Does it have two bedrooms?"

"Of course, but—"

"Then it will be perfect!" he exclaimed.

"Perfect? For what?"

"Krista and myself."

"I don't know…"

His eyes grew dark. "It's the perfect solution to our problem."

Her breath caught in her throat. "I didn't know that we had a problem," she returned, and began to place her undergarments in the open suitcase on the bed. Was he actually going to tell her what had been bothering him, why he had been so wary of her?

He came up behind her and let his arms encircle her waist. His words fanned her hair and the sensitive skin at the back of her neck. He captured the black silk and entwined it in his fingers. Burying his face in her hair, he groaned. "The problem is that I want to be near you…always!" The confession was a tortured, unwanted admission.

"What are you saying?" she asked, and a tightness constricted her breath.

"I want to live with you!"

Her voice was unsteady. "And what about Krista? What would she think about her father and his business associate living together? What kind of example would we set? No, Kane…" She shook her head sadly. "It wouldn't work!"

"Lots of people…"

"I'm not 'lots of people,'" she interrupted.

"So I noticed," he agreed, and his hands slowly kneaded the softness of her abdomen. Warm curling sensations grew to life within her. Slowly he stopped his seductive movements. "I'm sorry," he whispered. "I'm pushing you too quickly. Let's forget the entire suggestion—for the time being. But, please come and spend the weekend with me…"

Pulling herself away from him, she planted a fist firmly against her hip and forced back a smile that flirted with her lips. "I'll come with you—on one condition!"

Kane crossed his arms over his chest and leaned against the dresser. The sweater strained across his shoulders. "Okay. I'm game. What's the condition?"

"That for once you tell me where you plan on taking me!"

"Spoilsport!"

"Kane!"

"Where's that girl who loves mystery and old movies?" he inquired, a twinkle coming to his eyes.

"You're not going to tell me, are you?"

"Not unless you think of some wildly erotic torture that will force me into submission."

"Dreamer," she shot back at him, before turning to pack.

The small motorboat churned through the cold gray waters of Puget Sound and out toward the Pacific Ocean. When Erin had stepped into the tiny vessel, she had guessed that Kane was taking her to San Juan Island, but he had preferred to keep the destination and his secret to himself. Now, as the frigid salt spray tickled her nose and clung to her hair, she was grateful that she had had the foresight to bring her down jacket with her. She drew the warm collar closer to her neck in an effort to keep the moisture-laden air off her skin.

By the time they reached Orcas Island the sun had set, and only a long orange glow remained along the horizon. Night was closing in, and the lights of Deer Harbor winked like silvery diamonds against the black island as the launch continued on its journey around the small piece of land.

Erin rubbed her hands together, and then pushed them deep into her pockets in an effort to warm herself. At that moment the rhythmic rumble of the small craft's engine slowed, and Kane maneuvered the boat inland. It was difficult to see clearly in the evening light, but Erin made out a small cove with a relatively private beach and a ramshackle cabin.

Kane cut the engine and jumped out onto the private dock. He secured the craft and helped Erin out of the boat. Her eyes swept the beach until she spotted the cabin. A slow smile spread over her features.

"Well, what do you think?" Kane asked, his arm draped possessively over her slim shoulders.

"I think this all looks suspiciously like a set from one of those 1940s, black-and-white, slice-of-life movies," she commented as her eyes studied the small cozy cabin and its state of apparent neglect.

"I knew you'd like it," Kane replied with a self-satisfied smile. "Come on. Let's take a look inside..."

The cabin was, if nothing else, rustic. A broad, sagging front porch protected the front door. The cabin was constructed of cedar, and to Erin's discriminating eye, had never been painted. It bore the weathered look of exposed gray wood blanched by the salt of the sea. At one end of the porch a worn rope hammock swung in the breeze coming off the ocean. The front door groaned as it was opened, and the interior of the cabin had a musty, unused odor. There was no electricity, but running water was pumped into the kitchen. A woodstove in the kitchen and a massive stone fireplace at one end of the living area provided the only sources of heat in the building. Erin surveyed the cabin with a skeptical eye. She had never been much of a believer in "roughing it" when modern conveniences were the available alternative.

Kane unpacked the boat and started searching for firewood, while Erin lit the rose-colored kerosene lamps and removed the dustcovers from the furniture. To air out the interior, she opened all the windows, heedless of the chill in the air, and felt the tickle of salt air burn in her lungs.

The cabin was rather barren, and what little furniture there was appeared threadbare. But she had to admit that once she had swept the dust from the floor, and the fire was lit, the warm scent of burning wood mingled with the fresh fragrance of the salt sea air, and the cabin seemed bearable, if not cheerfully inviting. Fortunately Kane had the foresight to stop off at a delicatessen in Seattle before picking up Erin, and he had purchased sandwiches and a bottle of wine. Erin rummaged in the old-fashioned kitchen and was able to find an unopened package of paper cups along with a tarnished but necessary corkscrew for the wine.

Pleased with her discoveries, she retraced her footsteps back into the living area. Brandishing the corkscrew dramatically in the air, she captured Kane's attention. *"Voilà!"* she announced theatrically, and placed the cups on the floor next to the couch.

Because of the chill of the evening sea breeze, Kane was closing the final window in an effort to retain the heat from the fireplace when Erin reentered the room. He snapped the window latch closed and turned to face Erin, who wondered aloud, "How in the world did you ever find this place?"

"It's not exactly moonlight and roses, is it?" he asked, crossing the room to the fireplace. He squatted near the golden flames and warmed his palms against the heat that the fire offered.

"Who needs moonlight and roses?" she asked rhetorically, and shrugged.

"Don't you?" Gray eyes searched her face as if she were a puzzle to him.

"I'm a little too much of a realist to think that the world revolves around silver moonlight, cut flowers and soft music," she admitted dryly.

"Are you?" A smile of disbelief tugged at the corners of his mouth.

"Does it matter?" she asked, and unwrapped the sandwiches. "Anyway, you're avoiding my question—how did you come to find this private little hideaway?"

After dusting his hands on his jeans, Kane sat down next to her on the floor, allowing the slightly weathered couch to support his head and shoulders. His long legs stretched in front of him, and nearly reached the warm red coals of the fire. Erin silently offered him a sandwich, which he gratefully accepted, and between bites he explained.

"As you already know, I'm looking for a permanent residence for Krista and myself in Seattle. I read the classified ads every day, hoping to find something suitable." He paused to open the wine and poured the cool clear liquid into the paper cups. The light from the fire reflected and danced against the deep green bottle and in his clear gray eyes.

"Anyway—" he shrugged, as if it wasn't all that important "—I came across an ad for this place. I've always had a fascination for the sea and the wilderness, not to mention rustic old cabins. And I thought it would be good for Krista. This place sounded perfect."

Erin nearly choked on the wine that she had been sipping. She eyed the interior of the cabin speculatively. "You're not telling me that you bought this place sight unseen?" she gasped, unable to shake the astounded look from her face. It hardly seemed "perfect" for anyone, much less an eleven-year-old girl bound to a wheelchair! Erin surveyed the living quarters more closely. The old cabin needed a lot of work. The cleaning alone would take several days, and the varnish on the pine walls was cracking and beginning to peel. There was no hot water, the floors needed to be refinished, and the furniture—all of it needed to be replaced or repaired. The list of jobs seemed endless to her practiced eye.

Kane watched Erin with obvious amusement. The deep-timbred tones of his laughter drew her attention back to him. "No," he laughed, "I haven't bought this place. In fact, this weekend is just a trial run. A widow owns the place, but she hasn't been up here since her husband died a couple of years ago. She knows that I'm interested in buying it, but she agreed to rent it to me for the weekend—to look around for myself."

"You're really serious about buying it?" Erin gasped. "It doesn't even have electricity!"

"Part of its charm, wouldn't you say?" He grinned at her obvious dismay.

"It's your money," she conceded with a dismissive shrug, and took another sip of her wine. The bright embers from the fire and the heady effect of the wine lured her into a serene sense of complacency. She watched Kane over the rim of her cup, and noticed the mood swing that seemed to come over him.

At her offhand comment about money, Kane stiffened. "That it is," he agreed almost inaudibly. He set the remains of his uneaten dinner aside, and stared into the orange and black coals of the fire. His mood had indeed shifted, and Erin, even in her peaceful state, could sense that the tension was coiling within him again.

The fire crackled and popped as it burned the pitch-darkened wood. The movements of the flames reflected in menacing shadows over the angular structure of Kane's masculine face. His question surprised Erin.

"Did you know that Mitchell Cameron's arraignment hearing is scheduled for late this week?" he asked in an accusatory voice. Gray eyes slid sideways, trying to catch her reaction. His pose was relaxed, his hands crossed comfortably over his chest, but Erin could sense the strain due to the twist in the conversation, and saw the tense rigidity of the muscles in his face.

"I read about it in the paper," she replied unevenly. Carefully, with nervous hands, she set aside the rest of her suddenly unappetizing sandwich and took another drink from her cup. The cool wine felt smooth against the rough texture of her throat. Mitchell Cameron had become a taboo subject between Erin and Kane, a topic that was never brought out into the open. It was as if, by silent agreement, neither person would chance the subject of Mitch. For reasons Erin didn't understand, the subject of Mitch was a potential powder keg. Why then, tonight, would Kane turn the conversation in Mitch's direction?

Kane's voice broke into her fragmented thoughts. "There's a chance that I'll be out of town at the time of the hearing."

"But don't you have to testify?"

"I've already signed a sworn deposition," was the clipped reply. "I'm sure it will satisfy the court."

"Oh, Kane." Erin sighed, suddenly feeling very tired and unnerved. "Are you sure that you want to prosecute Mitch?" she asked, her hand reaching out to touch his shoulder.

He withdrew as quickly as if he had been seared by her touch. Twisting his head to meet her startled gaze, he drew his lips into a thin and menacingly grim line. "Is that what this is all about?" he demanded, and grabbed her wrist harshly.

"What—I don't understand!"

"Is that what you want, for me to drop the charges against your ex-employer? Is that why you've been so willing?" Steely eyes swept over her body and charged her with a crime she couldn't understand.

"Why, you…bastard!" she gasped, suddenly understanding at least a part of his vicious accusation. Involuntarily she drew her free hand backward in an effort to slap him. But she stopped in midswing as the same tortured look that she had seen so often in the past softened the severity of his dark gaze.

He dropped her wrist and closed his eyes for a second. "I'm sorry," he whispered huskily.

"You should be!"

"All right!" He reached a hesitant hand to her cheek and caressed its regal lines with exploring and sensitive fingers. "I have no choice," he assured her. "I have to prosecute Cameron. The board of directors would insist upon it, the bonding insurance company.…"

"But if you did have a choice?" Liquid violet eyes melted into his, and he drew his caressing hand away from her face.

"Nothing would change! I would still prosecute!" He stood up and put some distance between her body and his. He found it difficult to think when he looked at her or touched her. She was too close to him and to the truth. Perhaps, even now, she knew that he suspected her of involvement in the embezzlement. He had to be cautious with her—or did he? Damn it! Never in his life had he let a woman come between him and his purpose in life. Never had a woman been so intimately involved in his private thoughts. Dear God, why did it have to be this woman who attracted him so achingly? His thoughts weighed heavily on him, and he leaned against the broad mantel of the fireplace and let his head rest against the worn wood. He needed time to think, time alone, to put his life in perspective. It was a mistake bringing her to this isolated haven; he should have realized that before he insisted that she accompany him. How could he have been such a fool? Where was his common sense? His voice, a throaty whisper, crept across the thick silence that separated them.

"Can't you understand, Erin?" he pleaded. "Mitchell Cameron is a crook, and he has to pay."

"But surely, as president of the bank, with your influence..."

His gray eyes held hers frozen. "Oh, God, Erin. My influence has nothing to do with my *responsibility!*"

"Why is the subject of Mitch always so difficult?"

"You tell me!"

"I don't know!" she admitted honestly.

The silence was an electric current that seemed to bind them together and yet sever whatever peace they had shared. Kane eyed Erin with a haunted wariness that seemed to tire him, and Erin watched him with eyes naked in love and confusion. What was he trying to say?

He leaned against the mantel and rubbed the base of his head with his palm. He closed his eyes and gritted his teeth, as if he were trying to rid his body of tension. Slowly he seemed to relax; his tight muscles lengthened. With the effort his weight sagged wearily against the fireplace. "I think," he managed to say, "that you and I should drop the subject of Mitchell Cameron until after the arraignment hearing."

Erin let out a steadying breath. "Do you really suppose that I can just ignore the fact that Mitch's fate depends on your decision?"

"Correction," he cautioned sharply. "His fate depends upon his decision, one that was made quite some time ago. Not mine! I had nothing to do with it except unfortunately to catch a thief."

"I don't know that I can just erase it from my mind—as if we've never had this conversation."

"Just for the weekend?" he suggested, and bent near to her. He took both of her hands in his and forced her to look deeply into his eyes. "I'm sorry for the outburst. The past two weeks have been a strain on both of us," he said in an effort at apology. "But let's just spend this time together and get to know each other a little better." Deep lines of intense thought creased his forehead. "I—well, I need some time with you. Alone. Apart from Mitchell Cameron and the rest of the world." His voice was a reluctant plea, and before she could answer him, he buried his head between her breasts and held her close to him. "Oh, Erin," he whispered, his hot breath tantalizing her skin and arousing her breasts to an aching tautness. "Why do you tempt me so?"

Ignoring the doubts and warnings that still crowded her mind, she felt herself surrender to him, and her hands wound themselves in the thick strands of his burnished hair. Feeling her reaction, he slowly pulled his head away from the softness of her body and looked longingly into her eyes. Her breath came in short gasps, and she felt the warmth of desire curling upward in her body. A nearly wicked grin stole over his face as his fingers played with the buttons of her blouse. She made no move to stop him, and when the blouse finally parted, his gaze sought and found the swollen ripeness of her breasts.

She longed to be touched by him, to feel the heat of his body capture her soul and the essence of her being. Red and orange flames were reflected in the burning passion of his gaze.

"Do you know, do you have any idea, just how much I need you?" he asked, before covering her lips with his and seeking the open invitation of her warm, moist mouth. She couldn't get enough of him. The delicious scent and tantalizing taste of his body, in kisses flavored by the wine, lingered upon her lips and teased her senses into a yearning ache that she couldn't control. His lips explored the length of her body, all of her, gently nuzzling the hollow of her shoulder, rimming her ear, searching out the soft flat contour of her abdomen. "Dear God, how I want you," he admitted.

"Then love me, Kane, love me," she pleaded.

"I will, Erin," he vowed, and moved over her, gently probing the most intimate part of her. Even in her drugged sense of well-being, she realized that he was speaking only of physical love, not the eternal love that she had requested. But for the moment it was enough.

Chapter 9

The two days that they spent together on the island were carefree and warm. After a light cover of morning fog, the late autumn sun would warm the sand, and for the most part the days were crisply cool and invigoratingly clear.

Erin taught Kane how to dig for razor clams along the edge of the tide, and after a few hesitant tries, he became rather adept at kneeling in the wet sand and furiously shoveling after the escaping mollusks. Once, when a particularly large wave caught him off guard and sent him sprawling headlong into the bitter, cold surf, Erin laughed, only to find herself dragged down into the icy water by Kane.

"That will teach you not to make sport of me," he quipped, before kissing her soundly on her bluish lips. Another cold wave climbed over them, and they both hurried indoors to escape the frigid water and the cool air of autumn. They stripped off the wet, sandy clothes in front of the fire, while warming hot water to clean up the grit from the beach that had clung to their skins.

For most of the two short days, they spent their time beachcombing or taking the boat into nearby Deer Harbor for sight-seeing and browsing in the various antiques stores. It was a wonderful time to be together, and by the end of the week-end, Erin found herself more in love with Kane than she ever imagined possible. She hated the thought of leaving the island and dreaded returning to the city, the job and the pressures that always seemed to build between them at home. She en-joyed the freedom that the island provided and loved being alone with Kane, loved touching him whenever she had the desire, and loved kissing him in the light of day, unafraid of what others might think. Disturbingly she wondered if it was such a fairy-tale existence that it could never be recreated, only remembered. All too soon it would end.

During the nights they spread a large sleeping bag on the floor in front of the fire, rather than chancing the well-worn and musty bed in the attached bedroom. They spent hours in front of the fire, talking, laughing and making love until dawn.

It was a glorious, heady experience. The entire weekend was too good to last.

When, finally, after what seemed a short afternoon, the sun began to set against the cold gray sea, Erin found Kane stand-ing studiously on the porch. She had packed together all of her things, and she knew that it was well past the hour that Kane had planned to leave. And still he lingered. He half stood, half leaned against the railing and stared endlessly out toward the broad expanse of the ocean and into the beckoning twilight.

Quietly Erin watched him. She knew that he, too, was hesitant to leave the solitude of the romantic haven that this otherwise miserable excuse for a cabin had provided for them. She lowered her body into the rope hammock, which sagged and groaned against her weight. The noise distracted Kane, and he slowly turned to face her. His eyes were distant; his mind was light-years away. Lazily he leaned against the post that supported the roof of the porch and let his eyes slide caressingly over her body.

"I'm…ready to go," she stated. It was a poor attempt at conversation.

"Are you?" he drawled.

"Everything's packed. We really should get going."

"I know," he agreed reluctantly, and looked longingly once more at the ceaseless gray tide. He spoke softly, as if to himself. "It surprises me that I'm not itching to get back to the office. Usually I'm anxious and just can't wait to get back behind my desk. But tonight—I don't know—it all seems so pointless."

When he faced her once again, his gray eyes moved over her face, as if he were memorizing every contour of her creamy skin. He made a simple statement with measured slowness. "I'm going to buy this cabin. We'll come back together."

"I hope so," she breathed, and wondered why it was so important to her. Unconsciously she clung to the first promise that hinted of a future that they might somehow share together.

The week that followed was a dismal and lonely time for Erin. As Kane had promised, he refused to keep their affair quiet or in the dark. Although he didn't actually make an announcement of the fact, his cold indifference in the office had disappeared, and it was with difficulty that Erin had managed to keep up appearances during working hours. His eyes caressed her, and his affection was never hidden. Although inwardly Erin was pleased, she couldn't help but notice the reaction of the other employees of the bank, the expressively uplifted eyebrows whenever she was with Kane and the accusatory glances that were cast her way when she wasn't with him. She tried to ignore the gossip that was blazing through the bank, but she couldn't calm the churning of her stomach.

When Kane had to leave on Wednesday for California, Erin

was slightly relieved that the pressure of keeping him at arm's length at the office would be relieved for a while.

It was on Friday morning when everything seemed to happen at once. Kane's absence, as expected, had created a little extra work for Erin as well as the rest of the staff, but what she hadn't anticipated was an outbreak of the flu, leaving the office very shorthanded. Nor had she expected that the bank's main computer would break down, slowing the month-end posting to a snail's pace. It was a hectic, frustrating day, and when the telephone rang for what seemed to be the twentieth time within the span of five minutes, Erin couldn't keep the tight strain of anxiety out of her normally composed voice.

"Miss O'Toole," she nearly shouted into the mouthpiece.

"Erin?" a familiar voice inquired.

"Mitch? Is that you? I've been trying to reach you for weeks," she exclaimed, and felt a pang of regret that she had answered the phone so harshly. "How are you?" she asked with genuine interest.

"I've been better," was the matter-of-fact reply.

"Oh, Mitch. I'm so sorry," she began, suddenly at a loss for words. What could she say to him? Any condolence sounded foolish.

"I know, Erin," he replied as if he really did understand that she still cared for him and considered him her friend.

There was an uncomfortable pause in the conversation, before Mitch cleared his throat indecisively and stated the reason for his call. "I was wondering if you would like to go to lunch with me today?" he inquired.

"Oh, Mitch, I'd love to, but I'm absolutely swamped," Erin replied as she gazed at the stack of unanswered telephone messages that had been growing on the corner of her desk.

"Too busy for lunch with an old friend?" he joked, but the humor fell flat.

"Of course not. It's just that…well, Kane is out of town, and everyone here is down with the flu—including the computer."

There was a harsh laugh on the other end of the line. "Yeah, well, I get the message" was the curt retort. "Some other time…"

Indecision tore at Erin. She knew that today was the day of Mitch's arraignment hearing, and she also knew that if the judgment was turned against him, it was unlikely that she would see him again for an indefinite period of time. Kane wouldn't approve of a meeting with Mitch; Erin was sure of it, and yet he had no control over her friendship with Mitch. For once her reason was cast aside as she thought about the lonely man on the other end of the telephone line.

"Oh, Mitch," she said suddenly. "I'm sure I can meet with you today," she choked out. "I'll just have to make some room."

"Good!" Was there excessive relief in his voice? "How about Shorty's at one-thirty?"

"Perfect," she agreed lamely, and felt herself something of a traitor.

The few short hours until her agreed rendezvous with Mitch flew by, and with an uneasy feeling in the pit of her stomach, Erin set out on the short walk to a local pub known for its specialty: barbecued spareribs. Located in an older hotel in Pioneer Square, Shorty's had become a favorite with some of the employees of the bank, as much for its earthy San Francisco atmosphere as its flavorful food. Erin had been to the restaurant bar with Mitch several times in the past, but today, under the shroud of the allegations against him and the twisted set of circumstances surrounding them, she felt apprehensive about the lunch. *Don't be silly,* she chided herself. *This is the same old Gay Nineties restaurant, and he's the same old Mitch. Don't let any of this talk of embezzlement go to your head.* But still her stomach knotted, and without thinking, she pulled her pewter raincoat more closely around her throat and shook off a chill that ran up her spine.

She swung the heavy wooden door inward, and stepped into the dimly lit and secluded restaurant. The tangy odor of honey and tomato sauce assailed her nostrils, and she felt herself relax a little with the familiar aroma. It was forced, but she even managed a smile for the blond hostess who led Erin to a table where Mitch was already seated. She hadn't seen her ex-boss for over three weeks, and it was difficult to hide her surprise and embarrassment for the shell of a man that Mitch had become. Although more sober than the last time she had faced him, he carried with him a haunted look that destroyed the pleasantness of his face. His features, once bold, appeared gaunt, and his once-bright eyes had faded to a watery blue. A small, thin cigar was burning unattended in the ashtray.

At the sight of Erin, Mitch visibly brightened. His smile, though slightly strained at the corners, appeared genuine as he rose from the table while she was being seated. After she was comfortably settled in her chair, Mitch reached across the small table for her hand and clasped it warmly. "Erin," he shook his graying head in wonderment. "If possible, you're looking lovelier than ever!"

"Thank you," she murmured, and nervously pulled the napkin from the table in an effort to steady her hands. It wasn't like Mitch to gush, at least not the Mitch she remembered, and his bubbling enthusiasm seemed somehow phony and out of character. The uneasy feeling grew in the pit of her stomach. Perhaps it was the way he didn't quite meet her gaze, or the way he played with his cigar, but something about him made Erin definitely uncomfortable.

"So," he said with forced joviality, "how's it going at the old salt mine? Still as busy as ever?"

He had asked the question, but Erin had the distinct impression that he was totally uninterested in the topic that he had introduced.

"We're busy—all the time," she admitted, and when he didn't immediately respond, she continued chattering to break the uncomfortable silence that was building. "Kane—that is, Mr. Webster, has been out of town for a few days, and well, that just tends to make things all the more hectic for everyone else...." Why did she feel compelled to rattle on about the bank, and why did she feel so nervous around a friend whom she had once respected? She wiped her damp palms on the napkin in her lap.

The waiter deposited two platters of ribs on the table, and Erin turned her attention to the saucy food, hoping to dream up a polite way of excusing herself at the earliest possible moment. She knew now that it was a mistake to have met with Mitch; she wasn't ready to deal with him or any of the problems in his life. Loathing herself for her turn of feelings, she managed to continue to feign interest in her ribs, wondering why Mitchell Cameron had changed so much, and how she could manage an escape from the uncomfortable and intimate lunch.

It was then that Mitch brought up the subject of his courtroom hearing. "I suppose you know that the arraignment hearing is this afternoon?" he began slowly, and lit another cigar. His faded eyes waited to study her response.

"Oh, Mitch...I wish that all of this—problem—could be avoided," Erin claimed, and he could read the honesty in her eyes.

"Yes, well, it's a little too late for that now, isn't it?"

"I suppose so," she sighed, touching her napkin to her lips and pushing the uneaten ribs aside. Her appetite had diminished. "If there's anything I can do to help you, just let me know."

Blue eyes lighted. "There is something." His voice was bitter cold.

"Oh? What?"

Mitch shifted uncomfortably in his chair. "Nothing much." He shrugged his shoulders and reached inside of his jacket for a neatly folded piece of paper. "I was hoping that you could borrow a little information from the bank…."

"What?" she asked, perplexed, and ran a shaky hand through her sleekly restrained hair. "Information? What information?"

Mitch waved off her questions dismissively with the clean white envelope. "Well, it's really not all that important, except that I can't get my hands on the records, as I'm no longer employed with the bank." He puffed furiously on his cigar, cloaking his head in a thin veil of blue smoke as he offered her the envelope.

Reluctantly she reached for the paper, as her uneasy stomach began to churn. "This information—what do you need it for?"

"I know it's rather sudden," Mitch rattled on, "but I need documents that would help clear my name. Bank records, trust documents, computer printouts on the dividend accounts, stock certificate registrations…nothing all that important…."

"You're not serious!"

"Of course I'm serious. Everything I need is listed in there." He pointed dramatically to the envelope that Erin was holding. She dropped it onto the table.

"Mitch!" Erin's cool voice was tightly formal. "Are you suggesting that I confiscate private bank records and give them to you?"

"Not give…I just want to borrow the stuff, until I can get this embezzlement fiasco straightened out."

"But you know that I can't do that," Erin exclaimed. "For one thing it's against the law. All that information is confidential!"

"Erin!" Mitch interrupted her. "This is my life that we're talking about. I face more years in prison than you'd want to count!" His eyes beseeched her, but she didn't waver. She spread her hands against the linen-clad table, and looked him directly in the eyes.

"Mitch, you know I'd love to help you out, but you can't expect me to do anything illegal, for God's sake!"

He chewed on his cigar and rolled it from one side of his mouth to the other. All the while, his watery blue eyes impaled her.

"Can't your attorney subpoena the information that you need? Why come to me?"

"It would be better for me this way, Erin. Otherwise I'd never put you on the spot. You know that. But any information that my attorney subpoenas will be sifted through by the prosecution. If they don't know about the information until the time of the hearing, I could get the jump on them. You know, surprise the court, confuse the D.A., perhaps avoid the indictment!"

Erin began to shake her head in a negative sweep. "You're just putting off the inevitable. You can't expect me to take such a chance. I…can't…"

"And I counted on you as a friend," Mitch spat out with a bitterness that chilled the air.

"I—we are friends."

"No, you've got that one wrong, Erin, dead wrong!" he snapped, waving an angry accusatory finger and his cigar within inches of her face. "We were friends when it was convenient for you—when I was your boss, and I could help you. Especially when that jerk of a husband dumped on you and you needed a shoulder to cry on. But now, when the tables have turned, our friendship seems to be wearing a little thin, doesn't it?"

Erin drew in an unsteady and disbelieving breath. "You can't possibly mean what you're implying. You know that I care for you—I always have—but you're asking the impossible!"

"Ha!"

"Mitch…don't…"

"Don't what, Erin?" he taunted, all of his hatred coming to the surface. "Don't overextend your friendship? Don't ask you to help me, after I helped pull you back together during your divorce? Don't ask you to do anything that might endanger your fragile relationship with your new boss?"

"What?" she gasped, but the meaning of his words was clear.

"Don't give me that wide-eyed shocked virgin routine, Erin. It won't work. Besides, it's demeaning. I know that you're Kane Webster's mistress, and that you've been hopping in and out of bed with him since he first set foot in this town!"

All of the color in Erin's face washed away with Mitch's cruel words, and little protesting, choking noises came from somewhere in her throat. But Mitch's vicious tirade wasn't finished.

"You're surprised, aren't you. Well let me tell you this—it's all over town!"

"No!"

His eyes narrowed evilly. "I never thought you would stoop so low as to sleep with such despicable scum as Webster. But then you've never had very good taste when it came to men, have you?"

"That's enough," she gasped, finding her voice and her purse at the same moment. "I'm leaving!"

"What's the trouble, Erin? Am I getting too close to the truth? I should never have promoted you over Olivia Parsons eight years ago. That's where I made my mistake."

Erin's lilac eyes flashed fire. "I'm sure she would agree with you." She stood and hurriedly pulled on her coat. "I don't know what it is that's making you so bitter...."

"The prospect of prison, Erin. It can be very frightening!"

"I'm sorry, Mitch, but there's absolutely nothing I can do." Her poise was beginning to come back to her. She sighed heavily. "But no matter what, if it's any consolation, I do wish you luck today."

"Sure you do," he echoed sarcastically. "Thanks but no thanks. I don't need your good wishes, Erin. Not now, not ever!"

Erin turned on her heels and didn't bother to say goodbye. Her back was rigidly straight as she marched to the door and never looked over her shoulder. She felt tears begin to pool in her eyes, but she determinedly pushed them backward. She refused to cry over Mitch, not after the way that he had treated her today. She knew that she was trembling and weak-kneed by the time she reached the rain-dampened streets, but she ignored her weakness and the drizzle that collected on her hair and ran down the back of her neck. A queasy, nervous feeling of desperation was churning in her stomach.

How had Mitch changed so much? she wondered. What had happened to the kind and caring man she had once known and respected? And how—how had he guessed about her affair with Kane? Erin's mind was spinning in circles, and her face, now covered with drops of rain, had lost all of its color. Her sleek ebony hair had begun to curl in the rain, and tiny tendrils began to spring out of the tidy black knot at the base of her head. She walked along the rain-puddled streets, absorbed in her own distant thoughts for over an hour. With her head bent against the wind, her small fists thrust into the pockets of her raincoat and her jaw clenched at an angle, she hardly looked her pert businesslike self. She felt a burning sense of betrayal that Mitch would stoop so low as to ask her to confiscate bank records secretly for his personal use. How far did friendship reach? How much would he ask of her? Again, she was reminded of Mitch's initials on the chart showing that Erin had possession of a key that she had never seen. Had Mitch, somehow, tried to implicate her in his crime? Was it possible that she had been wrong about Mitch all this time? She stamped her booted foot impatiently on the sidewalk.

Suddenly aware of the passing time, she hurried back to the bank. She was oblivious to the fact that her usually neat appearance was disheveled from the wind and the rain and that her normally clear eyes were clouded and preoccupied. As she rushed into her office, she paused only to pick up her messages and remind her secretary more curtly than she had intended that under no circumstances, other than a telephone call from Kane, was she to be disturbed.

For the remainder of the afternoon Erin holed up behind her desk, and tried to immerse herself in paperwork. But all her concentration seemed to shift to Mitch, and she found it impossible to forget the hollow look of despair on his face or the nervousness of his hands or his eyes, once clear and blue, now gray and pasty. Erin's stomach twisted violently as she remembered him and realized just how suspicious she had become of a man she had once trusted completely. Was she being paranoid, or had she been a fool to trust him in the past? She let her forehead drop to her hand, and hoped to God that the afternoon would slide by without any further complications.

The little yellow car couldn't hurry home fast enough for Erin, and the snail's pace of the late afternoon traffic as it snarled in the rain only added to her frustration. Maneuvering the Rabbit through the hilly streets of the downtown area of Seattle, she made it to the freeway, but to no avail. Tonight, even the freeways were choked with commuters anxious to get home, semis on their assigned routes and recreational vehicles hoping to get a head start on the wet weekend. As the windshield wipers danced rhythmically before her eyes, Erin sighed, realizing that because she usually worked much later than six o'clock, she had forgotten how difficult and frustrating rush hour could be.

It took her nearly an hour to get home. As she guided her car to a halt she jerked on the emergency brake before racing up the sidewalk and taking the steps to her third-floor apartment two at a time. With unsteady fingers she unlocked the door, hurried into the apartment and switched on the local news. She was too preoccupied to bother shaking the rain from her coat or umbrella.

The sullen-faced newscaster was already making predictions about the upcoming statewide elections as the television snapped on. From habit Erin began to unbutton her coat, but she never let her eyes waver from the small black and white screen that held her attention. At the next commercial break, she managed to slip out of her coat and toss it next to her on the couch just as the dark-haired newsman began to recount the story that was uppermost on her mind: an alleged case of embezzlement at a downtown Seattle bank.

Erin's eyes were riveted to the set, and nervously she began to bite at her lower lip. As the scene on the television changed to the district courthouse, the eye of the camera sought Mitch and caught him hurrying out of the double doors of the marble courthouse. He was accompanied by a rather short and balding attorney who attempted to protect his client by fending off persistent questions from the group of anxious reporters clustered at the courthouse doors. Mitch, shielding his face with his hands, rushed to a waiting car. Erin only caught a glimpse of her former boss, and she felt a rush of pity for the man as his watery blue eyes darted anxiously back to the attorney before he climbed into the waiting automobile and sped away from the newsmen.

"Yes," the mustached anchorman was stating, "Mitchell Cameron, once considered one of Seattle's most prestigious and trusted bankers, was indicted today on seven counts of embezzlement. If Cameron is found guilty, the maximum sentence…" Erin couldn't listen to the rest of the broadcast. She was too numbed by the chilling realization that Mitch actually had been indicted! Rubbing her temples with her slender fingers, she tried to think rationally—indicted, what exactly did that mean? It took her a few minutes to understand that Mitch hadn't been found guilty of a crime, at least not yet. But apparently there was enough evidence against him to warrant a serious investigation and a trial. Erin sunk onto the sofa, mindless of the water that had started to collect around her boots on the Persian rug.

The TV continued to talk to her. A picture of the bank building, looking somehow more foreboding in the variegated gray tones of the set, flashed onto the screen. Consolidated First Bank stood out in bold letters, while a reporter recounted the bank's recent history along with the fact that, within the last month, the ownership of the prestigious building had changed hands. The smug newsman noted that when the president of Consolidated, Mr. Kane Webster, was summoned by the television station to remark on the alleged embezzlement, Mr. Webster declined. He was, of course, unavailable for comment—supposedly out of the state.

Erin had heard enough, and she clicked off the television with cold, numb fingers. Drawing her knees beneath her chin, she wrapped her arms about her legs and sat on the couch, staring at the black Seattle evening through the window. A loneliness settled upon her and she thought about Kane, thousands of miles away in Southern California. The smoky gray drizzle and the heavy purple cloud cover that cloaked the city only added to her gloom. Unconsciously she began to take the pins from her hair, and shake loose the tight, confining chignon. She ran her fingers through her black tresses and rubbed her scalp, hoping to deter the headache that was starting to throb against her temples. If only Kane were here now—perhaps the lonely desperation that was closing in on her would fade....

She must have been staring into the oncoming darkness for quite a while, but she was too lost in her own black thoughts to realize that time had escaped her. The urgent ringing of the telephone startled Erin back to the present, and she rushed into the kitchen to answer its incessant call. As she spoke, she tried to conceal the note of depression that had crept into her voice.

"Hello?"

"Erin?" a concerned voice inquired.

"Oh, Kane!" She sighed, and let her knees give way in relief. Resting against the counter, she found herself overwhelmingly grateful for the thin wire that stretched the length of the West Coast and tied her to Kane.

"Are you okay?" he asked, and she recognized a tremor of concern in his voice.

"I'm fine," she assured him. "It's been a long, hectic week without you. I'm just a little tired, that's all."

There was a weighty pause in the conversation before Kane spoke again. "Have you heard about the indictment?" he asked, and his voice seemed to have become suddenly reserved.

"Yes...I saw the evening news...." She hesitated a moment. Should she tell him about her meeting with Mitch this afternoon and his proposition? Erin knew that Kane would be angry and upset when he found out about it, and she reasoned it would be better to tell him face-to-face. A long-distance call was too short and too impersonal. Too many misunderstandings could occur.

"I know that you care a lot about Cameron," Kane began, wondering to himself why he continued to pursue a subject that only incensed him.

"I did, and I suppose I still do…but, really, it's okay. This is the way it had to be, didn't it?"

Why did he feel that there was a trace of hesitation in her voice? His fist involuntarily balled at his side, and his grip on the telephone receiver tightened until his knuckles showed white. It had been a difficult week for him also. Dealing with his strong-willed daughter had proven to be nearly impossible. And the fact that Erin was alone and over fifteen hundred miles away only added to his irritation and short temper.

"Krista and I will be home late Sunday afternoon," he was saying. "Probably around six. And the moving company has promised to have the bulk of our belongings in Seattle by Monday—or so they claim. What won't fit into the apartment, I'll have stored. Will the apartment be ready for us?"

Erin couldn't hide the disappointment that swallowed her. She had hoped that Kane would be home this evening or, at the very latest, Saturday.

"What? Oh, yes," she agreed distractedly. "Mr. Jefferies moved out at the beginning of the week, and the cleaning people were here earlier today. I'm sure it will be ready by Sunday evening…."

"Good—I'll see you then."

"Good night, Kane," Erin whispered, not wanting to hang up the phone and sever the frail connection that bound her so distantly to him.

"Erin?"

"Yes…"

A pause. "Good night."

Erin felt an incredible loneliness as she hung up the phone.

"Oh, darling!" Kane murmured to himself as he heard her

ring off. He slammed the receiver down in mindless frustration and rubbed his hands together anxiously, all the while leaning against the wall and staring at the clean, white telephone in his sister's apartment. How was he going to handle his emotions for Erin? God, had it only been four days since he had last seen—or touched—her?

Somehow he had expected and silently hoped that once he had put some distance between himself and her, the miles would erase the goddesslike image of her body and that her likeness in his mind would fade, cooling his hot-blooded need for her. But he had been mistaken, grievously mistaken, and just the reverse had occurred. Instead of forgetting her, the image of her body was burned savagely on his mind and achingly in his loins. He felt an urgency, a driving *need,* warm and molten, that throbbed against his temples and fired his blood. He had to see her again, and he had to see her soon, or he would surely go out of his mind!

And the lies! Oh, God, how he hated his lies. The duplicity of his situation was eating at him, tearing at him from the inside out. He slammed a powerful fist against the wall. How could he lie to her and to himself? How long could the tense charade continue?

Kane had convinced himself that it would be a good idea to live near Erin, in the same building, in order that he might watch her more closely. But now, as he stood staring at the phone, he knew that it was only his mind playing games with him again. Another lie to justify his urgent need to be near her and protect her.

Protect her? He laughed mirthlessly at himself and reached for the tall glass of Scotch that he had poured before placing the long-distance call. Erin needed to be protected all right, from Kane Webster, from himself! *He* was the one who continued relentlessly and mercilessly to track her down, stalking her like some wild, criminal creature. He was suspicious of her and too much of a coward to admit it for fear of losing her. A damned hypocritical bastard, that's what he was, he conceded to himself.

Kane's hands were shaking from the turbulent emotions that were battling cruelly within his mind. He took a long drink, and groaned as the Scotch hit the empty bottom of his stomach. His thoughts were black and excruciating as he strode into the living room and levered himself down on his sister's uncomfortable floral couch.

Why couldn't he just forget about Erin O'Toole and her crazy connection with the embezzling scam? Why did he continue to torture himself with the memory of the gentle curve of her neck, the slim, feminine contour of her legs or the longing way that her near-violet eyes could reach out and touch him?

Damn it, Webster, his persistent mind scolded, *control yourself! For all you know that woman is just another two-bit thief, and you're letting her rip you to shreds! She's destroying your objectivity! Erin's a witch,* his mind warned, *the less you have to do with her, the better!*

Kane shifted his weight uncomfortably on the prim blue cushions of the couch and took another long dissatisfying swallow of the potent warm liquor. He needed to break away from Erin and the spell she was casting over him, he reasoned.

Then, why the hell couldn't he convince himself to leave her alone?

Chapter 10

Sunday morning dawned as gloomy as the rest of the Seattle weekend had, but Erin felt somewhat lighthearted at the prospect of seeing Kane again. It seemed like forever since he'd been gone. She stretched out on the bed, and discovered that she ached all over. The muscles in her arms and legs seemed to be all knotted and twisted this morning, but she smiled to herself in spite of the pain. In order to keep her mind off Mitch's indictment and Kane's absence, Erin had run out on Friday night and purchased several gallons of paint. That night and all day Saturday she had spent repainting Mr. Jefferies' old apartment and the massive entry hall. This morning her aching muscles rebelled.

Against the silent protests of her body Erin got up and showered. The new paint job had been such an improvement to the building that she had decided to continue the project. She had almost finished with the entry hall, and today she planned to tackle Mrs. Cavenaugh's apartment. Ever since the repairmen had insulated the flooring and the windows, parts of the little old lady's apartment had suffered, and a new coat of paint would hide the dirt and chips of paint that had been loosened during the repairs. Erin shuddered when she realized that she had nearly depleted her savings with the insulation and painting projects. But it just had to be done!

Mrs. Cavenaugh had embraced the idea of repainting her apartment, and by the time Erin had swallowed a cup of coffee, looked over the headlines and nibbled on a bit of toast, it was only eight-thirty. Yet Mrs. Cavenaugh was already up and ready to help Erin with the task at hand.

For as long as Erin could remember, she had never seen Mrs. Cavenaugh in anything other than a prim housedress and a single strand of pearls. But this morning the half-bent figure of Mrs. Cavenaugh sported a garishly loud green-and-purple scarf that was wound tightly over her hair, oversize trousers and tennis shoes that were presumably antiques. She was a comical sight in the outlandish outfit, but her blue eyes sparkled with eagerness, and against Erin's protests, the elderly woman grabbed a brush and began to tackle the job at hand, only pausing to grumble about working on the Sabbath. Erin ignored her complaints and to her amazement found that Mrs. Cavenaugh was handy with the brush and had the endurance of a woman half her age.

"This is a wonderful idea," Mrs. Cavenaugh exclaimed, "even if we are working on the Lord's day." Her blue eyes were carefully checking over some of Erin's work with a practiced eye. Not able to complain about Erin's painting, she continued, "Adds a lot to this apartment, don't you think?" A pleased smile crept over her features. "You really are a dear. You know that don't you?"

"Keeping up the place comes with being a landlord, especially when I can get some free labor from my tenants," Erin laughed, and smiled at the little old lady's compliment.

"Is the apartment across the hall ready for the new renters? When are they moving in?"

Erin slid a suspicious glance at the old woman, who seemed intent on trimming the windowsill. "As a matter of fact I expect them this afternoon."

"Young couple?" Mrs. Cavenaugh asked, a mischievous twinkle lighting her eyes.

"No...it's my boss...Mr. Webster. I believe you've met?" Erin watched Mrs. Cavenaugh carefully.

"Charming man," the older woman agreed, and paid even more attention to the windowsill. "So he's moving in today?"

"Why do I get the feeling that I'm giving you yesterday's news?" Erin asked suspiciously. "You've already talked to Kane about this, haven't you?"

A smile spread across the wrinkled face. "Someone's got to look out for your best interests."

"And so you just appointed yourself guardian angel. Is that it?"

"Close enough," the little old lady averred. "Now don't you go jumping off the deep end, Erin," Mrs. Cavenaugh cautioned, and wagged a warning finger at Erin. "I just happened to mention in passing that there was an apartment available...."

"In passing! When did you see him?"

Mrs. Cavenaugh's face puckered for a moment. "Now listen here, young lady. I may not be as young as I used to be, but I have a pretty good idea of what goes on around here. I've seen Kane come and go, and I've also got it figured out that, for some reason, the good Lord only knows why—" she threw her hands heavenward in supplication "—you keep running away from him."

Erin began to protest, but the gray-haired lady would have none of it. "It's a mistake, pure and simple, for you to run from him. That man is hopelessly in love with you, Erin. Only a fool would let him slip through her fingers!"

"Oh, Mrs. Cavenaugh," Erin sighed, smiling wistfully. "If it were only that simple."

"It's as simple as you want to make it!" The old lady eyed Erin speculatively, and noticed the resigned droop of her shoulders. "Why don't you call it a day—the apartment looks fine. You go and get ready for your Kane and his daughter. They'll be here this evening, won't they?"

"Just where do you get all of your information?"

"Like I said before, I know what's going on around here!" Before Erin could voice any further questions or objections, the little bent figure hustled her out the door. "And don't you dare accuse me of snooping," she cautioned. "It's just that I care."

"I know you do," Erin replied thoughtfully, "but you do seem to have an uncanny sense about some things...."

"Comes with age, don't you know? My eyesight isn't what it used to be, and my hearing's, well, you know, a little less than it should be. But I can still see love when it stares me in the face. Now you hurry up and change into something pretty and make that man something to eat. I bet he'll be starved by the time that he gets home—the girl too."

Erin started to protest, but Mrs. Cavenaugh pursed her lips, and balanced the wet paintbrush on one of her hips. "Scoot," she ordered authoritatively, and slammed the door tightly shut.

Several hours had passed, and somewhat reluctantly Erin had taken Mrs. Cavenaugh's well-meant advice, although she doubted that the little old lady downstairs would consider her slim designer jeans and print cotton blouse as "something pretty." But Erin had made dinner for Kane and his daughter, and then, realizing that Krista probably wouldn't be able to manage the two flights of stairs to Erin's loft, Erin had moved the meal downstairs to Kane's new apartment.

She paced nervously while waiting for Kane and glanced at her watch for the sixth time in the space of two minutes. The trying weekend without Kane had made Erin anxious and tired, and she found that her nerves were stretched as tightly as a piano string. How would she react to Kane's daughter, and how would Krista take to Erin? she wondered.

Erin had attempted to bring as much warmth as possible to the small first-floor apartment by bringing down a few pieces of her own furniture. To her credit, the interior did look a little less stark and more comfortable for all her efforts. The creamy new coat of vanilla paint gleamed against the walls, and the few small pieces of furniture, though sparse, added a homey familiarity to the otherwise vacant rooms. Erin had even managed to cover the card table with a linen cloth and centered a basket of freshly cut flowers on it. All in all, she had done a decent job of making the tiny apartment attractive, but she found it impossible to shake the feeling of apprehension that shrouded her.

The sound of feet shuffling in the hall snapped her attention to the doorway. She knew in an instant that Kane and Krista had made it home. Nervously she wiped her suddenly wet palms against her jeans and pasted what she hoped appeared to be a pleasant smile upon her face. The door swung open, and father and daughter entered the room. At the sight of Kane, Erin's heart turned over. How, in less than a week's time, could anyone change so dramatically? He was dressed casually in jeans and a dove-gray sport shirt, but that's where the casual part of his image stopped. Erin could sense the signs of strain that hardened his features, the thin light lines of worry that crowded his forehead, and the somber tilt of his dark eyebrows that were drawn thoughtfully together. His eyes met hers for an instant, and a small flicker of relief and affection lessened the severity of his gaze.

At the whirring sound of the electric wheelchair, Erin's attention shifted from Kane to his daughter. Krista was beautiful in the classical sense: a small, evenly featured madonna-like face was surrounded by thick sun-kissed curls, and her deep-set, perfectly round icy blue eyes held a sparkle and a vibrancy of youth. Krista's cheekbones were high and noble-looking with just a hint of pink on her otherwise cream-colored skin. Even in the awkward stage of adolescence, it was apparent that Krista was an uncommonly beautiful girl. Only the mechanical apparatus of the wheelchair detracted from her wholesome, California-fresh appearance. The presence of the chair served to remind Erin just how difficult the past year of Krista's life must have been for the girl. Krista was much too young to have lived through the trauma of witnessing the death of her mother. Erin felt her heart go out to the attractive young girl in the mechanical beast.

There was a tense, uncomfortable moment as Kane dropped a bundle of blankets that he had carried into the apartment and shoved them into the corner of the room. For a split second Erin faced Krista alone and was surprised at the frigidity in the pale blue eyes of the girl. Uncontrollably Erin shuddered and hoped that she could somehow warm the cool look that hardened Krista's gaze.

After unsuccessfully arranging the pillows and blankets on the floor, Kane gave up and turned his attention to Erin and his daughter. He seemed to appraise the uncomfortable situation with knowing eyes, and in a minute, he stood near to Erin. He was smiling, but the grin was tight, forced as if it had been slapped on his face out of courtesy. He showed Erin no outward signs of affection, but his stormy gray eyes reached out for hers, and Erin realized that he was asking her indulgence with Krista. It was as if he had expected a confrontation.

"Krista," Kane said softly, and Krista's blue eyes sparked

upward to him. "This is Erin. You remember, I told you all about her. She works with me at the bank, and she'll be our landlord until we can find a house of our own."

Krista's eyes skimmed over the interior of the apartment, and from the bored expression on her face, Erin sensed that Krista disapproved of her new, temporary home. The girl remained silent, and for a moment Erin wondered if the child had even heard the introduction. Kane's black eyebrows melted together at Krista's rudeness, but for the moment, he chose not to reprimand her.

Continuing the stilted introduction, he said more firmly, "Erin, this is Krista."

Erin ventured a sincere smile for Kane's daughter and wondered if the young girl in the wheelchair was just being shy, or if she was purposely giving Erin the cold shoulder.

"Hello, Krista. It's nice to meet you. I hope you like it here." Erin offered her outstretched hand to the girl.

Krista didn't immediately respond to Erin's attempts at warmth or friendliness. In fact, Erin was sure that if Kane hadn't been in the room, the blue-eyed girl would have ignored the greeting altogether. As it was, Krista hesitated and then gave Kane an accusatory glare before finding her manners and answering. "Hello," Krista muttered, almost to herself, and reached for Erin's open hand. Her eyes never met Erin's puzzled gaze.

There wasn't time for a proper handshake. The instant that Krista's smaller fingers touched Erin's open palm, Krista withdrew her hand as rapidly as if Erin's touch were white-hot. Erin found herself standing with her open palm suspended in midair and an astonished expression of disbelief disturbing her features. Was the girl always so rude, or did she just dislike Erin?

Rather than commenting on Krista's complete lack of courtesy, or asking about Krista's negative reaction to her, Erin forced herself to remain calm and hang on to the dwindling amount of control she had left. Excusing herself, she turned her attention back to the kitchen and preparation of the meal. She could hear the quiet reprimand that Kane was giving his daughter, but Erin tried to ignore the tension between father and daughter—tension that she somehow felt guilty about. Perhaps she shouldn't have intruded on the homecoming. It was obvious that Krista would have preferred that she had never met Erin.

As Erin extracted the platter of warm rolls from the oven, she tried to convince herself that she was overreacting to Krista's indifference. After all, the girl was crippled and probably extremely self-conscious about her condition. Aside from the obvious, it couldn't be easy moving away from the only family and friends she had ever known to start a new life with a father she barely knew in an unfamiliar city. It was no wonder that the child was frightened and misbehaving. *Give the girl a chance,* Erin told herself. *It's barely been a year since the young girl witnessed her mother's death.* Armed with a new sense of conviction, Erin decided to ignore Krista's coolness.

As she carried the meal to the table, Erin forced herself to smile and say, "Let's get started. I bet you're both hungry!"

"We ate on the plane!" Krista announced, and Kane threw his daughter a grim reproving glance. Krista ignored it.

"That we did," Kane acknowledged, "but that was several hours ago, and it wasn't particularly good." His steely eyes never left his daughter—it was as if he dared her to act up again. "As I recall, you didn't eat much." The muscle cords in his neck stood out clearly against the collar of his shirt, and Erin could tell that he was holding on to the rags of his patience. He was about to explode. Erin hoped that Krista realized how dangerous the situation was becoming.

Erin tried to steady her rapidly disintegrating nerves as she went back to the kitchen for the rest of the food. She couldn't gloss over it, not even to herself. For some reason Krista was determined to hate her. Erin mentally counted to ten, took several deep breaths, and once again poised, returned to face father and daughter. It took a lot of determination, but she was able to hide her discomfort and take some pleasure in serving the dishes that she had so meticulously prepared, although Krista's discriminating eye took a little of the satisfaction away from her. Though the aroma of the food was tantalizing, and the marmalade-glazed game hens looked delicious as they sat on a platter of steaming wild rice and mushrooms, the meal was tense and uncomfortable. Everything seemed to have soured slightly under Krista's disapproving blue-eyed gaze.

"This looks great!" Kane exclaimed a little too heartily as he helped Erin to her chair. His fingers brushed against her arm, and startled by the intimate gesture, Erin turned her eyes away from the meal to look more closely at him. He seemed more than tired—he seemed weary. She could tell his jovial words were just a cloak for the tension coiling rigidly within him. Although his voice was cheerful, the lines on his forehead, the muscle cords strung tightly at his neck, and the darkness of his gaze betrayed his calm exterior.

"Doesn't this look delicious, honey?" he asked his daughter as he took his seat. Krista remained silent. Kane cleared his throat and rubbed his hands together. "I'm famished!" He looked at Krista with concern. Her large, liquid eyes met his, but still she didn't speak.

Finally she broke her gaze from that of her father, and stared instead at the napkin in her lap. Kane's forced smile disappeared into a frown. He was obviously distressed by Krista's coolness and lack of manners, but he wisely said nothing, preferring to wait until he was alone with his daughter before having the argument that he knew was brewing between them.

The meal began in silence, and Erin thought that she would scream if some of the icy tension in the air didn't melt. Fortunately the telephone rang, and Kane excused himself to answer it. The conversation was extremely one-sided and uncomfortable.

"Not tonight," Kane argued but was apparently interrupted. "No—it's absolutely impossible! I just got in from California with my daughter. You'll have to handle it yourself!" A pause, and the muscle in Kane's rigid face tightened again. "Can't Jones handle it? No—how about Martin?" Another long pause. "For God's sake, Jim, doesn't anyone down there know what they're doing?" Kane was shaking his head, raking his fingers through the burnished copper of his hair and pacing the length of the telephone cord. "All right, all right! I get the picture. I'll be there in—" he checked his watch "—about twenty minutes!" He slammed the receiver down viciously and uttered a curse under his breath.

"I'm sorry," he apologized sincerely, once he had subdued his temper. His gray eyes pleaded with Erin to understand. "It seems that there are major problems in the computer center tonight. I have to go to the bank for a little while…."

"No…" Krista began to wail, looking frantically from her father to Erin and back again. "Don't go…."

"I'm sorry, honey," Kane responded with a fond pat on her silky blond curls. "But, really, I have to go—just for a little while…"

"No…no…" Krista pleaded, clinging to her father's shirtsleeve.

"I'll be back in a couple of hours. You can stay here with Erin."

"Daddy! No!"

Kane's expression became confused, and for a moment Erin thought that he might reconsider. She fervently hoped so, but when his dark brows straightened again, she knew that the decision had been made. He was leaving Erin with the adolescent girl who obviously hated her.

"Erin, do you mind?" he asked, ignoring Krista's pleading eyes.

"Not at all," Erin agreed, as kindly as she could, and rained a warm smile on Krista. "We'll get along just fine!" Kane's gray gaze was dubious.

"Daddy, *please,* don't go!" Krista cried in a shaky voice. Her frightened blue eyes skittered over to Erin and back to her father.

"Look, honey," Kane answered, taking both of Krista's hands in his. He squatted next to the chair, so that the child could look him squarely in the eyes. "You know I don't want to go, so let's not make it any harder than it already is. I'll be back soon. I promise." He planted a loving kiss on the top of her forehead as if to ward off any further protests. His silvery eyes locked with Erin's for a moment, begging her to understand, but there was something more—the same old sense of wariness seemed to flicker across his face for an instant as he grabbed his jacket and walked to the door. Krista stared at her plate, unable to watch her father leave, but Erin followed him.

Kane stretched into his coat, took Erin's hand in his and gently guided her out into the semiprivacy of the hallway. "Thank you," he stated and his eyes held hers. Erin could see a question in their steely depths.

"It's no problem," she replied, doubting her own words as she thought about the headstrong blonde girl.

Kane looked at her and seemed unconvinced. "You don't have to mince words with me. I know that Krista's a handful!"

"I can handle her," Erin insisted.

"I know." Still he hesitated, and in the dimly lit hallway Erin could sense an uneasiness creep over both of them. It was the same feeling that seemed to keep them from completely trusting each other. He began to reach for her and then let his hand drop. "I'll be back as soon as I can...."

"I'm sure it won't be long," she agreed, knowing that her voice sounded feeble. What was it that was bothering her? Something didn't seem right. "I thought that the repairmen fixed the computer on Friday," she puzzled, shaking her head in an effort to remember the details of Friday afternoon. "Yes, I'm sure that we got a call around five o'clock, stating that all systems were go."

Kane's jaw flexed. "Apparently there have been additional problems." His voice was strangely devoid of emotion—cold.

"Odd, isn't it?" she murmured. "Oh, well." She lifted her shoulders and managed a sincere smile. "Try to hurry home...."

His sudden and powerful embrace surprised and baffled her. His arms held her closely, tightly, as if he were afraid she might disappear. His strength imprisoned her, and she could hear the hammering of his heart, belying his calm exterior of a few moments before. His breathing was labored and uneven. She couldn't see his eyes as her face was crushed, almost savagely, against his chest. There was anger in his strength and passion in his words. They were torn from him as if his admission were painfully traitorous.

"God, but I've missed you, Erin," he breathed, and the pressure against the curve of her spine increased. "I've had dreams about you, ached for you..."

"Shhh..." Before he could utter another word, Erin checked his speech by placing a trembling finger against the warmth of his lips. "Later," she whispered, cocking her head toward the open doorway to his apartment. "I'd better go inside and check on Krista." Erin knew that she was shaking from the intensity of his passion, but she controlled the urge to reach up and trace the angled contour of his cheeks with her fingers.

Kane reluctantly let his embrace loosen and an unreadable, agonized expression passed over his face. "I won't be gone long—it should only take a minute...."

"Don't be too sure," she laughed hollowly as she stepped back toward the apartment. "Computer problems tend to be complicated...."

"That they do," he whispered cryptically, and let his eyes rove over her face searchingly. What did he expect to find? Finally he tore his gaze away from her and threw open the door before stepping into the night. If only Erin could guess the *real* reason that he had been summoned to the bank on this black, rain-drenched night, Kane thought sardonically. If only she knew that he was aware of the fact that another three thousand dollars had slipped out of the dividend account during his absence. *Oh, Erin,* he thought as he drove toward the winking lights of Seattle. His grip tightened on the steering wheel, and the tires of the black sports car screamed against the pressure of a corner taken too recklessly. *Why,* he wondered—*oh, God, why?*

Erin straightened her shoulders before she entered the tiny apartment and let the door whisper shut behind her. At the sound of the soft noise Krista stirred and looked longingly at the door with cold disbelieving eyes.

Mentally Erin fortified herself. She could tell that the upcoming evening was going to be a test of will between herself and Kane's stubborn daughter. And although Erin was an adult, and the old Victorian house was "her turf," she felt at a distinct disadvantage to the blonde girl who had folded her arms defiantly over her small chest. Erin dreaded the argument that she knew was simmering in the air. Forcing herself to appear more collected than she felt, she walked back to the table and ignored Krista's wounded look as she spoke softly to the child. Erin's voice was friendly but firm.

"Is there anything else I can get you?" she asked the girl, and motioned to a basket of sourdough rolls at her end of the table.

Silence.

Erin gritted her teeth together in frustration and noticed that Krista hadn't touched any of the food on her plate. Once again Erin attempted to communicate. "How about a glass of milk?"

Nothing.

"Krista," Erin said, commanding the girl's attention, and bracing herself for the inevitable confrontation. "I'd like it very much if we could be friends."

Cold fearful blue eyes surveyed Erin as if seeing her for the first time. Pouty pink lips pressed into an insolent line. "I don't like you!" Krista hissed in a trembling voice.

Erin sucked in her breath but bravely continued the stilted conversation. "Why? Why don't you like me? Is it because I'm a friend of your father's?"

"I don't want to like you—and I won't!" Defiance and anger were evident in the tilt of Krista's finely shaped chin.

Erin sighed wearily and sat down in the chair opposite the rebellious girl with the fearful eyes. Their gazes locked and Erin found herself folding and refolding the napkin in her lap, while contemplating a way to bridge the gap that existed between her and Kane's daughter. She took in the challenging look on the girl's face, the proud carriage of Krista's head, and then Erin's gaze touched upon the empty wheelchair. Compassion washed over Erin. Krista was bearing a heavy cross.

"You don't have to like me," Erin stated simply, and a look of astonishment softened Krista's defiant features. "It's up to you."

Once again Erin paid full attention to her meal and hoped it seemed that she was enjoying her food, while all the time her stomach was twisting into knots of revulsion against the meal. It took all of Erin's will to finish the cold and suddenly tasteless meal.

It was several minutes before the silence was broken. Krista's small voice trembled and Erin politely looked at the girl. "They were getting back together, you know!" Krista announced, and toyed with the food on her plate.

"Pardon me?"

"Mother and Daddy. They were going to get married again. Mother told me so!" Krista's face was set for the denial she expected from Erin.

"Were they?" Erin asked calmly.

"You bet!" the girl nearly shouted. "And it would have been soon too. And...and...we were all going to be a family again!"

Erin listened intently, not knowing exactly how to respond to Krista's outburst. She studied Krista and saw the turbulent play of emotions that was contorting the beautiful child's face.

"We were going to be together again. We were!" she proclaimed, tears glistening in her round eyes. "If only Mama hadn't died...I know we would!" Her frail voice caught and tears began to flow freely down her cheeks.

Erin's heart bled for the small girl at the other end of the table. Dropping her fork onto the plate, she got up and hurried to Krista's side. She let her hand touch the sobbing shoulders.

"I'm so sorry," Erin whispered.

"No, you're not!" the child sniffed. "If Mama was alive, then you couldn't have Daddy. He loved her! He did!" By this time Krista's body was racked with her uncontrolled weeping, and Erin let her arm reach tentatively around the slim shoulders.

"Don't touch me," Krista screamed. "Don't you dare touch me!" She pushed her chair back from the table and attempted to reach for the wheelchair. Erin knew that the situation was getting dangerously out of control, and she tried to help Krista by pushing the wheelchair in the girl's direction.

"I can do it myself!" Krista declared, and to Erin's surprise, the slender girl braced herself on the table's edge and took a few hesitant steps before falling into her mechanical chair.

They faced each other as if they were opponents on a battlefield. Each one eyed the other distrustfully. Hesitantly Erin drew herself up to her full height, and her lilac gaze rested on her ward for the evening. How was it possible to handle Krista? There was no answer but the obvious.

"Krista," Erin said, and offered the girl a tissue to dry her eyes. "I want you to know that there's no rule stating that you have to like me. All I ask is that you give me a chance, an honest chance. And, for your father's sake, I'm asking you to be, at least, civil to me. Is that so much to ask?"

"I don't want a new mother!" the girl cried, nearly hysterical.

"I understand that, and...I respect it," Erin agreed, still holding the tissue out to the child. "No one has the right to step into someone else's shoes, unless they're asked. I'm sure that your mother was a very wonderful woman, and that she loved you very much, but, unfortunately, I can't bring her back to you. Nobody can." Erin's eyes had begun to fill with tears as she looked into a face that was much too young to understand death. "I hope you know that whatever happens between your father and me, that I would *never* attempt to take the place of your mother—that's a promise!"

Krista stared silently at Erin for what seemed an eternity before taking the tissue and wiping the stain of tears from her cheeks. Assured that the girl was poised again, Erin turned toward the kitchen and hastily wiped her own tears with the cuff of her blouse. She hoped that Krista hadn't seen her tears or her weakness.

For the rest of the evening, while Erin cleared the table and cleaned the dishes, Krista brooded in a corner of the room, pretending interest in the empty fireplace. Erin offered to build a fire, but Krista had withdrawn back into her shell and didn't respond to the invitation. Therefore, Erin shrugged her shoulders and acted as if it didn't matter in the least to her, one way or the other, before turning back to the task of straightening the kitchen. But she sensed that beneath Krista's cold exterior, the girl had begun to thaw.

Whenever Krista didn't think that Erin would notice, she studied the black-haired woman with interest. So this was the lady that her father was falling to pieces over. Although this Erin creature was very unlike her mother, Krista couldn't help but admire Erin's mettle. Maybe Seattle wouldn't be quite as bad as she had imagined.

It was late when Kane returned to the apartment house. He parked the car and sat motionless for several minutes, just staring into the darkness of the night. He was emotionally drained to the point of exhaustion, and he had the urge to restart the car and head to the closest tavern. He wanted a drink—make that several drinks—and then he wanted to fall into bed and sleep for days. He didn't want to face Krista and endure another fight, and he couldn't face Erin, not now.

He groaned when he thought about the scene at the bank: the evidence, the fear and the anger as Jim Haney explained about the latest development in the embezzling operation. Not only was three thousand dollars missing, but Jim had learned from Olivia Parsons that Erin had met with Mitchell Cameron on the day of his arraignment hearing—the very day the money was transferred from the dividend account. The only good news was that Jim had traced the money's path and it would only be a matter of days before he had sifted through all of the departmental checks to find one that was out of balance with the general ledger. At last the torture of the unknown would end, and Kane realized bitterly that Erin would be caught.

Erin was sitting in a chair, engrossed in a mystery novel, when Kane let himself into the apartment. Her black hair was wound into a loose ponytail, her glasses were perched on the end of her nose, and her legs were curled comfortably beneath her. As Kane saw her he was reminded of the first time he had seen her, dressed much the same and crouched in a pile of legal documents at the bank. He felt the same, now-familiar male response that he'd had several weeks ago. He wanted to run to her, to scoop her up in his arms, to crush her against him and to bury his head in the soft warmth of her breasts. Even now, suspecting what he did about her and knowing he was deathly close to the truth, he wanted her as he had never wanted another woman.

"Hi," Erin greeted him, and pulled her glasses off her face. She laid the book and the glasses on an upturned box that she was using as a table, stood up and stretched. It was an unconscious and provocative gesture that made Kane's blood heat as he watched the fabric of her clothes mold tightly to her body. Her eyes found his. "Can I get you anything? There's quite a few leftovers...."

He stood in the doorway, his shoulders drooped in resignation. Though she could tell that he, in his own way, was glad to see her, there was a strange look on his face.

"Are you well?" she asked.

"What? Oh, yeah. I'm fine," he responded, and rubbed the back of his neck.

"Were the computer problems that difficult?"

"The what? Oh, no, the computer is fine. But you know how it is, one problem seems to lead to another, and before you know it, the half-hour that you planned to be gone has stretched into three." His voice was vague, distant, and Erin wondered if he was trying to tell her something.

"How's Krista?" Kane asked, and dropped to the floor. He grabbed a loose pillow for his head and patted the floor next to him, inviting Erin to sit next to him on the floor.

"We got along fine," Erin replied, and leaned against Kane, who cocked a dubious eyebrow. "Well, it wasn't easy—not at first," she admitted hesitantly. "But we worked things out."

"Did you?"

"Well, somehow we managed to get by...." Erin's voice drifted off. Kane seemed remote this evening, and she could see the evidence of exhaustion on his face. She hated to add to his problems, but she thought that he should know about Krista. "Did you know that she can walk?" Erin asked in a near whisper.

Kane stiffened. "What do you mean? Did she actually walk while I was gone?" His voice had lost all of its distance, and his fingers dug into her upper arm.

"Not exactly..."

"But you said..."

"I know what I said. Just listen a minute. Krista and I had an argument. It wasn't serious," Erin added hastily, and felt guilty for the lie. "And when I tried to help her to the wheelchair, she wouldn't stand for it. She braced herself on the table and took two—three—possibly four steps until she made it to her chair."

"You're certain?"

"Kane! I was right there—only inches from her! She walked."

"Oh, God," he murmured, and covered his face in his hands. "If only I could believe that she would be able to walk again. If only..."

"Have you spoken to a doctor in Seattle?"

"Not yet…I thought I'd wait until she was settled into a routine." He rubbed his chin thoughtfully. "The tutor comes on Tuesday for her evaluation, and then I thought I'd call the doctors that were referred to me by Krista's doctor in L.A."

"Good." Kane was weary, and now disturbed. It had been a long, tiring day for both of them. Erin stood up and tightened the thong around her hair. "Krista went to bed at ten. She wanted to wait up for you, but the poor thing was exhausted. Maybe you should go in and let her know that you're back…." Had he even heard her suggestion? He was looking at Erin intently, but for some reason, she felt that he was light-years away from her. "Well…I'd better be getting upstairs," she said, and then added more lightly, "Work, tomorrow, you know. And my boss is a very punctual person."

"Don't go," Kane breathed, ignoring her joke and reaching for her wrist. "Stay with me tonight…." His face seemed so earnest, his gray eyes so intent, that Erin had trouble resisting him.

"I'd like to stay, you know that." She hesitated. "But I can't…"

"Why not? Erin, I need you."

"Oh, Kane. You know the reason why I can't stay with you—she's sleeping in the next room. You're the one who said she needed a more normal family existence," she reminded him, and lovingly touched his forehead. "What do you think she would do if she knew that you and I were sleeping together? You said yourself that her paralysis is psychosomatic, and now we know for sure—because she walked tonight!" Erin was on her knees, placing both of her hands on his cheeks. "Oh, Kane—perhaps the doctors were right, maybe she did need a change to get her motivated to walk. But…we, you and

I, we mustn't do anything to blow it with her. We can't take the chance and set her back, don't you see?"

Kane's eyes agreed with her, although he cursed his frustration.

"Damn!" he spat. "You're right," he conceded, "but just how long do you expect me to keep my hands off you?"

"It's not what I want, and you know it. But I think that we, both of us, need to give Krista some time for adjustment."

"You're right," he sighed, and taking her hands in his, pulled the two of them upright. The passion in his eyes simmered for a minute, and he dropped her hands. "Thanks for staying with Krista. I'll see you tomorrow at work." He seemed calm, only his clenched fists gave any indication of the restraint he was placing upon himself. "I'll be in late, because of Krista and the moving company, but when I get to the office, I...I think that we should have a talk."

"Oh?"

"You and I have a lot to discuss."

She smiled up at him and tried to ignore the unreadable expression in his eyes. "I'm glad you're back," she whispered. "I missed you."

He started to respond, but stopped and closed his eyes for a second before rubbing his temple. "I'm glad to be back," he admitted, trying to rub away the deep ridges of concern that were creasing his forehead. Erin thought that he had finished speaking.

"Good night," she called over her shoulder, but his voice whispered to her and stopped her as she started to ascend the steps.

"Erin?" he beckoned.

"Yes?" Her face turned to him, and even in the semidarkness he knew it was the most beautiful face he had ever seen, the most incredible woman he had ever made love to.

"You would tell me, wouldn't you? I mean, if you were in any trouble, you would tell me about it so that I could help you?"

"Of course I would. Honestly! Don't you know that?" She couldn't hide the smile that played on her lips.

"Sure," he agreed absently, as if totally unconvinced.

"Good! Then trust me!" She laughed, and shook her hair loose from the ponytail as she sprinted up the two flights of stairs. What was Kane talking about so seriously? Sometimes, she admitted to herself, he was a bit overly dramatic.

As Kane closed the door to his apartment, he leaned heavily against the cool hardwood. Erin's final words echoed and re-echoed in his ears. "Then just trust me…trust me…"

Chapter 11

Several days had passed, and Erin found it nearly impossible to spend any time alone with Kane. Even the meeting at work had to be postponed indefinitely. During the days at work, whenever their paths would cross, it seemed that there wasn't any time for the lengthy discussion that Kane had alluded to on Sunday evening. Most of the staff was still out with the flu, the computer was working erratically, and the general disorganization of the office kept Erin from seeing Kane. Also, Kane was in and out of the office, dividing his time between the office and home, hoping to get Krista settled. Fortunately for him, Mrs. Cavenaugh had been more than willing to be with his daughter when it was impossible for him to be at home. But the strain of the situation was wearing on him; Erin could see it in his eyes.

In the evenings, although Erin would eat with Krista and Kane, there wasn't much time spent relaxing. Kane's things had made it up to Seattle Tuesday afternoon, and after dinner each night for the next four days, Erin would help him and Krista get the apartment organized. It was a nearly impossible task. Although Kane had most of his belongings in storage, it still seemed to Erin that he had overstuffed the apartment with furniture, books, clothes and whatever else he could imagine. For the first time she realized how different Kane's lifestyle in California must have been. The expensive leather furniture, an endless wardrobe of clothes, everything he owned spoke of money.

Although Kane seemed to become more tense with each passing day, Erin decided it had to do with the added responsibilities of being a full-time father. All in all, Krista seemed to be adjusting better than Kane to their new life together in Seattle. Slowly Krista was coming out of her shell. She adored Mrs. Cavenaugh and had even accepted Erin. It was difficult, but the girl had begun to take hesitant steps in her father's presence, and at those times, all of the tension would drain from Kane and he would relax. The brooding sense of distrust in his eyes would die, and he would seem to enjoy life again.

The hectic week passed quickly, and Erin let a sigh of relief escape from her lips at six o'clock on Friday when she could forget about the flu, the computer, and the inheritance tax auditors. She grabbed her coat and hurried out of the bank building. Knowing that Kane was working late this evening, she hadn't even bothered to knock on his office door to let him know she was leaving. Tonight she had special plans.

She hurried along on foot for several blocks before locating the pet shop that she had found just this week. As promised, the owner had kept his store open the extra ten minutes that Erin needed.

Erin entered the little building and tried to keep her nose from wrinkling at the pungent odor within. Several fat puppies yipped to get her attention, and longingly she patted a black fluff of fur with sparkling eyes. The puppy's entire rear end was set in motion and a long pink tongue licked Erin's fingers.

"Oh, Miss O'Toole," the bearded shopkeeper smiled. "Have you changed your mind and decided on a dog?" He held up the fat black puppy, who responded by washing the shopkeeper's broad face.

"No, unfortunately, I don't have the space for a puppy." She wavered a moment, and then shook her head resolutely. "No, I think a kitten is a better choice. It's a gift for a friend."

The round shopkeeper held his hands out helplessly and shrugged his broad shoulders. "If you're sure. Just give me a couple of minutes. I know which one you picked out earlier." He hurried to the back of his store and came back with a tiny black and white kitten that couldn't have been more than six weeks old. "This is the one, right?" he asked.

Erin held out her hands and petted the warm powder puff of black fur. The kitten began to purr noisily and scratched its tiny paws against Erin's jacket. "She's perfect!" Erin breathed, raising the kitten to eye level and inspecting it.

The shopkeeper tugged on his beard. "That one's a male— is that acceptable?"

"It doesn't matter. This is the one I want!"

Erin couldn't hide her excitement as she tapped lightly on the door to Kane's apartment. The little cat was perched contentedly on her arm as she called through the door. "Krista? Mrs. Cavenaugh?"

"Where have you been?" Mrs. Cavenaugh scolded as she opened the door. "Kane's already called twice. Finally decided to leave a message with me…say, what's that you've got there?"

Erin breezed into the room, looking for Krista. "What does it look like, Mrs. Cavenaugh?" Erin asked in a whisper. "He's a surprise for Krista."

"Oh-ho," Mrs. Cavenaugh said, shaking her head, but reaching a tentative hand out to pat the kitten's soft, downy fur.

The whir of the electric wheelchair caught Erin's attention

as Krista came into the room. The defiant look of rebellion had left her features several days ago, and for the first time since their meeting, Erin was sure that Krista was glad to see her.

"Oh, there you are. Look!" Erin announced with a wide, infectious grin as she proudly held up the black and white kitten for Krista's inspection. The blonde girl let out a squeal of delighted excitement at the sight of the small cat. "I brought him home for you—you do like cats, don't you?"

"Oh, Erin," Krista stammered, wheeling more closely to the object of her delight. Erin placed the black ball of fur on Krista's lap. The kitten stretched and curled into a sleepy ball purring contentedly. "He's...beautiful...." Krista's sparkling blue eyes swept from the drowsy kitten to Erin. "Thank you."

Erin smiled back at the girl and was surprised to feel a lump in her throat. "You're welcome, Krista," she murmured, and for a moment her breath caught. Erin kneeled next to the wheelchair and stroked the dozing kitten. "Now, if you decide to keep him, you'll have to take care of him. Feed him, take him outside...."

"I will," Krista agreed hurriedly. "Does he have a name?"

Erin shook her head. "That's for you to decide, unless Mrs. Cavenaugh has any suggestions...." Erin looked at the elderly lady and caught the gray-haired woman taking in the scene before her with teary eyes.

"What? Me?" Mrs. Cavenaugh coughed back her tears. "Oh, no. I've never been much of a cat person myself."

"Then it's up to you, Krista," Erin said. She cocked her head and stroked her thumb against her chin as she studied the cat with feigned thoughtfulness. "What do you think?"

"How about—Figaro. You know, like the cat in Pinocchio?" the bright-eyed girl asked, and Erin realized that for the first time since they had met, Krista had asked for and needed her opinion.

"I think Figaro's a great name," Erin agreed. "Now," she said as she stood up and adjusted her skirt, "I'll hurry upstairs and change my clothes before I cook us all some dinner."

Mrs. Cavenaugh and Krista exchanged knowing, conspiratorial glances. "Don't bother," Mrs. Cavenaugh suggested. "Krista and I are going to eat a pizza and watch *The Late Show.* I suppose the cat will too. Remember I told you that Kane called earlier. He wants the two of you to go out alone."

"I don't know...." Erin looked pensively at the blonde girl in the wheelchair and the cat nestled comfortably in her lap. "Are you sure that Kane wanted only me? I thought he wanted to spend some time with Krista."

"It's already been decided," Mrs. Cavenaugh stated firmly. "He called a few minutes ago. It was his idea. You're supposed to meet him at a place called The Tattered Sail or some such nonsense. I think he said that it's on the waterfront."

"Are you sure?" Erin still wasn't convinced. "He didn't say anything to me about dinner...."

Mrs. Cavenaugh clucked her tongue and interrupted, "That's why he called. He missed you. He'd been in some sort of a meeting with a fellow from California, a Mr...."

"Haney," Erin supplied.

"That was it. Anyway, by the time he got out of the meeting, you had already gone." Mrs. Cavenaugh noted the puzzled expression on Erin's face. "Now, don't ask me any more questions, because I don't know anything else."

Erin turned her attention to Kane's daughter. The girl had managed to take a few steps on her own and flop down on the couch with the cat. Krista's progress was encouraging. "Krista, wouldn't you like to join us?"

The girl rolled her head negatively against the back of the couch and playfully scratched the kitten's belly. "Naw—not tonight. I think I'd rather stay here with Figaro. Besides, we've already ordered the pizza, and the movie is going to be great!"

Erin glanced at Mrs. Cavenaugh, who lifted her shoulders. A tiny hint of a smile pulled at the corner of the wrinkled mouth. "Well, if you're sure, but somehow I feel that I'm the innocent victim of a conspiracy."

"No one could accuse you of a lack of imagination. Conspiracy, ha!" Mrs. Cavenaugh rejoined, but her wise old eyes brightened. "Now, you'd better get going. You don't want to be late. Kane said he'd meet you at about eight o'clock."

Convinced that both Mrs. Cavenaugh and Krista were satisfied with their plans for the evening, Erin made her way up the stairs and began changing for her dinner date with Kane. She couldn't hide the feeling of excitement that surged within her. It seemed like an eternity since she had spent some time alone with him. It wasn't that she begrudged him the time he shared with his daughter, it was just that Erin missed the intimate and quiet times she had shared with him in the past. He had seemed so remote lately.

The cool amethyst silk dress that she chose for the date slid easily over her body. It was simple, smart and understated with its modest V-neck and long sleeves. The slit that parted the hem added just the right amount of flair to be called sexy in a discreet manner. Erin eyed herself speculatively in the mirror and was pleased with her reflection. Her ebony hair cascaded in loose curls to her shoulders and brushed against the neckline of the dress. Her skin was already rosy with the blush of excitement and only a few touches of makeup were necessary to add to the effect. She reached for her coat and purse and headed out the door.

Just as she had closed the door, the telephone began to ring insistently. Erin was late already, and she considered letting the maddening instrument ring, but she couldn't. It might be something important, possibly Kane rearranging their hastily made plans. Reluctantly she threw her coat over the arm of the couch and hurried to the kitchen to answer the relentless ringing.

"Hello?"

"Erin! I can't believe that I finally got through to you. I've been trying to get in touch with you for days. You never called me, you know," the male voice accused, and Erin could picture the pouting lips and hurt expression in Lee's boyish blue eyes.

"I'm sorry, Lee. I did try, but there wasn't any answer."

"You could have tried again."

"I...I decided that it probably wouldn't be wise."

"What if it had been an emergency?"

Her conscience felt a twinge. "It wasn't, was it?"

"No...but it could have been!"

Erin leaned heavily against the wall, and let her head fall backward. Why tonight? Why was Lee calling again? "Look, Lee," she whispered. "I'm in a hurry for an appointment. Was there something that you wanted?"

There was a heavy pause in the conversation before he replied. "I just...wanted to see you again...."

Erin bit at her fingernail. "Bull!"

"I need to talk to you," he pleaded, and his image flashed in her mind's eye: wavy blond hair, cut-off jeans, old tennis shoes, a grass-stained football jersey that she had given him for Christmas one year.

"So talk," she managed, her voice unsteady.

"Can we meet?"

"I told you I've got a date...." She glanced at her watch.

There was silence, then a deep, theatrical sigh. "Is he someone special?"

"Yes, Lee. He is. Very special. But what do you care, after all these years?" She blinked back the tears that threatened to spill.

"Believe it or not, babe, I've always cared about you."

"Don't lie to me, Lee. I've heard it all before. I don't think this is the time to go into all that. Not now."

"When?" he demanded.

"Oh, Lee, don't you understand? It's over for us. It's been over for a long time—probably before you met Olivia."

"Okay, Erin," he retorted testily. "I deserved that. I was a louse and I admit it. But can't you believe that I want to see you again?"

"No."

"Erin, I have to."

The tears she was choking back began to slide down her cheeks. "No!"

"But, babe…"

"And don't call me that! Just what is it you want, Lee? Money?"

Silence. Incriminating silence.

"Look, Lee, do us both a favor and don't call back—ever! We've been through this scene too many times, and I for one won't repeat it ever again. It's too hard on me and it's too hard on you."

"Erin, baby, listen to me…"

He was still talking when she hung up the phone. Hastily she brushed back the tears and attempted to recapture the sense of exhilaration she had felt before she answered the phone. Why did he insist on calling? There was only one reason, the same one that she'd heard in the past: money. Damn! How could she get him out of her life once and for all?

Erin pushed her wayward thoughts aside and dashed out to her car. Soon she would be with Kane alone. Soon everything would be all right, as it should be, and she would be able to forget about Lee, the telephone call, the past.

The Tattered Sail had a reputation for being one of the best restaurants in the Northwest for fresh seafood, and tonight

Erin found the rumor to be true. Once in the intimate old, barnlike structure, Erin could feel herself beginning to relax. The atmosphere was smoky and dark, and Erin was sure that if she listened closely, above the light contemporary music and the quiet chatter of the patrons, she would be able to hear the waters of the sound lapping quietly against the pier that supported the restaurant.

The succulent house specialty, fresh Dungeness crab in a tangy sauce, was superb, and the sparkling bottle of chilled champagne that Kane had ordered added just the right touch of elegance to the otherwise casual Pacific Coast cuisine. The dimmed lanterns, the massive ship's rigging that covered the walls and ceilings and the view of the inky water of Puget Sound all served to enhance the romance and intimacy of the evening. Erin ate quietly, entranced by the setting and her powerful feelings for Kane. His eyes, two dark silver orbs, never left her face, and the smile on his face spoke more clearly than words of the depths of his feelings for her.

Somehow he seemed to have shaken off the tension that had been boiling within him for the past few days. All the heavy undercurrents that were usually evident in his eyes had disappeared, at least for the night. The dinner was a thoroughly enjoyable experience, and Erin found herself unwinding as she hadn't since the weekend in the San Juans. They talked little and spoke mostly with their eyes, but Erin did mention that she had brought Krista the kitten, and Kane seemed more than pleased when he heard about his daughter's affection for the little black cat. The tender light that illuminated his face when he spoke of Krista touched Erin's heart.

The romance of the evening extended past dinner, and as they drove home together in her small car, Erin was overwhelmed by just how desperately she had grown to love the man sitting next to her. She couldn't deny to herself that she loved him with an unspoken passion that was consuming in its intensity. For the first time in weeks she wondered if, indeed, she and Kane and Krista might have a future together. Everything seemed to be falling into place. Perhaps someday, given enough time and affection, Kane could learn to love her. The little car climbed the hill that supported the Victorian apartment house. Its broad-paned windows winked cheerfully in the night.

As she shut off the engine, Erin felt the warmth of Kane's hand when it covered hers. "Let's not go in, not just yet," he suggested in a husky voice.

"But Krista..." The protest was feeble. Already she could feel the heat of desire beginning to warm her.

"She's fine," Kane assured her, and pushed a wayward wisp of her hair back into place. "She and Mrs. Cavenaugh planned to sit up and watch old movies all night long."

"But don't you think we should check on her?"

"In a minute," he insisted, and his face moved closer to hers. The warmth of his breath, laced with the clinging vapors of champagne, whispered over her face. "I'd just like to spend a few more minutes alone with you..." His fingers reached out and traced the curve of her cheek, the length of her throat, the neckline of the dress. Erin's breath began to constrict in her chest, it became ragged as she breathed. His hand found the slit in her dress and moved gently, heatedly against her inner thigh.

"Kane," she gulped, seeing the undying passion in his gaze. "I...we...can't possibly, not here...."

"Shhh..." he commanded, and rimmed her lips with his tongue. She was melting in his embrace, feeling herself begin to blend with him. "Walk with me," he suggested intimately. "The night's warm, and so am I."

His lips found hers, and he nibbled at them gently, persuasively. His hand moved in sensuous circles against her thigh. "Well," she agreed, her eyes closing, "a walk...a short one..."

He was right, she thought raggedly as they walked together in the clear October evening. Was it the night itself or Kane's presence that made it seem so special, so eternal? The cool nip of fall was in the air, and yet, under the stars winking in the ethereal moon glow, Erin was warm despite the season. Even in the half light, she could see the spiraling vapor of Kane's breath as it mingled with the chilly night air.

He held her hand tightly, as if he were afraid that his grasp would slip and that he might lose her in the shadows. It was a wonderful, exotic feeling; his magnetic touch and the magic of the night wound together. Erin felt drugged as together they made their way to the gazebo in the backyard. It was old and in sad disrepair. But against the backdrop of the clear night, its flaws hidden by the darkness and the stand of fir trees near the worn steps, it seemed intimate and regal with its undisturbed beauty of another era. Silently Kane helped her up the two weathered steps, and she felt herself begin to tremble.

"From the first time I saw this place, I knew that I wanted to make love to you here," he stated. The silver moon glow was reflected in the intensity of his gaze, and his head bent down slowly and seductively to find her chilled lips. He crushed her against his chest with a savage urgency that seemed to be ripping him apart. "Make love to me, Erin," he pleaded. "I don't think I can stand another moment of this agony. Touch me, love me!" His lips wet a trail of desire leading from her lips down her throat, to nestle hotly against her partially exposed breast. Once there he paused to moan, "God, I want you!" Her breathing began to come in short, uneven breaths in the cold night air. Kane fell to his knees and continued to press the warmth of his face against the frail fabric that covered her abdomen. "Love me," he commanded as his hands moved in circular seductive movements against her hips, and she felt the smooth fabric of the silk dress sweep gently upward to brush against her thighs.

"I want you, too," she whispered huskily, and her hands wound themselves in the thick strands of his hair. "Oh, Kane. I need you so much!" she confessed.

"I know," he murmured. Erin felt the cold shudder of autumn pierce her skin as the zipper of her dress was lowered and the silky fabric parted to expose her back and shoulders. The dress slipped to the floor of the gazebo, and Kane's gentle hands and mouth caressed her exposed skin, raining hot moist kisses against her flesh. He dragged her down to lie beside him and tentatively touched one rounded breast with the delicacy of a sculptor. An animal growl escaped from his throat as he watched her, and in wet, heated strokes, his tongue found the ripeness of her nipples.

His mouth seared against her skin, and his tongue licked and pressed hot moistness against her body. She felt the warmth of her desire spread from her innermost core through all of her body. Rivers of passion ran in her veins, and desire, hot and molten, pounded against her temples. She felt tides of feverish passion wash over her until she wanted to drown in its molten embrace. Despite the cool of the evening, a dusting of perspiration covered her body. On their own, without conscious thought, her fingers found the buttons of his shirt, the zipper to his slacks, the proud hardness of his desire. She arched her body heatedly against his, aware only of her agonizing love for him.

His lips teased and satisfied her, toying with her until she thought she would go mad, only to arouse her to still-untouched heights. His eyes, smoldering in the night, took in all of her: the look of yearning in her large luminous eyes, the way her provocative tongue continued to flick against her lips, the full, rounded breasts with nipples proudly erect, and her soft, sensuous hips, inviting him to explore her more intimately. He thought he would lose all control in the instant she arched against him, and he wanted to give in to his virile male urge to take her. God, he'd waited so long, and he felt a need, strong and inflexible, to make love to her, but he forced himself to wait, somewhat impatiently, caught up in the heat of his lovemaking, until he was certain she was ready for him.

Erin wondered if she would fall apart and crumble into fiery bursts of passion as Kane lowered himself onto her. With a sigh of long-denied pleasure, she wound her arms and legs around him, entrapping him and tempting him to make love to her. He could resist no longer.

"Oh, God, Erin. You're so beautiful, I need you..."

His words trailed off into the night in an unspoken confession as he found his way to her. In the shadow of the gazebo, his hot pulse at war with the cool night, he watched her as he loved her, and he saw the heat of desire blossom into the ecstasy of satisfaction. Together they found a love so exquisite that he knew it could never be recaptured. Only his own traitorous duplicity marred the perfect enchantment that he knew as he fell against her and felt the warmth of her breasts flatten against his weight.

It was several minutes before he spoke, as if he were unable to break the peaceful spell of enchantment that covered them. When at last he broke the silence, it was to murmur her name over and over in the night, as if trying to impress her memory upon his lips. It was so difficult to say all the things that he wanted so urgently for her to know. And the questions that had to be asked plagued him. He knew that it was time for explanation and discussion. Too much was at stake to continue to hide behind the truth. He needed her so desperately, yet his duplicity was eating at him. The fear of los-

ing her gripped him more savagely each day. It was time for
something to be done.

"What is it?" Erin asked suddenly, staring at the dread in his
eyes. Once again she sensed the wariness had appeared, and
the knowledge frightened her. She had hoped that all Kane's
reservations had melted away. Shivering more from Kane's obvious apprehension than from the coolness of the night, she felt
the same cold doubts crawl up her spine. He noticed the chill,
rolled off her and pulled his jacket lightly over her shoulders.

His hands trembled as they pressed against her face. "Marry
me, darling," he whispered in a voice dry with emotion. For
a moment Erin's heart turned over. Her first impulse was to
throw her arms around his neck and confess the depth of her
love, but something in his face made her pull the reins in on
her excitement.

"What?" she asked quietly, looking deeply into his eyes for
the trace of love she hoped to find.

"I'm asking you to marry me. Now—as soon as possible,"
he clarified, and pressed her fingers against his lips. "We need
to be together."

She wanted to accept his proposal, to take part in the ela-
tion that was beginning to burst in her veins. But there was
the strong scent of accusation that hung between them and
made her pause.

"I would love to marry you," Erin breathed, trying to think
rationally. The stars, the moon, the wind of the night were
all closing in on her, and she found it difficult to concentrate
on anything but the feelings of love that were swelling in her
veins. "You must know that...."

"Then, get packed. We'll fly to Reno tonight—or early in
the morning. The sooner the better." He began to slide into
his pants in his urgency to persuade her.

"We have time...."

"No!" he nearly shouted. And then, in a somewhat calmer voice, he continued, "No—we don't have any time."

"But, Kane," she argued, fearing the continuation of the discussion, but unable to stop herself. "You have to put certain things into perspective. We have to take Krista's feelings into consideration—surely you can understand that. And the bank—"

"Erin!" He grabbed her shoulders roughly, and forced her to look up at him. His grip tightened on her forearms, and his face was a harsh mask of determination. "It's got to be soon. You know that."

"Why? We have the rest of our lives..."

"No, we don't!" he snapped. "Don't you understand?" His eyes were shadowed by the darkness of the gazebo, but Erin could feel the pain and torture of his words without being able to probe his desperate gaze. Why was he so insistent? A cold strange feeling passed over her, transferred from him by the urgency of his forceful grasp on her upper arms.

With an unsteady voice, she asked, "Kane, just what is it that you're trying to say?"

"I'm asking you to be my wife, pure and simple. Is that so difficult to understand?"

She wasn't convinced. "There's more, isn't there? Has it got something to do with Krista, because she's already made it plain to me that she doesn't have room in her life for a 'new mother.'" In the blackness Erin tried to read the expression on Kane's face. Hoping to find love, she was disappointed. A cloud passed over the moon, and once the pale light was restored, she found his eyes torn with an emotion she couldn't understand. She tried to draw away from him but still he held her desperately, passionately.

Slowly the grip on her forearms relaxed, and resignation

covered Kane's features. "Get dressed," he commanded softly. "And then I promise you we'll talk."

Hurriedly she did as he instructed her, running her panty hose in her hasty efforts. Was it the chill of the night that made her shudder, or the cold look of determination heightening the masculine angles of Kane's face that cooled her blood?

As she was smoothing the silk dress over her hips, he began to speak in a distant voice that was dry with dread.

"When I was in California," he started, stepping away from her and pacing the length of the gazebo, "some more money was embezzled from the dividend account...three thousand dollars to be exact." He whirled to face her, and his guarded eyes found hers. The expression on her face was one of confusion.

"I don't understand—I thought that Mitch was the suspect...."

He cut off her conjecture. "Of course he's the prime suspect, but it's become apparent that he has an accomplice in the department!"

"No!" she gasped.

"Yes!"

Her voice was faint, barely a whisper. "But who?"

"Why don't you tell me?" he suggested, his voice taking on the quality of a smooth courtroom lawyer.

"But I don't know."

"Don't you?" Accusation singed his words.

"No...I can't imagine...." She was so taken aback by his supposition of an accomplice for Mitch that she hadn't noticed the suspicion in his eyes, the way his arms crossed over his chest, the grim hard angle of his jaw. But now, after the shock of his statement had dissipated, she knew what he was thinking.

"You're not...you couldn't be," she was stammering, but she couldn't control herself. Slowly she stood up and watched the play of emotions that rampaged over his face. "I don't be-lieve that you would think I could somehow be involved. You wouldn't be suggesting anything like that...would you?" Be-fore the anger took hold of her, disbelief and agony tortured her eyes.

"Why don't you explain..."

"No!" She stamped a bare foot on the thin floor of the gazebo. "I don't have to explain anything to you...." Tears burned in her eyes, but she tilted her head defiantly in spite of them. As they began to flow slowly down her face, they caught the moonlight in tiny rivers of outrage. "Are you ac-cusing me of embezzlement?" Her voice was as chilling as the wind that rustled the leaves overhead.

"Erin," he said in a calm voice devoid of emotion. "I just want to know the reason for certain facts...."

"Facts? You mean evidence? I don't believe it. You don't have any evidence—you couldn't, just an overactive and sus-picious imagination!"

He tried to interrupt, but she wouldn't let him. "I won-dered, from the beginning, why all the questions about Mitch, why all the vague insinuations and especially why you would look at me the way you did. But I must have been a fool, a damned idiot, not to have put two and two together." She took a gasp of cold autumn air, only to find that her entire body was quivering with rage and betrayal. "How can you stand there and accuse me, after all that we've shared together? Oh, Kane—why?"

"If you could just be reasonable."

"Reasonable?" she shrieked, and then laughed from the tension that was capturing her in its angry claws. "Reason-able? How can you expect me to be 'reasonable' after you ask me to marry you and accuse me of a crime I didn't commit?"

"Erin, don't make this any harder than it already is," he

pleaded, and leaned against a beam that supported the roof. "I can't ignore the facts, as much as I'd like to. I know that you need money—the employee loan application states as much—"

A protesting sound gurgled in her throat, but he ignored it.

"And your ex-husband, Lee Sinclair—" the name came out in a snarl of disapproval "—you loaned him money once, and he's back in town."

"How?"

"It doesn't matter." He shook his head, and continued in a flat, dry voice. "And there was the securities key discrepancy. You were one of the people who had access to the bearer bonds that were taken, and suddenly, somehow, you find the money to paint the apartment house and fix it up for the winter. An odd set of circumstances, wouldn't you say?"

"Exactly that, circumstances," she commented indignantly.

"That first morning in the bank I found you alone in your office. You had the perfect opportunity...."

"Enough!" she stammered, and started down the two weathered steps of the gazebo. "I've heard enough." She paused for a minute, her hands supporting her weight on the railing. "What I don't understand is why, if you suspected me from the start, you didn't tell me—or ask me? Didn't you have the decency to respect my innocence and ask me about all those 'facts'?"

"It doesn't matter, not now," he said with a rush of enthusiasm. "We can get married, and I'll find a way to replace the money." He strode over to her and captured her wrist. "Don't you see, no more money will be taken, and all the cash that's missing since Mitch left the bank will be replaced."

"Just like that?" she asked incredulously. Her eyes narrowed and she surveyed the hand on her wrist suspiciously. "You really think that I was a part of this, don't you?"

"Erin," he sighed disconsolately as he tilted her face with his thumb. "I know that you met Mitch on the day of his arraignment. I also know that the money was taken on that day...."

"You bastard!" Before she could think, her free hand arched upward and slapped Kane's cheek. The loud smack echoed in the night, and Kane's eyes grew black with suppressed fury. His jaw clenched, and for a moment Erin wondered if he was going to retaliate and hit her.

His voice, suddenly soft, reached out to her. "Erin..."

"Don't! I don't want to hear anything more! Not ever again. I'll...I'll hand in my resignation tomorrow...and I think it would be best for all of us if you would move out of the apartment as soon as possible. You...you can...have two weeks...." The sobs that she was quietly withholding began to rack her body, and she felt as if she were about to be torn in half by his betrayal. At the pressure from Kane's hand on her shoulder, she drew away as if wounded and started stumbling toward the house.

"Erin, wait!" Kane ordered, but she ignored his plea. "You can't resign. If you're innocent, you can't resign. It will appear more incriminating!"

Whirling to face him, nearly tripping on the exposed root from a nearby fir tree, she replied bitingly, "I'm quitting. I...I don't want anything more to do with you...or your bank!"

"Erin, don't!" He was beside her in a minute, and his features had softened. "Don't you understand? I need you, I want you...I love you!"

"Love? You don't have any idea what the word means. And, as for *needing* and *wanting,* I think you're getting them confused with *using.* Because that's what you did to me, wasn't it? You used me—tried to get close to me so that you could 'look into my darker, private side.' Isn't that how you phrased it? I didn't know what you meant, not at the time, but I know

now, don't I? You wanted to get inside my head and find a way to incriminate me for a crime that I had no part of...."

"Please try and understand...."

"Just leave me alone!" Her eyes met his, and even though they were filled with tears, he could see that she meant every word she was speaking.

"I don't want it to end this way."

"There isn't any alternative. You took care of that!"

"I'm sorry."

"Not good enough, Kane, not good enough." Her words were colder than the autumn wind that pushed her black hair away from her face, and highlighted the proud, near-perfect oval with its fine cheekbones and luminous violet eyes.

"All right, Erin. If that's the way you want it."

"That's the way it has to be," she sighed, and stepped aside to let him pass. She watched him silently as he walked toward the front of the house and disappeared around the corner. When he was finally out of her range of vision, she let herself slump against the tall fir tree near the gazebo. "You are a fool," she muttered under her breath. "And he is a bastard!" The tears started to flow again. How could he even think that she would stoop so low? How could he have misjudged her so? And how, in God's name, how could he be so gentle and caring one minute and so ruthless the next?

It was past midnight when Erin found the strength to return to the loft that she had once shared with the man she still loved.

Chapter 12

An insistent, impatient knocking awoke Erin from a night whose fitful sleep had been interrupted by dismal nightmares. The dull ache in her head increased with each knock on her front door. "I'm coming," she groaned, running her fingers through her tangled hair and hoping that her response would stop whoever it was from making any further racket.

Jerking on her peach-colored terry robe, she cinched the belt tightly around her waist and glanced haphazardly into the mirror over the bureau. The reflection that stared back at her was disheartening—the long, anxious night had taken its toll on her face. Large blue circles under her eyes intensified the pale, washed-out complexion of her face. The large eyes that had always sparkled seemed lifeless, and her black hair hung in tangled curls against her neck.

The pounding started up again. "I'm coming," Erin repeated loudly, and wondered who would be calling so insistently at seven in the morning. The knocking subsided for a minute. Erin half expected to see Kane when she opened the door and braced herself for whatever confrontation might occur when she came face-to-face with him. "Just a minute," she called through the wood panels, and tugged the door open.

What she hadn't expected to see on her doorstep—not in a million years—was Lee. His blond hair was meticulously combed and his blue eyes were as brilliant as ever, perhaps even more so. He was perched atop the polished wood railing of the landing. One arm was bent around a carved banister to aid his balance. His casual slouch, accented by faded jeans and a lightweight sport shirt was a theatrical display of relaxation by design, belied only by the tiny muscle that worked constantly near the back of his jaw.

"Hi, babe." He greeted her with a wink and gave her a long, suggestive head-to-toe appraisal. "Rough night?" A smile, boyish yet sinister, curved his thin lips.

After the initial shock of seeing him, Erin regained her composure and propped her shoulder against the doorjamb, keeping a careful distance between them. Without conscious thought, she tugged on the belt of her robe and pulled it more tightly around her slim waist.

"I'll ignore your insinuations for now," she replied with a plastic copy of his smirk pasted on her face. "What are you doing here?"

Hopping off the railing in a lithe movement, he responded, "I couldn't seem to get through to you on the phone. So I decided if Mohammed wouldn't come to the mountain...."

"I get the gist," she retorted coldly. She could feel an uneasy caution tighten the muscles of her back. "That doesn't explain why you're here, banging on my door loudly enough to wake up the entire neighborhood at seven in the morning. What do you want?"

"How about a cup of your coffee, for starters. From there, who knows how far our relationship can progress?" There was another long, suggestive look.

"I'm sorry, Lee, but as you already guessed, I did have a rough night last night. I'm tired and I'm not up to playing word games with you. Why don't you just tell me what it is you want? Then you can leave." She crossed her arms over her breasts to shield herself from his gaze. Lee made her uncomfortable, but she did her best to hide her apprehension.

"Why are you always so suspicious of me?" he asked in a low voice that was meant to be hypnotic.

"Because I know you."

"Erin, baby," he cooed, coming more closely to her. Involuntarily she shrank back. "What's happened to you? Let me make you feel better."

"And just how do you think you could do that?" she asked wryly, a grim smile twisting her lips and her black brows cocking nervously.

"We used to get along just fine," he suggested smoothly, and his hand reached out to trace the neckline of her robe.

Jerking away from him, Erin glared at his bemused face. "Look, Lee, just say whatever it is you think you have to say to me and then leave." She paused for a moment, and then continued. "What is it? Do you need money again?"

Sandy-blond eyebrows shot up with undisguised interest. "Ah, well, that's not the main reason that I came over here, but now that you mention it, I could use a few bucks." He smiled his most winning smile and shrugged his shoulders. Erin was surprised at her reaction, total disinterest in his most becoming grin. "You know how it is—I had a run of bad luck."

"Haven't we all?" she muttered under her breath, and raked her fingers through her tangled black curls.

"Ah, come on, Erin. Don't give me that. The way I hear it, you're loaded."

"Is that the way you hear it?" She laughed tightly, despite

the headache that was pounding relentlessly in her ears. "I guess you've got the wrong information."

"What do you mean?" he asked, a sudden seriousness killing his smile. *He looks old,* Erin thought to herself. The sunny college-boy looks only survived when he smiled.

"What I mean, Lee, is that I'm out of a job," she explained, her words a little less caustic than they had been. "I'm sorry. I can't loan you any money. I just don't have it."

"You? You've got to be kidding!"

"I'm not!" She shook her head to emphasize her point.

"You must have a savings account—*something!*"

"Not much," she admitted. "And anyway, I don't feel that I owe you any favors. That might sound a little cold-blooded, but it's the way I feel."

Lee began to bite his lower lip, and his eyes darted around the landing. "Look, babe, I'm desperate. I need to get my hands on some bread, and fast!"

"Why don't you get a job?" she asked, and hated herself for the acidic sound of the sarcasm.

A stricken expression covered Lee's face. "A job? I've been looking for a job night and day. It's…just that the right…opportunity hasn't presented itself."

Erin rubbed her hands against her temples and gave Lee a final sorrowful expression. "I'm sorry about that too," she said honestly, "but if you don't mind, I'm tired, and I'm going back to bed." He must have misinterpreted her feelings, because as she reached for the handle of the door, Lee was against her, his body molding tightly to hers. She tried to wriggle out of his embrace, but there was no escape.

"Erin, baby," he growled. "Why do you enjoy teasing me?"

"What? Lee, let go of me. What are you doing?" She felt the power of his body push against her and force her rigidly against the cold hardwood. His hands reached for the knotted belt of her robe, and she could feel his long, cold fingers probe against the flimsy fabric of her nightgown. A shudder of fear stiffened her spine.

"Let me go," she hissed, but his lips, dispassionately cool, descended on her open mouth. A sinking sensation of fear swept over her as his tongue pressed ruthlessly against her gums. With all the strength she could gather, she lifted her bare foot and hoisted her knee sharply upward, but Lee had anticipated the move and dodged the misplaced blow.

"So you want to play rough," he growled, and pulled her hands over her head to pin them cruelly against the door frame.

"Lee! Stop this. You're acting like a lunatic," she asserted, but the command in her voice was diminished by the fact that her words were trembling.

"Let her go!" Kane's voice commanded from the lower landing. At the sound Lee turned.

"What?" Lee studied the source of the noise. The man, tall and dark, was stripped to the waist, wearing only faded jeans as he began to slowly ascend the stairs. "Hey, look, mister," Lee said guardedly. "Why don't you mind your own business? This is my wife…." Lee jerked his head in Erin's direction. "We're just having a little disagreement…."

"I don't think so." Kane mounted the stairs and stood only a few feet from Lee. His gray eyes glinted like steel, and though his voice was outwardly calm and solicitous, his clenched fists and hardened jaw reinforced his words. "Do you have a hearing problem?" he asked. "I told you to let her go!"

Reluctantly Lee stepped away from Erin and glowered menacingly at Kane. "Just who the hell do you think you are?" he snapped, while Erin crumpled in the doorway. The smell of a fight was in the air.

"I was just about to ask you that same question," Kane's calm, hard voice rejoined.

"I'm her husband!" Lee snarled, tossing a look of red-hot anger and rage toward Erin.

"Ex-husband," Kane corrected. "And what sort of power does that title give you? The right to rough up the lady?"

"I wasn't…"

Kane's fury snapped and his eyes sparked disgusted fire. "Don't bother with any of your explanations. Just get out before I throw you over this railing!" Kane's voice had risen with his anger, and Erin saw Lee gulp and hesitate, casting a final threatening glance in her direction.

"I'd just like to see you try," Lee warned back to Kane. A light of grim satisfaction warmed Kane's face. Lee saw the reaction and slowly, carefully backed down the stairs.

"And just one more thing, Sinclair," Kane cautioned with an evil smile. "If I ever so much as hear that you've been bothering Erin again, I won't wait for you to show up. I'll come looking for you!"

Lee hastened down the remainder of the stairs, the front door crashed closed, and for a few seconds there was silence. Only the feeling of electricity crackling in the air disturbed the tranquillity of the moment until the noise of a racing engine split the silence as it roared angrily down the hill. Erin sighed as she realized that Lee was finally gone.

"I can't say much for your taste in husbands," Kane commented dryly. The grim set of his jaw hadn't relaxed.

"He's not so bad," Erin replied uneasily, as if convincing herself. "Not really, he's just had a run of bad luck…."

"Bad luck?" Kane threw his hands over his head in exasperation. "That gives him the right to come in here and force himself on you?" He regarded her ruefully, since she looked so small and vulnerable this morning. "Erin, you are incredibly naive! What is it with you anyway?"

"What do you mean?" she asked, feeling herself start to bristle, partially because she knew that he was close to the truth.

"I mean, first, Mitchell Cameron—you defend him to the hilt when he's an A-1 jackass—"

"Now, wait a minute," Erin gasped.

"No, you wait a minute! And now your husband, pardon me, your unfortunate ex-husband who's had 'a run of bad luck,' so he takes it out on you by almost..." His pause was effective, and Erin's face flooded with color. "Erin, don't you see? Sinclair's a bastard, a loser. You should know that better than anyone. As far as I can see, so far you've had a pretty poor track record of picking male companions!"

"Is that a fact?" she fired back at him, her temper sparking. "Does that include the latest man in my life? You remember him—a wonderful guy. I trusted him completely only to discover that he thinks I'm a crook!" Sarcasm flavored her words with bitterness.

Kane looked as if he'd been slapped. The stunned expression on his face and the sudden dead look in his eyes tore at Erin's heart, but she proudly held her ground. It would be too easy to forgive him, too easy to let him back into her heart.

His shoulders relaxed, the firm muscles slackening. "So that's how it stands, does it? You won't let me help you?"

"I don't need any help. I'm innocent," she maintained defiantly.

"Would it make you feel better to know that I believe you?"

"Ha! Then why did you accuse me of thievery last night? Why did you wait all this time? Why didn't you just ask me what I knew about the embezzlement and the fact that there is supposedly an accomplice? Why did you wait," she asked, her voice quaking, and her eyes meeting his with accusation, "all the while silently condemning me with your eyes!"

"Oh, God, Erin," he groaned. "I'm so sorry—I was hoping that maybe you had changed your mind...."

"No!" She shook her head firmly, but her voice softened. "Look." She reached out to touch his arm, but he jerked away from her. "I want to thank you for helping me with Lee. He... was...getting a little out of hand."

"Erin," Kane's voice was steady and low. He stood half-supported by the railing, his head drooping down and facing the lobby two stories below him. "I want you to marry me. I need you to be my wife, and Krista needs a mother. Perhaps I judged you too quickly, but it was only because I was afraid of the truth. I wanted to talk to you about it earlier." His eyes rolled heavenward and his voice became husky. "God, how many times did I try?" He shook his head disconsolately and continued to stare blankly ahead of him. "But I just couldn't."

"Because you didn't trust me. You couldn't find it in your heart to accept my innocence," Erin added in a flat, dead voice.

"There are other possibilities. The accomplice has to be in the legal department...."

"But I was the most convenient choice. The easiest target, right?"

His silence was as condemning as the pained droop of his shoulders. "Oh, God, Erin. Just believe that I love you!" he pleaded.

"I guess you and I have a different meaning for the word," she replied, her voice broken by emotion. "Goodbye, Kane," she whispered as she slipped through the door and listened to the sound of his footsteps retreating heavily down the stairs. Biting back the tears that were struggling to fill her eyes, she hurried to the bedroom and pulled out her worn leather suit-case. She tossed it recklessly on the bed. "You're a coward," she snipped at herself, "running from the truth that you love him, and no matter what he's done, the one thing that you want most in life is to be his wife." Her tiny fist balled up and crashed down on the suitcase. *Damn! Why am I such a fool?* For an instant she thought about running after him and throwing herself into his arms, but her pride forced her to restrain herself. He thinks you're a thief, she reminded herself, and the feeling of cold betrayal once again settled upon her. Hurriedly she tossed the rest of her things haphazardly into the suitcase and snapped it shut. She looked around the bedroom to see if she needed anything else but found that she had to get out of the room. It was too crowded with memories, gloriously happy memories of making love to Kane in her bed.

With shaking, unsteady hands she dialed the phone and made reservations for the week. Then, as calmly as possible, she wrote down the phone number and address of the hotel and placed it in an envelope before sitting down near the window and waiting. It wasn't long, maybe only ten minutes, but it felt like an eternity to Erin before she saw Kane walk out toward his car. Fortunately Krista was with him. Erin managed a smile through her tears as she saw that Krista was able to walk to the car with her father's assistance. Although she leaned heavily on Kane, the girl stumbled only once and he was able to catch her. The playful little kitten followed along. There appeared to be a slight argument of some sort, and Erin guessed that it had to do with the cat. Kane was shaking his head, but in the end, the black ball of fur was allowed to tag along for the ride.

After Kane's car was out of sight, Erin hurried out of her apartment and sprinted down the stairs to knock on Mrs. Cavenaugh's door. Erin tapped lightly against the wood, and the door was opened in an instant. The little old woman was up and dressed, as if she were expecting company.

"Good morning," the gray-haired lady said cheerily, her wise blue eyes flicking from Erin's distressed face to the suitcase in her hands. "Good morning, Mrs. Cavenaugh," Erin replied. "I...I've got to leave town for a while...."

Mrs. Cavenaugh's gray eyebrows shot upward and her mouth pursed into an expression of distaste. Erin continued. "Urgent business...I'll be gone for a week, maybe longer. In this envelope is the telephone number and address of the hotel where I can be reached in case of an emergency...."

"Erin," Mrs. Cavenaugh's calm voice broke into her chatter. "You know that I hate to pry, but what's the matter? Did something happen between you and Kane?" Kind, concerned blue eyes probed Erin's rigid face.

"What...what do you mean?"

"I mean 'leaving town because of urgent business' is a trifle overused." A wry smile twisted the wrinkled face. "Honestly I would have expected something with a little more imagination."

"Well, it's the truth," Erin maintained.

"And you're a terrible liar."

"Mrs. Cavenaugh, I'm not lying, honestly. Something has come up, something I can't deal with. I need a little time and distance in order to sort things out."

Mrs. Cavenaugh's knowing smile broadened. "Well, at least you're opening up a little. I understand that you might need a little space, isn't that what they say these days? I can't argue with that, but...."

"What?"

"Well, don't let your pride come between you and something you really want."

Erin sucked in her breath. "You mean Kane, don't you?" she sighed dismally and broke eye contact with her elderly tenant.

"He's a man who loves you dearly. And his daughter!" The old lady threw up her hands and shook her head at the incredulity of the situation.

"Krista? What about Krista?" Erin asked, her voice full of concern.

"Oh, nothing other than the fact that she worships the ground you walk on."

"Be serious!"

"I am—I've never seen the likes of it! Oh, at first, I'll grant you she was determined to hate you. But can you blame the child—losing a mother the way she did? All she had left was her father, and she didn't want to share him. But now—" Mrs. Cavenaugh moved her head thoughtfully "—that poor girl can talk of nothing but you—except for the kitten of course."

The lump in Erin's throat began to swell, and some of her firm resolve began to be chipped at. Mrs. Cavenaugh was working on her; Erin knew it, but she couldn't help but hope that there was just a sliver of truth in the sweet old woman's words.

"I'm sorry, Mrs. Cavenaugh," Erin managed, looking hastily at her watch, "but I've really got to run. Now, promise me that under no circumstances will you tell Kane where I am!"

"I don't know if I can do that," the older woman replied honestly.

"You have to! I *need* time to myself."

"Well, if you're so dead set against it, I'll give you my word," Mrs. Cavenaugh unwillingly agreed.

"Thanks," Erin sighed, kissing her friend lightly on the cheek. "I'll see you soon."

"Dear," Mrs. Cavenaugh said, placing a bony hand on Erin's sleeve. "Do be careful."

"I will," Erin promised, and turned to leave the apartment building. She could feel Mrs. Cavenaugh's kind eyes boring into her back as she walked to her car, but she didn't have the heart to turn and wave. It took all her strength to hoist her suitcase into the car, start the engine and race down the hill toward the city and the waterfront.

Once back in Deer Harbor on Orcas Island in the San Juans, Erin realized what a disastrous mistake she had made in returning to the island where she had had such a carefree and loving existence with Kane only a few weeks earlier. Although she was far removed from the rustic cabin that they had shared together, memories of the small town still burned in her brain, and it seemed that she couldn't walk anywhere without coming face-to-face with memories of Kane. The pain in her heart didn't disappear.

The seasons had changed in the past weeks, and each day was as gray and cold as the Pacific Ocean. Wind and rain deluged the coastal town, and although Erin tried several kinds of outdoor amusements, she found that most of her days were spent inside her tiny hotel room staring vacantly at the television or brooding about the turn of events in her life. Knowing that her attitude was as discouraging as the somber, gray rain-washed days, she attempted to pull herself out of her depression, but found it impossible. Nothing seemed to work. And thoughts of Krista and the fact that she hadn't even bothered to say goodbye to the lonely girl only made Erin more miserable and guilt-ridden. While the island had once been a haven, now it seemed like a prison, but Erin elected to continue her confinement until she could no longer afford it. How could she possibly go home to an empty house and no job?

It had been over a week, and the depression still clung to her like a heavy shroud when she picked up the Seattle newspaper to look through the classified advertisements in search of employment. As usual, the openings for legal assistants were few, and Erin faced the fact that it would be more difficult than she had first imagined to find a decent position. Disinterestedly she perused the rest of the paper and stopped at the financial section. A photograph of the bank building with a caption concerning the embezzlement caught her eye. With more interest than she had felt for days, she began to read the article. As the meaning of each sentence in the column became clear to her, Erin began to feel her stomach churn with emotions of rage and disgust. According to the article, Mitchell Cameron had in fact worked with an accomplice—a woman with whom he had shared responsibility for years—Miss Olivia Parsons. The article explained the scam more fully and the fact that the scheme was so elaborate that it had taken the auditing staff and the president of the bank a lengthy amount of time to prove the guilt of the parties involved.

Erin felt a growing nausea as she read the article, and when she had finished, she tossed the newspaper into the wastebasket near her bed. Never would she have suspected Olivia of doing anything illegal. Just like Mitch, Olivia seemed far too professional to stoop to thievery. The delight that Erin should have experienced as she realized that she was no longer under suspicion of the crime seemed to have soured as she thought of Mitch and Olivia, two respected members of the banking industry who had tossed away their careers and possibly their lives for greed. Erin wondered what could have caused their joint journey into crime.

Two days later Erin began preparing for her trip home to Seattle. She had been gone far too long already, and her money was running out. She realized that she couldn't run away from Kane and her love for him, and there was really no reason to linger on the island.

Just as Erin began to pack her things, the telephone jarred the stillness of the hotel room. For several seconds Erin just stared at the telephone, wondering who would be calling her.

Kane? Unlikely. A wrong number? Perhaps. Her heart began
to thud wildly in her chest as she reached for the receiver.

"Hello?" she inquired, and felt a welling sense of dread when
she recognized Mrs. Cavenaugh's unsteady voice.

"Erin—Erin, is that you?" the old lady demanded.

"Yes, it's I….what happened?" Erin asked, convinced that
Mrs. Cavenaugh wouldn't call unless there was an emergency
of some sort. Nervously she bit at her thumbnail.

"Oh—I know that he told me not to call, but I knew that
you would want to know. It's just awful—I really don't know
what to do. Dear Lord in heaven!" The little old lady continued to ramble in endless circles of words and phrases that meant
nothing to Erin. Apprehensively Erin interrupted.

"Mrs. Cavenaugh! What's wrong? Try and pull yourself
together and just tell me what's the matter." The hairs on the
back of Erin's neck began to stand on end.

"It's Krista," Mrs. Cavenaugh moaned in a voice so low that
Erin thought perhaps she had misunderstood.

"Krista?" Erin echoed. "Oh, God, what's happened to her?"
Erin's heart leaped to her throat and her pulse began to race.
Tiny droplets of perspiration moistened her skin, and she felt
her knees give way as she sank against the bed.

"Oh, Erin, it's so awful. Ever since you've been gone, Kane,
well he hasn't been himself—in a terribly foul mood." Erin
swallowed hard and tried to press back the feelings of guilt
that assailed her. "And Krista, well, she didn't fare any better.
She…withdrew. You know. You remember what she was like
when she first arrived in Seattle…." Erin gasped, and the little lady reassured her. "It wasn't nearly that bad, you understand, but still she just wasn't her cheery self. I'm afraid that
she's missed you terribly."

Erin closed her eyes and leaned her head against the headboard of the bed for support. "She didn't stop walking, did she?" Erin held her breath.

"Thank goodness—no." Erin let the air escape from her lungs in a rush. "However, she was distracted, wouldn't eat, was thoroughly depressed." Erin felt as if a knife were being slowly twisted in her stomach. How could she have been so heartless as to have left Krista without explaining anything? Mrs. Cavenaugh continued. "And then, late this morning... well, Krista was chasing that little kitten of hers, and it scrambled up the stairs. She tried to follow it but fell. She hit her head on the bottom step."

"Oh, no," Erin gasped, the color draining from her face. "Is—is she seriously injured?"

"Well, that's just it. No one seems to know for sure. She's still in the hospital for observation, been there all day as far as I know. I think she regained consciousness, but I'm not really certain." The elderly woman's voice had begun to quake, and Erin felt herself shiver.

"Mrs. Cavenaugh, where is Krista?"

"Virginia Mason Hospital on First Hill, but you shouldn't go there. Kane's there and he specifically instructed me not to tell you."

Erin stifled the sob that threatened to belie her calm words. "Don't worry about Kane. I can handle him—I'm leaving as soon as possible. I'll see you when I get home."

"Good."

"Oh, and Mrs. Cavenaugh?"

"Yes?"

"Thanks for calling."

"I knew that you'd want to know," came the somber reply.

Erin stripped her things out of the closet and dresser. As hastily as possible she threw them into her case, paid the hotel bill and rented a small boat back to the mainland. It wasn't easy to find someone who was willing to take her out in the stormy weather, but fortunately she found a young sailor with a sense of adventure who loved to make a quick buck.

The rain washed down in torrents and the small craft rocked and lurched against the rough whitecapped waters of the sound. Several times the boat rocked so crazily that Erin was sure that they would capsize, but the steady hand of the dark-complexioned young man kept the tiny craft miraculously on course. The wind tore at Erin's face, pelting it with cold rain, and whipping her long black hair away from her neck. But she continued to watch the shoreline and prayed that Mrs. Cavenaugh had exaggerated Krista's condition.

"Hey, lady," her companion called to her over the roar of the boat's engine and the howl of the wind. "Would you like something to drink? I've got a thermos of coffee, or…something stronger, if you like rye whisky."

Erin shook her head. The thought of something in her already-knotted stomach made her want to gag. "No…thank you. I'm fine."

"You sure?" he asked, not convinced. The young woman was pale and scared, and deep lines of concern creased her otherwise beautiful face.

"Yes, really," Erin asserted, and managed a wan smile. The young man lifted his shoulders and turned his attention back to the sea. The remainder of the trip was made in silence. It seemed an eternity before Erin was on solid ground once again.

Virginia Mason Hospital stood out starkly white against a threatening charcoal-gray sky. Inside, the corridors were hushed, and the white walls were only made more severe by the garish splotches of color in the modern-art prints that hung on the walls. The bustling, white-uniformed staff, the mechanical groans of the elevators, and the overall oppressive silence gave Erin a strange sense of impending doom.

Room 538 was easy enough to find, and Erin braced herself to enter the white cubicle just as a portly nurse in a neatly starched uniform approached her.

"Looking for someone?" the nurse asked in a professional voice. There was a calm smile on the broad face that spoke of authority and efficiency. "Can I help you?"

"I hope so. I'm a close friend of Krista Webster. I just found out about the accident today, and I hurried over here as quickly as I could." The disapproving brown eyes of the nurse studied Erin, and for the first time she realized what she must look like in her rain-drenched clothing and wet hair.

"You're not a member of the family?"

"No…not exactly." Erin shook her head.

The nurse placed a friendly hand on Erin's arm. "I'm sorry, but only family members are allowed to visit Miss Webster. Perhaps you would like to wait in the lobby? There's a coffee machine and some magazines…."

Erin refused to be brushed off. "Can you at least tell me how she is? Will she be all right? I…I have to know!"

"I understand," the nurse replied, and Erin felt that those wide, brown eyes and large, kindly face wouldn't lie. "Krista had a very bad fall and suffered a concussion, but Dr. Sampson is caring for her and the prognosis is very hopeful."

"But…what does that mean, exactly? Will she recover? Will she be able to walk again?"

The nurse was steering Erin toward the waiting room. "Don't worry. Dr. Sampson is a very capable doctor, and he has the entire staff of the hospital to support him." With that, the nurse excused herself to answer another patient's call, and Erin found herself alone in the clinically clean waiting room with its ancient magazines and battered plastic furniture. She waited impatiently, staring out the window at the gloomy city, and ignored the stacks of outdated magazines that cluttered the table, while she sipped bitter coffee from a machine that looked as old as the hospital.

The sound of a familiar voice startled her, and she pulled her gaze from the dismal gray sky and the gathering dusk into the direction of the deep-timbred sound that made her heart leap. For several seconds she found it impossible to move or to speak as she studied Kane, his face lined with concern. He was speaking in low tones to a short, balding man with heavy glasses. The identification tag indicated that he was Dr. Sampson. The conversation was short and one-sided, with Dr. Sampson explaining Krista's condition in medical terms. Although the doctor seemed optimistic, Kane's entire bearing was a slouch of resignation and grim defeat. Erin felt her eyes burn with tears as she saw the pain and confusion in Kane's normally clear gaze. *He loves Krista so much,* Erin thought, *and he is hurting so badly.* She felt the urge to run to him, to comfort him, to love him, but she restrained herself.

Dr. Sampson excused himself, and Kane stood transfixed in the waiting area. He hadn't noticed Erin yet; he was too preoccupied with his own black thoughts. Suddenly she felt very out of place, an intruder. How would he feel when he finally saw her? How could she explain how she felt about him and his daughter, the love that was smothering her in its encompassing grasp? He had instructed Mrs. Cavenaugh not to call Erin. Perhaps he truly didn't want to see her. What would he do?

Her conjecture was cut short as Kane whirled to face her. It was as if he had sensed her presence and her uncertainty. His expression was cold, guarded, and Erin felt her heart stop as her eyes clashed with his brittle gray gaze.

"Erin?" His dark brows drew together. "How did you know?"

"Mrs. Cavenaugh told me."

"That woman can't keep a secret to save her soul!" He bit

out the words and Erin wondered once again if she had made a grave mistake by intruding into his private grief. She took a step toward him and stopped. There was so much to say, so great a misunderstanding to bridge, and she wondered if it was at all possible.

"I'm sorry about Krista," she whispered, and the pain in her eyes was undeniable.

She saw him hesitate for a moment. He closed his eyes and seemed to give into the pressure that was battering against him. When he opened his eyes, they were clear once again, and in swift strides, he was by her side.

"I'm glad you came," he admitted, his voice rough from the strain of the day.

"Didn't you know that I would?"

"Erin, I don't know anything, not anymore!" His confession was a sigh of disgust.

"How—how is Krista?"

Lowering himself onto the edge of the plastic orange couch, he rubbed the tension from the back of his neck and ground his jaws together. When he spoke, it was in a monotone. "Dr. Sampson seems to think that she'll be fine, even taking into consideration her previous problem. She's got a concussion, but supposedly it's not serious, or at least not too serious. She was unconscious for a while, but she came to. Now she's resting. They gave her something—a sedative. The doctor thinks she'll wake up soon and that I can see her. God, I hope so. This waiting and not knowing is driving me up a wall." His long fingers raked deep gorges in his thick chestnut hair.

Erin sat next to him, not knowing the comforting words that would soothe him. They sat only inches apart, and yet Erin felt as if it might have been miles. Kane's eyes remained closed as if he were frighteningly weary and unable to face the trauma that was in store for him.

At the sound of Dr. Sampson's clipped footsteps Kane's eyelids flew open, and he was on his feet in a moment. "How is she?" he asked.

The pudgy doctor smiled. "You worry too much, Mr. Webster. Krista is going to be just fine. As a matter of fact, she's coming around now. You can see her if you like."

Erin couldn't keep up with Kane's swift strides as he nearly ran back to Krista's room. The frail figure in the hospital bed brought back Erin's earlier feelings of apprehension and dread. Krista's complexion was nearly as white as the stark bedsheets that draped her, and the bandage on her head only seemed to add to her fragile appearance. A colorless fluid dripped into Krista's arm from a suspended I.V. bottle positioned near the bed. The tiny arm was secured to the bedrail by a strip of gauze.

Krista's eyes fluttered open after what seemed like hours, and a look of utter confusion and fear crossed her small face as she called to her father.

"Daddy?"

Kane's voice cracked with emotion as he responded. "Krista, honey, I'm right here." His fingers reached out and touched her cheek. "Oh, sweetheart, you don't know how good it is to hear your voice," he sighed.

Krista tried to lift her head, but her small face cringed in pain. "Oooh, where am I?"

"You're in the hospital, honey. Remember you hit your head while chasing the kitten?"

"Figaro? Where is he?" she asked with childish concern.

Kane smiled despite his tension. "Don't worry about him, honey. He's in good hands. Mrs. Cavenaugh promised to take care of him until you get home."

Krista's eyes moved around the room until she spotted Erin. A smile brought back a little of the color to her face. "You're back!" Krista's enthusiasm shined in her eyes. "I knew that you'd come back!"

"You were right," Erin choked out, stepping nearer to the bed. "You should have known better than to think that I'd ever leave you."

"I did. I knew you wouldn't go without saying goodbye. See, Dad, I told ya she'd be back!"

"That you did," Kane whispered, and his eyes locked with Erin's questioning gaze.

Dr. Sampson came back into the room with his usual quick, short stride. "Well, little lady—so you did decide to wake up after all. About time, I might add! Your father here, he was beginning to worry." The little man's expert fingers probed Krista, and his knowing eyes studied her as he talked.

"That's okay. Dad always worries."

"Is that so? Well, maybe next time you'll be more careful on those stairs," the doctor reprimanded teasingly. When his examination was over, he studied Krista with feigned concern. "I think you should get some rest, young lady, before I send down for a special dinner for you. I'm going to send your dad home for a while, but he can come back and visit you later— what do you say?"

Disappointment crowded Krista's fine features, but she gave in. "All right," she agreed, and turned her attention back to her father. "But you will come back tonight, won't you?"

"You can count on it, pumpkin," Kane said huskily.

"And you, Erin?" Krista asked, her sky-blue eyes searching Erin's face.

Erin cast a quick glance at Kane and then smiled tenderly down at the child. "Sure, Krista. I'll be back," she promised.

As they stepped out of the room, Dr. Sampson gave Kane a quick report on Krista, assuring him that the little girl was responding well to treatment, and Erin felt a tide of relief wash over her. Kane, too, seemed visibly encouraged by the news. They walked out of the hospital together, and Erin wondered what their futures would be—together or apart. Kane was lost in his own thoughts but shook his head when Erin offered him a lift home.

"No, thanks," he said, "I've got my own car." Disappointment shattered Erin, but she tried not to show her feelings. "I have to stop off and talk to Mrs. Cavenaugh. I know she's worried about Krista."

"Will…will I see you later?" Erin blurted, unable to restrain herself.

"Do you want to?"

"Of course I do!" She shook her head in frustration. "I've missed you so badly."

"Shhh," he held her close to him for a moment, and she could hear the clamoring of his heart. "I'll meet you back at your place in an hour," he promised. "It's important that I speak to Mrs. Cavenaugh—you understand that, don't you?"

"Of course," she whispered as he walked away from her.

The hour stretched out to two, and Erin found herself nervously pacing the floor of her apartment. Where could he be? Was he even coming at all? She had tried to fill the time by taking a hasty shower, unpacking and finally brewing a strong cup of tea. The minutes ticked slowly by. What was he doing?

When at last he arrived, she steeled herself for the rejection that she knew was coming. Too much had happened— too many bitter words had been lashed out—it was just too damned late.

She didn't bother to get up when he opened the door and came into her antiques-filled loft.

"I'm sorry I'm late," he apologized, but didn't move to take off his jacket. "I've spent the last two hours driving in circles, wondering how on earth I can say the things that have to be said."

"I know," she whispered.

"I appreciate the fact that you came to the hospital."

A wry smile curved her lips. "You don't have to thank me. I had to come. Krista means a great deal to me."

"Erin." She let her eyes melt into his as he spoke her name. "I feel as if I owe you this incredibly large apology about the embezzling."

"Oh, Kane, not tonight, not after everything that's happened to Krista. It…doesn't matter."

"Damn it, Erin! The least you could do is let me explain. Then, if you want to throw me out of here, I'll go." Kane walked into the living room and sat on the small antique coffee table, positioning himself directly in front of Erin. She found it impossible to take her gaze from his. She was compelled to listen to him.

"After our last fight, I began thinking about alternate suspects in the embezzlement. You were right and I feel like a fool admitting it, but I was so blinded by my love for you, so afraid that you were the culprit, that I couldn't see the facts correctly. It was an unforgivable injustice to you."

Erin started to protest but he ignored her. "Just let me finish," he commanded. "I started putting some of the pieces together and discovered that Mitch was having an affair with Olivia. It really wasn't all that difficult to see, once I knew you were innocent. Olivia was the one person who seemed to know too much—everything about you, the securities key, the meeting with Mitch on the day of the arraignment. She was clever and subtle, but she took great pains to mention that you and Mitch had always been friendly, and Cameron, the bastard, didn't deny it."

Erin shook her head in disbelief as Kane continued. "At the

point that I began to suspect Olivia, I was inhibited because of Krista's depression. I'm sorry, Erin, if you can only guess how really sorry I am that I thought, even for a moment..."

"It's okay," she whispered, and reached to touch his arm.

"No, it's not!" He closed his eyes and shook his head. "And what makes it worse is the fact that I fell in love with you the moment I saw you sitting in the office on the floor with all those books spread around you, and still I thought that you were involved with Cameron. I must have been out of my mind."

Erin's head was reeling with the magnitude of Kane's confession. He had said it over and over—that he loved her. Was it really possible?

"I want you to know that it doesn't matter, not anymore. When I heard about Krista from Mrs. Cavenaugh, I realized that nothing matters—nothing except for you and Krista," she admitted, smiling into his face.

His eyes opened slowly. "Erin, just what are you saying?" he asked quietly.

"I'm saying that I love you, and the only reason that I wouldn't marry you before was because I didn't think that you loved me."

"How could you have been so blind?" he asked, reaching for her and crushing her to him. "It was so evident!" He didn't wait for an answer. His lips came crashing down on hers with a fiery passion that was soon exploding in her veins. "I'll never let you get away again," he vowed. "We're getting married as soon as Krista is out of the hospital."

"You haven't heard any disagreements from me, have you?" she asked.

"Thank God for small favors!" He sighed, and let the weight of his body fall against hers.

★ ★ ★ ★ ★

Book Two:
TEARS OF PRIDE

To Mary Clare, my editor,
with love and affection.

Chapter 1

He stood alone, and his vibrant blue eyes scanned the horizon, as if he were looking for something…or someone. The cold morning fog on the gray waters of Elliott Bay hampered his view, but the lonely, broad-shouldered man didn't seem to notice. Haggard lines were etched across his forehead and an errant lock of dark brown hair was caught in the Pacific breeze. Noah Wilder didn't care. Though dressed only in a business suit, the icy wind blowing across Puget Sound couldn't cool the anger and frustration burning within him.

Realizing that he had wasted too much time staring at the endlessly lapping water, he began to walk along the waterfront, back to a job he could barely stomach. He gritted his teeth in determination as he continued southward and tried to quiet the anger and fear that were tearing him apart. Just half an hour earlier he had been notified that his son was missing from school. It had happened before. Noah closed his mind to the terrifying thoughts. By now, he was used to the fact that his rebellious son hated school—especially the school into which he had been transferred just two months before. Noah hoped that Sean wasn't in any real trouble or danger.

He paused only once as he walked back to the office and that was to buy a newspaper. Knowing it was a mistake, he opened the paper to the financial section. Although this time the article was buried, Noah managed to find it on the fourth page. After all this time, he had hoped that the interest in the scandal would have faded. He was wrong. "Damn," he muttered to himself as he quickly scanned the story.

It had been four weeks since the fire, but that had been time enough for Noah Wilder to have the opportunity to curse his father too many times to count. Today was no exception. Actually the fire and the scandal surrounding it were only a couple of problems on a long list that seemed to grow daily. The fire and the suspected arson complicated matters for Noah, and until the entire business was resolved, he knew that he would suffer many more long hours in the office and endure countless sleepless nights. It was just his luck that the blaze had started while his father was out of the country. At the thought of Ben Wilder, Noah's frown deepened.

The early morning was still thick with fog, the air thick with the smell of the sea. A few shafts of sunlight pierced the gray clouds and reflected on the water collected on the concrete sidewalk, but Noah was too preoccupied with his own black thoughts to notice the promise of spring in the brisk air.

An angry horn blared, and a passing motorist shouted indignantly at Noah as he stepped onto the street against the traffic. He ignored the oath and continued, without breaking stride, toward the massive concrete and steel structure that housed Wilder Investments, his father's prosperous holding company. Damn his father! This was one helluva time for Ben to be recuperating in Mexico, leaving Noah to clean up all of the problems at the company. If it weren't for his father's recent heart attack, Noah would be back in Portland where he belonged, and perhaps Sean wouldn't be missing from school again. At the thought of his rebellious son, Noah's stomach tightened with concern. The lines deepened on his forehead, and his thoughtful scowl gave him a ragged, anxious appearance. Unfortunately, Noah could blame no one but himself for his son's attitude.

Noah should never have let Ben talk him into taking control of Wilder Investments, not even for a short period of time. It had been a mistake, and Sean was the person who was paying for it. Noah shouldn't have let his emotions dictate the decision to move to Seattle, and Ben's heart attack shouldn't have made any difference in that decision. Noah uttered an oath under his breath and slapped the rolled newspaper against his thigh in frustration. It had been difficult enough trying to raise a son alone in Portland. But now, in Seattle, along with the problems of managing Wilder Investments, it was nearly impossible for Noah to find enough time for his son.

Noah pushed open the wide glass doors of the Wilder Building and strode angrily to the elevator. It was early in the day, and the lobby was nearly empty. Silently the elevator doors parted and Noah stepped inside, grateful that he was alone. This morning he had no use for small talk with the employees of his father's multimillion dollar corporation. Anyone or anything that reminded him of Ben Wilder only served to deepen Noah's simmering anger.

After pushing the button for the thirtieth floor, he glared at the headlines of the financial section of the paper and reread the beginning of the article that had ruined his morning. His stomach knotted as the headline jumped up at him. "Burned" Wilder Investments Suspected of Insurance Fraud. Noah gritted his teeth and tried to control his anger. The first paragraph was worse than the condemning headline: *Noah Wilder, act-*

ing president of Wilder Investments, was unavailable for comment against the rumor that Wilder Investments might have intentionally started the blaze at Cascade Valley Winery. The fire, which started in the west wing of the main building, took the life of one man. Oliver Lindstrom, the deceased, was in partnership with Wilder Investments at the time of the blaze...

The elevator stopped, and Noah drew his eyes away from the infuriating article. He'd already read it, and it only served to make him more frustrated with his father and his decision to prolong his stay in Mexico. To top things off, Sean had taken off from school this morning and couldn't be found. Where the hell could Sean have gone? Noah bit at his lip as his eyes glinted in determination. Regardless of anything else, Noah promised himself that he would find a way to force Ben to return to Seattle to resume control of Wilder Investments. This time Sean came first. There was just no other alternative.

Noah stepped from the elevator and headed for his father's auspicious office. He paused only slightly at Maggie's desk to order a terse directive. "See if you can get Ben on the phone immediately." He forced a smile that he didn't feel and entered the spacious, window-lined office where all the decisions for Wilder Investments were made. Pitching the bothersome newspaper onto the contemporary oak desk, Noah shrugged out of his suit jacket and tossed it unceremoniously over the back of a well-oiled leather couch.

The bank of windows behind the desk overlooked Pioneer Square, one of Seattle's oldest and most prestigious areas. Brick buildings, set on the sides of the rolling hills overlooking the sound, boasted turn-of-the-century architecture contrasting sharply to the neighboring modern skyscrapers. The area was packed with an interesting array of antique shops, boutiques and restaurants.

Beyond Pioneer Square were the soothing gray waters of

Puget Sound, and in the distance were the proud Olympic Mountains. On a clear day, they stood as a snow-laden barrier to the Pacific Ocean. Today they were merely ghostly shadows hiding in the slate-colored fog.

Noah cast a glance at the calm view over the rooftops of the city before sitting stiffly down in his father's leather chair. It groaned against his weight as he leaned back and ran an impatient hand through his thick, coarse hair. Closing his eyes, he attempted to clear his mind. Where was Sean?

He shook his head and opened his eyes to see the newspaper lying flat on the desk. The picture of the charred winery met his gaze. The last thing he wanted to think about this morning was the fire. One man was dead—arson was suspected—and the Northwest's most prominent winery, Cascade Valley, was inoperable, caught in a lawsuit contesting the payment of the insurance proceeds. How in the world had he been so unlucky as to get trapped in the middle of this mess? The intercom buzzed, interrupting his thoughts.

"I've got your mother on line two," Maggie's voice called to him.

"I wanted to speak with Ben, not my mother," was Noah's clipped, impatient reply.

"I wasn't able to reach him. It was hard enough getting through to Katharine. I swear there must be only one telephone in that godforsaken village."

"It's all right, Maggie," Noah conceded. "I shouldn't have snapped. Of course I'll talk to Katharine." Noah waited, his temper barely in check. Although he was furious with himself and his father, there was no reason to take it out on Maggie. He told himself to calm down and tried to brace himself against the wall of excuses his mother would build for his father. After pushing the correct button on the telephone, he attempted to sound casual and polite—two emotions he didn't feel at the moment. "Hello, Mother. How are you?"

"Fine, Noah," was the cool automatic response. "But your father isn't feeling well at all." Beneath Katharine's soft, feminine voice was a will of iron.

Noah's jaw tightened involuntarily, but he managed to keep his voice pleasant and calm. "I'd like to speak to him."

"I'm sorry, Noah. That's out of the question. He's resting right now." His mother's voice continued to drone in low, unemotional tones, giving Noah an updated prognosis of his father's condition. As he listened, Noah rolled up the sleeves of his shirt and began to pace angrily in front of the desk. He rubbed the back of his neck with his free hand while he clutched the other in a death grip around the telephone receiver. His knuckles whitened in annoyance as Katharine continued to speak tonelessly to him from somewhere in northern Mexico. Noah cast a dark glance out of the window into the rising fog and hoped for a break in the one-sided conversation.

It was obvious that Katharine Wilder was protecting her husband from the demands of his son. Noah could envision the tight, uncompromising line of his mother's small mouth and the coldness in her distant blue eyes as she spoke to him from some three thousand miles distance.

"So you can see, Noah, it looks as if we have no other choice but to stay in Guaymas for at least another two months...possibly three."

"I can't wait that long!"

There was a long unyielding sigh from his mother. Her voice sounded a little more faint. The frail telephone connection to Mexico seemed to be failing. "I don't see that you have much of a choice, Noah. The doctors all agree that your father is much too ill to make the exhaustive trip back to Seattle. There's no way he could hope to run the company. You'll just have to hang on a little longer."

"And what about Sean?" Noah demanded hotly. There was no response. Noah's voice quieted slightly. "Just let me talk to Ben."

"You can't be serious! Haven't you heard a word I've said? Your father is resting now—he can't possibly come to the phone!"

"I need to talk to him. This wasn't part of the bargain," Noah warned, not bothering to hide his exasperation.

"Perhaps later…"

"Now!" Noah's voice had risen as his impatience began to get the better of him.

"I'm sorry, Noah. I'll talk to you later."

"Don't hang up—"

A click from a small town in Mexico severed the connection.

"Damn!" Noah slammed the receiver down and smashed one fist into an open palm. He uttered a stream of invectives partially aimed at his father, but mainly at himself. How could he have been so gullible as to have agreed to run the investment firm while Ben was recuperating? It had been an emotional decision and a bad one at that. Noah wasn't prone to sentimental decisions, not since the last one he had made, nearly sixteen years before. But this time, because of his father's delicate condition, Noah had let his emotions dictate to him. He shook his head at his own folly. He was a damned fool. "Son of a…"

"Pardon me?" Maggie asked as she breezed into the office in her usual efficient manner. Nearly sixty, with flaming red hair and sporting a brightly colored print dress, she was the picture of unflappable competency.

"Nothing," Noah grumbled, but the fire in his bright blue

eyes refused to die. He slumped into his father's desk chair and attempted to cool his smoldering rage.

"Good!" Maggie returned with an understanding smile. She placed a stack of correspondence on the corner of the desk.

Noah regarded the letters with a frown. "What are those?"

"Oh, just the usual—except for the letter on the top of the pile. It's from the insurance company. I think you should read it." Maggie's friendly smile began to fade.

Noah slid a disgusted glance at the document in question and then mentally dismissed it as he looked back at the secretary. She noticed his dismissive gesture, and a perturbed expression puckered her lips.

"Would you put in a call to Betty Averill in the Portland office? Tell her I won't be back as soon as I had planned. Have her send anything she or Jack can't handle up here. If she has any questions, she can call me."

Maggie's intense gaze sharpened. "Isn't your father coming back on the first?" she asked. Maggie normally didn't pry, but this time she couldn't help herself. Noah hadn't been himself lately, and Maggie laid most of the blame on his strong-willed son. The kid was sixteen and hell-on-wheels.

"Apparently not," Noah muttered in response.

"Then you'll be staying for a few more months?"

Noah narrowed his eyes. "It's beginning to look that way, isn't it?"

Maggie tried to ignore the rage in Noah's eyes. She tapped a brightly tipped finger on the correspondence. "If you're staying on as head of Wilder Investments—"

"Only temporarily!"

Maggie shrugged. "It doesn't matter, but perhaps you should read this insurance inquiry."

"Is it that important?" Noah asked dubiously.

Maggie frowned as she thought. "It could be. That's your decision."

"All right...all right, I'll take a look," Noah reluctantly agreed. Before Maggie could back out of the office, he called to her. "Oh, Maggie, would you do me a favor?" She nodded. "Please keep calling the house, every half an hour if you have to. And *if* you do happen to get hold of my son, let me know immediately. I want to talk to him!"

Maggie's smile was faintly sad. "Will do." She closed the door softly behind her.

When Maggie was gone, Noah reached for the document that she had indicated. "What the hell is this?" he muttered as his dark brows pulled together in concentration. He scanned the letter from the insurance company quickly and several phrases caught his attention: *nonpayment of benefits...conflict of interest... lawsuit contesting the beneficiary...Cascade Valley Winery.*

"Damn!" Noah wadded the letter into a tight ball and tossed it furiously into the wastebasket. He pushed down the button on the intercom and waited for Maggie's voice to answer. "Get me the president of Pac-West Insurance Company on the phone, *now!*" he barked without waiting for her response.

The last thing he needed was more problems with the insurance proceeds for the winery located in the foothills of the Cascade Mountains. He had hoped that by now the insurance company would have straightened everything out, even with the suspected arson complicating matters. Apparently he had been wrong, very wrong. Maggie's efficient voice interrupted his conjecture.

"Joseph Gallager, president of Pac-West Insurance, is on line one," she announced briskly.

"Good." He raised his hand to connect with Gallager, but paused. Instead he spoke to the secretary. "Do you have the name of the private investigator that my father uses?"

"Mr. Simmons," Maggie supplied.

"That's the one. As soon as I'm off the line with Gallager, I might want to talk to Simmons." An uneasy feeling settled over him at the mention of the wily detective. "Oh, Maggie... did you call the house?"

"Yes, sir. No one answered."

Noah's blue eyes darkened. "Thanks. Keep trying," he commanded through tightly clenched teeth. Where was Sean? Noah turned his dark thoughts away from his defiant son and back to the problems in the office. Hopefully, the president of Pac-West Insurance could answer a few questions about the fire at the winery and why the insurance benefits hadn't been paid to Wilder Investments. If not, Noah would be forced to contact Anthony Simmons. Noah's lip curled into an uncompromising frown as he thought about the slick private investigator that Ben insisted upon keeping on the company payroll. Though he hated to rely on the likes of Simmons, Noah didn't have much of a choice. If the insurance company refused to pay because of the suspected arson, maybe Simmons could come up with a culprit for the crime and get rid of any lingering suspicion that Wilder Investments had had something to do with the blaze. Unless, of course, Ben Wilder knew something he wasn't telling his son.

The law offices of Fielding & Son were sedately conservative. Located on the third floor of a nineteenth-century marble bank building, they were expensively decorated without seeming garish. Thick rust-colored carpet covered the floors, and the walls gleamed with finely polished cherrywood. Verdant Boston ferns and lush philodendrons overflowed the intricately woven baskets suspended from the ceiling. Leather-bound editions of law texts adorned shelves, and polished brass lamps added a warmth to the general atmosphere.

Despite all of the comfortable furnishings, Sheila was tense. She could feel the dampness of her palms, though they were folded on her lap.

Jonas Fielding mopped the sweat from his receding hairline with a silk handkerchief. Although it was only late May, the weather in the valley was unseasonably warm, and the small, delicately framed woman sitting opposite him added to his discomfort. Her large gray eyes were shadowed in pain from the recent loss of her father. There was an innocence about her, though she was dressed in a tailored business suit. Jonas couldn't help but remember Sheila Lindstrom as a little girl.

Jonas had practiced law for nearly forty years. Though he could have retired years ago, he hadn't, and it was times like this that he wished he had left the firm to his younger associates. Looking at Sheila, he felt very old, and the burden of his seventy years seemed great.

He should have become accustomed to grieving relatives long ago, but he hadn't, especially when the deceased had been one of his friends. Working with family members for the estate was a dismal part of his job, one that he would rather sluff off on a young associate. However, in this case it was impossible. Oliver Lindstrom had been a personal friend of Jonas Fielding. Hence, he had known Oliver's daughter, Sheila, all of her thirty-one years.

Jonas cleared his throat and wondered why the devil the air-conditioning in the building wasn't working properly. The offices seemed uncomfortably confining this afternoon. Perhaps it was his imagination. Perhaps dealing with Sheila was the cause of his irritability. He detested this part of his job. To give himself a little space, he stood up and walked over to the window before addressing her.

"I understand that all of this business about your father's will and the complication with the insurance proceeds is a bit much for you now, because of your father's death." Sheila's small face whitened and she pinched her lower lip between her teeth. "But you have to face facts…"

"What facts?" she asked shakily. Her voice was dry with emotions that wouldn't leave her. "Are you trying to tell me something I already know—that everyone in this valley, and for that matter the entire Pacific Northwest, thinks my father committed suicide?" Sheila's hands were shaking. It was difficult but she held on to her poise, holding back the tears that were burning in her throat. "Well, I don't believe it, not one word of it! I won't!" Nervously she ran her fingers through the thick, chestnut strands of her hair. "You were a friend of my dad. You don't think that he actually took his own life, do you?" Round, gray eyes challenged the attorney.

The question Jonas had been avoiding made him squirm against the window ledge. He rubbed his hands on the knees of his suit pants, stalling for time to compose a suitable answer. He wanted to be kind. "I don't know, Sheila. It seems unlikely…. Oliver had such zest for life…. But, sometimes, when his back is up against the wall, a man will do just about anything to preserve what he has worked for all of his life."

Sheila closed her eyes. "Then you do believe it," she whispered, feeling suddenly small and very much alone. "Just like the police and the press. They all think that Dad started the fire himself and got caught in it by mistake…or that he took his own life."

"No one suggested—"

"No one had to! Just look at the front page of the paper! It's been four weeks, and the newspapers are still having a field day!"

"Cascade Valley employed a lot of people from around here. Since it's been closed, unemployment in the valley has doubled. There's no two ways about it, Sheila. Cascade Valley is news. *Big news.*" Jonas's voice was meant to be soothing, but Sheila refused to be comforted.

"I guess I don't see why everyone seems to think that my father killed himself. Why would he do that—for the money?"

"Who knows?" Jonas shrugged his aging shoulders as he made his way to the desk. "All of the talk—it's only speculation."

"*It's slander!*" Sheila accused, lifting her regal chin upward defiantly. "My father was a decent, law-abiding citizen, and nothing will change that. He would never…" Her voice cracked with the strain of the past month as she remembered the gentle man who had raised her. Since her mother's death five years before, Sheila had become closer to her father. The last time she had seen him alive, just last spring vacation, he had been so robust and healthy that Sheila still found it impossible to believe he was gone. When she had visited him, he had been remote and preoccupied, but Sheila had chalked it up to the problems that the winery was experiencing at the time. Although her father had seemed distant, Sheila was sure that no problem at Cascade Valley had been serious enough to cause him to take his life. He had been stronger than that.

Sheila managed to compose herself. There was too much pride in her slender body to allow Jonas Fielding to witness the extent of her grief. "Is there any way I can get the winery operating again?"

Jonas shook his balding head. "I doubt it. The insurance company is balking at paying the settlement because of the possibility of arson."

Sheila sighed wearily, and her shoulders sagged. Jonas hesitated before continuing. "There's more to it than that," he admitted.

Sheila's head snapped up. "What do you mean?"

"The papers that were in your father's safety deposit box—did you read them?"

"No...I was too upset at the time. I brought everything here."

"I didn't think so."

"Why?"

"I found the partnership papers among the rest. Did you know that Oliver didn't own the business alone?"

"Yes."

The elderly attorney seemed to relax a little. "Have you ever met his business partner?"

"Years ago—when I was very young. But what does Ben Wilder have to do with anything?" she asked, confused by the twist in the conversation and Jonas's inability to meet her gaze.

"As I understand it, when the business was purchased nearly eighteen years ago, Ben and Oliver were equal partners." Sheila nodded, remembering the day when her father had made the ecstatic announcement that he had purchased the rustic old winery nestled deep in the eastern foothills of the Cascades. "However, during the course of the last few years, Oliver was forced to borrow money from Wilder Investments...to cover expenses. He put up his share of the business as collateral."

A tight, uneasy feeling gripped Sheila's stomach. "You didn't know about that?"

Jonas shook his head. "All the legal work was done by Ben Wilder's attorneys. I would have advised Oliver against it."

Sheila suddenly felt guilty as she remembered the course of events over the past five years. "Why exactly did Dad borrow the money?"

Jonas was evasive. He rubbed his palms together. "Several reasons...the economy had been rotten...and then there was a problem with the tampered bottles in Montana. From what I can see in the ledgers, sales have been down for several years."

"But there's more to it than that, isn't there?" Sheila whispered. Her throat became dry as she began to understand the reasons for her father's debt to Ben Wilder. *It was her fault!* Guilt, in an overpowering rush, settled in her heart.

Jonas dreaded what he had to say. "Your father took out the loan four years ago."

Sheila blanched. Her suspicions were confirmed.

Hesitating only slightly, the old attorney continued. "As I remember, there were several reasons for the loan. The most important thing at the time was that Oliver wanted to help you recover from your divorce from Jeff. Your father thought you should go back to school for your master's degree. He didn't want for you or Emily to be denied anything you might need, just because your marriage had failed."

"Oh, God, *no!*" Sheila sighed. She closed her eyes against the truth and sank lower into the chair. At the time of the divorce she hadn't wanted to take her father's money, but he hadn't given her much of a choice. She was a single mother without a job or the skill for decent employment. Her father had insisted that she attend a private school in California where the tuition along with the living expenses for herself and Emily were outrageous. Oliver had forced the money upon her, telling her that the California sun would help her forget about Jeff and the unhappy marriage. Begrudgingly she had accepted her father's help, assuring herself that she would pay him back with interest.

That had been over four years ago, and so far, Sheila hadn't managed to pay him a penny in return. *Now her father was dead.* He had never once mentioned that Cascade Valley was in financial trouble. Then again, Sheila had never asked. Guilt took a stranglehold of her throat.

Jonas handed her the partnership papers. She glanced through them and saw that the attorney's assessment of the situation was correct. After perusing the documents, Sheila raised her head and handed the papers back to her father's elderly friend.

"If only your father had come to me," Jonas offered. "I could have avoided this mess."

"Why didn't he?"

"Pride, I'd guess. It's all water under the bridge now."

"There's a letter demanding repayment of the loan to Wilder Investments," Sheila thought aloud.

"I know."

"But it wasn't written by Ben Wilder. The signature is…" Sheila's voice failed her, and her brows drew together as she recognized the name.

"Noah Wilder. Ben's son."

Sheila became pensive. She didn't know much about the man; Noah Wilder had always been a mystery to her. Despite her grief for her father, she was intrigued. "Is he in charge now?"

"Only temporarily, until Ben returns from Mexico."

"Have you talked to either Ben or his son and asked them if they might consider extending the loan?" Sheila asked, her tired mind finally taking hold of the situation. Without help from Wilder Investments Cascade Valley Winery was out of business.

"I've had trouble getting through to Noah," Jonas admitted. "He hasn't returned any of my calls. I'm still working on the insurance company."

"Would you like me to call Wilder Investments?" Sheila asked impulsively. Why did she think she could get through to Noah Wilder when Jonas had failed?

"It wouldn't hurt, I suppose. Do you know anything about Wilder Investments or its reputation?"

"I know that it's not the best, if that's what you mean. Dad never mentioned it, but from what I've read, I'd say that the reputation of Wilder Investments is more than slightly tarnished."

"That's right. For the past ten years Wilder Investments has been walking a thin line with the S.E.C. However, any violations charged against the firm were never proven. And, of course, the Wilder name has been a continued source of news for the scandal sheets."

Sheila's dark eyebrows lifted. "I know."

Jonas tapped his fingers on the desk. "Then you realize that Wilder Investments and the family itself are rather…"

"Shady?"

Jonas smiled in spite of himself. "I wouldn't say that, but then I wouldn't trust Ben Wilder as far as I could throw him." His voice became stern. "And neither should you. As sole beneficiary to your father's estate, you could be easy prey for the likes of Ben Wilder."

"I guess I don't understand what you're suggesting."

"Don't you realize how many marginal businesses have fallen victim to Wilder Investments this year alone? There was a shipping firm in Seattle, a theater group in Spokane and a salmon cannery in British Columbia."

"Do you really believe that the Wilder family wants Cascade Valley?" Sheila asked, unable to hide her skepticism.

"Why not? Sure, in the last few years Cascade has had its trouble, but it's still the largest and most prestigious winery in the Northwest. No one, even with the power and money of Ben Wilder, could find a better location for a vineyard." Jonas rubbed his upper lip and pushed aside the moisture that had accumulated on it. "Your father might not have been much of a businessman, Sheila, but he did know how to bottle and ferment the best wine in the state."

Sheila leveled her gaze at Jonas's worried face. "Are you

implying that Wilder Investments might be responsible for the fire?"

"Of course not...at least I don't think so. But regardless of who started the blaze, the fact stands that Wilder Investments is the only party who gained from it. Ben Wilder won't pass up a golden opportunity when it's offered him."

"And you think the winery is that opportunity."

"You'd better believe it."

"What do you think he'll do?"

Jonas thought for a moment. "Approach you, unless I miss my guess." He rubbed his chin. "I'd venture to say that Ben will want to buy out what little equity you have left. You have to realize that between the first and second mortgages on the property, along with the note to Wilder Investments, you own very little of the winery."

"And you don't think I should sell out?"

"I didn't say that. Just be careful. Make sure you talk to me first. I'd hate to see you fleeced by Ben Wilder, or his son."

Sheila's face became a mask of grim determination. "Don't worry, Jonas. I intend to face Ben Wilder, or his son, and I plan to hang on to Cascade Valley. It's all Emily and I have left."

Chapter 2

The door to Ben's office swung open, and although Noah didn't look up, his frown deepened. He tried to hide his annoyance and pulled his gaze from the thick pile of correspondence he had been studying. It was from a recently acquired shipping firm, and some of the most important documents were missing. "Yes," he called out sharply when he felt, rather than saw, his father's secretary enter the room. He looked up, softening the severity of his gaze with a smile that didn't quite reach his eyes.

"I'm sorry to disturb you, Noah, but there's a call for you on line one," Maggie said. Over the past few months she'd become accustomed to Noah's foul moods, provoked by his father's business decisions.

"I'm busy right now, Maggie. Couldn't you take a message?" He turned his attention back to the stack of paperwork cluttering the desk. Maggie remained in the room.

"I know you're busy," she assured him, "but Miss Lindstrom is the woman waiting to speak with you."

"Lindstrom?" Noah repeated, tossing the vaguely familiar

name over in his mind. "Is she supposed to mean something to me?"

"She's Oliver Lindstrom's daughter. He died in that fire a few weeks ago."

The lines of concentration furrowing Noah's brow deepened. He rubbed his hands through the thick, dark brown hair that curled above his ears. "She's the woman who keeps insisting I release some insurance money to her, isn't she?"

Maggie nodded curtly. "The same."

All of Noah's attention was turned to the secretary, and his deep blue eyes narrowed suspiciously. "Lindstrom died in the fire, and according to the reports, arson is suspected. Do you suppose that Lindstrom set the fire and inadvertently got trapped in it?" Without waiting for a response from Maggie, Noah reached for the insurance report on the fire. His eyes skimmed it while he posed another question to the secretary. "Didn't I write to this Lindstrom woman and explain our position?"

"You did."

"And what did I say? Wasn't it a phony excuse to buy time until the insurance investigation is complete?" He rubbed his temple as he concentrated. "Now I remember…I told her that everything had to wait until Ben returned."

"That's right." Maggie pursed her lips in impatience. She knew that Noah had complete power over any business decision at Wilder Investments, at least until Ben returned from Mexico.

"Then why is she calling me again?" Noah asked crossly. That fire had already cost him several long nights at the office, and the thought of spending more time on it frustrated him. Until the insurance report was complete, there wasn't much he could do.

Maggie's voice was tiredly patient. She had become familiar

with Noah's vehement expressions of disgust with his father's business. The insurance problem at the winery seemed to be of particular irritation to him. "I don't know why she's calling you, Noah, but you might speak to her. This is the fifth time she's called this afternoon."

Guiltily, Noah observed the tidy pile of telephone messages sitting neglected on the corner of his desk. Until this moment he had ignored them, hoping that the tiny pink slips of paper might somehow disappear.

"All right, Maggie," he conceded reluctantly. "You win. I'll talk to—"

"Miss Lindstrom," the retreating secretary provided.

In a voice that disguised all of his irritation, he answered the phone. "This is Noah Wilder. Is there something I can do for you?"

Sheila had been waiting on the phone for over five minutes. She was just about to hang up when Ben Wilder's son finally decided to give her a little portion of his precious time. Repressing the urge to slam the receiver down, she held her temper in tight rein and countered his smooth question with only a hint of sarcasm. "I certainly hope so—if it's not too much to ask. I'd like to make an appointment with you, but your secretary has informed me you're much too busy to see me. Is that correct?"

There was something in the seething agitation crackling through the wires that interested Noah. Since assuming his father's duties temporarily last month, no one had even hinted at disagreeing with him. Not that Noah hadn't had his share of problems with Wilder Investments, but he hadn't clashed with anyone. It was almost as if the power Ben had wielded so mightily had passed to Noah and none of Ben's business associates had breathed a word of opposition to Ben's son. Until now. Noah sensed that Miss Lindstrom was about to change all of that.

"On the contrary, Miss Lindstrom. I'd be glad to meet with you, but we'll have to make it sometime after next week. Unfortunately, Maggie's right. I'm booked solid for the next week and a half."

"I can't wait that long!" Sheila cried, her thin patience snapping.

Her response surprised Noah. "What exactly is the problem? Didn't you get the letter I sent?"

"That's precisely why I'm calling. I really do have to see you. It's important!"

"You're hoping that I'll reverse my decision, I suppose?" Noah guessed, wondering at the woman's tenacity. He thumbed through his phone messages. Maggie was right. Sheila Lindstrom had called every hour on the hour for the past five.

"You've got to! If we hope to rebuild the winery and have it ready for this season's harvest, we've got to get started as soon as possible. Even then, we might not make it—"

Noah interrupted. "I understand your problem." There was a hint of desperation in her voice that bothered him. "But, there's really nothing I can do. You understand that my father is out of the country and—"

"I don't care if your father is on the moon!" Sheila cut in. "If you're in charge of Wilder Investments, you're the man I have to deal with. Surely you can't be so much of a puppet that you can't make a simple business decision until your father returns."

"You don't understand," Noah began hotly in an attempt to explain, and then mentally cursed himself for letting this unknown woman force him into a defensive position. It really was none of her business.

"You're right, Mr. Wilder. I *don't* understand. I'm a businesswoman, and it seems utterly illogical to me that you would let a growing concern such as Cascade Valley sit in disrepair, when it could be productive."

Noah attempted to keep his voice level, even though he knew that the woman was purposely goading him. "As I understand it, Miss Lindstrom, Cascade Valley has been running at a loss for nearly four years."

There was a pause on the other end of the line, as if Sheila Lindstrom was studying the weight of his words. Her voice, decidedly less angry, commanded his attention. "I think it's evident from this discussion that you and I have a lot to talk over," Sheila suggested. Though she sounded calm, a knot of tension was twisting her stomach. "If it isn't possible for you to meet with me today, perhaps you could come to the winery this weekend and get a firsthand impression of our mutual problem."

For a moment the soft, coaxing tone of her voice captivated Noah, and he was tempted to take her up on her offer. He would love to leave the problems at Wilder Investments, if only for a weekend, but he couldn't. There were situations in Seattle that he couldn't ignore. It wasn't just the business; there was Sean to consider. A note of genuine regret filled his voice. "I'm sorry, Miss Lindstrom," he apologized. "It's out of the question. Now, if you would like to make an appointment, how about the week after next—say, June eighth?"

"No, thank you," was the curt reply. She was furious when she slammed the receiver back into the cradle of the pay telephone. The city of Seattle, usually a welcome sight to her, held no fascination today. She had come prepared to push her pleas on Noah Wilder, hoping to make him understand her desperate plight. She had failed. After being put off by his secretary, placed on hold forever, and making five fruitless telephone calls, Sheila wondered if it was possible to reason with the man. He was obviously just a figurehead for his father, a temporary replacement who held no authority whatsoever.

Sheila was lost in thought as she walked down the rain-washed sidewalk before wandering into a quiet bistro that had a view of Puget Sound. The cozy interior of the brightly lit café didn't warm her spirits, nor did the picturesque view of the shadowy sound. Her eyes followed the flight of graceful seagulls arcing over the water, but her thoughts were distant.

Absently, she stirred a bit of honey into her tea. Though it was past the dinner hour, she wasn't hungry. Thoughts of the winery sitting charred and idle filled her mind. It just didn't make sense, she reasoned with herself. Why would Ben Wilder leave town and let his obviously incapable son run a multimillion dollar investment business? Pensively sipping the tea, Sheila tried to remember what she could about her father's business partner. Tiny, fragmented thoughts clouded her mind. Though her father had been partners with Ben Wilder for over seventeen years, the two men had had little personal contact. Ben's son, Noah, was a mystery. He was the only heir to the Wilder fortune and had been a rebel in his youth.

Sheila ran her fingers through the thick strands of her shoulder-length hair as she tried to remember what it was about Noah Wilder that kept haunting her? Slowly, vague memories surfaced.

Although she hadn't been meant to hear the whispered conversation between her father and mother some sixteen years in the past, Sheila had listened at the closed kitchen door with all the impish secrecy of a normal fifteen-year-old. From what she pieced together, Sheila understood that her father's business partner's son had gotten some girl in trouble. The family disapproved. At the time Sheila had been puzzled by the conversation and then had quickly forgotten it. Although she had always been interested in Noah Wilder, she didn't know him and had dismissed her parents' secretive conversation.

The recent problems of the Wilder family were just as cloudy in her mind. Her father had mentioned that some of the bottles of Cascade Valley Cabernet Sauvignon had been tampered with and discovered in Montana, and Sheila remembered reading about the supposed SEC. violations in one of Wilder Investment's takeover bids. However, she had ignored the gossip and scandals concerning her father's business partner. At the time Sheila had not been interested in anything other than the fact that her marriage was breaking apart and that she would have to find some way to support her young daughter. Her father's business concerns hadn't touched her. She had been too wrapped up in her own problems.

Sheila set down her teacup and thoughtfully ran her fingertips around its rim. If only she had known what her father was going through. If only she had taken the time to help him, as he had helped her. As it was, his name was now smeared by the speculation and gossip surrounding the fire.

Thinking about her daughter's welfare and her father's reputation spurred Sheila into action. She pushed her empty teacup aside. Despite the warnings of Jonas Fielding against it, Sheila knew it was imperative that she talk with Ben Wilder. He had been a friend of her father as well as his business partner, and if anyone could see the logic in her solution to the problem at the winery, it would be Ben.

She opened her purse and withdrew a packet of old correspondence she had discovered in her father's private office. Fortunately the papers in the fireproof cabinet hadn't burned, and on an old envelope she found Ben Wilder's personal address. The envelope had yellowed with age, and Sheila realized that her plan was a long shot. Ben Wilder could have moved a dozen times since he had mailed the letter. But how else would she find him? He was a man who prized his privacy.

Despite the odds against locating him, Sheila knew she had to find someone who might be able to get in touch with him. A phone number was all she needed. If she could convince him that it was in his best interest to reopen the winery, Ben would be able to order the reconstruction of Cascade Valley. *Wouldn't his arrogant son be burned!* Sheila smiled to herself and felt a grim sort of pleasure imagining Noah's reaction when he found out about her plans. He would be furious! Sheila grabbed her purse, quickly paid the check and nearly ran out of the restaurant.

When Noah hung up the telephone, he had a disturbing feeling that he hadn't heard the last from Sheila Lindstrom. The authoritative ring in her voice had forced him to reach for the file on the fire. After glancing over the letters from Sheila a second time and thinking seriously about the situation at the winery, Noah felt a twinge of conscience. Perhaps he'd been too harsh with her.

In all fairness, the woman did have an acute problem, and she deserved more than a polite brush-off. Or did she? Anthony Simmons, Ben's private detective, hadn't yet filed his report on the arson. Could Oliver Lindstrom really have been involved? What about Lindstrom's daughter, sole beneficiary to the old man's estate? Noah shifted restlessly in his chair. Perhaps he should have been more straightforward with her and told Sheila about Simmons's investigation into the cause of the fire. Was he getting to be like his father, preferring deceit to the truth?

Noah's jaw tightened. He felt the same restless feeling steal over him that had seized him countless in the past. There was something about the way his father did business that soured his stomach. It wasn't anything tangible, but there was just something wrong. If only he could put his finger on it. Wilder Investments put him on edge, just as it had in the past. That was one reason Noah had quit working for his father seven years before. The quarrel between Ben and Noah had been bitter and explosive. If it hadn't been for his father's recent heart attack and the one, large favor Ben still kept hanging over Noah, he would never have agreed to return, not even temporarily. Noah's face darkened with firm resolve. At least now he was even with his father, out of the old man's debt. They were finally square after sixteen unforgiving years.

Maggie knocked on the door before entering the office. "You wanted me to remind you of the probation meeting," she announced with a stiff smile. This was the part of her job she liked least, dealing with her boss on personal matters. In this case it was like rubbing salt into an open wound.

"Is it three o'clock already?" Noah asked, grimacing as his wristwatch confirmed the efficient secretary's time schedule. "I've got to run. If there are any more calls, or people who need to see me, stall them until tomorrow...or better yet, till sometime next week. Unless, of course, you hear from Anthony Simmons. I want to speak to him right away. He owes me a report on that fire at Cascade Valley."

Maggie's eyebrows lifted slightly. "Yes, sir," she replied before stepping back into the hallway.

Noah threw his coat over his shoulder and snapped his briefcase closed. He half ran out of the office and down the hallway before stopping. On impulse he turned to accost his father's secretary once again. "Oh, Maggie?"

The plump redhead was a few paces behind him. "Yes?"

"There is one other thing. If Sheila Lindstrom should call again, tell her I'll get back to her as soon as possible. Get a number where she can be reached. I'll check back with you later."

The smug smile on Maggie's round face only served to irritate Noah further. Why did he feel a sudden urge to amend his position with the intriguing woman who had called him earlier in the day? For all he knew, Sheila Lindstrom might be involved with the arson. He didn't know anything about her. It was crazy, but he felt almost compelled to speak to her again. Perhaps it was the mood of the letters she had sent him, or maybe it was her quick temper that had sparked his interest in her. Whatever the reason, Noah knew that it was very important that he talk with her soon. She was the first one of his father's business associates who had shown any ounce of spunk. Or was it more than that?

He shrugged off the unanswered question as he slid behind the wheel of his silver Volvo sedan and headed for the meeting with Sean's probation officer. Noah had been dreading this meeting for the better part of the week. Sean was in trouble. Again. When the school administrator had called last week and reported that Sean hadn't shown up for any of his midmorning classes, Noah had been worried. Then, when he finally found out that his son had cut classes with a group of friends and later had been picked up by the police for possession of alcohol, Noah had become unglued. He was angry and disgusted, both at himself and his son.

If Sean was in trouble, Noah had himself to blame. Sixteen years ago he had begged for the privilege and responsibility of caring for his infant son, and he was the one who had insisted on raising the child alone. Unfortunately, he had made a mess of it. If Sean didn't straighten out soon, it could spell disaster.

Although it wasn't quite three-thirty, the Friday afternoon traffic heading out of the city was thick, and driving was held to a snail's pace. Even Seattle's intricate freeway system couldn't effectively handle the uneven flow of motorists as they moved away from the business district of the Northern Pacific city.

The high school that Sean attended was near Ben's home, and in the twenty minutes it took to get to the school, Noah found himself hoping that the probation officer would give Sean another chance. Noah knew that he had to find a way to get through to his son.

Noah's car crested a final hill, and he stopped the car in front of a two-story brick building. At the sound of the afternoon bell, he turned all of his attention to the main entrance of the school. Within minutes a swarm of noisy teenagers burst through the doors of the building and began to spill down the steps. Some held books over their heads, others used umbrellas, still others ignored the afternoon drizzle altogether.

Noah's eyes scanned the crowd of teenagers as it dispersed over the school yard. Nowhere did he see his blond, athletic son. The thought that Sean might have stood him up crossed Noah's mind, but he pushed it quickly aside. Surely the kid wouldn't be that stupid! Sean knew the importance of today's meeting with the juvenile officer. He wouldn't blow it. *He couldn't!*

Noah continued to wait. His hands gripped the steering wheel more tightly with each passing minute. There was no sign of his son. The teenagers on the steps thinned as they dashed across the lawn, heads bent against the wind and rain. The roar of car engines and rattling school buses filled the air. Still no Sean. Noah's impatience was beginning to surface, and he raked his fingers through the thick, coarse strands of his near-black hair. *Where the devil was that kid?* The appointment with the juvenile officer was in less than thirty minutes, and Sean was nowhere in sight.

Angrily Noah opened the car door, pulled himself to his full height, slammed the door and pushed his hands deep into his pockets. He leaned against the car, oblivious to the rain that ran down his back. His eyes skimmed the empty school yard. No sign of his son. He checked his watch once, uttered a low oath and continued to lean against the car.

Chapter 3

It was dusk when Sheila found the address listed on the torn envelope, and even though twilight dimmed her vision, she could tell that the house Ben Wilder called home was immense. The three-story structure stood high on a cliff overlooking the banks of Lake Washington, and the grounds surrounding the manor encompassed several acres. The stately stone house was surrounded by a natural growth of sword ferns and ivy. To Sheila, the building seemed strangely cold and uninviting. Even the sweeping branches of the fir trees and the scarlet blossoms of the late-blooming rhododendrons didn't soften the hard, straight lines of the manor.

An uneasy feeling that she was intruding where she didn't belong nagged at Sheila's mind, and she considered retreating into the oncoming night. She chided herself for her case of nerves. What would it hurt to knock on the door and inquire as to the whereabouts of Ben Wilder? Nothing ventured; nothing gained. Wasn't that the phrase?

It was obvious that someone was home. Not only was there smoke rising from one of the chimneys, but also, several windows in the stone mansion glowed brightly from interior lights. Even the porch lanterns were lit. It was almost as if her presence were expected. A cold chill of apprehension skittered up her spine.

Ignoring her mounting misgivings, Sheila parked her car behind the silver Volvo sitting in the long, circular drive. Before she could think twice about the consequences of what she was about to do, she slid out of her car, gathered a deep breath of damp air and walked to the door. A quiet rain had begun to settle over the city, and droplets of moisture clung to Sheila's hair. After hiking the collar of her raincoat more tightly around her throat, she knocked softly on one of the twin double doors. As she nervously waited, she wondered who would answer her knock and what his reaction would be to her inquiry. Would she really be able to procure information as to the whereabouts of Ben Wilder or was this just one more leg in the wild-goose chase she had been participating in all afternoon?

The door opened suddenly. Sheila wasn't prepared to meet the forceful man standing in the doorway. In a house the size of a Tudor, she had expected a servant to greet her, but she had been mistaken. The tall, well-built man standing in the light from the hallway presented himself with an arrogance that spoke of power rather than servility. His face was handsome, though not in a classical sense. His features were even, but severe. The angle of his jaw was strong, and dark, ebony brows hooded deep-set delft-blue eyes. The lines of worry on his face intensified his masculinity and the power of his gaze. His eyes sparked with interest as he looked down on Sheila. Involuntarily her pulse quickened and fluttered in the hollow of her throat. Surely he could sense her unease.

"Is there something I can do for you?" he asked with practiced boredom. Sheila instantly recognized his voice. It belonged to Noah Wilder. Of course! Why hadn't she expected him...*or had she?* Had her subconscious sought him out? She swallowed with difficulty while her heart clamored in her chest.

"I was looking for Ben Wilder," was her inadequate response.

"Ben?" He cocked a wary black eyebrow before crossing his arms over his chest and leaning on the doorjamb. The light fabric of his shirt strained over his shoulder muscles. A lazy smile softened the severe planes of his face. "You want to see Ben? Who are you?"

There was something disturbing in Noah's deep blue eyes, something that took hold of Sheila and wouldn't let go. With difficulty she drew her eyes away from the alluring depths of his gaze. She drew in a steadying breath and ignored both her racing pulse and the strong desire to run back into the safety of the night. "My name is Sheila Lindstrom. I believe I spoke with you earlier this afternoon."

He didn't seem surprised by her announcement. His smile broadened to show the hint of a dimple. He was interested but cautious. "You're the lady with the urgent problems at Cascade Valley, right?"

"Yes." At least he remembered her. Was he amused? Why the crooked, knowing grin?

"You called the office and Maggie told you where you could reach me?" he guessed, rubbing his chin while his eyes inched slowly up her body. What was it about her that he found so attractive?

Before she could answer his question, his eyes left her face. A car engine whined on a nearby road, and Noah's head snapped upward. His eyes followed the sound, and every muscle in his body tensed as he looked past her toward the sound.

The car drove past the main gates and turned into another

driveway. "No," Sheila said, responding to his question of a few moments before.

"No?" Noah's interest was once again on the conversation. His eyes searched hers.

"I told you I'm looking for your father."

"And I told you he was out of the country." Something in his gaze seemed to harden.

"I was hoping that someone here might be able to give me an address or a telephone number where he might be reached," she admitted, pressing onward despite the chill in Noah's gaze.

His lips tightened into a scowl, and his voice became still colder. "Come in, Miss Lindstrom, and get out of the rain. You were right. Earlier today you indicated that we have a few things to iron out, and I agree with you. Let's get on with it." He moved out of the doorway as if he expected her to enter.

Sheila hesitated for a moment as her resolve faltered. When his eyes had darkened in disdain, she felt her poise crumbling. She was the intruder. "I think it would be better if I talked to your father. If you could just give me the number...."

"I asked you to come inside! I think it's an excellent suggestion, as it's getting dark and the wind is beginning to pick up. I'm not about to stand here and get wet while I argue with you. The choice is yours; either you can come into the house and talk to me or you can stand out on this porch alone. I'm not going to stand out here much longer. You were the one who was so desperate to talk to me this afternoon. Now you have the opportunity. Take it!"

It was a mistake to enter this man's home. Sheila could feel it, but she was cornered. With what little dignity she could piece together, she reluctantly accepted Noah's invitation and quietly strode into the formal entry hall. Antiques and portraits adorned the walls of the expansive foyer. A large crystal chandelier warmed the entrance in a bath of filtered light, which reflected against the polished wood floor and the carved walnut staircase. Expensive Persian carpets, rich in hues of burgundy and navy, seemed to run endlessly along several of the corridors that branched from the central reception area.

Noah closed the door behind her and indicated the direction she should follow. Sheila tried to hide the awe that was flooding through her at the ostentatious display of Wilder wealth. Although the Wilder name was familiar throughout the Northwest, never had Sheila guessed her father's business partner to be so affluent. The size and elegance of the gracious old house overwhelmed her, and she had to remind herself of Ben Wilder's infamous reputation for gaining his wealth. Nothing stood in his way when he wanted something; no amount of money was an obstacle that couldn't be overcome. She slid a glance toward the tall man walking silently at her side. Was he the same as his father?

Without breaking stride Noah touched Sheila's elbow, nudging her into a room near the back of the house. A dying fire and a few table lamps illuminated the room, which appeared to be a library. Hardcover editions rested on an English reading table, and other books were stored behind the leaded glass of the built-in cabinets. A leather recliner sitting near the fireplace was partially extended, and a half-finished drink rested on a side table, indicating that Noah had been in this room just moments before, waiting. But for whom? Certainly not Sheila. He had no idea that she would grace his doorstep this evening. Once again the overwhelming sensation that she was intruding upon him cut her to the bone. Noah Wilder was just as mysterious as she had imagined.

"Sit down, Miss Lindstrom," Noah suggested as he stood near a bar. "May I get you a drink?"

"No...thank you." She sat on the edge of a wingbacked chair and prayed that she looked calmer than she felt.

"Coffee, perhaps?"

She looked up at him and shook her head. She could feel his eyes on her face; they were the bluest eyes she had ever seen, erotic eyes that mystified her. "No...nothing, thanks."

Noah shrugged, pulled at his tie and dropped into the ox-blood red recliner facing her. In the warm glow from the smoldering embers he studied her face. His stare was so intense that after a moment of returning his direct gaze, she let her eyes fall and pretended interest in the dying fire. But the blackened logs and the quiet flames reminded her of her father and the inferno that had taken his life. Unconsciously she bit at her lower lip and tried to concentrate on anything but the nightmare of the last month.

Noah was disgusted with himself when he realized how fascinated he was becoming with the beguiling woman he had found on his doorstep. Earlier today he had known that she interested him, but never had he expected to become so utterly captivated by her beauty and unconscious vulnerability. Lines of worry etched across her otherwise flawlessly complected forehead, and a deep sadness lingered in her eyes. Still, she was beautiful. The combination of her thick chestnut-colored hair, her delicately structured oval face and her large, nearly luminous gray eyes bewitched him. Noah didn't fall easy prey to beautiful women; most of them bored him to death. But this intriguing woman with her sharp tongue and gorgeous eyes captivated him. It was difficult for him to disguise his interest in her.

Sheila was nervous, though she proudly attempted to shield herself with a thin veil of defiant poise. Her cheeks were flushed from the cold, and tiny droplets of moisture clung to her dark hair, making it shine to the color of burnished copper.

Noah took a swallow from his drink. What bothered him most was the shadow of despair in her eyes. It puzzled and nagged at him, and he wondered if he had inadvertently contributed to that pain. An odd sensation swept over him. *He wanted to protect her.* He felt the urge to reach out and soothe her…comfort her…make love to her until she forgot everything else in her life other than him.

His final thought struck him savagely. What was he doing, fantasizing over a woman he had barely met, a virtual stranger? He reined in his emotions and blamed his traitorous thoughts on the long, tense day and the worry that was eating at him. What did he know of Sheila Lindstrom? He tried to convince himself that she was just another woman. One that, for all he knew, wanted nothing more from him than a piece of his father's fortune. He drained his drink.

"All right, Miss Lindstrom," Noah said, breaking the heavy silence. "You have my undivided attention. What is it that you want from me?" He folded his hands and leaned back in the recliner.

"I told you that I want to get in touch with your father."

"And I told you that your request was impossible. My father is in Mexico, recuperating from a recent illness. You'll have to deal with me."

"I've tried that," she pointed out.

"You're right. You did try, and I wasn't very accommodating. I apologize for that…. I had other things on my mind at the time. But right now I'm prepared to listen. I assume that you want to talk about the insurance claim for Cascade Valley Winery?"

Sheila nodded, a little of her confidence returning. "You see, Ben was a personal friend of my father's. I thought that if I could reason with him, I could convince him of the importance of rebuilding the winery before the fall harvest."

"Why do you think Wilder Investments would want to continue operating Cascade Valley?"

Sheila eyed Noah dubiously. "To make money, obviously."

"But the winery wasn't profitable."

"Only in the last few years," she countered. Was he testing her? "It's true that we've had a run of bad luck, but now—"

"*We?*" he interrupted abruptly. "Do *you* manage the operation?"

"No," Sheila admitted honestly. Her face clouded in thought. "No…I don't. Dad took care of that…." Her voice faded when she thought of her father.

Noah's question was gentle. "Your father was the man who was killed in the fire?"

"Yes."

"And you think that you can take over where he left off?"

Sheila squared her shoulders and smiled sadly. "I know I could," she whispered.

"You worked in the winery?"

"No…yes…only in the summers." Why couldn't she think straight? It wasn't like her to be tongue-tied, but then Noah Wilder was more intimidating than any man she had ever met. "I helped Dad in the summers, when I was free from school and college. I'm a counselor at a community college." Sheila purposely omitted the five years she had been married to Jeff Coleridge. That was a part of her life she would rather forget. Her daughter, Emily, was the only satisfying result of the sour marriage.

Noah regarded her thoughtfully. He pinched his lower lip with his fingers as he turned her story over in his mind. His eyes never left the soft contours of her face and the determination he saw in her gaze. "So what, exactly, qualifies you to manage the operation—a few summers on the farm?"

She recognized his ploy and smile. "That along with a master's degree in business."

"I see." He sounded as if he didn't.

Noah frowned as he stood and poured himself another drink. The woman was getting to him. Maybe it was all of the worries over his son, or the anxiety that plagued him at the office. It had been a long, hard day, and Sheila Lindstrom was getting under his skin. He found himself wanting to help her, for God's sake. Without asking her preference, he poured a second drink and set it on the table near her chair. After taking a long swallow of his brandy he sat on the edge of the recliner and leaned on his elbows. "What about the vineyards? It takes more than a college education to oversee the harvest and the fermentation."

Sheila knew that he was goading her, and although she was provoked at the thought, she replied in a calm voice that overshadowed his impertinent questions. "The winery employs a viticulturist for the vineyards. Dave Jansen is a respected viticulturist who grew up in the valley. His research has helped develop a stronger variety of grape, hardier for the cold weather. As for the actual fermentation and bottling, we employ an enologist who is more than capable—"

"Then what about the losses?" he demanded impatiently as he frowned into his drink. Why did he care? "Assuming that your father knew what he was doing, he made one helluva mess of it, according to the latest annual report."

Sheila's throat was hoarse and dry. The pent-up emotions she had kept hidden within her for the last month were about to explode, and she knew that if prodded any further, her restrained temper would be unleashed. She had expected a rough business meeting with a member of the Wilder family, but she was unprepared for this brutal inquisition from Noah and the way his overpowering masculinity was affecting her. She found it impossible to drag her eyes away from his face. "As I stated before…we've had a run of bad luck."

"*Bad luck?* Is that what you call it?" Noah asked. He wondered why his words sounded so brittle in the warm den. "The tampered bottles found in Montana, and the expensive recall? The damaged crops last year because of the early snowfall? The ash and debris from the Mount Saint Helens' eruption? And now the fire? From what I understand, the fire was set intentionally. Do you call that bad luck?" His eyes had darkened to the color of midnight as he calculated her reaction.

"What would you call it?" she challenged.

"Mismanagement!"

"Natural disasters!"

"Not the fire."

For a moment there was a restless silence; Sheila felt the muscles in her jaw tightening. She made a vain effort to cool her rising temper. It was impossible. "What are you inferring?' she demanded.

"That your father wasn't exactly the businessman he should have been," Noah snapped. He was angry at himself, at Ben and at Oliver Lindstrom. "I'm not just talking about the fire," he amended when he noticed that the color had drained from her face. "That loan to him from Wilder Investments. What was it used for—improvements in the winery? I doubt it!"

Sheila felt the back of her neck become hot. How much did Noah know about her? Would she have to explain that most of the money her father had borrowed was given to her?

Noah's tirade continued. "I don't see how you can possibly expect to turn the business around, considering your lack of experience." His fingers tightened around his glass.

Sheila's thin patience snapped, and she rose, intending to leave. "Oh, I see," she replied, sarcastically. "Cascade Valley doesn't quite hold up to the sanctimonious standards of Wilder Investments. Is that what you mean?"

His eyes darkened before softening. Despite his foul mood

a grim smile tugged at the corners of Noah's mouth. "Touché, Miss Lindstrom," he whispered.

Sheila was still prepared for verbal battle and was perplexed by the change in Noah's attitude. His uncompromising gaze had yielded. When he smiled to display straight, white teeth and the hint of a dimple, the tension in the air disintegrated. Sheila became conscious of the softly pelting rain against the windowpanes and the heady scent of burning pitch. She felt her heart beating wildly in her chest, and she had the disturbing sensation that the enigmatic man watching her wistfully could read her mind. He wanted to touch her…breathe the scent of her hair…make her forget any other man in her life. He said nothing, but she read it in the power of his gaze. Was she as transparent as he?

Sheila felt an urgency to leave and a compulsion to stay. Why? And why did the needs of Cascade Valley seem so distant and vague? The closeness of the cozy room and the unspoken conversation began to possess her, and though she didn't understand it, she knew that she had to leave. Noah Wilder was too powerful. When he took hold of her with his eyes, Sheila wanted never to be released. She reached for her purse. When she found her voice, it was ragged, torn with emotions she didn't dare name. "Is…is it possible to meet with you next week?"

Noah's eyes flicked to her purse, the pulse jumping in the hollow of her throat and finally to her face. "What's wrong with right now?"

"I…have to get back…*really*." Who was she trying to convince? "My daughter is waiting for me." She started to turn toward the door in order to break the seductive power of his gaze.

"You have a daughter?" The smile left his face, and his dark brows blunted. "But I thought…" He left the sentence unfinished as he got out of the chair.

Sheila managed a thin smile. "You thought I wasn't married? I'm not. The divorce was final over four years ago. I prefer to use my maiden name," she explained stiffly. It was still difficult to talk about the divorce. Though she didn't love Jeff, the divorce still bothered her.

"I didn't mean to pry." His sincerity moved her.

"I know. It's all right."

"I'm sorry if I brought up a sore subject."

"Don't worry about it. It was over long ago."

The sound of tires screaming against wet pavement as a car came to a sudden halt cut off the rest of her explanation. Sheila was grateful for the intrusion; Noah was getting too close to her. The engine continued to grind for a moment and then faded into the distance. Noah was instantly alert. "Excuse me," he muttered as he strode out of the room.

Sheila waited for just a minute and then followed the sound of Noah's footsteps. She had to get out of the house, away from the magnetism of Noah Wilder. As she walked down the hallway, she heard the sound of the front door creaking open.

"Where the hell have you been?" Noah demanded. The worry in his voice thundered through the hallways. At the sound Sheila stopped dead in her tracks. Whoever he had been waiting for had finally arrived. *If only she had managed to leave earlier.* Why hadn't she listened to her common sense and left Noah Wilder the moment she had met him? The last thing she wanted was to be caught up in a family argument.

There was a muted reply to Noah's demand. Sheila couldn't hear the words over the pounding of her heartbeat. She was trapped. She couldn't intrude on a very personal confrontation. She had to find a way to escape.

Noah's voice again echoed through the house. "I don't want

to hear any more of your pitiful excuses! Go upstairs and try to sleep it off. I'll talk to you in the morning, and believe you me, there are going to be some changes in your behavior! This is the last time you stumble into this house drunk on your can, Sean!"

Sheila let out a sigh of relief. It was Noah's son who had come home, not his wife. Why did she feel some consolation in that knowledge? Sheila retreated to the library, but Noah's harsh words continued to ring in her ears. Why was Noah so angry with his son, and why did it matter to her? It was better not to know anything more about Noah Wilder and his family. It was too dangerous.

Once back in the den, Sheila fidgeted. She knew that Noah was returning, and the knowledge made her anxious. She didn't want to see him again, not here in this room. It was too cozy and seemed seductively inviting. She needed to meet with him another time, in another place...somewhere *safe*.

She rushed through the room and paused at the French doors. She pushed down on the brass handle and escaped into the night. A sharp twinge of guilt told her she should make some excuse for leaving to Noah, but she didn't know what she would say. It was easier to leave undetected. She couldn't afford to get involved with Noah Wilder or any of his personal problems. Right now she was a business partner of Wilder Investments, nothing more.

Sheila shuddered as a blast of cold air greeted her. She had to squint in the darkness. Soft raindrops fell from the sky to run down her face as she attempted to get her bearings in the moonless night. "Damn," she muttered under her breath when she realized that she hadn't walked out of a back entrance to the house as she had hoped but was standing on a spacious flagstone veranda overlooking the black waters of Lake Washington. She leaned over the railing to view the jagged cliff and saw that there was no way she could hope to scale its rocky surface. She couldn't escape.

"Sheila!" Noah's voice boomed in the night. It startled her, and she slipped on the wet flagstones. To regain her balance, she tightened her grip on the railing. "What the devil do you think you're doing?" In three swift strides he was beside her. He grabbed her shoulders and yanked her away from the edge of the veranda.

Sheila froze in her embarrassment. How stupid she must look, trying to flee into the night. It seemed that her poise and common sense had left her when she had met Noah.

"I asked you a question—what were you doing out here?" Noah gave her shoulders a hard shake. His eyes were dark with rage and something else. Was it fear?

Sheila managed to find her voice, though most of her attention remained on the pressure of Noah's fingers against her upper arms. "I was trying to leave," she admitted.

"Why?"

"I didn't want to hear your argument with your son."

The grip on her shoulders relaxed, but his fingers lingered against her arms. "You would have had to have been deaf not to hear that argument. I'm just glad that you weren't considering jumping from the deck."

"What? Of course not. It must be over fifty feet straight down."

"At least."

"And you thought I might jump?" She was incredulous.

"I didn't know what to think," he conceded. "I don't know you and I don't really understand why you came out here or why you were leaning over the railing." He seemed honestly perplexed.

"There's nothing mysterious about it, I just wanted to leave. I was looking for a back exit."

"Why were you in such a hurry?" He examined her more closely. It was hard to tell in the darkness, but he was sure that she was blushing. Why?

"I don't feel comfortable here," she admitted.

"Why not?"

Because of you. You're not what I expected at all. I'm attracted to you and I can't be! "I've invaded your privacy and I apologize for that. It was rude of me to come to your home uninvited."

"But you didn't know it was my home."

"That doesn't matter. I think it would be best if I were to leave. We can meet another time…in your office…or at the winery, if you prefer." He was close to her. She could see the interest in his cool blue eyes, smell his heady male scent, *feel* an unspoken question hanging dangerously between them.

"I don't know when I'll have the time," he hedged.

"Surely you can find an hour somewhere," she coaxed. The tight feeling in her chest was returning.

"What's wrong with now?"

"I told you…I don't want to interfere in your private life."

"I think it might be too late for that."

Sheila swallowed, but the dryness in her throat remained. Noah looked into the farthest reaches of her eyes, as if he were searching for her soul. She felt strangely vulnerable and naked to his knowing gaze, but she didn't shrink away from him. Instead she returned his unwavering stare. His fingers once again found her arms. She didn't pull away, nor did she sway against him. Though she was drawn to his raw masculinity, she forced her body to remain rigid and aloof as his hands slid up her arms to rest at the base of her throat.

Raindrops moistened her cheeks as she lifted her face to meet his. She knew that he was going to kiss her and involuntarily her lips parted. His head lowered, and the pressure of his fingers against her throat moved in slow, seductive circles as his lips touched hers in a bittersweet kiss that asked questions she couldn't hope to answer. She wasn't conscious of accepting what he offered until she felt her arms circle his waist. It had been so long since she had wanted a man. Not since Jeff had she let a man close to her. Never had she felt so unguarded and passionate. Until now, when she stood in the early summer rain, kissing a man she couldn't really trust. She felt a warm, traitorous glow begin to burn within her.

His hands shifted to the small of her back and pulled her against his hard, lean frame. She felt the rigid contours of his body, and the ache in hers began to spread. Lazily he brushed his lips over hers, and softly his tongue probed the warm recess of her mouth. All of her senses began to awaken and come alive. Feeling she had thought dead reappeared.

When he pulled away from her to look into her eyes, her rational thought came thundering back to her. She saw a smoldering passion in the smoky blue depths of his eyes, and she knew that her own eyes were inflamed with a desire that had no bounds.

"I'm sorry," she swiftly apologized, trying to take a step backward. The hands on her waist held her firmly against him.

"For what?"

"Everything, I guess. I didn't mean for things to get so out of hand."

He cocked his head to one side in a pose of disbelief. "You must enjoy running out on me. Is that it? Are you just a tease?" Was he kidding? Couldn't he feel her response?

"I meant that I hadn't planned to become involved with you."

"I know that."

"Do you?"

"Of course. Neither of us planned any of this, but we can't deny that we're attracted to each other. We both felt it earlier in the study, and we're feeling it now." One of his fingers touched her swollen lips, challenging her to contradict him.

Her knees became weak as his head once again lowered and his lips, deliciously warm and sensitive, touched hers. She was drawn to him, but she fought the attraction. She pulled away. Her own lips were trembling and for an unguarded instant, fear lighted her eyes.

Noah was wary. "Is something wrong?"

She wanted to laugh at the absurdity of the situation. "Is anything wrong?" she echoed. "Are you kidding? How about everything? The winery is in a shambles, so I came to Seattle hoping that you would help me. Instead, I end up here looking for your father because I couldn't get through to you. On top of that I stumble onto your argument with your son, and finally, I fall neatly into your arms."

Noah put a finger to her lips to silence her. "Shhh. All right, so we've got a few problems."

"A few?"

"What I'm trying to tell you is that sometimes it's best to get away and escape from those problems. It gives one a better perspective."

"You're sure?"

"What I'm sure of is that I find you incredibly attractive." Noah's voice was soothing, and Sheila felt her body lean more closely to his.

"This won't work, you know," she whispered breathlessly.

"Don't worry about tomorrow."

"Someone has to." Reluctantly she wrenched herself free of his arms and straightened her coat. "I came here to find your father because you refused to see me."

"My mistake," he conceded wryly.

She ignored his insinuation. "That's the only reason I'm here. I didn't intend to overhear your argument with your son, nor did I expect to get this close to you. I hope you understand."

The smile that slid across his face was seductively charming. "I understand perfectly," he responded gently, and Sheila felt herself becoming mesmerized all over again. He was powerful and yet kind, bold without being brash, strong but not unyielding—the kind of man Sheila had thought didn't exist. Her attraction to him was compelling, but her feelings were precarious.

"I have to go."

"Stay."

"I can't."

"Because of your daughter?"

"She's one reason," Sheila lied. "There are others."

His smile broadened, and she saw the flash of his white teeth. "Come on, let's go inside. You're getting soaked."

"At least I'm wearing a coat," she taunted, noticing the way his wet shirt was molding to the muscular contours of his shoulders and chest.

"I didn't expect you to run out into the rain."

"It was a stupid thing to do," she admitted. "It's just that I didn't want to intrude. I didn't think you—"

"Have problems of my own?"

Embarrassment crept up her throat. "I'm sorry."

"Don't worry about it. I should have been a little more discreet when Sean came home. I lost control when I saw him drunk again." Noah wiped the rain from his forehead as if he were erasing an unpleasant thought. He touched her lightly on the elbow and guided her back into the house.

It was difficult for Noah to ignore any part of her; he couldn't help but notice the quiet dignity with which she carried herself, the curve of her calf as she walked, or the

shimmer of her chestnut hair, which had darkened into unruly curls in the rain.

"Thank you for seeing me," she said softly. "I don't suppose
you would consider telling me how to reach your father?"

"I don't think that would be wise."

Sheila smiled sadly to herself. "Then I'll be going. Thank
you for your time."

"You're not really planning to drive back to the valley tonight?" he asked, studying the tired lines of her face. How far
could he trust her? She seemed so open with him, and yet he
felt as if she were hiding something, a secret she was afraid
to share.

"No. I'll drive back in the morning."

He stood with his back to the fire, warming his palms on
the rough stones. "But your daughter. I thought she was expecting you."

"Not tonight. She's probably having the time of her life.
That grandmother of hers spoils her rotten."

Noah rubbed his chin and his dark brows raised. "I didn't
realize your mother was still alive."

A pensive expression clouded Sheila's even features. "She's
not. Emily is staying with my ex-husband's mother…. We're
still close."

"What about your ex-husband? Are you still close to him,
too?" Noah asked, brittlely. Why the devil did he even care?
He watched a play of silent emotions darken Sheila's eyes, and
without knowing why, Noah Wilder immediately despised the
man who had caused Sheila so much pain. He could feel the
muscles in his jaw begin to tighten.

"Jeff and I are civil," Sheila replied, hoping to close the unwelcome subject.

"Then you still see him?" Noah persisted.

"It can't be avoided…because of Emily."

"Is he good with your daughter?"

"Yes...I suppose so. Does it matter?" Sheila asked, experiencing a hot flash of indignation. She didn't like discussing her feelings about Jeff with anyone, especially not a man she was beginning to admire.

"Doesn't it...matter, I mean?"

"To me, yes. But why do you care?"

His voice lowered at the bitterness in her words. "I didn't mean to bring up a sore subject."

Sheila stiffened, but pushed back the hot retort forming in her throat. It was none of Noah's business. Her divorce from Jeff had been a painful experience, one she would rather not think about or discuss.

"I think I had better leave," she stated evenly. She reached into the front pocket of her purse and fished for her keys. The conversation was getting far too personal.

"You mean you want to run away, don't you?"

"What?"

"Isn't that what you were doing when I found you out on the veranda, leaning over the rail? Weren't you attempting to avoid a confrontation with me?"

"You were arguing with your son! I was only trying to give you some privacy."

His eyes darkened. "There's more to it than that, isn't there?"

"I don't know what you're suggesting."

"Sure you do." He moved from the fireplace to stand only inches from her. "Anytime the conversation turns a little too personal, you try to avoid me," he accused. A dangerous glint of blue fire flashed in his eyes.

Sheila stood her ground. "I came here to talk about business. There was nothing personal about it."

"Save that for someone gullible enough to believe it."

She glared at him defiantly but held on to her poise. "Quit

beating around the bush and just say what it is that's bothering you."

"You came over here with the intention of contacting Ben.
You were sidestepping me. Don't take me for such a fool. I
know that you were deliberately trying to avoid me."

"Only because you were being completely unreasonable!"
she snapped. He was impossible! When she looked into his intense cobalt eyes, she felt as if she wanted to float dreamily in
his gaze forever. The smell of burning logs mingled with the
earthy scent of Noah's wet body. Raindrops still ran down the
length of his tanned neck.

"I'm not an unreasonable man," he stated calmly. His hand
reached up to touch her chin, and Sheila felt a shiver skitter
down her spine. His eyes studied her face, noting in detail
the regal curve of her jaw, the blush on her creamy skin and
the seductive pout on her full lips. "Please stay," he implored.

"Why?" She longed for an excuse, *any* excuse to spend some
more precious time with him.

"We could start by talking about the winery and your plans
for it."

"Would you change your position on the insurance settlement?"

The corners of his mouth quirked. "I think you could persuade me to do anything." His finger trailed down her chin
and throat to rest against the collar of her coat. Her heart fluttered.

She stepped away from him and crossed her arms over her
chest. Eyeing him suspiciously, she asked, "What would it
take?"

"For what?"

"For you to listen to my side of the story."

He shrugged. "Not much."

"*How* much?"

Noah's smile spread slowly over his face and his eyes gleamed devilishly. "Why don't we start with dinner? I can't think of anything I'd rather do than listen to you over a glass of Cascade Valley's finest."

He was mocking her again, but there was enough of a dare in his words to tempt Sheila. "All right, Noah. Why not?" she countered impulsively. "But let's set out the ground rules first. I insist that we keep the conversation on business."

"Just come with me," he suggested wickedly. "The conversation...and the night will take care of themselves."

Chapter 4

The restaurant Noah selected was located on one of the steep hills near the heart of the city. It was unique, in that the original Victorian structure had been built by one of Seattle's founding fathers. The old apartment building had been remodeled to accommodate patrons of *L'Epicure,* but the structure retained its authentic nineteenth-century charm. White clapboard siding, French gray shutters and an elegant touch of gingerbread adorned the entrance. Flickering sconces invited Sheila inside.

A formally dressed waiter led them up a narrow flight of stairs to a private room in the second story of the gracious old apartment house. An antique table sat in an alcove of leaded glass, giving the patrons a commanding panorama of the city lights. Raindrops lingered and ran on the windowpanes, softly blurring the view and creating an intimate atmosphere in the private room.

"Very nice," Sheila murmured to herself as she ran her fingers along the windowsill and looked into the night.

Noah helped her into her chair before seating himself on

the other side of the small table. Though he attempted to appear calm, Sheila could sense that he was still on edge. The quiet, comfortable silence they had shared in the car had been broken in the shadowy confines of the intimate restaurant.

Before the waiter left, Noah ordered the specialty of the house along with a bottle of Chardonnay by Cascade Valley. Sheila lifted her brows at Noah's request, but the waiter acted as if nothing were out of the ordinary.

"Why would a European restaurant carry a local wine?" she inquired after the waiter had disappeared from the room.

Noah's smile twisted wryly. "Because my father insists upon it."

The waiter returned with the wine and solemnly poured the wine first into Noah's glass, and upon approval, into Sheila's. After he had left once again, Sheila persisted with her questions.

"*L'Epicure* keeps wine for your father?"

"That's one way of putting it. *L'Epicure* is a subsidiary of Wilder Investments," he explained tonelessly.

Sheila's lips tightened. "I see. Just like Cascade Valley."

Noah nodded. "Although the restaurant carries a full cellar of European wines, Ben insists that Cascade Valley be fully represented."

"And your father is used to getting what he wants?"

Noah's blue eyes turned stone cold. "You could say that." Any further comment he would have made was repressed by the appearance of the waiter bearing a tray overloaded with steaming dishes of poached halibut in mushroom sauce, wild rice and steamed vegetables. Sheila waited until the food was served and the waiter had closed the door behind him before continuing the conversation.

"I take it you don't like working for your father?" she guessed as she started the meal.

Noah's dark eyebrows blunted, and the fork he had been holding was placed back on the table. He clasped his hands together and stared at her over his whitened knuckles. "I think we should get something straight: I do *not* work for Ben Wilder!"

"But I thought—"

"I said I do not work for Ben! Nor do I collect a salary from Wilder Investments!" His clipped words were succinct and effectively closed the subject. The angry edge of his words and the tensing of his jawline left little doubt that he preferred not to speak of his father or his business.

"I think you owe me an explanation." Sheila sighed, setting her uneaten food aside. Somehow she had to keep her temper in check. What sort of game was he playing with her? "Why am I sitting here wasting my time, when you just intimated that you have nothing to do with Wilder Investments?"

"Because you wanted to get to know me better."

Sheila found it difficult to deny the truth, and yet she couldn't help but feel betrayed. He had tricked her into coming with him, when all along he couldn't help her in her quest to save the winery and her father's reputation. Was it her fault for being so mystified by him? Ignoring his wish to avoid discussing Wilder Investments, Sheila continued to push her point home. "I'm listening," she said quietly. "I want to know why you led me on—or have you forgotten our ground rules?"

"I didn't lead you on."

"But you just said that you don't work for Wilder Investments."

"I said that I don't work for *my father,* and I'm not on the company payroll."

"That doesn't make a lot of sense," Sheila pointed out, her exasperation beginning to show. "What is it exactly that you do?"

Noah shrugged, as if resigned to a fate he abhorred. "I do owe you an explanation," he admitted thoughtfully. "I used to work for Ben. From the time I graduated from college I was groomed for the position Ben's only heir would rightfully assume: the presidency of Wilder Investments, whenever Ben decided to retire. I was never very comfortable with the situation as it was, but—" he hesitated, as if wondering how much of his private life he should divulge "—for personal reasons I needed the security my position at Wilder Investments provided."

"Because of your wife and son?" Sheila immediately regretted her thoughtless question.

Noah's eyes darkened. "I've never had a wife!" He bit out the statement savagely, as if the thought alone were repulsive to him.

Sheila flushed with color. "I'm sorry," she apologized hastily. "I didn't know.... You have a child...."

Noah's glare narrowed suspiciously. "You didn't know about Marilyn? If that's the truth, you must have been the only person in Seattle who didn't know the circumstances surrounding Sean's birth. The press couldn't leave it alone. All of Ben's money couldn't even shut them up!"

"I've never lived in Seattle," she explained hurriedly, still embarrassed. Surely he would believe her. "And—and I didn't pay any attention to what my father's business partner was doing, much less his son.... I was only a teenager and I didn't know anything about you."

Noah's anger subsided slightly as he noticed the stricken look on Sheila's near-perfect face. "Of course not—it happened years ago."

Sheila's hands were trembling as she reached for her wineglass and let the cool liquid slide down herparched throat. She avoided Noah's probing gaze and pushed the remains of her dinner around on her plate. Although the food was delicious, her hunger had disappeared.

Noah speared a forkful of fish and ate in the thick silence that hung over the table. It was a long moment before he began to speak again. When he did, his voice was calm and toneless, almost dead from the lack of emotion in his words. "There were many reasons why I quit working for my father… too many to hope to explain. I didn't like the idea of being treated as 'Ben Wilder's son' by the rest of the staff, and I had never gotten on well with my dad in the first place. Working with him only served to deepen the rift between us." His teeth clenched, and he tossed his napkin onto the table as he remembered the day that he had broken free of the cloying hands of Wilder Investments.

"I stayed on as long as I could, but when one of my father's investments went sour, he ordered me to investigate the reasons. A manufacturing firm in Spokane wasn't making it. Although it wasn't the manager's fault, Ben had the man fired." Noah took a drink of wine, as if to cast off the anger he felt each time he remembered the painful scene in his father's office, the office Noah now reluctantly filled. The image of a man near fifty, his shoulders bowed by the wrath and punishment of Ben Wilder, still haunted Noah. How many times had he pictured the tortured face of Sam Steele as the man realized Ben was really going to fire him for a mistake he hadn't made? Sam had looked to Noah for support, but even Noah's pleading was useless. Ben Wilder needed a scapegoat and Sam Steele presented the unlikely sacrificial lamb, an example to the rest of the employees of Wilder Investments. It didn't matter that Sam wouldn't be able to find another job at a comparable salary, nor that he had two daughters in college. What mattered to Ben Wilder was his company, his wealth, his *power*. Though it had all happened years ago, Noah felt an uncomfortable wrench in his gut each time he remembered Sam's weathered face after leaving Ben's office. "It doesn't matter, boy," Sam had said fondly to Noah. "You did what you could. I'll make out."

Sheila was staring at Noah expectantly, and he quickly brought his thoughts back to the present. "That incident," he stated hurriedly, "was the final straw. By the end of the afternoon I had quit my job, yanked my kid out of school and moved to Oregon. I told myself I would never come back."

Sheila sat in the encumbering silence for a minute, watching the lines of grief still evident on Noah's masculine face while he reflected upon a part of his life she knew nothing about. She longed to hear more, to understand more fully the enigmatic man sitting across the table from her. Yet she was afraid, unsure of growing any closer to him. Already she was inexplicably drawn to him, and intuitively she realized that what he was about to tell her would only endear him to her further. Those feelings of endearment would surely only cause her suffering. She couldn't trust him. Not yet.

"You don't have to talk about any of this," she finally managed to say. "It's obviously painful for you."

"Only because I was weak."

"I…don't understand," she whispered, gripping the edge of the table for support as she lifted her eyes to meet the question in his. "And," she allowed ruefully, "I'm not sure that I want to understand you."

"You're the woman who insisted that I owed her an explanation," he reminded her.

"Not about *all* of your life."

"But I thought you wanted to get to know me."

"No…I just want to know how you're connected with Wilder Investments," she lied. She ignored the voice in her mind that was whispering, *Dear God, Noah, I don't understand it, but I want to know everything about you...touch your body and soul.* Instead she lowered her eyes. "You are in charge of the company, aren't you?"

"Temporarily, yes."

"And you do make all of the decisions for Wilder Investments."

"Unless the board disapproves. So far they haven't." The mindless members of the board wouldn't dare argue with Ben's son, Noah thought to himself.

Sheila held her breath as the truth hit her in a cold blast of logic. "Then you were lying to me when you said that you couldn't make a decision about the winery until your father got back into the country."

Noah's mouth twitched in amusement. "I prefer to think of it as stalling for time."

"We haven't got time!"

His smile broadened and his eyes lightened over the edge of his wineglass. "Lady, that's where you're wrong. We've got all the time in the world."

His gaze was warm. Though the table separated them, Sheila could feel the heat of his eyes caressing her, undressing her, bringing her body closer to his. Under the visual embrace she felt her skin begin to tremble, as if anticipating his touch. *Don't fall for him,* she warned herself. *Don't think for a minute that he cares for you. You're just a handy convenience that stumbled onto him tonight. Remember Jeff. Remember the promises. Remember the lies. Remember the pain. Don't let it happen again. Don't fall victim to the same mistake. Don't!*

Carefully she pieced together the poise that he could shatter so easily. "Perhaps we should go."

"Don't you even want to know why I'm back at Wilder Investments?" he invited.

"Do you want to tell me?"

"You deserve that much at the very least."

"And at the very most?"

"You deserve more—much more."

She waited, her nervous fingers twirling the stem of her glass. She cocked her head expectantly to one side, unconsciously displaying the curve of her throat. Why did he work for his father in a position he found so disagreeable? "I had assumed that you took command because of your father's heart attack."

"That's part of it," he conceded reluctantly. "But a very small part." She was quiet, and her silence prodded him on. "Actually, when Ben had the first attack and asked me to take over for a couple of weeks, I refused. I didn't need the headache, and I figured he would have half a dozen 'yes-men' who could more than adequately fill his shoes while he was recuperating. So I refused."

Sheila's eyebrows drew together as she tried to understand. "What changed your mind?" she asked quietly.

"The second attack. The one that put Ben in the intensive care unit for a week." Noah's fingers drummed restlessly on the table as he thought for a moment. "My father hadn't trusted anyone to run the company other than himself. When I refused to help him, he ignored the advice of his doctor and picked up where he left off."

"That's crazy," she thought aloud.

Noah shook his head. "That's getting his way. The second attack almost took his life, and when my mother pleaded with me to help him out, I agreed, but only until a replacement could be found."

"And you father didn't bother to look for one," Sheila surmised.

"Why would he? He got what he wanted."

"But surely *you* could find someone—"

"I've looked. Anyone I've suggested has been turned down by the powers that be."

"Ben."

"Exactly."

Sheila was confused. When she thought of her family and all of the love they had shared, she found it hard to imagine the cold detachment between Ben Wilder and his only son. "Surely there must be some way of solving your problem. Can't you talk to your father?"

"It doesn't do any good. Besides, that's only part of the story. I owed my father a favor—a big favor."

The uneasy feeling that had been threatening to overtake Sheila all evening caused her to shudder involuntarily. "And you're repaying him now, aren't you?"

"In my opinion, yes. You see," he continued in a flat, emotionless voice, "when my son, Sean, was born, there were problems I wasn't able to handle alone. I was too young. I was forced to ask and rely upon my father for help. He complied, and the bastard has never let me forget it."

"But what about Sean's mother?" Sheila questioned. "Certainly she could have helped if there were a problem with the child. Sean was her responsibility as well as yours."

"Marilyn?" Noah's face contorted at the irony of the suggestion and the memory of a young girl he had once thought he loved. "You don't seem to understand, Sheila. *Marilyn* was the problem, at least the most evident problem, and it took all of my father's money and power to deal with her effectively."

"I shouldn't have asked—it's none of my business," Sheila stammered, stunned by the look of bitterness and hatred on the angled planes of Noah's proud face.

"It doesn't matter anymore. Maybe it never did. Anyway, it's all a part of the past, dead and buried."

Sheila pushed herself onto unsteady legs beginning to rise from the table. "There's no reason for you to tell me all of this."

His hand reached out and captured her wrist, forcing her to stay near him. "You asked," he reminded her.

"I'm sorry. It was my mistake. Perhaps we should go."

"Before you see all of the skeletons in the Wilder closets?" he mocked.

She felt her spine become rigid. "Before I lose track of the reason I came here with you."

Her dark eyebrows lifted elegantly, and Noah thought her the most intriguingly beautiful woman he had ever met. "Am *I* coercing *you?*" she asked as her eyes dropped to her wrist, still shackled in his uncompromising grip.

"If you are, lady, it's only because I want you to," he rejoined, but the tension ebbed from his face and his hand moved slightly up her forearm, to rub the tender skin of her inner elbow. "Let's go," he suggested, helping her from the chair. His hand never left her arm as he escorted her down the stairs and into the night. He carried her coat and wrapped his arm over her shoulders to protect her from the damp breeze that still held the promise of rain.

The drive back to the Wilder estate was accomplished in silence as Noah and Sheila were individually wrapped in their own black cloaks of thought. Though separated from him in the car, Sheila felt mysteriously bound to the darkly handsome man with the knowing blue eyes. *What's he really like?* her mind teased. In the flash of an instant she had seen him ruthless and bitter, then suddenly gentle and sensitive. She sensed in him a deep, untouched private soul, and she longed to discover the most intimate reaches of his mind. What would it hurt? her taunting mind implored. What were the depths of his kindness, the limits of his nature? He'll hurt you, her bothersome consciousness objected. A man hurt you in the past, when you opened yourself up to him. Are you foolish enough to let it happen again? Just how far do you dare trust Noah Wilder, and how far can you trust yourself?

The Volvo slowed as Noah guided the car past the stone pillars at the entrance of the circular drive. The headlights splashed light on the trunks of the stately fir trees that guarded the mansion. As Ben Wilder's home came into view, Sheila pulled herself from her pensive thoughts and realized that she had accomplished nothing toward furthering her purpose. She had intended to find a way, any way, to get the insurance proceeds to rebuild the winery, and she had failed miserably. She didn't even know if Noah had the power or the desire to help her. Had the insurance company paid off Wilder Investments? The car ground to a halt as Sheila discovered her mistake. Caught in her fascination for a man she had been warned to mistrust, she had lost sight of her purpose for making the trip to Seattle.

"Would you like to come in for a drink?" Noah asked as he flicked off the engine and the silence of the night settled in the interior of the car.

"I don't think so," she whispered, trying to push aside her growing awareness of him.

"We have unfinished business."

"I know that. You've found a way to successfully dodge the subject of the winery all evening. Why?"

Noah smiled to himself. "I didn't realize that I was. Would you like to come inside and finish the discussion?"

Sheila caught her breath. "No."

"I thought you were anxious to get the insurance settlement," he replied, his eyes narrowing as he studied her in the darkness.

"I am. You know that, but I happen to know when I've been conned."

"Conned?" he repeated incredulously. "What are you talking about?"

"It was difficult to get you on the phone and when I finally did, you refused to see me with some ridiculous excuse that any decision about the winery had to be made by your father. Then you agreed to talk about it over dinner, but conveniently avoided the issue all night. Why would I think that anything's going to change? You haven't listened to me at all...."

"That's where you're wrong. I've listened to everything you've said all evening," he interrupted in a low voice.

"Then what's your decision?"

"I'll tell you that, too, if you'll join me for a drink." His hand reached for hers in the car. "Come on, Sheila. We've got the rest of the night to talk about anything you want."

Again she felt herself falling under his spell, her eyes lost in his and her fingers beginning to melt in the soft, warm pressure of his hands. "All right," she whispered, wondering why this man, this *stranger,* seemed to know everything about her. And what he didn't know, she wanted to divulge to him....

The fire in the den had grown cold, and only a few red embers remained to warm the room. Noah quickly poured them each a drink and took a long swallow of his brandy before kneeling at the fire and adding a wedge of cedar to the glowing coals. As he stood, he dusted the knees of his pants with his palms. Sheila sipped her drink and watched him, noticing the way his oxford cloth shirt stretched over his shoulders as he tended the fire and then straightened. In her mind she could picture the ripple of muscles in his back as he worked.

When Noah turned to face her, she couldn't hide the embarrassed burn of her cheeks, as if she expected him to read the wayward thoughts in her eyes.

"Can I get you anything else?" he asked, nodding toward the glass she held tightly in her hands.

"No…nothing…this is fine," she whispered.

"Good. Then why don't you sit down and tell me what you intend to do with the insurance settlement, should it be awarded you."

Sheila dropped gratefully into a wingback chair near the fire and looked Noah squarely in the eyes. "I don't expect you to hand me a blank check for a quarter of a million dollars, you know."

"Good, because I have no intention of doing anything of the kind." Sheila felt butterflies in her stomach. Was he playing with her again? His face was unreadable in the firelight.

"What I do expect, however, is that you and I mutually decide how best to rebuild Cascade Valley, hire a contractor, put the funds in escrow and start work immediately." Her gray eyes challenged him to argue with her logic.

"That, of course, is assuming that the insurance company has paid the settlement to Wilder Investments."

"Hasn't that occurred?" Sheila asked, holding her breath. Certainly by now, over a month since the fire, payment had been made.

"There's a little bit of a hitch as far as Pac-West Insurance Company is concerned."

Sheila felt herself sinking into despair. "The arson?" she guessed.

Shadows of doubt crowded Noah's deep blue eyes. "That's right. Until a culprit is discovered, the insurance company is holding tightly on to its purse strings."

Sheila blanched as the truth struck her. "You think my father had something to do with the fire…. You think he deliberately started it, don't you?" she accused in a low voice that threatened to break.

"I didn't say that."

"You *implied* it!"

"Not at all. I'm only pointing out the insurance company's position...nothing else."

"Then I'll have to talk to someone at Pac-West," Sheila said. "One of those claims adjusters, or whatever they are."

"I don't think that will do any good."

"Why not?"

His smile didn't touch his eyes. "Because, for one thing, I've already tried that. The insurance company's position is clear."

"Then what can we do?" Sheila asked herself aloud.

Noah hedged for a moment. How much could he tell her? Was she involved in the arson? Had her father been? He rubbed his thumbnail pensively over his lower lip and stared at Sheila. Why did he feel compelled to trust this beguiling woman he didn't know? As he studied the innocent yet sophisticated curve of her cheek, the slender column of her throat and the copper sheen to her thick, chestnut hair, he decided to take a gamble and trust her...just a little. His intense eyes scrutinized her reaction, watching for a flicker of doubt or fear to cross her eyes.

"What we can do is investigate the cause of the fire ourselves," he explained thoughtfully.

Her eyebrows furrowed. "How?"

"Wilder Investments has a private investigator on retainer. I've already asked him to look into it."

"Do you think that's wise? Doesn't the insurance company have investigators on its staff?"

"Of course. But this way we can speed things up a little. Unless you're opposed to the idea."

If she heard a steely edge to his words, she ignored it and dug her fingernails into the soft flesh of her palm. "I'll do anything I can to clear my father's name and get the winery going again."

"It's that important to you?" he asked, slightly skeptical. "Why?"

"Cascade Valley was my father's life, his dream, and I'm not allowing anyone or anything to take away his good name or his dreams."

"You want to carry on the Lindstrom tradition, is that it? Follow in your father's footsteps?"

"It's a matter of pride...and tradition, I suppose."

"But your father bought his interest in the winery less than twenty years ago. It's not as if Cascade Valley has been a part of your family's history," he observed, testing her reaction. How much of what she was saying was the truth? All of it? Or was she acting out a well-rehearsed scene? If so, she was one helluva convincing actress.

Sheila was instantly wary. The doubts reflected in Noah's eyes lingered and pierced her soul. "What do you mean?"

He shrugged indifferently. "Running the day-to-day operation at the winery is a hard job. You'll have to be an accountant, manager, personnel director, quality control inspector... everything to each of your employees. Why would a woman with a small child want to take on all of that responsibility?"

"For the same reasons a man would, I suppose." Her eyes lighted with defiance.

His voice was deathly quiet as he baited her. "A man might be more practical," he suggested, inviting her question.

"How's that?"

"He might consider the alternatives."

"There are none."

"I wouldn't say that. What about the option of selling out your interest in the winery for enough money to support you and your daughter comfortably?"

Sheila tried to keep her voice steady. "I doubt that anyone would be interested in buying. The economy's slow, and as you so aptly pointed out earlier, Cascade Valley has had more than its share of problems."

Noah set his empty glass on the mantel. "Perhaps I can convince the board of directors at Wilder Investments to buy out your share of the winery."

Jonas Fielding's warning echoed in Sheila's ears. Noah was offering to buy out her interest in Cascade, just as the crafty lawyer had predicted. A small part of Sheila seemed to wither and die. In her heart she had expected and hoped for more from him. In the short time she had known him, she had learned to care for him and she didn't want to let the blossoming feelings inside her twist and blacken with deceit. She couldn't be manipulated, not by Ben Wilder, nor by his son. "No," she whispered nearly inaudibly as she lifted her eyes to meet his piercing gaze. "I won't sell."

Noah saw the painful determination in the rigid set of her jaw and the unmasked despair that shadowed her eyes as she silently accused him of a crime he couldn't possibly understand. She had tensed when he had mentioned the possibility of buying out the winery, but it had only seemed logical to him. What did she expect of him...more money? But, he hadn't even named a price. "I can assure you, Sheila, that Wilder Investments would be more than generous in the offer."

Her quiet eyes turned to gray ice. "I don't doubt that, but the point is, I'm not interested in selling."

"You haven't even heard the terms."

"It doesn't matter. I won't sell," she repeated coldly. How much like the father he so vehemently denounced was Noah Wilder?

Noah shrugged before draining his glass and approaching the chair in which she was seated. "It doesn't matter to me what you do with your precious winery," he stated evenly as he bent over the chair and placed his hands on each of the silvery velvet arms, imprisoning her against the soft fabric. "I only wanted you to be aware of your options."

His voice was gentle and concerned. Sheila felt as if she had known him all her life rather than a few short hours, and she wanted to melt into his soft words. "I...understand my options," she assured him shakily.

"Do you?" His blue eyes probed deep into hers, further than any man had dared to see. "I wonder." His lips were soft as they pressed gently against her forehead, and Sheila sighed as she closed her eyelids and let her head fall backward into the soft cushions of the chair. A small, nagging voice in her mind argued that she shouldn't give in to her passions; she shouldn't let the warmth that he was inviting begin to swell within her. But the sensuous feeling of his lips against her skin, the mysterious blue intensity of his eyes, the awareness in her body that she had presumed to have died in the ashes of her broken marriage, all argued with a twinge of conscience and slowly took over her mind as well as her body.

His hands were strong as they held her chin and tipped her lips to meet his. A sizzling tremor shook her body in response when the kiss began, and she sighed deeply, parting her lips and inviting him quietly to love her. When his passion caught hold of him and he tasted the honeyed warmth of her lips, he gently pushed his tongue against her teeth and entered the moist cavern of her mouth. Her moan of pleasure sent ripples of desire hotly through his blood. His hands slid down the length of her neck and touched the fluttering pulse that was jumping in the feminine hollow of her throat. His thumbs gently outlined the delicate bone structure in slow, swirling circles of sensitivity that gathered and stormed deep within her.

Sheila heard nothing over the resounding beat of her heart fluttering in her chest and thundering in her eardrums. She thought of nothing other than the cascading warmth and desire that were washing over her body in uneven passionate waves. Feelings of longing, yearning, desires that flamed heatedly, flowed through her as Noah kissed her. Involuntarily she reached up and wound her arms around his neck. The groan of satisfaction that rumbled in his throat gave her a deep, primeval pleasure, and when he pulled his lips from hers, she knew a deep disappointment.

He looked longingly into her eyes, asking her silent, unspoken questions that demanded answers she couldn't ignore. How much did he want from her? What could she give—what would he take?

"Sheila, dear Sheila," he murmured against her hair. It was whispered as a plea. She wanted him, ached for him, but remained silent.

His persuasive lips nuzzled against the column of her throat to linger at the inviting feminine bone structure at its base. His tongue drew lazy circles around Sheila's erratic pulse, and Sheila felt as if her very soul were centered beneath his warm insistent touch. Her fingers entwined in the dark, coffee-colored strands of his hair, and she leaned backward, offering more of her neck… more of her being. When his wet tongue touched the center of her pulse, quicksilver flames darted through her veins, and she pushed herself more closely against his body.

His fingers found the buttons on her blouse, and cautiously he opened the top button. As he did so his head lowered, letting his lips caress the gaping space between the two pieces of silken cloth. Sheila moaned against him, asking for more of his gentle touch. He unbuttoned the next pearly fastener, and once more his lips dipped lower, touching her soft, warm flesh. Molten fire streamed through Sheila's veins at his expert touch and in anticipation of his next move. His hot lips seared her skin, and she was not disappointed when his fingers unhinged an even lower button, parting the soft, rose-colored fabric and exposing the gentle swell of her breasts straining achingly against the flimsy barrier of her bra. When his mouth touched the edge of her bra, outlining the lace with the moistness of his tongue, she thought the ache within her would explode. His breath fanned heatedly over her sensitive skin, and she felt her breath come in short gasps. There didn't seem to be enough air in the room to keep her senses from swimming in the whirlpool of passion moving her closer to this man she had barely met and yet known a lifetime. She was drowning in his velvet-soft caresses, losing her breath with each passing instant of his arduous lovemaking *Take me*, a voice within her wanted to scream, but the words never passed her lips.

She felt the wispy fabric of her blouse as he eased it gently past her shoulders, kissing her exposed neck and arms.

"Let me love you..." he moaned.

Her eyes, shining with a burning passion, yielded to his demands. But still the words froze in her throat.

Softly he pulled her out of the chair and gently eased her onto the carpet with the weight of his body. She felt the soft pile of the Persian rug against the bare skin of her back, and she knew that if she wanted to turn back, it would have to be soon, before all of the long-buried desire became alive again. His hands fitted warmly against her rib cage, outlining each individual bone with one of his strong, masculine fingers. A trembling sigh of submission broke from her lips.

He plunged his head between her breasts, softly imprinting his lips on the firm, white skin in the hollow. Her fingers traveled up his neck to hold his head protectively against her as one of his hands reached up to lovingly cup a breast. She took a quick intake of breath at the command of his touch. His fingers dipped seductively beneath the lace and her nipple tightened, expecting his touch.

"You're beautiful," he moaned before kissing the soft fabric of her bra and teasing the nipple bound within the gossamer confinement of lace and satin. Sheila felt her breast swell with desire and a flood of foreign, long-lost emotions raced through her blood.

Gently Noah lowered the strap over her shoulder, and her breasts spilled from their imprisonment. He groaned as he massaged first one, and then the other. Sheila thought she would melt into the carpet as he kissed his way over the hill of one of the shapely mounds before taking it firmly in his mouth and gently soothing all of the bittersweet torment from her body.

"Let me make love to you, beautiful lady," Noah whispered, quietly asking her to give in to him. "Let me make you mine," he coaxed.

In response, Sheila felt her body arching upward to meet the weight of him. Whether it was wrong or right, she wanted him as desperately as he wanted her.

"Sheila." His voice was flooded with naked passion. "Come to bed with me." Her only response was to moan softly against him.

Slowly he raised his head to stare into the depths of her desirous gray eyes. The red embers from the fire darkened his masculine features, making them seem harsher, more defined and angular in the bloodred shadows of the dimly lit room. His eyes never left hers, and they smoldered with a blue flame of passion that he was boldly attempting to hold at bay.

"Tell me you want me," he persuaded in a raspy, breathless voice.

Her dark brows pulled together in frustration and confusion. Why was he pulling away from her? Of course she wanted him, needed him, longed to be a part of him. Couldn't he *feel* the desperate intensity of her yearning?

"Tell me!" he again demanded, this time more roughly than before. Her eyes were shadowed; was there a flicker of doubt, a seed of mistrust in their misty gray depths? He had to know.

"What do you want from me?" she asked, trying to control her ragged breathing and erratic heartbeat. Had she misread him? Suddenly she was painfully aware of her partially nude condition, and the fact that he was *asking* rather than *taking* from her.

"I want to know that you feel what I'm feeling!"

"I…I don't understand."

His fingers, once gentle, tightened against the soft flesh of her upper arms and held her prisoner against the carpet. As he studied the elegant lines of her face, his eyes narrowed in suspicion. Never had he been so impulsive, so rash, when it came to a woman. Why did this woman bewitch him so? Why did she make him feel more alive than he had in years? Was it the provocative turn of her chin, the light that danced in her eyes, the fresh scent of her hair? Why was he taken in by her beauty, which was in the same instant innocent and seductive? For the last sixteen years of his life he had cautiously avoided any commitment that might recreate the scene that had scattered his life in chaos. He had been careful, never foolhardy enough to fall for a woman again. But now, as he stared into Sheila's wide, silver-colored eyes, he felt himself slipping into the same black abyss that had thrown his life into disorder long ago. Not since Marilyn had he allowed himself the luxury of becoming enraptured by a woman. And if he had been truthful, none he had met had deeply interested him. But tonight was different. Damn it, he was beginning to care for Sheila Lindstrom, though he knew little of her and couldn't begin to understand her motives. How far could he trust such a lovely, bewitching creature as the woman lying desirously in his arms?

Noah's death grip on Sheila relaxed. "I want you," he said simply in a hoarse voice that admitted what he had felt from the first moment she had appeared on his doorstep.

"I know." She sighed. She crossed her arms over her breasts, as if to shield herself from the truth. But her eyes met Noah's unwaveringly. "I want you, too," she conceded huskily.

The silence in the room was their only barrier, and yet Noah hesitated. "That's not enough," he admitted, wiping the sweat that had begun to bead on his upper lip. "There has to be more."

Sheila shook her head slowly in confusion, and the sweep of her hair captured red-gold highlights from the flames. Try as she would, she couldn't understand him. What was he saying? Was he rejecting her? Why? What had she done?

Noah witnessed the apprehension and agony in Sheila's eyes and regretted that he was a part of her pain. He wanted to comfort her, to explain the reasons for his reservation, but was unable. How could he expect her to understand that he had loved a woman once in the past and that that love had been callously and bitterly sold to the highest bidder? Was it possible for Sheila to see what Marilyn had done to him when the bitch had put a price on her illegitimate son's head when Sean was born? Was it fair for Noah to burden Sheila with the guilt and agony he had suffered because of his love for his child? No! Though he wanted to trust her, he couldn't tell her about the part of his life he had shoved into a dark, locked corner of his mind. Instead, he took an easier, less painful avenue. "I get the feeling that you think I'm rushing things," he whispered as he pressed a soft kiss against her hair.

She smiled wistfully and blushed. "It's not your fault...I could have stopped you...I didn't want to."

"Don't blame yourself," he murmured quietly.

In the thickening silence, Sheila could sense Noah struggling with an inner battle, resisting the tide of passion that was pushing against him. She reached for her blouse, hoping to pull it back onto her body so she could leave this house... this man before he ignited the passions in her blood and she was once again filled with liquid fire. If possible she hoped to leave the quiet room and seductively intense man with whatever shreds of dignity she could muster.

"Wait!" he commanded as he realized she was preparing to leave. His broad hand grabbed her wrist, and the silken blouse once again fell to the floor.

Sheila felt her temper begin to flare, and the tears that had been threatening to spill burned in her throat. She was tired, and it had been a long, fruitless evening. She had accomplished nothing she had intended to do, and now she wasn't sure if she was capable of working with Ben Wilder or his son. Too many emotions had come and gone with the intimate evening, too many secrets divulged. And yet, despite the growing sense of intimacy she felt with Noah, she knew there were deep, abysmal misconceptions that she couldn't possibly bridge. "What, Noah?" she asked in a tense, raw whisper. "What do you want from me? All night long I've been on the receiving end of conflicting emotions." Her breath was coming in short, uneven gasps. Tears threatened to spill. "One minute you want me and the next...you don't. Just let me go home, for God's sake!"

"You're wrong!"

"I doubt that!" She pulled her hand free of the gentle manacle of his grip, scooted silently away from him, snatched up the blouse and quickly stretched her arms through the sleeves. Her fingers fumbled with the buttons, so intent was she on getting out of the house as rapidly as possible...away from the magnetism of his eyes...away from the charm of his dimpled, slightly off-center smile...away from the warm persuasion of his hands....

Noah dragged himself into a sitting position before standing up and leaning against the warm stones of the fireplace. He let his forehead fall into the palm of his hand as he tried to think things out rationally. The entire scene was out of character for him. What the devil had he done, seducing this woman he had barely met? Why was she so responsive to his touch? He knew instinctively that she wasn't the type of woman who fell neatly into a stranger's arms at the drop of a hat, and yet she was here, in his home, warm, inviting, yielding to the gentle coaxing of his caresses. His mouth pulled into a grim frown. How did he let himself get mixed up with her...whoever she was? And what were her motives? "Don't go," he said unevenly, turning to face her.

She had managed to get dressed and was putting on her raincoat. She paused for only a second before hiking the coat over her shoulders and unsteadily tying the belt. "I think it would be best."

"I want you to stay, here, tonight, with me."

Sheila took in a long, steadying breath. "I can't."

"Why not?"

"I don't know you well enough."

"But if you don't stay, how will you ever...'know me well enough'?" he countered. He stood away from her, not touching her. It was her mind he wanted, as well as her body.

"I need time...." she whispered, beginning to waver. She had to get out, away from him. Soon, before it was too late.

He took a step toward her. "We're both adults. It's not as if this would be a first for either of us. You have a daughter and I have a son."

She paused, but only slightly. "That doesn't change things. Look, Noah, you know as well as I that I would like to fall into bed and sleep with you. But...I just can't...." She blushed in her confusion. "I can't just hop into bed with any man I find attractive.... Oh, this is coming out all wrong." She took a deep breath and lifted her eyes to meet his. They were steady and strong, though tears had begun to pool in their gray-blue depths. "What I'm trying to say," she managed bravely, "is that I don't have casual affairs."

"I know that."

"You don't understand. I've never slept with any man, other...other than Jeff."

"Your ex-husband," Noah surmised with a tightening of his jaw.

Sheila nodded.

"It doesn't matter," Noah said with a shrug.

"Of course it does. Don't you see? I almost tumbled into bed with you...on the first night I'd met you. That's not like me, not at all... I don't even know you."

His scowl lifted, and an amused light danced in his eyes. "I think you know me better than you're willing to admit."

"I'd like to," she conceded.

"But?"

It was her turn to smile. "I'm afraid, I guess."

"That I won't live up to your expectations?"

"Partially."

"What else?"

"That I won't live up to yours."

Chapter 5

Noah took a step toward her, leaving only inches to separate their bodies. "I doubt that you would ever disappoint me," he whispered. His fingers softly traced the line of her jaw and then continued on a downward path past her neck to rest at the top button of her coat. Easily it slipped through the buttonhole.

Sheila sucked in her breath as Noah took each button in turn. When he reached her belt, he worked on the knot with both of his hands. Sheila felt fires of expectation dance within her while his incredibly blue eyes held hers in a passionate embrace.

The coat parted. Noah's hands moved beneath it and found her breasts. A small sigh came unexpectedly from her lips, and Sheila knew that she wanted Noah more desperately than she had ever wanted any man. It had been so long since she had been held in a man's embrace. As Noah's thumbs began drawing delicious circles against the sheer fabric of her blouse, Sheila told herself that he was different from Jeff. He wouldn't hurt her. He *cared*.

The soft coaxing of Noah's fingertips made Sheila weak

with longing. She leaned against him, tilted her head and parted her lips in silent invitation. Warm lips claimed hers and Noah's arms encircled her, crushing her against him. His tongue probed into her mouth to find its mate and touch her more intimately. Sheila wanted more of this mysterious man.

When he guided her to the floor, it was her hands that parted his shirt and touched the tense, hard muscles of his chest. It was her lips that kissed his eyes as he undressed her. She felt the warmth of his hands as each article of her clothing was silently removed.

It felt so good to touch him. Her fingers traced the outline of each of his muscles on his back and crept seductively down the length of his spine. When her fingertips touched the waistband of his pants, she hesitated. How much would he expect from her—how much did he want?

"Undress me," he persuaded, his eyes closing and his breath becoming shallow. "Please, Sheila, undress me."

She couldn't resist. He groaned as she unclasped the belt and gently pushed his pants over his hips. She stopped when she encountered his briefs.

"Take them off," he commanded, guiding her hand to the elastic band of his shorts. She paused, and he read the uncertainty in her eyes. He smiled wickedly to himself.

Slowly his hands moved over her breasts, massaging each white globe until the rosy tip hardened with desire. He teased her with the soft, whispering play of his fingers against her skin. "You're exquisite," he whispered as his head bent and his tongue touched the tip of her breast, leaving a moist droplet of dew on the nipple.

Sheila moaned in pleasure as the cold air touched the wet nipple, and she once again craved the sweet pressure of his mouth against her skin. As if to comply, he again lowered his head and ran his tongue over the soft hills of her breasts, lingering only long enough over her nipples to warm and then leave them.

Sheila felt a hot, molten coil begin to unwind within her and race like liquid fire through her veins. His kisses touched her breasts and then lowered to caress the soft skin of her abdomen. Lazily his tongue rimmed her navel, and Sheila felt her hips shift upward, pressing against his chest, demanding more from him.

"Please," she whispered hoarsely.

Noah was trying to control himself, to give as well as get pleasure. He was vainly fighting a losing battle with his passion. The last thing he wanted to do was come on like some horny college kid. Already, though he couldn't explain it, Sheila was important to him, and he wanted to please her. It had been difficult, but he had restrained himself to the point where he thought he would burst from the aching frustration in his loins.

Sheila's eyes reached for his, begging him to end her torture and take her. He could resist no longer. He slipped out of his shorts and lay beside her. The length of his body was pressed against hers, and his need for her was unhidden.

"I want to love you, Sheila," he whispered into her ear, while his hands cupped and stroked her breast.

"Yes."

"I want to make love to you and never stop...."

She sighed her willingness. She could feel his breath on the back of her neck and the musky smell of brandy mingled with the scent of burning moss. Everything about the night seemed so right. She moved her legs and parted his. A strong, masculine hand pressed against her abdomen and forced her more intimately against him. Her body seemed to mold against his. It was as if she could feel each part of him, and she had to have more.

His hands moved leisurely up and down the length of her body, touching her breasts softly with his fingertips and then pressing a moist palm to her inner thighs with rough, demanding pressure. Involuntarily her legs parted, and she felt the heated moisture of his lips as he kissed each vertebra of her spine. Sharp, heated needles of desire pierced her when at last he gently rolled her onto her back and positioned himself above her.

Beads of sweat moistened his upper lip and forehead. His dark brow was furrowed, as if he were fighting an inner turmoil. The fire's glow gave his skin a burnished tint and his blue eyes had deepened to inky black. In a ragged breath, with more control than he had thought possible, he whispered, "Sheila, are you sure that this is what you want?" He grimaced, as if in pain, against a possible rejection.

She wrapped her arms around his chest and pulled him down upon her. Her breasts flattened with the weight of his torso. "I'm sure," she returned, caught up in the raw passion of the night.

With a growl of satisfaction he parted her legs with his knees and came to her to find that she was as ready as he. Never had he felt so desperate with need of a woman—not just any woman, but *this* woman with the mysterious gray eyes and the softly curving, voluptuous mouth. This woman with the vibrant chestnut hair that caught the reflection of the fire's glow and framed an intelligent, evenly featured face. As he moved with her, attempting to withhold the violent burst of energy within him, he found himself falling more desperately under her bewitching spell. What was happening to him?

Sheila moaned beneath him, and the tension mounting steadily within him threatened to explode. He didn't care who she was, he had to have her. With a sudden rush of heat, he ignited into a flame that consumed the both of them. Sheila's answering shudder told him that she, too, had felt the ultimate consummation.

He lay upon her, continuing to kiss her cheeks while running his fingers through her hair. She looked at him through eyes still shining in afterglow. "Oh, Noah," she sighed contentedly.

"Shhh…." He placed his finger to her lips to quiet her and reached behind him to pull a knitted afghan off the couch. Still holding her in his arms, he wrapped the soft blanket over their bodies. "Don't say anything," he whispered quietly.

Sheila wanted to stay with him. It was so warm and comfortable in the shelter of his arms. But as the afterglow faded and the reality of what she had done hit her, she was horrified. A deep crimson flush climbed steadily up her throat. What was she doing lying naked with a man she had only met a few hours earlier? What had happened to her common sense? It was true that Noah had surprised her with his commanding masculinity and seductive blue eyes, but that was no excuse for making love to him. It wasn't that she hadn't enjoyed it—quite the opposite. The passion that had risen in her was wilder than she had ever imagined, and even now she could feel her body stirring with traitorous longings at the nearness of this enigmatic man. She tried to loosen herself from the strength of his embrace.

"What are you doing?" he asked.

"I think I'd better leave."

"Why?"

"This is all wrong," she began, trying to slide away from him. His fingers clamped over her shoulders.

"This could *never* be *wrong*." The afghan slipped, exposing one swollen breast. He kissed the soft, ripe mound.

Sheila trembled at his touch. "Don't," she pleaded.

"Why not?" His rich voice had taken on a rough tone.

"I've got to go."

"Don't leave."

She pushed her palms against his chest. "Noah... please...."

"Please what?"

"Please let me go."

"Later."

"Now!" Her voice quivered, and she felt tears of frustration burning in her throat. She longed to stay with him, feel his weight upon her, fall victim to his lovemaking. But she couldn't.

"We have the rest of the night."

"No...no, we don't," she said waveringly. Her gray eyes lifted to his and begged him to understand.

Slowly he released her and ran his fingers through his unruly hair. "What is this, some latent Victorian morality?"

"Of course not."

"Then I don't understand."

"Neither do I, not really." She pulled the afghan over the exposed breast, feeling a little less vulnerable under the soft covering.

"Sheila." His finger reached out and carefully raised her chin so she could meet his confused gaze. "We're in the 1980s."

"I know."

"But?"

"I just need time, that's all," she blurted out. How could she possibly explain her confused jumble of emotions. He was so close. She had only to stretch her hand and touch him to reignite the fires of desire. She shuddered and reached for her clothes.

"How much time?"

"I don't know... I don't understand any of this."

"Don't try."

Sheila closed her eyes and took a deep breath, hoping to clear her mind. "Look, Noah. I don't even know you, and I'm really not sure that I *want* to know you this well."

"Why not?" he persisted.

She struggled into her blouse. "You and I, whether we like it or not, are business partners."

"Don't give me any of that sanctimonious and overused line about not mixing business and pleasure."

"I don't think of sex as pleasure!"

An interested black eyebrow cocked mockingly. "You're not going to try and convince me that you didn't enjoy yourself."

"No."

"Good, because I wouldn't believe you. Now, what's this all about?"

"When I said that I don't consider sex to be pleasurable, I meant *merely* pleasurable. Of course I enjoyed making love with you; I'd be a fool to try and deny it. The point is, I don't go in for 'casual sex' for the sake of pleasure...or any other reason."

"And you think that I do?"

"I don't know."

"Sure you do," he replied seductively. "I'm willing to bet that you know more about me than you're admitting."

"That's no excuse for hopping into bed with you."

"You don't need an excuse, Sheila. Just stay with me tonight. Do it because you want to."

"I can't." She had managed to pull on all of her clothes and stand upright. Noah didn't move. He sat before the fire, his chin resting on his knees, but his eyes never let go of hers.

"Do whatever it is that you think you must," he whispered.

Sheila swallowed a lump that had been forming in her throat. She pulled on her raincoat and wondered if she was making the biggest mistake of her life. "Goodbye, Noah," she murmured. "I'll...I'll talk to you later...." She ran out of the

house before he could answer and before she could change
her mind.

Noah waited and listened to the sounds of her leaving. The
front door closed, and a car engine coughed before catching
and fading into the night. When he realized that Sheila wasn't
coming back, he straightened and pulled on his pants. He was
more disturbed by his reaction to her than anything else. How
could she have so easily gotten under his skin? Had all of the
pressures of the office made him such an easy prey to a beautiful woman? There had to be more to it than met the eye. Why
had she so easily responded to his touch? What the hell did she
want from him—certainly more than a quick one-night stand.
Or did she? He had thought that she had been hinting that
she wanted out of the partnership with Wilder Investments.
But when he had suggested buying her out, she had seemed
indignant, as if she had already anticipated his offer and was
more than ready to discard it before hearing the exact price.

Noah's clear blue eyes clouded with suspicion. Without
thinking, he reached for the brandy bottle and poured himself
a drink. He took a long swallow before swirling the amber liquor in the glass and staring into the glowing coals. What was
Sheila Lindstrom's game?

Disregarding the fact that it was after two in the morning,
Noah walked over to the desk and picked up the telephone.
He looked up a number and with only a second's hesitation
dialed it. Several moments and nine rings later a groggy voice
mumbled an indistinct greeting.

"Simmons?" Noah questioned curtly. "This is Noah
Wilder."

There was a weighty pause on the other end of the line.
Noah could imagine the look of astonishment crossing the detective's boyish face. "Something I can do for you?" Simmons

asked cautiously. He hadn't dealt much with Ben Wilder's son, especially not in the middle of the night. Something was up.

"I want a report on the Cascade Valley Winery fire."

"I'm working on it."

Noah interrupted. "Then it's not complete?" he asked sternly.

"Not quite."

"Why not?"

The wheels in Simmons's mind began to turn. Wilder was agitated and angry. Why? "It's taken a little longer than expected."

"I need it now," Noah rejoined. His words were tainted with mistrust; Anthony Simmons could feel the suspicion that hung on the telephone line.

"I can have a preliminary report on your desk tomorrow afternoon," he suggested smoothly.

"And the final?"

"That will take a little longer."

"How much longer?"

"A week or two I'd guess," Simmons responded evasively.

"I can't wait that long! What's the hang-up?" Noah inquired. He waited for the slick excuses, but they didn't come.

"I'd like some time to check out the winery myself. You know, look for a few skeletons hanging in some locked closets...."

Noah debated. He didn't like the thought of Anthony Simmons being in such close proximity to Sheila. He had never completely trusted his father's private detective. However, he saw no other recourse; Noah needed information—and fast. Anthony Simmons could get it for him. "All right," Noah heard himself saying, "go to the winery and see what you can find out. Tell the manager, her name is Sheila Lindstrom, that you work for Wilder Investments and that you're trying to speed up the arson investigation in order to get the insurance money."

Simmons was hastily scratching notes on a small white pad on the nightstand. It had been some time since he had pocketed expense money from Wilder Investments and the thought of it warmed his blood. "Is there anything special you want on this Lindstrom woman?" he asked routinely. The moment of hesitation in Noah's response caught his attention. He had been trained to read people, be it in person, from a distance or over the phone. The slight hesitation in Noah's response triggered Simmons's suspicious instincts. There was more here than met the eye.

"Yes, of course," Noah said with more determination than he felt. "Anything you might find out about Miss Lindstrom or any of the employees could be useful."

"Right," Simmons agreed, making a special note to himself about the manager of the winery. He hadn't missed the interest in Noah's voice.

"Then I'll expect a full report in a week."

"You'll have it." With his final words Anthony Simmons disconnected the call and smiled wickedly to himself. For the first time in quite a few years he smelled money—lots of money.

When Noah hung up the telephone, he had an uneasy feeling in the pit of his stomach. Simmons had been too accommodating, too confidently obliging; so unlike the Anthony Simmons Noah had dealt with in the past. His hand hesitated over the receiver as he thought fleetingly of redialing Simmons's number and pulling him off the case. Why did he feel that his final directive to Simmons was somehow dangerous?

Noah shook his head, walked away from the desk and finished his drink in one long swallow. He was beginning to get paranoid. Ever since he had laid eyes on Sheila Lindstrom, he had been acting irrationally. Whether she had intended it or not, Sheila Lindstrom was beginning to unbalance him. The corners of Noah's mouth tightened, and after forcing all thoughts of the intimate evening aside, he walked out of the den and began to mount the stairs. There wasn't much of the night left, but he had to try and get some rest; tomorrow promised to be another battle with his son. Also, Anthony Simmons had promised the preliminary report on the fire. For some reason that Noah couldn't quite name, he felt an impending sense of dread.

Sheila drove as if the devil himself were on her tail. She had checked out of the Seattle hotel without really understanding her motives. All she knew was that she had to get away from this city, the city Noah Wilder called home. The feelings he had stirred in her had blossomed so naturally in the warm embrace of his arms. But now, as she drove through the pelting rain, a cold despair began to settle over her. Why had she fallen such an easy victim to Noah's charm? Why did she still taste the lingering flavor of brandy on her lips where he had kissed her? Unconsciously her tongue rimmed her lips, and she could almost feel the power of his impassioned kiss.

Wrapped in her clouded thoughts, Sheila took the next corner too quickly. The tires skidded on the wet pavement and the car swung into the oncoming lane. Severe headlights bore down upon her, and she was forced to swerve back onto her side of the road. By the time the oncoming car had managed to get around her, Sheila's heart was hammering in her ears. She had never been a careless driver, but tonight she couldn't seem to concentrate on the rain-washed highway winding through the dark mountains. "Dear God," she whispered in prayer as she clutched the steering wheel more tightly and realized that her palms were damp. Was it from the near collision—or the man who had played havoc with her senses?

Why did she feel as if she were walking a thin line with Noah? It was dangerous to become involved with anyone working for Wilder Investments. Jonas Fielding's fatherly voice echoed in her mind, reissuing the warning he had given Sheila in his office: "I wouldn't trust Ben Wilder as far as I could throw him.... *I'd hate to see you fleeced by him or that son of his.*" No, she argued with herself, Noah wouldn't cheat me...he couldn't! But hadn't he offered to buy out her portion of the winery, just as Jonas Fielding had warned?

The headache that had been threatening all day began to throb at the base of her skull. She attempted to concentrate on the thin white line in the center of the road, and managed to slow the pace of the car to a safer speed. It had been a long, strained day and Sheila was dog-tired by the time she crossed the Cascades.

Dawn was beginning to cast irregular purple shadows over the valley as Sheila drove down the final hills surrounding the small town of Devin. Located west of Yakima, it was hardly more than a fork in the road. Originally just a general store, the small hamlet had grown slowly and taken on the family name of the owners of the combined hardware, grocery and sporting goods store. That was years in the past, and by the 1980s, several shops lined the two streets that intersected near the original Devin store. Buildings, some eighty years old, complete with false wood facades, stood next to more recent postwar concrete structures. It wasn't a particularly beautiful town, but it was a friendly, comfortable place to live and a welcome sight to Sheila's weary eyes. She had only left Devin yesterday, but it seemed like a lifetime.

The outskirts of the town were beautifully tended farmlands. Softly rolling hills covered in sweet-smelling new hay gave the air a fresh, wholesome scent. Sheila rolled down the window of the car and let the wind stream past her face to revive her. Her dark hair billowed behind her, and despite the weariness of her bones, Sheila was forced to smile. With the rising sun, her problems seemed to shrink and fade.

The compact wagon rounded a final bend in the road before starting the slow, steady climb up the hill to the winery. From the gates the winery looked as proudly welcoming as ever. The main building was the most prominent, and could be seen from the drive. It had been designed with a distinctly European flair. French château architecture, two storied and elegantly grand, was complete with stucco walls painted a light dove gray. Narrow-paned windows, graced with French blue shutters, were the full two stories in height, and the broad double doors gleamed in the early morning sunshine. With the stately, snow-laden Cascade Mountains as a backdrop, the parklike grounds of the winery gave the impression of wealth and sedate charm.

If only the truth were known, Sheila thought wryly to herself as she unlocked the rear door of the wagon and extricated her suitcase. It was fortunate, for appearance's sake, that the portion of the winery destroyed by the fire wasn't visible from the road. Sheila placed her luggage on the front porch and strolled lazily past the rose garden to the rear of the main buildings. She picked a single peach-colored blossom and held it to her nose. How long ago had her father planted this particular rosebush? One year? Fifteen? She couldn't remember. Each spring he had planted another variety to add to the abundance of the garden.

Sheila looked at the imposing buildings and meticulously tended grounds that supported the winery. All of the years Oliver Lindstrom had put into the operation of Cascade Valley seemed to slowly pass through her thoughts. He had worked so hard to make the Cascade Valley label nationally known and recognized. Sheila rubbed her palm over her forehead, and her shoulders slumped with a renewed sense of grief for her father. The guilt she bore took hold of her as she silently vowed to find a way for Cascade Valley once again to begin producing the finest wines in the Northwest. She couldn't hide from the fact that it was her fault her father had taken out the loans from Ben Wilder in the first place. If she hadn't needed money after her divorce from Jeff, maybe Oliver Lindstrom wouldn't have needed to borrow the money, maybe he wouldn't have felt so trapped, *maybe he would be alive today.*

Don't think that way, she chastised herself. She again smelled the brilliant peach-hued blossom and tried to shake her thoughts back to a viable solution to her problem. It was impossible; her thoughts were too dark and black, and for a fleeting moment she wondered if perhaps her father did start the fire.

She didn't answer the question and hurried to the back of the buildings. The charred west wing of the manor house, a black skeleton of sagging timbers, was still roped off. A garish sign with bold red letters was nailed to one of the surrounding pine trees. It stated, quite unequivocally, that there was no trespassing allowed, by order of the sheriff's department for the county. *Suspected Crime Area* the sign pronounced boldly, and Sheila's heart cringed at the meaning of the words. The sign, an intruder on her father's personal life, increased the fires of determination burning within Sheila's heart. No one, including Noah Wilder, would take away her father's dream; not if she could help it.

At the thought of Noah, Sheila felt suddenly empty and hollow. As crazy as it sounded, she felt she had left part of herself in the warm den of the stone mansion high on the shores of Lake Washington. The vague thought that she might be falling in love with Noah Wilder flitted through her mind, but she resolutely pushed it away. What she felt for the man was sexual attraction, physical chemistry, that was all. Sheila was too much of a realist to consider falling in "love at first sight." The Cinderella story just never came true. The one love she had experienced had turned sour, and her marriage had become a dismal, humiliating sham. That feeling of love she had foolishly convinced herself she shared with Jeff Coleridge had taken months to grow. But, fortunately, not so long to die, she added ironically to herself.

She kicked a small stone on the flagstone path that led from the garden. There was no way she could be falling in love with Noah Wilder. It was ludicrous even to consider another side to the coin. She had met him only hours earlier in particularly seductive surroundings. She knew virtually nothing about him, except that he was perhaps the most magnetically powerful man she had ever laid eyes on. But what was it that made him tick? Yes, he was mysterious and alluring, but to try and call purely sexual attraction love was sheer folly, at least in Sheila's pragmatic estimation. Too many women fell into that vicious trap.

Sheila knew herself well enough to understand her guilt. Because of her uncharacteristic display of passion in the early hours of the morning, her subconscious was trying to soothe her by substituting love for lust. But Sheila wouldn't allow herself that leisure. To consider what had happened in the Wilder mansion an act of love was pure fantasy, and the easy way out—merely an appropriate, if false, excuse.

Sheila sighed to herself as she closed the garden gate. The problem was that there was no way she could avoid Noah Wilder or his enigmatic blue eyes. How could she hope to reopen the winery without his help? Unless his father came back to Seattle to take command of Wilder Investments, she was stuck with Noah. Just at the thought of seeing him again, her pulse began to race. Realistically she attempted to find an alternate solution to her problem, but found no way out of the inevitable conclusion: No one would lend her enough money to buy out Ben Wilder's interest in Cascade Valley. And even if she were lucky enough to get another mortgage on the property, Wilder Investments was unlikely to sell.

Before opening the back door to the undamaged portion of the château, she took one final look at the blackened west wing. "There's got to be a way to save it," she muttered to herself before hurrying inside the house and letting the screen door slam behind her.

Chapter 6

The following Tuesday evening Sheila decided once again to attempt to assess the damage to the west wing of the manor building and try and come up with a temporary solution to the disrepair. She had spent the entire weekend and the last two evenings cleaning up that portion of the rubble that was not considered evidence in the ongoing police investigation. And yet, for all her efforts, the entire west wing was in shambles.

The late afternoon sun cast dark shadows on the charred walls of the château that had housed the commercial end of the winery. The living quarters, attached by a covered portico, hadn't been severely damaged. Sheila looked at the building apprehensively. What would it take to save it? Though parts of the grayish stucco walls had blackened, the elegance of the architecture remained. Several panes from the narrow windows had shattered from the intensity of the heat and a couple of the cobalt-blue shutters hung at precarious angles from their original placement adorning the windows. But the walls of the building had remained intact, and even the gently sloping roof hadn't sustained too much damage.

Sheila sighed deeply to herself. Daylight was fading, she had final term papers to grade, and she had to get Emily into bed. Right now she couldn't spend any more time working on the winery.

"Emily," she called in the direction of the duck pond, "come on, let's get ready for bed."

Emily emerged from a stand of trees near the edge of the pond and reluctantly obeyed her mother. When she was within shouting distance, she began to voice her disapproval. "Already? It's not even nine o'clock."

"I didn't say you had to go to bed; I asked you to get ready," Sheila pointed out.

Emily's large green eyes brightened. "Then I can stay up?"

Sheila smiled. "For a little while. Right now, why don't you take a shower and I'll fix us some popcorn."

"Let's watch the movie," Emily suggested.

"I don't think so—not tonight. You still have school for another week."

"But next week, when school's out, I can stay up and watch the movie?"

"Why not?" Sheila agreed, fondly rumpling Emily's dark auburn curls.

"Great." Emily ran up the steps and flew through the front door leaving Sheila to wish that she had only half the energy of her eight-year-old daughter. From the exhausting work of the past few days, every muscle in Sheila's body rebelled. She hadn't realized what a soft job she had; teaching accounting to college students didn't entail much physical exercise.

Sounds of running water greeted her when she finally got inside the house. She and Emily were "temporarily" camping out in the lower level of the house. It was the least damaged. Sheila wondered how long this temporary condition would continue. She had used some of her small savings to have the electricity reconnected and the plumbing repaired, but as to the rest of the house, she was still waiting for the insurance settlement. Fortunately she did have a few dollars left in the savings account, but she was steadfastly holding on to them. After paying the expenses of Oliver's funeral she had less than a thousand dollars in the bank and hoped to stretch it as far as possible. With the coming of summer, she was out of a job until school started in the fall.

The interior of the château had suffered from the fire. As Sheila walked through what had been the living room toward the kitchen, she tried to ignore the smoke-laden lace draperies and the fragile linen wallpaper that had been water stained. Several of the broken windows were now boarded, and a fine, gritty layer of ash still covered all of the elegant European antiques and the expensive burgundy carpet. No amount of vacuuming seemed to lift the soot from the interior of the manor.

The kitchen was in better shape. Sheila had taken the time to scrub it down with disinfectant before painting all of the walls. Even the countertop had been repaired, as the heat of the blaze had loosened the glue and caused it to buckle. The hot corn was just beginning to pop when Emily hurried into the kitchen. She was still soaked and attempting to put her wet arms and legs through the appropriate holes in her pajamas.

"It's easier if you dry yourself off first," Sheila reminded her daughter.

"Aw...Mom..." Emily's head poked through the soft flannel material, and her face, still rosy from the warm jets of shower spray, broke into a smile. "It's just about ready, isn't it?" she asked, running over to the popping corn.

"In a minute."

Emily stood on first one foot and then the other, eyeballing the kernels as they exploded in the hot-air popper.

"What were you doing down at the duck pond for so long?" Sheila asked.

"Talking.... I think it's done now."

Sheila looked up from the pan of butter on the stove. "Talking? To whom? Did Joey come over?"

"Naw... Joey couldn't come over...too much homework. Come on; let's put the butter on the popcorn."

Sheila's dark brows came together. "If it wasn't Joey, who were you talking to?"

Emily shrugged. "A man."

"*A man?* What man? Was it Joey's dad?" Sheila studied her young daughter intently, but Emily didn't seem to notice. She was too engrossed in fixing a bowl of her favorite snack.

"If it was Joey's dad, I would have told you.... It was just some guy."

Sheila could feel her face drain of color. "What guy?"

"Don't know his name." Emily replied with all the matter-of-factness of a confident eight-year-old.

Sheila attempted to sound calm, but the thought of a stranger talking to her young daughter made her quiver inside. "Surely it was someone you know...maybe someone you met in town...."

Emily shook her dark, wet curls. "Nope." She began to attack the bowl of popcorn without another thought to the stranger.

Sheila didn't want to frighten her daughter. Emily had grown up in a small, Northwest town where there were few strangers and nearly everyone knew each other on a first-name basis. "What did the man want to talk about?" she asked, pretending interest in the dishes.

"Oh, you know, all about the fire...the same old thing."

Sheila felt herself relax. "Oh, so a deputy from the sher-

iff's department came by.... He should have stopped at the
house first."

"Wasn't a policeman or a deputy."

Once again Sheila's nerves tightened. She turned from the
sink and sat in a chair opposite Emily's. "The man was a complete stranger, right?"

"Um-hum."

"Not a policeman?"

"I told you that already!"

"But maybe he was a detective? They don't always wear
uniforms."

Emily sighed, and with a concern greater than her few years,
looked at her mother. "Is something wrong?"

"Probably not...I just don't like the idea of you talking to
strangers. From now on you stick a little closer to the house."

"I don't think he would hurt me...if that's what you're
afraid of."

"You don't know that."

"But I like to go down to the duck pond."

"I know you do, sweetheart," Sheila said with more confidence than she actually felt, "but from now on I want to go
with you."

"You're afraid of something, aren't you?" Emily charged,
her innocent green eyes searching her mother's worried face.

"Not really," Sheila lied. It wouldn't help matters to scare
Emily, but the child had to learn to be more cautious. "But
sometimes...it's better not to talk to strangers. You know that,
don't you? From now on, if you see anyone you don't know
hanging around, you come and tell me, before you talk to
them, okay? No one should be on the property while the winery's shut down, so if someone comes, I want to know it immediately. Fair enough?"

"I guess so."

"Then you do understand why I don't want you to wander off too far from the house when you're alone?"

Emily nodded gravely. Sheila's message had gotten through.

"Good!" Sheila said, attempting to display a lighthearted enthusiasm she didn't feel. "We'll go feed the ducks together tomorrow. It will be lots of fun." Somehow she managed a confident smile for her daughter.

Emily continued to nibble at the popcorn while leafing through a math textbook. Sheila got up to clear the dinner dishes and turned on the radio to cover the sudden silence. Nightfall was imminent, and the lengthening shadows made Sheila nervous. She had always loved warm summer nights in the foothills of the Cascades, but tonight was different. She felt alone and vulnerable. The nearest house was over a mile away, and for the first time in her life the remote location of the winery put her on edge. A stranger had been lurking on the property, talking to her child. Why? Who was the man and what did he want from Emily? Information on the fire? Unlikely. Sheila let her gaze wander out the window and she squinted into the dusky twilight. She attempted to tell herself that the man was probably just an interested tourist who wondered why the daily tours of the winery had been suspended. But if that were so, certainly he would have come up to the main building. The entire incident put Sheila's nerves on edge.

That night, before going to her room, Sheila checked the bolts on all of the doors and windows of the house. When she finally got to bed, even though her tired body ached for sleep, it didn't come. Instead she found herself staring at the luminous dial of the clock radio and listening to the soft sounds of the early summer night. Everything sounded the same. Why then was she so nervous and tense?

Lack of sleep from the previous night made Wednesday unusually tedious. The lengthy hours of teaching distracted students coupled with the forty-five minute drive from the community college seemed more tiresome than it usually was. Thank goodness there were only a few final days of the school year left. Next week was finals week, and after that Sheila could concentrate on the reopening of the winery. By the end of the summer the harvest season would be upon her.

Emily stayed with a friend after school. Since Oliver Lindstrom's death, Sheila hadn't allowed her daughter to stay at home after school because Emily would be alone. In light of the events the day before with the stranger, Sheila was more grateful than ever that she could trust Emily with Carol Dunbar, the mother of Emily's best friend, Joey. Emily was waiting for her when Sheila arrived, and after a quick stop at the market, mother and daughter finally headed home.

Sheila had contemplated calling the police about the trespasser, but had decided against it. No harm had been done, and if the man was still hanging around, Sheila hadn't seen any evidence of him. When he turned up again, then Sheila would alert the authorities, but right now, due to the unsolved arson and the suspicion cast upon her father, the last thing Sheila wanted to do was talk to someone from the local sheriff's department.

An unfamiliar car was sitting in the driveway near the house when Sheila and Emily arrived home. Sheila's thoughts turned back to the stranger and she felt her heart leap to her throat. Trying to appear calmer than she felt, she braked the small wagon to a halt near the garage and tried to pull together a portion of her poise. Who was he?

"That's the man I was talking to yesterday, Mom. You know, down at the duck pond." Emily was openly staring at the individual who was sitting, slump-shouldered, behind the wheel of an old Chevrolet.

The stranger had been waiting. At the sound of the approaching vehicle he had turned in his seat, pushed back the brim of his felt hat and blown out a final stream of smoke from his cigarette. He tossed the hat onto the front seat as he pulled himself out of the car.

"Wait here," Sheila told Emily.

"Why?"

"Just for a minute. Stay in the car." The authoritative ring in Sheila's voice gave Emily no room for argument. Sheila grabbed her purse and hurried from the car, intent on meeting the man out of earshot of her young daughter. Her gray eyes were cool as she focused on the rather average-looking, slightly built visitor.

"Ms. Lindstrom?" the man in the worn suit coat asked. He strode boldly up to her and extended his hand.

Sheila nodded as she accepted the brief handshake. "I'm Sheila Lindstrom."

"Anthony Simmons," he retorted with a shadowy grin. He acted as if the name might mean something to her.

"Is there something I can do for you?" she asked calmly. The man looked trustworthy enough, but still she was jittery. It was his eyes, light brown and deep set over a nose that had obviously once been broken; they didn't quite meet her steady gaze. Instead, he seemed to be studying the angle of her face.

"I hope so," he replied, shifting from one foot to the other. His face broke slowly into a well-practiced and slightly uneven smile. "I work with Noah Wilder."

Sheila couldn't keep her heart from skipping a beat at the sound of Noah's name. This man standing before her was a friend of Noah's? Sheila doubted it.

"Mr. Wilder sent you?" she asked with a dubious and reserved smile.

"That's right. He wants me to look into that fire you had here a while back." Reading the skepticism on Sheila's even features, Simmons reached into his back pocket, extracted a wallet and withdrew a white card. He offered it to Sheila. Along with his name the card was inscribed with the nationally known logo for Wilder Investments.

Sheila kept the card and began to relax. "What is it exactly you're to do here?"

Simmons shrugged as if his job were entirely routine. "Mr. Wilder is hoping that I can speed up the investigation of the arson, help clear up the whole mess, in order for the insurance company to pay off on the policy. Didn't he tell you that I was coming?"

Sheila hedged. "He did mention that someone might be coming." Anthony Simmons was not what Sheila had expected.

The investigator's smile widened. "Then we're all set."

"For what?"

"Well, first I thought I'd check over the burned wing of the winery. Didn't the fire start in the aging room?"

"According to the fire department."

"I thought so. After I'm through poking around the burned building—"

"Are you sure you should go in there? What about the warnings posted by the sheriff's department?"

"I've taken care of that."

Sheila couldn't help but be dubious. The deputy had been adamant about the restraining orders surrounding the winery. "You have?"

"Sure. Don't worry about it. After I'm done with the building I'd like to take a look at Oliver Lindstrom's books," Simmons replied.

"Wilder Investments has copies of the winery's records. Didn't Mr. Wilder give them to you?" Sheila was puzzled.

Simmons nodded curtly. "I'm not talking about Cascade Valley. I need your father's *personal* records."

"Why?"

Simmons let out an exasperated breath. He hadn't expected any argument from this Lindstrom woman. Usually the crisp white card indicating that he worked for Wilder Investments gained him entrance to the most securely locked doors. But this lady was different. Even her sophisticated looks had surprised Anthony. He tried a different tactic with her. "Look, Ms. Lindstrom, it's no skin off my nose one way or the other. I just thought that your father's books might speed the investigation." He saw a look of doubt cross her gray eyes, and he pressed his point home. "Besides which, those records might possibly clear your dad's name."

"But the police have checked—"

"They might have missed something. It's my *job* to find what the police and the insurance company might have missed."

"I don't know…" But Anthony Simmons could tell that she would give him anything he wanted. He had found her weakness; he had read it in her startled eyes when he had mentioned her father's reputation.

"It's up to you," he called over his shoulder as he headed for the fire-damaged wing.

Sheila hurried back to the car and found an impatient child fuming in the front seat. "Well?" Emily queried.

"He's an investigator, sent by Grandpa's business partners."

"Then it's okay if I talk to him?"

Sheila hesitated. Something about Anthony Simmons bothered her. "I guess so, but, try to stay out of his way."

"Why?"

"Because he's busy, honey. He's here to do a job and you might bother him. If he wants to talk to you again, I'm sure that he'll come up to the house."

Partially placated, Emily scrambled out of the car. "Then I can play by the duck pond again?" she asked.

Sheila managed a smile for the eager young face that was cocked upward at her. "Sure you can, dumpling, but not now. Let's wait until after dinner and I'll go down with you."

For the next few days it seemed to Sheila as if Anthony Simmons was forever underfoot. She couldn't turn around without running into him and having to answer questions that seemed to have little to do with his investigation of the fire. She tried to tell herself that he was just doing a thorough job, for which she should be grateful, but she couldn't help but feel that there was more than "leaving no stone unturned" to Anthony Simmons's overly zealous pursuit of the truth. Maybe that was what kept nagging at the back of Sheila's mind; she didn't really believe that Simmons was looking for the truth. He seemed to her to be more interested in finding a scapegoat for the fire. The pointed way he asked the questions, the quickly raised brown eyebrows, and his cynical remarks didn't live up to the professionalism Sheila had expected. The fact that Simmons had been sent by Noah himself bothered Sheila even more than the short man's unprofessional attitude.

Simmons left within the week, and Sheila breathed a long sigh of relief. He hadn't explained what he had pieced together, and Sheila hadn't asked. She would rather hear Simmons's theories from Noah or even Ben Wilder. The less she had to do with a cockroach like Simmons, the better.

She waited to hear from Noah and was disappointed. Another week passed and school was out for the summer. She had turned in the final grades to the school administration and both she and Emily were home, able to spend a few weeks alone together until Emily left to spend four weeks with her father. In the custody arrangement, Jeff was allowed partial custody of his child. If he had wanted to see Emily more frequently,

Sheila wouldn't have objected; after all, Emily *was* his only child. However, the four weeks he took Emily in the summer were generally more than he could stand. Jeff Coleridge wasn't cut out to be a father—or a husband.

Every summer, because of Emily, Sheila was forced to think about her ex-husband and the five years of her marriage. Fortunately, as time had worn on, the pain she had suffered at Jeff's hands diminished, and this year, because of the fire, Sheila had other thoughts to occupy her mind. This year Cascade Valley and its reopening were her main concern.

Sheila saw the situation concerning the winery: the clock was ticking and time was running out. With the passing of each successive day, she became more anxious about the business. Surely Noah had Simmons's report, and certainly the insurance company had come to some sort of settlement. Why hadn't she been notified? If only Sheila knew where she stood with Wilder Investments and the insurance company, she could begin to make plans for the fall harvest. As it was, her hands were tied. The fate of Cascade Valley Winery rested in the palms of Noah Wilder, and he hadn't had the decency to call.

The one time she had tried to reach Noah, she hadn't gotten through, and her stubborn pride forbade her from leaving her name or phone number. Surely Noah must know how desperate she was.

She tried another angle, but the telephone call to Jonas Fielding was a disappointment. Sheila had hoped that the attorney could prevail where she had failed, but it seemed that both the insurance company and Wilder Investments were stalling. Why? What had Anthony Simmons found out?

Despite her hopes otherwise, Sheila began to understand that there was no way Cascade Valley could put its label on this year's harvest. It seemed there was no other option but to sell this year's grapes to a competitive firm. For the first time in the nearly twenty years in which the Lindstrom name had been a part of the winery, Cascade Valley would be unable to bottle or ferment any wine. Not only would the winery's reputation be further tarnished, but also the potential income from the crop would be considerably reduced. It looked as if she would have to renew her contract to teach and counsel at the community college at least for another year, or until the winery was operating again—if ever. Maybe Noah had been right when he suggested that running a winery was too big a job for a woman, she thought idly to herself as she stacked her father's personal records back in the scarred oak desk. Or maybe it was more than that. Perhaps Noah was stalling for time to add just the right incentive, a little more pressure, all the while knowing that she couldn't possibly save the winery without his help. Would he be so callous as to wait her out, backing her into a trap she couldn't possibly avoid?

She slammed the rolltop desk shut with a bang. What was she thinking? Noah would never use her for his own benefit; he couldn't. She walked crisply into the kitchen and tried to ignore her suspicions. What had Jonas said about Wilder Investments and the reputation of Ben Wilder's firm? Something about forcing businesses on the brink of bankruptcy to their knees with the influence of money. Wasn't that how Ben Wilder had amassed his wealth, by purchasing failing businesses and, one way or another, turning them into profitable ventures for Wilder Investments?

Her growing suspicion crawled coldly up her spine. Without thinking, she picked up the telephone receiver and dialed the number for Wilder Investments. It was nearly five, but with any luck, Sheila would be able to catch Noah at the office. The pride that had kept her from calling him seemed small when compared with the grim fact that he might be using

each passing day as a means of squeezing her out of ownership of the winery.

"Wilder Investments," answered a pleasant, if bored, voice.

"Yes…I would like to speak to Noah Wilder, please," Sheila
said boldly.

"I'm sorry, Mr. Wilder is out for the day."

"Do you know where I could reach him? It's very important."

"I'm sorry, miss. As far as I know Mr. Wilder is out of town
for the weekend and can't be reached until Monday. If you'll
leave your name and number, I'll leave a message for him to
call you back."

"No, thank you…. I'll try next week."

Sheila replaced the receiver and tried to think clearly. Why
hadn't he called? All of his questions and interest in the winery
seemed to have passed with the one night she had shared with
him. A flush rose in her cheeks as she considered the fact that
the interest he had shown in the winery was probably little
more than polite concern displayed as part of his seduction;
a seduction that had trapped her completely. Unfortunately,
it looked as if her entire trip to Seattle had been a waste. Not
only had she lost precious time in her battle to save the winery, but she had also been played for a fool. Willingly she had
begun to give her heart to a man who considered her only a
passing interest that had faded with the dawn.

"What's for dinner?" Emily asked as she breezed into the
kitchen and grabbed a cookie from the jar.

"Beef Stroganoff," Sheila replied.

"That all?"

"No. I'm making a spinach salad, and if you don't demolish
them all before dinner, we'll have cookies for dessert."

Emily, who was beginning to reach into the cookie jar

again, quickly withdrew her hand. "I can take a hint," she mumbled.

"Good. Dinner will be ready in about half an hour. I'll call you when it's time to come in."

Emily hesitated and rubbed her fingers in distracted circles on the countertop. Sheila had begun to put water on the stove for boiling the noodles, but she stopped, noticing instead the droop in Emily's slim shoulders. "Is something wrong?"

Emily's head snapped up, and she took a deep breath. "I don't want to go to Daddy's place this summer," she announced.

"Oh, sure you do," Sheila said with a smile. "You love being with Daddy."

"No, I don't." Emily's slim arms crossed defiantly over her small chest. "And...I bet he doesn't want me to come."

"That's ridiculous. Your father loves you very much."

"Will you come with me?"

Sheila turned from the stove and faced her daughter. "If you want me to, I'll take you to Spokane, but you know that your dad likes to come and get you himself."

"You mean you're not going to stay with me?"

"I can't, honey; you know that."

"But maybe if you call Daddy and tell him you don't want me to go, he might understand."

"Emily, what brought all of this on?" Sheila asked, placing her arm over Emily's shoulders.

The young girl shrugged. "I just don't want to go."

"Why don't you think about it for a couple of weeks? You're still going to be here for a little while longer. Let's see how it goes and then we'll make a decision—okay?"

Emily's downcast eyes lifted to look out the kitchen window. "I think someone's coming."

Sheila turned her attention to the open window and the sound of a car's rapidly approaching engine. "You're right," she agreed, trying to focus on the sporty vehicle winding its way up the long gravel drive. As the silver car crested the final hill, Sheila felt her breath catch in her throat. The car belonged to Noah.

She was both ecstatic and filled with dread. Noah must have come here with his answer about the winery.

Chapter 7

The lump in Sheila's throat swelled as she watched Noah's car approach.

"Who's that?" Emily asked, squinting into the sunset and straining to get a better view of the silver vehicle as she looked through the window. Noah braked the Volvo to a halt and got out of the car. He looked tired and hot. He was wearing tan corduroy pants and a loosely knit ivory sweater. The sleeves were pushed up over his forearms to display tanned skin and tight muscles. His dark hair was slightly windblown from the drive, and the shadow of his beard was visible against his olive skin. His mouth, set in a firm, hard line, tightened as the other passenger in the car said something that caught his attention. Sheila felt her pulse begin to race at the sight of him. No other man had ever affected her so deeply.

"Mom?" Emily asked, catching Sheila's attention. "Do you know that guy?"

Sheila managed a frail smile for her daughter. "I'm sorry, Em," she replied, realizing that she had ignored Emily's previous question. "Yes, I know him. His name is Noah Wilder, and he's in charge of the company that owns most of the winery."

"A big shot, huh?"

Sheila laughed. "I think his title is 'temporary president,' or something of the sort. Let's not call him a big shot. Okay?"

"If you say so."

"Just keep in mind that he is important. His decision on the winery is critical." Emily's puzzled expression was not lost on Sheila. "I'll explain more about him later. Right now let's go and meet him at the door." Sheila grabbed Emily's hand and hurried to the front entrance, hoping to forestall any more of Emily's questions about Noah.

When she opened the door, Sheila stood face-to-face with the one man who had touched her to the core, and she felt her poise beginning to slip. Noah wasn't alone. With him was a boy; his son, Sheila guessed. The resemblance between the man and teenager was strong. Though Sean's hair was blond, his skin was dark like his father's, and his eyes were the same piercing blue. Those blue eyes regarded Sheila intently with a deep-seated, undisguised hostility.

"I tried the bell, but I didn't hear it ring," Noah explained.

"It hasn't worked since the fire."

Noah seemed a little uncomfortable, but when his eyes found Sheila's, he held her gaze and spoke softly. "Earlier, you invited me to come and see the winery for myself. You asked me to spend a weekend here, and I've decided that there's no time like the present. Does the offer still stand?"

"Now? This weekend?" she asked.

"If it wouldn't inconvenience you...."

Sheila was caught in the power of his gaze, the warmth and invitation in his eyes. She had to force herself to smile and keep her voice cool and professional. "Of course you're welcome. I'm sure if you stay and see the magnitude of the problem, you'll understand why we have to begin rebuilding the winery as soon as we can."

"I'm sure," he agreed, dismissing the subject. "I'd like you to meet my son, Sean."

Sheila's smile spread as she turned her attention to the boy at Noah's side. She had always had a way with kids, especially teenagers. She genuinely liked them, and it showed in the interest in her eyes. "Hi, Sean. How are you?"

"Fine," was the clipped, succinct reply. His expression of hostility didn't diminish.

Sheila didn't press the issue. "This is Emily." She touched Emily's shoulders fondly.

Noah bent his knees so he could talk to Emily at her level. "It's nice to meet you, Emily." He extended his hand, and when Emily took hold of it, he gave the girl a warm handshake. "I bet you're a big help to your mom, aren't you?"

"I guess so," Emily mumbled before retrieving her hand and stepping backward to put some distance between herself and the forceful man.

"We were just about to have dinner," Sheila stated as Noah rose back to his full height. "Could you join us?"

Sean rolled his eyes and looked away. Noah spoke for the two of them. "If it's not too much trouble. I should have called before I left the office, but I was running late, so I just headed out of town." The lie slipped so easily off his tongue that Noah had no trouble smiling disarmingly down at her. His conscience twinged, but he ignored it.

"It's fine," Sheila was saying emphatically. "I always cook as if I'm expecting the army." She moved out of the doorway. "Come in. I still have a few things to do to get dinner on the table. Or, if you would prefer, you can look around the grounds. I'll give you a guided tour later."

"I'll wait. I think I'd prefer a *personal* tour."

Sheila felt the heat climbing up her throat. Somehow she managed to keep her voice level. "What about you, Sean? Dinner won't be ready for half an hour. You're welcome to come into the house; I've got several books and magazines you might be interested in, or you can do whatever you want out here."

"I don't like to read," Sean replied curtly, but after receiving a dark and admonishing glance from his father, he amended his brusque response with a shrug of his shoulders. "I'll stay outside."

Emily followed Sheila and Noah inside. Sheila busied herself with the finishing touches for the meal, and Noah lounged against the counter, watching her as she worked. Emily hovered near Sheila, uncertain about the upcoming evening.

"You out of school for the year?" Noah asked the girl.

"Uh-huh."

Sheila could feel Emily's embarrassment. Ever since Sheila's divorce from Jeff, Emily was shy with men to the point of wariness, especially any man who showed attention to her mother. To ease Emily's discomfort, Sheila changed the subject. "Dinner's going to take a little longer than I thought, Emily. Why don't you take a couple of cookies and—" she paused to inspect the contents of the refrigerator "—some of this pop outside for you and Sean."

Emily's wide green eyes lit up. "Really? Before dinner?"

"Why not?" Sheila asked with a smile and handed the cans of ginger ale to her daughter. "Tonight's special."

Emily balanced the cans against her chest while she reached into the cookie jar and withdrew a handful of macaroons. "Great," she whispered, hardly believing her luck at receiving goodies before a meal.

When the back door slammed shut and Emily could be heard in the distance, Noah moved from his position against the counter to stand behind Sheila. She could sense his presence behind her, but she tried to maintain her interest in the sauce she was preparing. It was impossible. His hands wrapped around her waist and drew her close to him. She closed her eyes as she felt his breath rustle the hair at the nape of her neck.

"Is it?" he asked.

"What?"

"Is tonight special?" His words caressed the air.

She attempted to misread him. "Of course it is. It's not often Emily and I have guests for dinner."

"That's not what I meant."

Sheila sighed and turned the burner to the lowest setting. She rotated in Noah's arms and tried to step backward. He didn't let go. "I knew what you meant."

"Do you?"

"Of course I do, Noah. I'm not exactly a naive innocent. I think you were the one that pointed it out to me. I assume you came here to talk about the winery..."

"And?" His half smile showed just a seductive hint of white, straight teeth, and a gleam of fascination flickered in his blue eyes.

"And you probably expect to take up where we left off." Sheila's heart was pounding so loudly she was sure he could hear it.

"The thought did cross my mind."

"You're wicked," she accused teasingly.

"No, I wouldn't say that...*captivated* would be a better word."

"Oh, Noah," Sheila murmured. His words had a magical effect upon her, and she felt unable to resist the spell of tenderness he was weaving. Though she attempted to deny it, she still found something enigmatic and intimately alluring in Noah. A crazy feeling of exhilaration climbed steadily up her spine as she realized that he wanted to be with her. Perhaps she had misjudged him. Perhaps despite everything holding them apart, there was a chance that they could find happiness with each other.

"You look great," he said. His eyes caressed her face and dropped to the tempting white column of her throat.

"In jeans and an old blouse?"

"In anything...." The pressure of his hands against her back drew her close to him; so close that she could feel the strength of his legs where they touched hers and the pressure of his chest against her breasts. "As I recall, you look incredible in absolutely nothing as well." His head lowered and his lips captured hers in a warm kiss that evoked passionate memories. In one instant she remembered his embrace in the rain and his touch in the silent afterglow.

Without thinking she entwined her arms around Noah's neck and parted her lips under the soft pressure of his mouth. His tongue rimmed her lips, and all of the doubts of the last weeks fled with the promise of his kiss. "I've missed you," he groaned when he lifted his head and pulled her roughly against him. "God, how I've missed you."

At the sound of his confession, Sheila felt tears begin to pool in her eyes. "I've missed you, too," she murmured into his sweater. Her voice caught, and she felt him stiffen. Slowly he released her.

"Is something wrong?" he asked.

"It's been a long day..." she hedged. How could she begin to explain the storm of emotions within her each time he held her closely?

"Is it a bad time for you? I should have called before I came racing over here."

"No...everything's fine. *Really.*"

"Is dinner ready yet?" Emily called just as she was entering the room.

Sheila managed to brush her tears aside. "Just about. You can help by setting the table."

"In the dining room?" Emily asked as she reached in the drawer for silverware.

"No. We'll have to eat in here." Sheila withdrew a linen tablecloth and put it on the small kitchen table. Looking skeptically at the makeshift dining arrangements, her mouth pulled into a pouty frown. "It's not exactly elegant, but it will have to do. The dining room is still a mess."

"From the fire?" Noah asked.

"And the water that was used to put out the flames. I'll show you everything after we eat. Maybe then you'll appreciate my position about the winery."

The door opened and shut with a resonating thud. Sean strode into the room wearing cut-off jeans, a sloppy red sweatshirt and a look of bored indifference. His face was shaped similarly to his father's, except that the sharp planes of Noah's face were softer on his son. There was still a hint of boyish naiveté in Sean that he obviously tried to hide under a guise of insolence.

"Time to eat?" Sean asked, directing his question to his father.

"I think you can sit down."

"Good." Sean slid into the nearest chair and avoided looking at Sheila. His fingers tapped restlessly on the edge of the table. Emily took a seat next to Sean and began to chatter endlessly about a hike she hoped to take with him. Sean responded with adolescent nonchalance about the prospect of spending more time with the eager eight-year-old, but Sheila's practiced eye saw the interest he was trying to hide. Three years of counseling teenagers had helped her understand both the kids and their motives.

The dinner was eaten under a thin veil of civility. Sheila had hoped that as the meal progressed the strain of the impromptu get-together would fade and a comfortable feeling of familiarity would evolve. She had been wrong. Before the dinner was over, even Emily could feel the tension building between Sean and Sheila.

Sheila attempted to bridge the gap. "Are you out of school for the summer?" she asked Sean.

Silence. Sean continued to wolf down his food.

She tried another ploy. "Would you like anything else to eat? How about a roll?"

Nothing. Noah's anger had been simmering throughout the meal, but he had decided not to discipline his son in front of Sheila and Emily. Sean's rude behavior forced the issue.

"Sheila asked you a question, Sean," he stated sternly.

"Yeah...I heard."

"Then could you be polite enough to answer."

Sean bristled. "Sure." His cool blue eyes sought Sheila's. "Naw...I don't want another roll." He turned his gaze back to his father. "Satisfied?"

Emily's eyes widened as father and son squared off.

"No, I'm not. I don't expect much from you, son, but I do think you can be civil."

"Why?" Sean demanded.

"Out of respect."

"For what? *Her?*" He cast his disdainful gaze at Sheila.

"Cut it out!" Noah stated tersely.

Sean ignored him. "Look, Dad, I don't need this."

"What you need is to learn about acting with just a modicum of decency and common courtesy." A muscle in Noah's jaw began to tense.

"Back off, Dad. What I don't need is some lady trying to be my mother!"

"Don't worry about that, Sean," Sheila interjected. "I have no intention of trying to become your mother." With that, she turned her attention back to her dinner and finished eating. Sean cast a skeptical glance in her direction, and Noah's dark eyebrows cocked. However, he didn't interfere. When finished with her meal, Sheila again looked at Sean. "No, I'm sure you've done very well without a mother for the past sixteen years, and I, for one, have no intention of changing that." She rained her most disarming smile upon the confused boy. "Now, is there anything else I can get you?"

"No!"

"Good." Sheila placed her napkin on the table. "Then, if we're all finished, you can clear the table while Emily gets the dessert."

Sean's face fell and his blue eyes sought those of his father, entreating Noah to help him. "Good idea," Noah agreed amicably, but the glint of determination in his eyes demanded that his son obey.

Sheila wasn't finished. She began stacking the plates and handing them to Sean. "Just put the dishes on the counter near the sink, and don't worry about washing them, I'll take care of that later. Let's see, the leftovers go in the refrigerator. Use the plastic wrap to cover them. Can you handle that?"

Sean's hot retort was thwarted by his father's stern glare. Rather than press the issue, Sean scowled and nodded curtly.

"All right, now, Emily; it's your turn." Emily fastened her frightened eyes on her mother. Never had she witnessed such hostility at a meal. Nor had she ever seen her mother so tough with a guest.

Sheila smiled at her daughter, and Emily's anxieties melted a bit. "You can bring the cookies out to the back patio. I'll bring the coffee and Noah will get the milk." If Noah was surprised that he, too, was issued an order, he didn't show it.

Sean's chair scraped insolently against the tiled floor as he rose from the table. His handsome face was clouded in an expression of disdain, but he managed to clear the dishes. Emily was uncommonly silent as she arranged the macaroons on a small plate. The tension that had been building throughout dinner continued to mount. Noah poured two glasses of milk and escaped out the back door. Emily soon followed. Sheila waited for the coffee to perk, while Sean put things away, making as much noise as he possibly could.

Just as Sheila was pouring the hot, black liquid, Sean exploded. "Maybe you can fool my dad, but you can't fool me!"

Sheila was startled and sloshed some of the coffee on her wrist. The scalding brew burned her skin, but she remained calm. As Sean watched her reaction, she set the cup down and put her hand under cold water from the tap. Her voice was even when she addressed him. "I have no intention of trying to fool you, Sean."

"Sure," he sneered.

Sheila turned to face the tall boy, and she leveled her cool gray eyes on his face. "Look, Sean, I'm not trying to deceive anyone, and I expect the same in return. I don't really care if you like me or not. You have the right to your own opinions, just as I have the right to mine...."

"Don't give me any of your psychiatric lines! I know you're a school counselor, and I'll just bet Dad dragged me up here so you could do a number on me; you know, analyze me— try and straighten me out." He threw up one of his hands in disgust. "I just want you to know that it won't work on me. Save your breath!"

Sheila managed a smile. "Do you really think that I would bother wasting my time or expertise on someone who didn't want it?"

"It's your job."

"No. I'm sorry, Sean, but you're wrong. I'm not going to beat my head against the wall for someone who doesn't want my help, and that includes you. As for what your father expects from me, it has nothing to do with you. We're business partners."

"Sure."

"I think I will take your advice," Sheila agreed. Sean tensed. The last thing he had expected was for this woman to concur with him. "I'm going to save my breath. I would like to try and convince you to relax and enjoy the weekend—"

"Fat chance," Sean interrupted under his breath.

"Pardon me?"

"This isn't my scene," he spat out, and turned to glare out the window.

"That's too bad, because it looks like you're stuck here for the duration of the weekend." Sean rolled his eyes heavenward, and Sheila poured the coffee into the second cup. When she picked up the tray, she cast a final glance in Sean's direction. "Why don't you come out to the patio and join the rest of us? Emily already took out the cookies."

Sean whirled angrily to face Sheila. "I'm here, okay? That's the end of it. I'm not going to sit with the rest of you and eat milk and cookies. That might be all right for Emily, but not for me. I'm not wasting my time babysitting your kid!" he shouted.

The screen door slammed shut and Emily came into the room. From the expression on her face it was evident she had heard Sean's final words. Tears sprung to her soft green eyes as she stared at Sean.

"Damn!" Sean muttered, and slammed his fist onto the counter. His face burned in his embarrassment as he strode angrily from the room.

"Why doesn't he like me?" Emily asked Sheila. The little girl tried vainly to swallow her tears. Sheila set the tray down.

"It's not that he doesn't like you, Em," Sheila replied, hugging her child. "He's just not sure of himself here. He doesn't know you or me, and he's not really sure how to act."

"He's mean!" Emily sniffed.

"He's not trying to be. Maybe he's jealous of you," Sheila whispered into her daughter's thick, dark curls.

"Why?"

"Sean doesn't have a mother."

Emily was puzzled. She pulled out of her mother's embrace and with a childish imitation of adult concern, looked deeply into Sheila's eyes. "I thought everybody had a mommy."

"You're right, sweetheart. Everybody does have a mother, including Sean. But, I think he's unhappy because he doesn't see her very much."

"Why not?" Emily was clearly perplexed, and Sheila wondered if she had broached a topic she couldn't fully explain. After all, what did she know of Sean's mother? If she had interpreted Noah's story correctly, Sean may never have met his mother. No wonder the kid had a chip the size of a boulder on his young shoulders. Sheila felt her heart go out for the stubborn boy with the facade of bravado. Emily was still staring at Sheila, and she knew she had to find a suitable answer for her daughter. "Sean's parents don't live together," she whispered.

Emily's sober expression changed to one of understanding. "Oh, they're divorced. Like you and Daddy."

Sheila's expression clouded. "Sort of," she replied vaguely. Emily seemed satisfied for the moment, and Sheila changed the subject quickly. "Let's go out on the patio and see Noah before this coffee gets cold."

"He's not there."

"He's not?"

Emily shook her head. "He's just walkin' around."

"Then we'll wait for him." Again Sheila picked up the tray,

and with Emily in tow, walked out to the brick patio that was flanked by Oliver's rose garden.

Noah had been familiarizing himself with the layout of the winery. His walk also gave him the excuse to vent some of the frustration and tension that had been boiling within him since he had left Seattle. The trip over the mountains had been strained; Sean had brooded because his weekend plans were canceled by his father's hastily organized trip. Sean had pleaded to be left alone in Seattle, and when Noah had refused, Sean had ridden the entire distance with his head turned away from his father while he pretended interest in the passing country-side. He had responded to Noah's questions with monosyllabic grunts. By the time they reached the winery, Noah's tension was wound tighter than the mainspring on a watch.

Noah had hoped that Sean would loosen up by the time they had come within sight of the winery, but he had been wrong—dead wrong. Sean was more petulant than ever. It was as if he were intent on punishing his father with his abrasive behavior.

Noah's frown twisted into a wry grin as he thought about Sheila's reaction to his strong-willed son. The embarrassment Noah had experienced at the table had faded into admiration for Sheila as he had witnessed the effective manner in which she had handled Sean. Even Sean had been set on his heels by Sheila's indifferent and coolly professional attitude. She had refused to be goaded by anything Sean had done. Noah had to hand it to her: she knew how to handle kids. Her own daughter was proof of that. It occurred to him that perhaps he would never be able to control his son. It was all too evident that Sean needed a mother as well as a father. Noah had been a fool to think that he could raise a son of his own. Ben's warning, issued sixteen years before, rang in his ears. "You want to raise that bastard on your own? You're an even bigger fool than I thought!"

The screen door slammed, breaking into Noah's thoughts. He lifted his eyes to observe Sean racing angrily from the house. There had obviously been another battle and it seemed as if Sean had lost one more round to Sheila. Noah shook his head as he watched his athletic son run across the backyard, hoist himself effortlessly over a pole fence without once breaking stride, and continue at a breakneck pace into the fringe of woods beyond the orchard.

Noah's thoughts returned to Sheila. There was more grit to her than met the eye. Stunningly beautiful, she was also independent and intelligent. Noah raked his fingers impatiently through his hair as he wondered if he had made a grave mistake in seeking her out. She was more intriguing than he had remembered, and seeing her in the setting of the burned winery seemed to add an innocent vulnerability to her large eyes. Noah felt as if he wanted to protect her, when in fact he had come to Cascade Valley expecting to confront her with the knowledge that her father did, in fact, start the fire at the winery. As yet, Noah hadn't found the right opportunity to broach the subject. The more he was with Sheila, the less he wanted to talk about the fire.

Anthony Simmons's report had been short and concise. Though the detective had produced no concrete evidence to name Oliver Lindstrom as the arsonist, the case Simmons had built against Sheila's father had been complete. Noah knew that the insurance company was bound to reach the same conclusion as he had: Based on circumstantial evidence, it was proven that Oliver Lindstrom set fire to Cascade Valley hoping to collect the insurance settlement and pay off a sizable debt to Wilder Investments. Inadvertently Mr. Lindstrom got caught in his own trap, was overcome by fumes of noxious gas and died in the blaze.

Noah's stomach knotted as he wondered how involved Sheila had been in her father's scheme. Had she known about it beforehand? Was she involved? Or was she, as she claimed, looking for a solution to the dilemma? According to Simmons, Sheila had been polite, but hadn't gone out of her way to help with the investigation. It had been like pulling teeth to get her to divulge anything personal about her father...or herself. Was she hiding something? Simmons seemed to think so. Noah didn't. Still, it didn't matter, the bottom line was that he had to tell her about her father and then gauge her reaction to the news. It wasn't going to be easy. Either way she lost. If she already knew that her father was a fraud, she would come out of this mess at the very least a liar; at the most an accomplice. If she didn't know that her father had started the fire, her dreams and respect for the dead man would be shattered. No doubt she would blame Noah for digging up the dirt on Oliver Lindstrom.

As Noah walked back to the patio he tried to find a way to help her rather than hurt her.

Chapter 8

Noah paced back and forth across the red bricks of the patio. The anxieties of the day were etched across his face in long lines of worry. It was nearly ten. The sun had set over an hour before and Sean hadn't returned. He was obviously back to his old tricks of vanishing without a word of explanation.

Emily was already asleep in her bed. Since overhearing Sean's unkind remarks, she had been quiet. The girl hadn't even put up an argument about going to bed, and Sheila's heart broke when Emily reasserted her earlier assessment of the situation. "Sean doesn't like me, and it's not because I've got a mommy. He doesn't like anybody."

"He's just trying to find out who he is," Sheila had responded.

"That's silly. He's Sean. He just doesn't like me."

"Maybe he doesn't like himself."

Emily hadn't been convinced as she snuggled under her comforter. Sheila had attempted to hand the child her favorite furry toy, but Emily pushed it onto the floor. "I don't need Cinnamon," Emily had stated. "Toys are for *little kids*." Sheila hadn't argued, wisely letting her child cope with the struggle of growing up. Instead she picked up the toy dog with the floppy ears and set him on the nightstand near Emily's bed.

"Just in case you change your mind." After her parting remarks she had kissed Emily lightly on the cheek and left the room.

"Is she all right?" Noah asked.

"I think so."

"What was bothering her?"

"She took offense to Sean's notion that she was a little kid. She thinks she has to grow up all in one evening."

"Sean's the one who has to grow up," Noah argued. "I don't know if he ever will!"

"It will get better," Sheila said quietly.

"How do you know?"

"It has to. Doesn't it?" The gray intelligence in her eyes reached out to him.

"What makes you so certain? How do you know I don't have the makings of a hardened criminal on my hands?"

Sheila smiled, and her face, captured in the moon glow, held a madonna-like quality that was only contradicted by the silver fire of seduction in her eyes. "Sean's not a bad kid," she pointed out. "He's just not certain of himself."

"He could have fooled me."

"That's exactly what he's trying to do."

Noah strode over to the chaise lounge where she was sitting. "How did a beautiful woman like you get so wise?" He sat next to her and his hand touched her thigh as he leaned over her to kiss her forehead.

"Don't you remember what it was like when you were in high school?"

"I try not to."

"Come on, admit it. Didn't you give your parents a few gray hairs?"

"I don't remember ever getting into as much trouble as Sean has."

"Maybe you were smarter and just never got caught," she suggested.

"Now you're beginning to sound cynical."

"Realistic."

"Yeah, so it's all business, is it?" Sean jeered, walking out of the darkness into the circle of light surrounding the patio. Noah, still leaning over Sheila, barely moved, but Sheila could feel all the muscles in his body become rigid. Slowly he turned to face his son.

"It's about time you got back. Where were you?"

Sean shrugged indifferently. "Around."

"I was beginning to worry about you."

"Yeah. I can see that," the boy snorted. His blue eyes sought Sheila's in a condemning gaze. "You told me you were business partners with him, nothing more!"

"I said that we were business partners and that I didn't think your father brought you up here for a counseling session. I should have added that your father and I are friends," Sheila explained calmly.

"Yeah. *Good* friends."

"Sean, that's enough!" Noah shouted, rising to his full height. Sean's defiance wavered under his father's barely controlled rage. "You apologize to Sheila!"

"Why?" Sean asked, managing to pull together one last attempt at asserting his pride.

"You tell me," Noah suggested.

Sean shifted from one foot to the other as he measured his father's anger. Noah didn't take his eyes off of his son. Realizing he had no other choice, Sean mumbled a hasty apology before entering the house.

"I'll show him his room," Sheila offered. "There's a Hide-A-Bed in my father's office. I just put clean sheets on it yesterday."

Noah objected. "*I'll* take him to the room. He and I have a few things to get straight. I'm not putting up with his cocky attitude any longer." He rubbed the tension from the back of his neck and followed his son into the house.

Pieces of the argument filtered through the thick walls of the château. Sheila began to clear the dishes off the patio and tried not to overhear the heated discussion. Noah's voice, angry and accusatory, didn't drown out Sean's argumentative tones.

The night was sultry and still. The tension from the argument lingered in the air, and Sheila felt beads of moisture beginning to accumulate on the back of her neck. She wound her hair into a loose chignon and clipped it to the top of her head before she carried the dishes into the house.

Noah and Sean were still arguing, but the hot words had become softer. In order to give them more privacy, Sheila turned on the water in the kitchen and rattled the dishes in the sink. It wasn't enough to drown out all of the anger, so she switched on the radio. Familiar strains of a popular tune filtered through the kitchen and Sheila forced herself to hum, hoping to take her mind off the uncomfortable relationship between Noah and his son. Just as Noah couldn't get along with Ben, Sean shunned his father. Why? Her loose thoughts rambled as she began to wash the dishes. She didn't hear the argument subside, didn't notice when Noah entered the room.

He leaned against the doorjamb and watched her as she worked. Her hair was piled loosely on her head, and soft tendrils framed her delicate face. A thin trickle of perspiration ran down her chin and settled below the open neck of her blouse.

He could almost visualize it resting between her breasts. Her sleeves were rolled over her elbows, and her forearms were submerged in water so hot it steamed. A vibrant rosy flush from the hot night and the even hotter water colored her skin. She was softly humming to the strains of music from the radio, and though the sound was slightly off-key, it caused Noah to smile. She had to be the most beautiful woman in the world.

"Don't you have a dishwasher?" he asked, not moving from the doorway. He enjoyed his vantage point, where he could watch all of her movements.

She laughed. "Oh, I've got one all right, but it doesn't work."

"Can't it be repaired?"

Sheila turned to face Noah, while still wiping her hands with the dish towel. "I suppose it can."

"But you haven't called a repairman?"

"Not yet."

"Why not?"

"Because I enjoy washing dishes," she snapped sarcastically.

Noah finally understood. "You're waiting for the insurance money, right?"

"Right." Sheila's expression softened. "A dishwasher is the last thing we need right now. Emily and I use very few dishes, so it's not exactly a hardship."

"That kind of thinking will send you back to the nineteenth century," he teased.

"That kind of thinking will keep me out of debt…at least for a little while." Sheila's eyes clouded with worry for an instant, but she bravely ignored her problems. The best way to solve them was to apprise Noah of the hopeless condition of the winery. She tossed the dish towel over the back of a chair and boldly reached for Noah's hand. "I promised you a tour of the grounds."

"I can think of better things to do," he suggested huskily.

"Not on your life." She pulled on his hand and attempted to ignore the laconic gleam in his eyes. "Now that I've got you on my territory, you're going to see exactly what I've been talking about." She led him to the front of the house. "Let's start with public relations."

"Public relations? For a winery?"

"Not just any winery, Noah. This is Cascade Valley, the Northwest's finest. My father always ran the winery with the opinion that the public comes first. Anyone who was even the slightest bit interested in Cascade Valley has always been treated as if he were an important dignitary." She led him down an asphalt path that led from the château toward the park grounds of the vast estate. Though the grass was overgrown, Noah could tell that in the past the grounds had been immaculately groomed. Stands of dark pine trees surrounded the long grass and the untrimmed shrubbery. The air was fragrant with the scent of pines and lilacs. A hazy moon gave an iridescent glow to the shadowy night.

"Sounds as if your father spent a lot of time and money humoring tourists."

Sheila refused to be baited. "It paid off, too. Word of mouth was our first form of advertising." Sheila glanced at Noah to interpret his reaction. Though it was dark, she could read the hardening of his gaze, feel the tensing of his hand over hers, sense the clenching of his teeth as his jaw tightened.

"What kind of tours did your father give?" Noah asked, pressing the issue.

"At first they were nothing out of the ordinary. One of the staff would just show the tourists around. But, as public interest grew, Dad had to hire a woman to pass out literature about the winery and give tours of the buildings every afternoon in the summer." Sheila motioned her hand toward a small lake shimmering in the moonlight. "Dad had the duck pond built about six years ago. Then he added the gravel paths through the woods. Later he installed the picnic tables and the benches."

"I'm surprised he didn't give away bottles of Cabernet Sauvignon, too," Noah muttered caustically.

"You didn't approve of my father, did you?" Sheila accused.

"I didn't know him."

"But you're passing judgment."

"Not on the man," Noah pointed out. He took his hand away from Sheila's and rubbed his chin. How could he explain to her that her father was an arsonist who had only wanted to get money from the insurance company to pay his debts? If Oliver Lindstrom had been a little more daring and a little less clumsy, it might have worked. "I'm only questioning some of his business practices. Public relations is usually sound, but not when it devours all of a company's profits. What's the point? If your father had paid less attention to putting on a show for anyone who happened to wander by and had more concern for his profits, maybe he never would have had to borrow money from Wilder Investments in the first place!"

Sheila felt the hairs on her neck prickle with anger. "The reason he borrowed the money had nothing to do with the tourists or the duck pond, Noah. That nearly paid for itself in the gift shop alone," she argued. Indignation flashed in her eyes as she came to the defense of her father. "Dad took a survey of all the people who came here one summer and it proved him right; nearly seventy percent of the tourists bought more than one bottle of Cascade Valley a month."

"What about the other thirty percent?"

"I don't know."

"Do you think those people, those who bought your product, were swayed because of a duck pond, or picnic tables?"

"No…but…"

"Of course not! Those people would probably have bought the wine without all of this…grandstanding. The money would have been better spent in production or research, even advertising. Sure, these grounds look impressive, but it's the quality of the product that counts! Wouldn't it be wiser to use this acreage for cultivation?"

"I don't know if the soil is right…" she hedged.

"So check it out."

Her simmering anger began to boil. "I guess you don't understand, Noah. We're not only selling the best wine on the West Coast, we're creating an image for the consuming public. We're not competing with cheap muscatel. Our opposition is the finest European wine on the market. Every summer we provide samples of our product at a wine-tasting celebration and the public is invited. We introduce the newest varieties, invite a few celebrities and generally promote the image of Cascade Valley wines as sophisticated, yet reasonably priced.

"Sounds expensive."

"It is," she admitted reluctantly. "But, most often, we get national media attention. That kind of advertising we can't afford to lose."

"But you didn't get any national attention for the last few years, did you?"

She shook her heard as if she had expected this question and seemed resigned to a fate she couldn't avoid. "No."

"Why not?" He knew the answer, but he wanted to hear it from her.

Sheila bit her lower lip nervously. Her words rang with honesty and despair. "Dad was afraid. With all of the news coverage on the tampered bottles of Cabernet Sauvignon found in Montana and the problems with the crop because of the early snowfall, Dad thought it would be best for Cascade Valley to keep a low profile." She paused for a moment to study the ribbon of silver moon glow on the pond. "This was the year he had hoped would change all of that."

"How?"

"Because we planned to introduce our reserve bottling of Cabernet Sauvignon."

"Reserve bottling?" Noah repeated. "Something new?"

"For Cascade Valley, yes." She turned to face him, her expression sincere. "It could be the biggest breakthrough we've had."

"Tell me about it." Noah was interested. This was the first hint of good news at the winery.

Sheila shook her head. "Not now. On Monday Dave Jansen will come by. He can tell you all about it…" She stopped mid-sentence, as if she'd assumed far too much about him. "You can stay until Monday, can't you?" Why was it so imperative that he remain for more than just one night? Now that he was here, she desperately wanted him to stay.

"Is it that important?" he asked, his voice as low as the soft breeze that had begun to whisper through the pines.

"Yes, it's important," she admitted, but lied about the reason. "I think you should see for yourself…."

His fingers lightly touched her shoulders, and through the light cotton fabric they warmed her skin. "What I meant was, is it important that I stay with you?"

Her lips felt desert dry. She had to lick them in order to find the courage for her truthful reply. "I'm glad you came here, Noah." She admitted with only a trace of reluctance. "And I'd like you to stay, not just to witness the damage from the fire, nor just to evaluate the winery. I *want* you to stay here with me, for *me*." Her honesty filtered softly through the warm night air. The words of confession surprised her. After Jeff, she thought she had lost the *need* of a man's embrace. She had never expected to admit how much she wanted a man, because she thought that part of her had died. She had assumed that Jeff had ruined her for a relationship with any man, that the cynical feelings he had created in her would remain forever.

But she had been wrong, hopelessly mistaken. The strong man touching her lightly on the shoulders had changed her mind about many things, one of which was love. Though she couldn't yet admit it to him, Sheila knew that she loved Noah as she had never loved before.

"Then I'll stay," he whispered. His thumbs smoothed the fabric over her collarbones. "I want to stay with you, sweet lady."

Sheila sighed through trembling lips as Noah reached up and unclasped her hair. It billowed down in a chestnut tumble to frame her face in copper-tinged curls. Noah gently kissed her eyelids, and Sheila felt her knees begin to give way. His arms came protectively around her waist and pulled her achingly against the length of him. Her thighs touched his, her breasts were crushed against his chest, her heartbeat echoed with his in the still night.

His lips caressed her eyelids before moving slowly downward, leaving a moist trail of midnight dew on her cheekbones and the soft skin below her chin. A warm passion uncurling within her made a shudder pass through her body, and her skin quivered under the touch of his hands. His lips moved gently against her throat, and his tongue stroked the white skin, leaving a heated, wet impression. Sheila sighed dreamily into the night, unconsciously asking for more from him.

Her lips quivered when met by his and her gentle moan of pleasure blended warmly with his answering sigh. Their breath mingled and caught, heated by the fires dancing in their bloodstreams. When his tongue touched hers, the tempo of her heartbeat quickened and she opened her mouth in a gasp, wanting all of him, craving more of his bittersweet love.

He felt her surrender, knew the moment when the passion began to thunder in her ears and her bones began to melt. Her tongue stroked his, teasing and flirting with him until he could stand no more of the painless agony. Gently he pushed against her until the weight of his body forced her to fall on the soft bed of grass beneath the towering Ponderosa pines. He let his weight fall against her, imprisoning her with the power of his body and the strength of his desire.

The ground felt cool against her back, a welcome relief to a sultry night. Noah's kisses inflamed her blood and awakened a savage beast of passion slumbering quietly within her. She felt hot blood pumping through her racing heart until she thought she would explode from the powerful surge of desire sweeping through her. She wanted him—all of him. There was a desperation to her need, an untamed craving that knew no bounds.

"Make love to me," she pleaded through fevered lips. He lifted his head and slowly extracted himself from her embrace.

After opening one of the buttons of her blouse, he kissed the warm skin between her breasts, tasting the salt of her perspiration on his tongue. His hand shook as he smoothed the hair away from her face. "I thought I'd go crazy," he confessed, watching the play of moonlight on her red-brown hair. "I wanted to follow you back here that first night I met you." His face was grave, his eyes earnest. "It was hell staying away."

"Why didn't you come sooner?" she asked, trying to keep her mind on the conversation. With his free hand he was toying with the collar of her blouse, letting his fingers dip deliciously below the lapels. Her skin still burned where he had planted the wet kiss between her breasts. Heat waves washed over her skin, which flushed a rosy hue.

"You were the one who needed time," he reminded her. "I didn't want to push you into anything you might regret later."

"I could never regret spending time with you," she confessed.

His forefinger circled the hollow of her throat, creating a whirlpool of sensitive longing deep within her. "Is...is that why you decided to come now, because you thought I might have come to some decision...about our relationship?" Why couldn't she keep her wandering mind on the subject? It was important that she learn more about this man, and yet all of her thoughts were centered on his slow, seductive touch at the base of her throat.

"No...I came because I couldn't wait any longer," he admitted. It wasn't a lie; he had felt an urgency to be with her again, but there was that sordid little business about Anthony Simmons's report and her father's implication in the arson. Dear God, how would he be able to tell her? He promised himself that he would find a way to break the news—when the timing was right. Just now, beneath a dusty sprinkling of midnight stars, he could only think of how hopelessly he wanted her.

She grabbed his finger, stopping its wandering journey on her neck. "I can't think when you touch me like that."

"Don't think," he persuaded, but she ignored the husky invitation in his voice.

"Why couldn't you wait?"

"I had to see you again."

She released his finger, and a smile crept slowly across the smooth contours of her face. Shadowy moonlight lingered in her gaze as she looked up at him. "It doesn't matter," she whispered, kissing his hand. "The only important thing is that you're here, *now*." Her fingers curved around the back of his neck, ruffling his coffee-colored hair and pulling his head down to meet hers in a kiss of naked longing. She willingly parted her lips, inviting him to touch her most intimate reaches.

"Oh, Sheila," he groaned, damning himself inwardly for his deception. How could he make love to her without telling her everything he knew about her, her father, the fire? A bothersome guilt nagged at him like a broken vow, and yet he pushed it savagely aside. "Some other time," he promised himself.

"What?" Her hand stopped caressing his head. "What are you talking about?"

His grip on her tightened. "Nothing, my darling...nothing that can't wait."

His lips came to hers in a kiss that dismissed her fears. She was conscious of the hot breeze singing through the trees as it carried the sweet scent of pine and honeysuckle to her. She could taste the salty masculinity that passed from his lips to hers and she felt the protective strength of his hands as they quickly unbuttoned the remaining buttons of her blouse. The fabric parted, letting her breasts caress the night air. Noah pushed the blouse off her shoulders and never took his eyes from hers as he unclasped the filmy bra and tossed it recklessly to the ground.

Sheila's breasts, unbound by clothing, glistening with a dewy film of sweat, were swollen from the flames of passion Noah had aroused within her. They stood out in the darkness as two white globes, small and firm, perfectly proportioned to her petite body. Noah held first one and then the other in his caressing hands. At his softly insistent touch, the dark nipples hardened.

Sheila sighed when he took one of the moonlit mounds of feminine flesh into his mouth. His fingers gripped the soft skin of her back, drawing her closer to him, letting him devour more of her. She felt the tip of his tongue and the ridges of his teeth against her sensitive skin, and she had the sensation of melting deep within her being. His fingers kneaded her back, persuading her muscles to respond to his intimate touch.

"You're gorgeous," he sighed, taking his head away from her breast long enough to capture her passion-drugged gaze with his knowing blue eyes. His hand took one of hers and guided it to the button above the zipper of his cords. "Undress me," he commanded, "and let me make love to you until the sun comes up."

"I want to," she admitted, removing her hand.

Once again he pulled her fingers against him, lifting the edge of his sweater and letting her hand touch the taut muscles of his abdomen. "Trust me," he whispered into her hair. "Come on, love, take my clothes off. Show me that you want me."

"Noah—"

"I'll help." In one quick movement he pulled the sweater over his head and discarded it against the trunk of a tree. Blue fire flamed in his eyes. She let her gaze travel slowly down his chest, taking in the ripple of each muscle, the mat of dark hair, his tanned skin, darker because of the night. "Now it's your turn," he coaxed with a wicked smile.

She raised her hand and placed it on his chest. Her fingers tentatively stroked the rock-hard muscles, tracing the outline of his male nipples. He groaned in pleasure and she let her finger slide down his torso to rest on his belt. She told herself she was being wanton, but she didn't believe it, not for a moment. Her love for this man stole all of the guilt from her mind.

The heat in his loins ached with restraint. The fires within him burned with a savage flame, and he had to use all of his willpower to control himself and the urge to rip off the remaining clothes that kept him from taking her. He wanted this night to be as important for her as it was for him. He wanted to love her as she had never before been loved. He wanted to take the time to draw out every feminine urge in her body and satisfy it. Beads of perspiration collected on his forehead and the back of his neck from the frustration of his self-imposed restraint.

"Take them off," Noah pleaded as her fingers hesitated at his belt buckle. Obediently she withdrew his belt and tossed it into the air. It landed silently on the sweater. Her fingers touched the button of his pants—it slid through the hole noiselessly. Every muscle in Noah's body strained with nearly forgotten control.

The zipper tab dropped easily and Noah let out a groan. "Dear God, woman, do you enjoy tormenting me?" He opened his eyes to search hers and saw the reckless gleam of pleasure in her eyes. "You're going to regret this," he warned, and a wicked smile of seduction curved his lips.

Picking up the pieces of his shattered self-control, he began extracting the same sweet agony from her as she did from him. Slowly, with barely concealed deliberation, he lowered her jeans inch by inch over her hips. He let his fingers graze the warm flesh of her inner thighs only to withdraw them. He again took her breast in his mouth and rekindled the passion that had earlier driven her mad with longing.

She arched against him, moaning into the night. Her fingers traced the contours of the lean muscles in his back, pulling him closer to her, letting him know without speaking how much she needed him, how deep the ache within her was. "Please, Noah," she cried into the night, her desire for him chasing away all other thoughts.

Her desperate cry ended the agony. With a groan he settled upon her, letting his weight fall against her, making her feel that the need in him was as great as hers. His lips caressed her and his breath warmed her skin. He threw off the last thin piece of his self-control and found her, became one with her and joined her in the exquisite union of body and soul. His body fused with hers completely, and his rhythm was as demanding as the ceaseless pounding of waves upon the shore. The tempo increased, pushing her to higher crests of rapture as they blended together in a rush of naked passion.

She shuddered beneath him, a quake ripping through her body as the final wave crashed her wildly in sublime surrender. His answering explosion sealed their union, and he let his weight fall gratefully against her body, flattening her breasts. Their arms entwined, the rapid breathing slowed, and they clung together, hoping to capture forever the moment when the two became one.

Words of love, honest thoughts that needed to be shared, came unbidden to her lips. "Noah...I..."

"Shhh, darling. Just listen to the sounds of the night," he whispered against her hair.

Chapter 9

"Tell me about yourself," Noah coaxed, whispering into Sheila's ear. They had managed to get dressed and were sitting together, propped by a pine tree. Noah's arms were wrapped protectively around her as she leaned against him, and his chin rested on her head.

"There's not much to tell." She snuggled deeper into his arms while she watched ghostly clouds move across the moon. It was a still night, with a mere hint of a breeze. The soft drone of insects and the occasional cry of an owl were the only sounds she could hear, aside from Noah's steady breathing and the rhythmic beating of his heart.

"Why don't you start by telling me why you want to stay on at the winery?" He felt her body become rigid.

"I think it's obvious."

"Good. Then you can explain it to me."

"It was my father's lifeblood, Noah. He spent his whole life dreaming of producing the best wines possible. I can't just give it up."

"I haven't asked you to."

"Not yet." She could feel the muscles in her jaw tensing. Not now, she thought to herself, don't ruin it now. We just made beautiful, heavenly love. I love you hopelessly. Don't betray me! Not now.

"But you think I will."

She ran a trembling hand through her hair. "You already offered to buy me out."

"And that bothers you. Why?"

He seemed sincere. She didn't want to think that he had the ugly ulterior motives of which her attorney had warned her. She didn't want to believe he was like his infamous father. "It's just too soon…after my father's death. I don't want to give up everything he believed in. Not yet."

His thumb persuaded her to turn her head and look at him. "Does it mean that much to you—what your father wanted?"

"We were very close."

Noah rubbed his thumbnail under his lower lip. "Close enough that you're willing to sacrifice everything in order to prolong his dream?"

"It's not a sacrifice. It's what I want to do."

Noah sighed and his breath ruffled her hair as he tightened his grip around her waist and pulled her closer to him. "Oh, beautiful lady—what am I going to do with you?" She was a puzzle to him; an intriguing, beguiling puzzle for which he had no answers.

"Trust me," she replied in answer to his rhetorical question.

"I do," he admitted fervently.

She wanted to believe him, but couldn't forget the dark shadows of doubt she had seen in his clear blue eyes.

"Tell me about your husband," Noah suggested, carefully changing the topic of conversation. The faceless man who had married Sheila, impregnated her and then left her had been eating at Noah since the first night they had been together.

"I don't like to talk about Jeff." It was a flat statement, intent on changing the subject.

"Why not?"

Her fingers curled into tiny fists, and she had to force them to relax. "It still bothers me."

"The divorce—or the marriage?"

"The fact that I made such a big mistake." She pulled herself out of Noah's warm arms.

"Then you blame yourself."

"Partially, I suppose—look, I don't want to talk about it."

"I didn't mean to pry…"

Sheila waved his apology aside. "No…you didn't. I don't know why it bothers me so much."

"Maybe it's because you're still in love with him."

Sheila's head snapped back as if his words had slapped her in the face. "You're wrong. The answer is probably just the opposite. I don't know if I ever loved him. I thought I did, but if I had loved him enough, perhaps things would be different."

"And you would still be married?"

She nodded mutely, trying to repress the urge to cry.

"Is that what you want—to be married to him?"

Sheila felt as if the blood were being drained from her as she told Noah her innermost thoughts, the secrets she had guarded from the rest of the world. "No, I don't want to be married to him—marrying Jeff might have been my biggest mistake. But, because of Emily, I wonder if I did the right thing."

"By divorcing him?"

"He divorced me," she sighed, rubbing her fingertips pensively over her forehead. "But maybe I should have fought it, tried harder for Emily's sake."

"Oh, so you think that it would be better for the child if the two of you hadn't split up." His voice sounded bitter in the dark night.

"I don't know what would have been right. It was difficult. I thought he was happy."

"Were you?"

"In the beginning, yes. And when I found out I was pregnant, I was ecstatic. Jeff wasn't as thrilled as I was, but I thought his reaction was normal and that he would become more involved with the child once she was born." Sheila paused, as if trying to put her emotions into some kind of order. Noah felt an intense dislike for Jeff Coleridge.

"It didn't happen," Noah guessed.

"It wasn't the baby so much…as the added strain on him to support the family. I couldn't work, not even in the part-time job I had kept before Emily was born. The cost of a good sitter would have eaten up all my salary. I guess the financial burden was too much for him." Sheila stopped, and the heavy silence enveloped her. Noah was waiting to hear the end of her story, but she found her courage sadly lacking. What she had hidden from her father and the rest of the world, she found impossible to say to the man whose fingers still touched her arm.

"He left you because of the money? What kind of man would leave a wife and a child when he couldn't support them?"

Sheila felt herself become strangely defensive. "He wasn't born to wealth, like you. He had to struggle every day of his life."

"That has nothing to do with a man's responsibility." His fingers dug into her arm. "What happened? There's something you're not telling me."

Sheila swallowed back her tears. "Jeff…he became…involved with another woman." She lowered her head, ashamed of what she had admitted.

When confronted with the truth he had suspected, Noah

felt a sickening turn in his stomach. He gritted his teeth to prevent a long line of oaths from escaping.

Compelled to continue, Sheila spoke again in the barest of whispers, as if the pain were too intense to be conveyed in a normal tone of voice. "This woman—her name was Judith— she was older than Jeff, mid-forties, I'd guess. Divorced and financially secure. She wanted a younger…"

"Stud?" Noah asked sarcastically.

"Man."

"Your husband was no man, Sheila!" he swore. "He's a bastard, and a stupid one at that."

Sheila bravely held her poise together, admitting to Noah what no one else had ever known. She had kept her secrets locked securely within her, hoping to keep any of her pain or anger from tainting Emily's image of her father. "It doesn't matter. Not now. Anyway, Jeff demanded a divorce, and when I realized that there was no hope for the two of us, I agreed. The only thing I wanted was my child. That wasn't much of a problem; Emily would only have gotten in Jeff's way."

Noah's fingers tightened and pulled her closer to his chest. "You don't have to talk about any of this…."

"It's all right. There's not much more to tell, but I think you should hear it," she stated tonelessly. "When the marriage failed, I went off the deep end. I didn't know where to turn. Dad encouraged me to move to California and go to school for my master's."

Sheila smiled wistfully to herself when she recalled how transparent her father had been. "I'm sure that he expected me to find some other man to take my mind off Jeff. So—" she let out the air in her lungs with her confession "—I took money from my dad, a lot of money that he probably couldn't afford to lend to me, and accepted his advice. I didn't know that payment for my out-of-state tuition and living expenses was more than Dad could afford. I thought the winery was profitable. But, it wasn't, and Dad had to borrow the money he loaned to me."

"From Wilder Investments," Noah guessed. Noah's frown deepened and the disgust churning in his stomach rose in his throat. So this was how Ben had cornered Oliver Lindstrom, by using the man's love of his daughter and capitalizing upon it. The muscles in the back of Noah's neck began to ache with the strain of tension.

"There are two mortgages on the winery," Sheila admitted. "Dad had nowhere else to borrow."

"And of course Ben complied."

"You make it sound as if he instigated the whole thing."

Noah's nostrils flared, and his eyes narrowed. "I wouldn't put it past him."

"Your father had nothing to do with the fact that my marriage fell apart. It's my fault that I hadn't paid back the loan.... I just thought there was more time. I never even considered the fact that my father was mortal." Her grief overcame her and the tears she had been fighting pooled in her eyes. "I thought he'd always be there."

"Don't," he urged, kissing her lightly on the top of the head. "Don't torture yourself with a guilt you shouldn't bear."

The little laugh that erupted from her throat was brittle with self-condemnation. "If only I could believe that."

"You're being too hard on yourself."

"There's no one else to blame."

"How about your ex-husband to start with?" Noah spat out, surprised at the hatred he felt for a man he didn't know. "Or your father. He should have told you about his financial problems."

She shook her head, and the tears in her eyes ran down her cheeks. "He didn't want to burden me, and I didn't even ask!"

"Shhh…love, don't," Noah whispered, holding her shaking form against him, trying to quiet a rage that burned within him. How did so beautiful a creature, so innocent a woman, get caught in the middle between two men who only meant to hurt her? Her husband was a wretch, and her father, while trying to shield her, had wounded her in the end. The fire and Oliver Lindstrom's part in its conception waged heavy battles in Noah's tired mind. If only he could tell Sheila what he knew about her father, if only he could bare his soul to her. But he held his tongue, fearful lest he reinforce her feelings of guilt.

Noah had never guessed why Sheila's father had borrowed against his interest in the winery. He had assumed that the money was used for personal use or folly, but he didn't doubt the authenticity of Sheila's tale. Too many events correlated with the ledgers at Wilder Investments, ledgers he had studied for hours before coming to the Cascade Valley. If the ledgers weren't evidence enough, the guilt-ridden lines on Sheila's face testified to her remorse and self-incrimination.

"Come on," he murmured, rising and pulling her to her feet. "Let's go back to the house. You need some sleep."

"Will you stay with me?" she asked, cringing in anticipation of possible rejection. She felt as if her confession would destroy any of the feelings he might have had for her.

"For as long as you want me," he returned, slowly walking up the hill toward the house.

Sheila woke to find herself alone in the bed. The blue printed sheets that she loved seemed cold and mocking without Noah's strong embrace. She knew why he wasn't with her. He had held her and comforted her most of the night, but sometime near morning, when she was drowsily sleeping, he had slipped out of her room to wait for dawn on the uncomfortable couch. It was somewhat hypocritical, but the best arrangement possible because of Emily and Sean.

The day began pleasantly, and even a makeshift breakfast of sausage and pancakes went without much of a hitch. Sean was still sullen and quiet, but at least he seemed resigned to his fate, and for the most part didn't bait Sheila.

After breakfast, while the kids washed the dishes, Sheila took Noah through the rooms of the château. It was a large building; it had originally been built as the country resort of a rich Frenchman named Gilles de Marc. Viticulture had been his hobby, and it was only when he discovered the perfect conditions of the Cascade Valley for growing wine grapes that he began to ferment and bottle the first Cabernet Sauvignon.

Other than a few rooms on the first floor that had been spared, the damage to the main house was dismal. Noah's practiced eyes traveled over the smoke-laden linen draperies and the gritty layer of ash on the carpet. It was obvious that Sheila had tried to vacuum and shampoo the once-burgundy carpet to no avail. Huge water stains darkened the English wallpaper, and a few of the windowpanes were broken and covered with pieces of plywood. The elegant European antiques were water stained, and with the grateful exception of a few expensive pieces, would have to be refinished. Everywhere there was evidence that Sheila had attempted to restore the rooms to their original grandeur, but the task had been too overwhelming.

Later, sitting in the office looking over Oliver Lindstrom's personal records, Noah noted they coincided with the events in Sheila's story. He pondered the entries in Oliver's checkbook, noting dismally when the money borrowed from Wilder Investments had come in. Some of the funds had been sent in quarterly installments to Sheila in California; other money had been used for the day-to-day operation of the winery in lean years. As far as Noah could tell, Oliver had used none of the funds for himself. That knowledge did nothing to ease his mind; it only made it more difficult to explain to Sheila that her father was involved with the arson.

Sheila attempted to help Noah, explaining what she knew of the winery. Noah sat at her father's desk, jotting notes to himself and studying her father's books as if they held the answers to the universe. She felt as if she were growing closer to him, that she was beginning to understand him. She knew that she could trust him with her life, and she quietly hoped that the love she was feeling for him would someday be returned. Perhaps in time the shadows of doubt that darkened his eyes would disappear and be replaced by trust.

Even Emily was beginning to open up to Noah, and the little girl's shyness all but disappeared by midafternoon. Though he was busy looking over the books, he always took the time to talk to her and show an interest in what she was doing. By late afternoon Emily seemed completely at ease with Noah.

The most surprising relationship that began to evolve was Emily's attraction to Sean. She adored the teenager and followed after him wherever he went. Though Sean tried vainly to hide his feelings, Sheila suspected that Sean was as fond of the tousled-headed little girl as she was of him. Things were going smoothly—too smoothly.

"Enough work," Sheila announced, breezing into Oliver's study. Noah was at the desk, a worried frown creasing his brow. One lock of dark hair fell over his forehead. As he looked up from the untidy stack of papers on the desk and his eyes found hers, a lazy grin formed on his lips.

"What have you got in mind?" A seductive glint sparked in his eyes as they caressed her from across the room.

She lowered her voice and dropped her eyelids, imitating his look of provocative jest. "What do *you* have in mind?"

"You're unkind," he muttered, seeing through her joke.

"And you're overly optimistic."

He leaned back in the leather chair and it groaned with the shifting of his weight. "*Expectant* might be a better word."

"I was hoping to hear that you were hungry."

His smile broadened. "That might apply," he admitted, his voice husky.

"Good." She threw off her look of wicked seduction and winked at him. "We're going on a picnic."

"Alone?"

"Dream on. The kids are joining us."

Before Noah could respond, an eruption of hurried footsteps announced Emily's breathless arrival into the study. "Aren't you ready yet?" she grumbled. "I thought we were going on a hike."

"We're on our way," Sheila laughed. "Did you pack your brownies?"

"Shhh…" Emily put her finger to her lips and her face pulled into a pout. "They're supposed to be a surprise!"

"I promise I won't tell a soul," Noah kidded, his voice hushed in collusion with the excited child. "This will be our secret, okay?"

Emily smiled, and Sheila couldn't help but wonder how long it had been since she had seen her daughter so at ease with a man. Emily was shy, and even when her father visited, it took time for her to warm up to him. But with Noah it was different; a genuine fondness existed between the man and child. Or was it her imagination, vain hopes that Emily would take to Noah….

Emily raced out of the room, and Sheila cocked her head

in the direction of the retreating child. "I think we'd better get going before Emily's patience wears out."

"I can't believe that little girl would ever lose her temper."

"Just wait," Sheila warned with a warm laugh. "You'll see, only hope that you're well out of range of her throwing arm if you ever cross her."

"Emily? Tantrums?"

"The likes of which haven't been seen in civilization," Sheila rejoined.

Noah rose from the chair. "I wonder where she gets that temper of hers?" he mused aloud. The corners of his eyes crinkled in laughter as he stared pointedly at Sheila. He crossed the room and encircled her waist with his arms. His fingers touched the small of her back, pressing her firmly against him. He pushed an errant lock of copper hair behind her ear as he stared down at her, a bemused smile curving his lips. His clean, masculine scent filled her nostrils.

She lifted an elegant eyebrow dubiously. "Are you accusing me of being temperamental?"

He shook his head. "Temperamental is far too kind. Argumentative is more apt, I think." His lips caressed her forehead and his voice lowered huskily. "What I wouldn't give to have just an hour alone with you," he growled against her ear.

"What would you do?" she asked coyly, playing with the collar of his shirt.

"Things you can't begin to imagine."

She felt a tremor of excited anticipation pierce through her. "Try me."

His eyes narrowed in frustration. "You're unbelievable, you know, but gorgeous. Just wait, you'll get yours," he warned as he released her and gave her buttocks a firm pat. "Let's go—we don't want to keep Emily waiting."

The hike up the steady incline of the surrounding hills took nearly an hour, but Sheila insisted that the view from the top of the knoll was well worth the strain on their leg muscles. Noah appeared openly doubtful, Emily was an energetic bundle of anticipation and Sean had once again donned his role of bored martyrdom.

The picnic spot Sheila had chosen was one of her favorites, a secluded hilltop guarded by a verdant stand of tamaracks and lodgepole pines. After selecting an area that afforded the best view of the surrounding Cascade Mountains, she spread a well-worn blanket on the bare ground and arranged paper plates and sandwiches haphazardly over the plaid cloth. The tension of the previous night was subdued, and Sheila relaxed as she nibbled at a sandwich and sipped from a soft drink. Even Sean began to unwind, letting his mask of rebellion slip.

"I know a good place to catch trout," Emily stated authoritatively. She was still trying to impress Sean.

"You do, do you?" Sean kidded, rumpling Emily's dark curls. A mischievous twinkle lighted his blue eyes. "How would a little kid like you know about catching trout?"

Emily's face rumpled in vexation. "I'm *not* a little kid!"

"Okay," Sean shrugged dismissively. "So how do you know how to fish?"

"My grandpa taught me," Emily declared.

Sean's indifference wavered as he sized up the little girl. She was okay, he decided, for a little kid. His expression was still dubious. "What kind of trout?"

"Rainbow…and some brook."

Sean's interest was piqued. "So how do you catch them?"

"With a pole, stupid," Emily replied haughtily.

Once again Sean was defensive. "But we didn't bring any poles."

"You think you know everything, don't you?" Emily shot

back. She reached into Sheila's backpack and extracted two tubes; within each was an expandable fly rod.

"You need more than a pole to catch a fish."

Emily shot him a look that said more clearly than words, *Any idiot knows that much.* Instead she said, "Give me a break, will ya?" Once again she reached into the open backpack and pulled out a small metal box full of hand-tied flies. She flipped open the lid and held it proudly open for Sean's inspection. "Anything else?"

Sean smiled, exposing large dimples as he held his palms outward in mock surrender. "Okay, okay—so you know all about fishing. My mistake. Let's go." He looked toward Noah and Sheila sitting near the blanket to see if he had parental approval.

Sheila, who had been witnessing the ongoing discussion with quiet amusement, grinned at the blond youth. "Sure you can go. Your dad and I can handle the dishes—such as they are. Emily knows how to get to the creek; she and her grandpa used to go up there every evening." Sheila's smile turned wistful. "Just be sure to be back at the house before it gets too dark."

Emily was already racing down the opposite side of the hill, her small hand wrapped tightly around the fly rod. "Come on, Sean. Get a move on. We haven't got all day," she sang out over her shoulder.

Sean took his cue and picked up the remaining pole and the box of flies before heading out after Emily.

Sheila began to put the leftover fruit and sandwiches into the basket. "You can help, you know," she pointed out, glancing at Noah through a veil of dark lashes.

"Why should I when I can lie here and enjoy the view?" His blue eyes slid lazily up her body. He was lying on his side, his body propped up on one elbow as he studied her. As she placed the blanket into her backpack, his hand reached out to capture her wrist. "Explain something to me."

The corners of her mouth twitched. "If I can."

His dark brows blunted, as if he were curiously tossing a problem over in his mind, but his thumb began to trace lazy, erotic circles on the inside of her forearm. "Why is it that you and that precocious daughter of yours can handle my son when I can't even begin to understand him?"

"Maybe you're trying too hard," Sheila answered. She bit into an apple and paused when she had swallowed. "Do you really think that Emily's precocious?"

"Only when she has to be."

"And when is that?"

"When she's dealing with Sean. He's a handful."

Sheila rotated the apple in her hand and studied it. "She's never had to deal with anyone like Sean before."

Noah seemed surprised. "Why not?"

Sheila shrugged dismissively. "All of my friends have children just about Emily's age. Some are older, some younger, but only by a few years. The winery's pretty remote and she hasn't run into many teenagers. That might be because they tend to avoid younger kids."

"Certainly you've had babysitters."

Sheila shook her head, and the sunlight glinted in reddish streaks on her burnished curls. "Not many," she explained, tossing the apple core into the trash. "I usually trade off with my friends, and when that doesn't work out, there's always Marian."

"Marian?"

"Jeff's mother. Emily's grandmother."

Noah's thumb ceased its seductive motion on her inner wrist. "Right," he agreed, as if he really didn't understand. He stood up abruptly and dusted his hands on the knees of his jeans. A dark scowl creased his forehead. As if dismissing an unpleasant thought, he shook his head and let out a long gust of wind. "You're still very attached to your ex-mother-in-law, aren't you?" he observed.

Sheila jammed the cork back in the wine bottle and stashed it in the backpack. "I suppose so," she said. "She's Emily's only living grandparent."

"And that makes her special?"

"Yes."

Noah snorted his disagreement as he picked up his pack and the light basket.

"Marian Coleridge is very good to Emily and to me. She adores the child, and just because Jeff and I split up doesn't mean that Emily should have to sacrifice a good relationship with her grandmother."

"Of course not," was Noah's clipped reply.

"Then why does it bother you?"

"It doesn't."

"Liar."

"I just don't like being reminded that you were married."

"You're reminded of it every time you see Emily."

"That's different."

"How?"

"Your child can't be compared to your ex-husband's mother."

Sheila sighed to herself as they began walking back to the house. "I don't want to argue with you. It's pointless. I'm a thirty-one-year-old divorced woman with a child. You can't expect me to forget that I was married."

"I don't. But then, I don't expect you to constantly remind yourself of the fact."

"I don't."

They came to a bend in the path, and Noah stopped and

turned to face Sheila. He set down the basket and gazed into the gray depths of her eyes. "I think you're still hung up on your ex-husband," he accused.

"That's ridiculous."

"Is it?"

Sheila's anger became evident as she pursed her lips tightly together. "The only reason I don't like to talk about Jeff is that I'm not proud of being divorced. I didn't go into that marriage expecting it to end as it did. I thought I loved him once, now I'm not so sure, but the point is, I had hoped that it wouldn't have turned out so badly. It's...as if I've *failed*." She was shaking, but tried to control her ragged emotions. She sighed as she thought of her daughter. "I am glad I married Jeff, though."

"I thought so." His blue eyes narrowed.

"Because of Emily!" Sheila was becoming exasperated. "If I wouldn't have married Jeff, I would never have had Emily. *You* should understand that."

"I didn't get married to have Sean!"

"And I wouldn't have a baby without a father."

Noah's jaw clenched, and the skin over his cheekbones stretched thin. "So you think Marilyn should have gotten an abortion, as she had planned."

"No!" Didn't he understand what she was saying? "Of course not. I don't even understand the circumstances surrounding your son's birth."

"Is that what you want, to hear all the juicy details?"

"I only want to know what you're willing to tell me and to try and convince you that I'm not in the least 'hung up' on Jeff. That was over long before the divorce."

The anger in Noah's eyes began to fade. His mouth spread into a slow, self-deprecating smile. "It's hard, you know."

"What?"

"Dealing with jealousy." He looked into the distance as he

sorted his thoughts. It was late afternoon; a warm sun hung low in the sky, waiting to disappear beneath the ridge of snow-capped mountains and he was with the only woman who had really interested him in the last sixteen years. Why did he insist on arguing with her? Why couldn't he just tell her everything he felt about her—that he was falling in love with her and couldn't let himself fall victim to her? Why couldn't he find the courage to explain about her father? Why couldn't he ignore the look of pride and love in her eyes when she spoke of her father? What did he fear?

Sheila was staring at him, her eyes wide with disbelief. "You're trying to convince me that you're jealous…of what… not *Jeff?*" If Noah hadn't seemed so earnest, so genuinely vexed with himself, she might have laughed.

He was deadly serious, his voice low and without humor. "I'm jealous of any man that touched you."

She reached down, picked up the basket and handed it to him. "Now who's exhibiting 'latent Victorian morality'?"

His dimple appeared as he carefully considered her accusation. "Okay, so you're right. I can't help it. I get a little crazy when I'm with you." He reached for her, but because he was hampered by the picnic basket, she managed to slip out of his grasp. A few feet ahead of him, she turned and walked backward up the sloping, overgrown path. "Is that such a crime?"

"That depends," she murmured, tossing her rich chestnut hair before lowering her lashes and pouting her lips provocatively.

He waited, his smile broadening, his dark brows arching. "Upon what?" he coaxed while striding more closely to her.

She touched her finger to her lips and then pressed it fleetingly to his. "On just how crazy you want to get…."

"You're wicked," he accused, "seductively wicked." This

time, when he reached for her with his free hand, his steely fingers wrapped possessively over her forearm.

"Only when I'm around you," she promised. A smile quirked on her full lips. "That makes us quite a pair, doesn't it? Crazy and wicked."

"That makes for an indescribably potent attraction," he stated, drawing her closer to him. "Just where are you taking me? Didn't you take the wrong turn back at the fork in the path a little while ago?"

"I wondered if you would notice."

"Did you think that you had captivated me so completely that I would lose my sense of direction?"

"Hardly," she whispered dryly.

"Is it a secret?"

"No."

"Then why are you being so mysterious?"

"Because I've never taken anyone up here before…aside from Emily."

"What is it, your private part of the mountains?"

Sheila smiled broadly, slightly embarrassed. "I guess I kind of thought of it that way. It's just a place I used to go, as a kid, when I wanted to be alone."

Noah's hand strengthened its grip on her arm. They followed the path around pine trees that had fallen across it and over a summit, until they entered a small valley with a clear brook running through it. The water spilled over a ledge from the higher elevations of the mountain, creating a frothy waterfall with a pool at its base. From the small lake the stream continued recklessly through the valley and down the lower elevations of the foothills.

They walked around the small pond together, arms linked, eyes taking in the serenity of the secluded valley. Noah helped her cross the stream, nearly slipping on the wet stones peeking from the rushing water. Once on the other side of the brook, Noah spread the blanket. They sat together near a stand of ponderosa pines, close to the fall of cascading water and able to feel the cool mist of water on their skin.

"Why did you bring me here?" Noah asked, his eyes following the path of the winding mountain stream.

"I don't know. I guess I just wanted to share the beauty of this place with you.... Oh, Noah, I just don't want to lose it."

Grim lines formed at the corner of his mouth. "And you think that I'll take it away from you."

"I think you have that power."

Noah rubbed his thumbnail over his lower lip. "Even if I did, do you honestly think I would use it?"

Her eyes were honest when they looked into his. Lines marred her forehead where her brows drew together. "I don't know."

"Don't you trust me?"

She took in a steadying breath. "Yes..."

"But?"

"I don't think you're telling me everything."

Noah tossed a stone into the pond and watched it skip, drawing circles on the clear surface of the water. "What do you want to know?"

"About Anthony Simmons's report on the fire."

"What if it isn't complete?" he heard himself ask, damning himself for hedging. The truth should be so simple.

"It has to be. He hasn't been here in two weeks. He strikes me as the kind of man who doesn't give up until he finds what he's looking for."

"And you think he has?"

"I think that if he hadn't, he would still be knocking on my door, digging through Dad's records, asking his inane questions."

Noah rested his forearms on his knees. "You're right about that much."

"And I'm right that his report is complete?" she asked, barely daring to breathe.

"Right again."

"Well?"

"Well, nothing."

"I don't understand."

"I'm not convinced that Simmons's report was conclusive. There are a few discrepancies."

"Such as?"

Noah found himself lying with incredible ease. Was this how it started, with a single deception that multiplied and compounded until it became an intricate network of lies? Is this what had happened to his father? "Nothing all that important…it's just that the insurance company needs some more documents to support his theories. Until Pac-West is satisfied, the entire report isn't considered valid."

Doubts darkened her eyes and her confidence in him wavered. The trust he had worked so hard to establish was flowing from her as surely as sand through an hourglass.

"I assume that means that Mr. Simmons and his questions will be back."

"Maybe not."

"Noah." Her voice was amazingly level for the sense of betrayal that was overwhelming her. "You're talking in circles. Just tell me the truth…all of it."

One lie begat another. "There's nothing to tell."

"Then why did you come here? I thought you had news about the winery. I thought we could finally put the fire behind us."

This time he didn't have to lie. His eyes were a clear blue, filled with sincerity. "Don't let the fire stand between us. I came here because I wanted to see you. Can't you believe that?"

"Oh, God, Noah, I want to," she whispered fervently. She let her forehead drop into the open palm of her hand. Noah's heart turned over, as he witnessed her defeat. "It's just that I feel that you're holding back on me. Am I wrong? Aren't there things you know that you should be sharing with me?"

He traced the sculpted line of her jaw with his finger. The curves of her bones neared perfection. "Just trust me, Sheila," he stated, feeling the traitor he was. He tilted her head with the strength of one finger and pressed his lips against hers. His lips were gentle but persuasive. His seduction began to work. Against her will, she thought less of the fire and the damage to the winery and concentrated with a growing awareness of the man. She realized that he was pushing against her, that she was falling backward, but she knew that his strong arm would break her fall and before her back would encounter the plaid blanket and cold earth, he would catch her. She wanted to trust him with her life.

His hands parted her blouse, slipping the cotton fabric easily over her shoulders, and his tongue rimmed her lips, which opened willingly to his moist touch. His fingers grazed her breast and finally settled against it, warming her skin and causing her to moan. She trembled with need of him and felt contentment welling from deep within her when he unclasped her bra and pressed his flesh against hers, molding his skin to hers.

Her nipple hardened under his erotic touch, and he growled hungrily in the back of his throat. "You do make me crazy, you know," he whispered against the pink shell of her ear. "You make me want to do things to you that will bind me to you forever," he admitted raggedly. "I want to make love to you and never stop.... Damn it, Sheila, I love you."

She swallowed the lump in her throat that had formed during his tortured admission. How could she possibly sort the fact from fiction? Tears began to collect in her eyes. "You…you don't have to say anything," she stammered, bracing herself for the denial that was sure to come once his passion had subsided.

"I don't want to love you, Sheila…but I just can't seem to help myself." His black brows knit in confusion as he looked down upon her, witnessing her tears and misreading them. "Oh, no, Sheila, darling, don't cry."

To still him and prevent any more half-truths to form on his lips, she kissed him, holding his head against hers and letting him feel the depth of her desire.

Her heart began to thud in her chest, and the blood rushing through her veins turned molten. His hands smoothed the skin over her breasts and down her rib cage, pressing against her with enough force to mold her skin tightly over her ribs and inflame the skin when his fingers dipped below the waistband of her jeans.

His lips followed the path of his hands, and his hungry mouth caressed each breast moistly as his tongue massaged a nipple. She felt the convulsions of desire rip through her body as he trailed a dewy path of kisses across the soft skin of her abdomen. Still, his hands kneaded her breasts. Involuntarily she sucked in her breath and arched against him. Her fingers pushed his shirt off his shoulders and dug into the hard, lean muscles of his upper arms.

When he removed her jeans, he tossed them aside and she sighed in contentment. Slowly he rose and took off his jeans, discarding them into a pile near hers. She stared at him unguardedly, devouring the contours of his tanned muscles as if her eyes were starved for the sight of him.

The sun was beginning to set, casting lengthening shadows across the valley. The fading light played over his skin, adding an ethereal dimension to the oncoming evening.

Noah was silent as he settled next to her and began caressing her with his lips and hands. He stroked her intimately, forcing the tide of her desire to crest, making the blood within her throb with fiery need as it pulsed through her body. They lay together, face-to-face, man to woman, alone except for the hungry need that controlled them.

He took her slowly, coupling with her as gently as if she were new to him. He waited until he felt her demand a faster rhythm, until he saw passion glaze her eyes, until the pain in his back where her fingernails had found his flesh forced him to a more violent, savage union.

Her breath came in short, uneven gasps, her body broke into a glow of perspiration, and the ache within her deepest core began to control her until she was rising with him, pushing against him, calling his name into the wilderness.

She began to melt inside, and convulsive surges of fulfillment forced her to cling to him. He groaned her name against the silken strands of her hair as he shuddered in an eruptive release of frustrated desire that turned his bones to liquid.

"I love you, Sheila," he whispered over and over again. "I love you."

Chapter 10

"You're out of your mind," Noah stated emphatically. Twilight was rapidly approaching and the last thing he wanted to do was take a quick dip in an icy lake.

"Come on…it's not that cold."

"Save that for someone who'll believe it, Sheila. That water is runoff from the spring melt on the Cascades. You've got another think coming if you think you can talk me into swimming in ice water."

"It could be fun," she suggested. He could see her body through the ripples in the water. The firm contours of her limbs were distorted against the darkening pool. He would catch a glimpse of one breast as she treaded in the water, and then it would be gone, covered by her arm as she kept herself afloat. Her hair was damp and tossed carelessly off her face. Dewy drops of water clung to her eyelashes and cheeks. "Come on."

"I've never done anything this irrational in my life," he admitted, testing the water and withdrawing his foot.

"Then it's time." She shoved her hand through the clear

ripples and set a wave of cold water washing over his body. His startled look was replaced by determination as he marched into the lake. Quickly she dove under the water and swam near the bottom, to resurface behind the waterfall. Just as she took in a gulp of air, her legs were pulled out from under her by strong arms. When she came up again, she was sputtering for air. Noah's arms encircled her waist.

"You lied," he accused. "This lake is *too cold*."

"Refreshing," she bantered back.

"Frigid." He captured her blue lips with his and kissed the droplets of water off her face. His hands and legs touched her intimately beneath the surface of the water; his kiss deepened and their tongues entwined. Her skin heated, but was cooled by the chilly temperature in the water.

His fingers touched her thigh, smoothing the soft skin and caressing her as they stood, waist deep in the lake. The waterfall was their flowing curtain of privacy as Noah kissed a hardened nipple and pushed her against the ledge.

"We should be going," she pleaded.

"Not now, you little witch. You coerced me into this lake with you, and you're going to suffer the consequences."

"And just what consequences are you talking about?"

"I'm going to make you beg me to love you."

"But Sean…Emily…" His hand continued its exploration, warming her internally while her skin was chilled by the water.

"They'll wait for us."

He kissed her again, his hand still extracting sweet promises from her. Her breasts flattened against him, and he licked the moisture from them.

Despite the temperature of the water, Sheila began to warm from the inside out. She felt her legs part and wanted more than the touch of cold lapping water on her skin. She yearned to be a part of the man she loved, ached for him to join with her. His kisses upon her neck enticed her. The dewy droplets of cold water on her breasts made her skin quiver. And his hands, God, his hands, gently stroked her, driving all thoughts from her mind other than the desire welling deep within her body.

"Oh, Noah," she whispered as she felt the excruciating ache within her beg for release.

"Yes, love," he whispered thickly.

"Please..."

"What?"

"Please love me," she murmured against his chest, stroking her tongue against the virile male muscles, wondering if it were possible ever to get enough of him. How long would it be before her love for him would consume her?

"I do love you, Sheila. I will forever," he vowed as he pushed her gently against the ledge beneath the water's surface. He placed his legs between hers, and the spray from the waterfall ran in lingering rivulets down her face and neck. The water lapped lazily around her hips and thighs and Noah came to her, burying himself in her with savage strokes.

She found herself clutching him, clinging to him, surging with him over the final barrier until satiation and exhaustion took its toll on her.

"I love you," she whispered, licking a drop of water from his temple, and the strength of his arms wrapped her more tightly to him, as if he were afraid that in releasing her he would lose her.

They shivered as they got dressed, packed their belongings and hiked down the path. Dusk began to shadow the hills in darkness, but when they were within sight of the château, they could see that no lights burned in the windows. It was obvious that Sean and Emily hadn't returned. Sheila became uneasy.

"I thought the kids would be back by now," she said, voicing her thoughts. "I told Emily to be home before dark."

"She might have had trouble convincing Sean," Noah muttered. "It's quite a hike, and the best fly-fishing is in the evening."

Sheila wasn't convinced. "They should be home."

"They will be. Don't worry. I bet they'll be here within the next half hour."

"And if they're not?"

"We'll go looking for them. You do know where Emily was headed, don't you?"

Sheila nodded and smiled in spite of her apprehension. "It's the same place Dad used to take me."

"Then let's not worry until we have to. There's something I want to talk about." He settled upon a rope hammock in the yard and indicated with a gesture that he wanted her to lie next to him.

She slid into the rope swing, careful not to lose her balance. "Okay—so talk."

"I think I should tell you about Marilyn."

"Sean's mother?"

Noah's lips twisted wryly. "I don't think of her as his mother, merely the woman who gave him birth."

"You don't have to explain any of this to me." Sheila wanted to know everything about him, and yet was unwilling to know his secrets more intimately. The past was gone; what was the point in dredging up bitter memories?

"I don't have to tell you anything, but I want to. Maybe then you'll understand my feelings for my son...and my father."

"Ben was involved."

Noah's entire body became rigid. "Oh, yes, he was involved all right—he couldn't help himself. You don't know my father, but if you did, you'd realize that he tries to dominate everyone or everything he touches."

"Your father's ill," Sheila reminded him gently.

Noah relaxed a little and stared at the stars beginning to peek through the violet-gray dusk. "He wasn't ill sixteen years ago," Noah asserted as he squinted in thought. "As a matter of fact he was in his prime."

Noah paused, conjuring up the period in his life he had tried to forget. "Marilyn was only seventeen when we first met. She came to a fraternity dance with a friend of mine. I thought at the time she was the most beautiful girl I had ever seen. Long blond hair, clear blue eyes and a smile that could melt ice. I was captivated.

"It wasn't long before I was dating her, and Ben told me to 'dump her.' In the old man's opinion, Marilyn wasn't quite up to par, socially speaking." Noah shook his head at his own young foolishness.

"You know that I haven't ever gotten along with Ben?" Sheila nodded, afraid to break the silence. "Well, Ben considered Marilyn a 'gold digger,' after the family fortune. Maybe she was. Hell, she was just a kid, barely seventeen. Anyway, I suppose that because my father was so hell-bent against her, it made her all the more attractive to me…at least for a while. We dated for about four months, I guess, and then we started arguing, over stupid little things. We never got along."

Noah absently ran his hand across his chin, rubbing the beard shadow that had begun to appear. "Anyway, just as I decided to break things off with her, she turned up pregnant. She was probably scared, but she didn't have the guts to tell me about it. I heard the news secondhand, through a friend of mine who was dating her sister.

"At first I was angry—furious that she hadn't come to me with the news. When I found out that she intended to have an abortion, I thought I would kill her myself. I drove around for four hours, and I had no idea where I'd been, but I had managed to calm down. By the time I went to her house, I knew that I wanted my child more than anything in the world and that I was willing to pay any price to get it.

"I tried pleading with her to keep the baby, but she didn't even want to talk about it. I told her that I would marry her, give my name to the child, whatever she wanted, if she would reconsider."

Noah closed his eyes, as if hiding from the truth. "She finally agreed and I thought I'd won a major victory because it was pretty evident that she was more concerned about being a cheerleader to the football squad than being a mother to my unborn child. And maybe I've been too rough on her—she wasn't much older than Sean is now. Just a kid. And I was just as foolish. Although we'd made one mistake, I thought we could correct it. Given time, I was sure that Marilyn would mature and learn to love the baby. I even thought she and I had a chance."

Bitterness made his voice brittle. "But I was wrong. Dead wrong. Ben couldn't leave it alone...and maybe it was better that he didn't...I don't know. Anyway, Ben was against the marriage from the first, baby or no baby, and he offered Marilyn a decent sum of money to go quietly away and give the baby up for adoption. The offer was attractive to her; she had no other means to afford college.

"I was outraged at my father's proposal and sickened by Marilyn's transparent interest in the money. I tried to talk her out of it and insisted that she marry me and keep the child. If she wanted to go to school, I was sure we could afford it, at least part-time. She was adamantly against any solution I provided. I didn't understand it at the time, not until she told me what she had come up with as an alternative solution."

Sheila was breathless as she watched the angry play of sixteen-year-old emotions contort Noah's face in pain. "In Marilyn's beautiful, scheming mind, she found the answer. The price was considerably higher of course, but she agreed to give the baby up for adoption to me, his father, for a discreet and large sum of money. Although Ben didn't like the idea of being manipulated by a girl he considered socially off-limits, he seemed to almost…enjoy her sense of values.

"It was obvious that a marriage to Marilyn under the best circumstances would be a disaster for both the baby and myself, so I swallowed my pride and pleaded with my father to agree to her demands, in order that I could gain custody of Sean. Sixteen years ago fathers' rights were virtually unheard of, and without Marilyn's written consent, I could never have gotten custody of my son. I wanted the only decent thing I could retrieve from that relationship with Marilyn—my unborn son.

"Ben thought I was completely out of my mind, but finally agreed. In the past sixteen years, every time he and I would disagree, Ben would remind me that it was *his money and his power* that gave me custody of Sean."

Noah ran an angry hand through his dark hair and uttered an oath under his breath. Sheila knew she was witnessing a rare side of him. As she watched the cruel emotions tighten his jaw, she understood that she was learning things about him that he kept hidden from the rest of the world. He was letting her become closer to him, divulging his innermost secrets. She leaned her head against his shoulder and listened to the steady beat of his heart.

"Ben even has the stubborn pride to think that he saved me from an unhappy marriage…. Maybe he did. Who can say? The point is that he's held it over my head for sixteen years. Finally, I've paid him back in full." He spat the words out with a vehemence that sent a shiver skittering down Sheila's spine.

"Because you've taken over the business while he's been recuperating in Mexico?"

"That's right. It took me this long to get out of the old man's debt." Sheila could see the emotional scars of pain etched on Noah's broad forehead; she could read the agony in his blue eyes.

Her voice caught as she began to speak. "I'm sorry."

"Don't be. It's over."

"It bothers you."

"I said, it's over." He shifted on the hammock and seemed to notice the darkness for the first time. His eyes searched the hillside. "The kids should be home."

Sheila, too, had been caught up in the complexity of his story. Panic began to take hold of her as she realized that night had descended and Emily was missing.

"Oh, my God," she whispered, clasping a hand over her mouth. "Where could they be?"

"You tell me. Do you have any flashlights?"

She nodded, and was on her way to the house before he could tell her to get them. She fumbled with the light switch in the kitchen in her hurry. Within two minutes she was back outside, listening for a response to Noah's shout. Nothing interrupted the stillness of the night.

"Damn," Noah muttered as he pinched the bridge of his nose. "I should have listened when you wanted to search for them earlier."

"You didn't know they wouldn't come home."

"But you did." He turned to look at her as they followed the bobbing circles of lights flashing on the ground before them. "Why were you worried—is it part of being a mother?"

"Emily's never late," Sheila asserted breathlessly. They were climbing the hill at a near run.

"Next time I'll pay more attention when you begin to worry."

"A lot of good that does us now," Sheila snapped back. She

knew she was being short with Noah and that it was unfair, but her concern for her daughter made her irritable.

Noah stopped and cupped his hands around his mouth to call Sean's name. From somewhere in the distance they heard his answering shout. Sean's voice sounded rough and frightened.

"Oh, my God," Sheila whispered, listening for Emily's voice and hearing nothing. "Something's happened." Fear took a stranglehold on her throat, and she started running up the path, jumping to conclusions and imagining scenarios of life without her daughter.

She stumbled once on an exposed root. Noah reached for her, but couldn't break the fall that tore her jeans and scraped her knee. Wincing in pain, she continued to race up the hill, mindless of the blood that was oozing from the wound.

Sean's shouts were louder, and within minutes his anxious face came into range of the flashlights. Sheila choked back a scream as she saw Emily in his arms. The child was dripping wet, her face was covered with mud and there were several scratches on her cheeks.

"Mommy…" Emily reached her arms out to her mother and tears formed in Sheila's eyes as Emily clung, sobbing to her.

"Hush…Emily, it's all right. Mommy's here." Emily burrowed her nose into Sheila's shoulder. The girl was visibly shaking and her teeth were chattering. Noah took off his shirt and placed it on Emily's small shoulders. "Shhh… Sweetheart, are you all right… Are you hurt?"

"It's her ankle," Sean interrupted. His face was ashen as he looked down at Emily.

"Let's take a look at that." Noah took the flashlight and illuminated Emily's right ankle. Gently he touched the swollen joint. Emily wailed in pain.

"Shhh…Em, Noah's just seeing how bad it is," Sheila whispered into Emily's bedraggled curls. Sheila's eyes drove into Noah's with a message that he had better be careful with her daughter.

"I don't think it's broken…but I can't really tell," Noah said softly. "Here, Emily, let me carry you back to the house. We'll call a doctor when we get there."

"No! Mommy, you hold me. *Please*." Emily clung to Sheila's neck as if holding on for dear life.

"Emily," Noah's voice was firm as he talked to the little girl.

"Don't, I can handle her."

"Forget it, Sheila." The beam of light swept from Emily's ankle to Sheila's torn, bloody jeans. "You'll be doing well if you can get back to the house on your own. I'll carry Emily."

"Mommy…" Emily wailed.

"Really, Noah, I'm sure I can manage," Sheila asserted, her gray eyes glinting like daggers.

"Forget it…. Sean, you carry the gear and the flashlights." Noah carefully extracted Emily from Sheila's arms, but still gave orders to his son. "Then you walk with Sheila; she's cut her leg. Now let's go. The sooner we get Emily home, the better."

Not even Emily argued with the determination in Noah's voice. Sheila pursed her lips together and ignored the urge to argue with him. The most important thing was Emily's well-being, and Sheila couldn't find fault with Noah's logic.

"Tell me, son," Noah said sternly, when the lights of the château were visible. "Just what happened?"

"We were fishing."

"And?"

"Well, it was getting dark, and I guess I was in kind of a hurry," Sean continued rapidly. "Emily kept getting behind, and when we crossed the creek, she slipped on a rock. I threw down the gear and reached for her, but the current pushed her off balance and pulled her under the water. It was lucky that the creek was shallow, and I got to her. Then she started crying and screaming about her ankle and, well, I just started carrying her down the hill as fast as I could."

"You should have been more considerate, Sean. If you weren't always hurrying to get where you should have been an hour ago, this might never have happened!" Noah declared gruffly.

"I didn't think…"

"That's the problem, isn't it?"

"Noah, don't," Sheila interjected. "It's not Sean's fault. Arguing isn't going to help anything."

It seemed an eternity to Sheila, but eventually they got Emily to the house. While she cleaned and dried the child, Noah called a local doctor who was a friend of Sheila's. Sean paced nervously from the living room to the den and back again until Emily was propped up in bed and the doctor arrived.

Dr. Embers was a young woman who had a daughter a couple of years younger than Emily. She was prematurely gray and wore her glasses on the end of her nose as she examined the child.

"So you took a tumble, did you?" she asked brightly as she looked into Emily's pupils. "How do you feel?"

"Okay," Emily mumbled feebly. Her large green eyes looked sunken in her white face.

"How about this ankle…does this hurt?"

Emily winced and uttered a little cry.

The doctor continued to examine Emily while Sheila looked anxiously at the little girl, who seemed smaller than she had earlier in the day. Lying on the white pillow, Emily seemed almost frail.

Dr. Embers straightened, smiled down at the child and gave

her head an affectionate pat. "Well, I think you'll live," she pronounced. "But I would stay off the ankle for a while. And no more jumping in creeks for the time being, okay?"

Emily smiled feebly and nodded. Dr. Embers took Sheila into the kitchen and answered the unspoken question hanging on Sheila's lips. "She'll be fine, Sheila. Don't worry."

"Thank goodness."

"She shouldn't need anything stronger for the pain than aspirin, but I do want you to bring her into the clinic on Monday for X-rays."

Alarm flashed in Sheila's eyes. "But I thought…"

Donna Embers waved Sheila's fears away with a gentle smile and a hand on her arm. "I said don't worry. I'm sure the ankle is just a sprain, but, I want to double-check, just in case there's a hairline fracture hiding in there."

Sheila let out a relieved sigh. "I really appreciate the fact that you came over tonight."

"No problem; what are friends for? Besides, you'll get the bill."

Sheila smiled. "Can you at least stay for a cup of coffee?"

Donna edged to the door and shook her head. "I'd love to, really, but I left Dennis with dinner and the kids, which might be just a shade too much responsibility for him."

Sheila leaned against the kitchen door frame and laughed. The last thing she would call Donna Ember's loyal husband was irresponsible. A feeling of warm relief washed over her as she watched the headlights of Donna's van fade into the distance.

"Is Emily going to be all right?" Sean asked when Sheila walked back into the kitchen and began perking a pot of coffee.

"She's fine."

Sean swallowed and kept his eyes on the floor. "I'm really sorry."

"It's not your fault," Sheila maintained.

"Dad thinks so," Sean replied glumly.

"Well, your dad is wrong."

Sean's head snapped upward, and his intense blue eyes sought Sheila's. "But I thought you liked Dad."

"I do…I like him very much," Sheila admitted, "but that doesn't mean he can't be wrong some of the time."

Sean sank into a chair near the table. "I should have been more careful."

"Even if you had, the accident might still have occurred. Just be thankful it wasn't any worse than it was."

Sean's face whitened at the thought. "I don't think it could have been worse."

"Oh, Sean, it could have been a dozen times worse." Sheila took a chair near Sean and touched him lightly on the shoulder. "Emily could have struck her head, or you could have fallen down, too…a thousand different things could have happened." Sheila fought the shudder of apprehension that took hold of her when she considered how dangerous the accident could have been. "Look, Sean, you did everything right. You got Emily out of the water and carried her to me. Thank you."

Sean was perplexed and confused. "You're thanking me… why?"

"For clear thinking, and taking care of my little girl."

"Miss Lindstrom—"

"Sheila."

Sean shifted uncomfortably on the chair. He was still carrying the weight of guilt for Emily's accident and had transformed from a tough punk teenager into a frightened boy. "Okay…Sheila…I'm…sorry for the way I acted last night."

"It's okay."

"But I was crummy to you."

Sheila couldn't disagree. "You were."

"Then why aren't you mad at me?"

"Is that what you want?" Sheila inquired, taking a sip from her coffee.

Noah had heard the end of the conversation and stood in the door awaiting Sean's response to Sheila's question.

Sean looked Sheila in the eye, unaware that his father was standing less than five feet behind him. "I don't know." He shrugged, some of his old bravado resurfacing. "I just didn't want to like you."

Sheila's eyes flicked from Sean to Noah and back again. "Because you were afraid that I might take your father from you?"

Again the blond youth shrugged.

"I would never do that, Sean. I have a daughter of my own, and I know how important it is that we have each other. No one could *ever* take me away from my child. I'm sure the same is true of your father."

Sean looked at Sheila, silently appraising her. His next words shattered the friendliness between them. "My dad still cares for my mom!" His look dared her to argue with him.

"I'm sure he does, Sean," Sheila agreed, silencing Noah with her eyes. "And I don't intend to change that." Knowing that Noah was about to break in on the conversation, and hoping to avoid another confrontation, Sheila changed the topic. "Emily made some brownies for you earlier, but she must have forgotten them with all of the excitement about fishing." She rose from the table and began putting the chocolate squares on a plate. Noah entered the room, but Sheila ignored him. "Why don't you take this into Emily—cheer her up?"

"Do you think she'll want to see me? She might be sleeping or something."

"She's awake," Noah stated. "I just left her, and believe it or not, I think she's hungry."

Sean grabbed the plate of brownies and, balancing them between two glasses of milk, left the kitchen in the direction of Emily's room. Without asking if he wanted any, Sheila poured Noah a cup of coffee.

"How's *your* leg?" Noah asked, eyeing Sheila skeptically.

"Never better. I cleaned it and it's okay. A little of the skin is scraped off, that's all."

Noah took an experimental sip from his coffee as he looked dubiously at her white slacks. "Did Dr. Embers look at it."

"No."

"Why not?"

"I told you I cleaned it and bandaged it. Look, it's really no big deal."

Noah didn't look convinced. "I'm just sorry that you and Emily had to suffer because of Sean's neglect."

"Noah, please. Don't blame him. He's just a child himself."

"He's sixteen and has to learn responsibility sometime. He should have been more careful."

"He knows that—don't reprimand him. It would be like rubbing salt into his wound. He feels badly enough as it is."

"He should."

"Why? Because he was careless? Noah, accidents will happen. Give the kid a break, will you?"

Noah set his cup down on the table and walked over to the sink. For a few silent moments he stared out the window into the night. "It's not just the accident, Sheila. It's his attitude. You were there the night he came home drunk. It wasn't the first time." He breathed deeply and tilted his head back while squinting his eyes shut. "He's in trouble at school and I've even had to pick him up downtown. Since he's a minor, he hasn't been in jail, but he's been close, damned close. He missed a couple of probation meetings, and so now he's walking a very thin line with the law."

"A lot of kids get into trouble."

"I know. I should count myself lucky that he doesn't use dope, I guess."

Sheila approached Noah and wrapped her arms around his waist. How long had he tortured himself with guilt for his son? "Sean will be all right, Noah. I've seen more kids than you'd want to count in my job, some easier to deal with than Sean, others more difficult. Sean will come through this."

He put his large hands over hers, pressing her fingertips into his abdomen. "Why did you let him lie to you?"

"About what?"

"His mother. You know how I feel about Marilyn."

"Sean probably does, too. But he can't admit it to me, not yet. He still considers me a threat."

"I think you're reading more into this than there really is."

"Adolescence is tough, Noah, or don't you remember? Add to that the fact that Sean knows his mother rejected him. It makes him feel inferior."

"Lots of kids grow up without one parent…even Emily."

"And it's hard on her, too," Sheila sighed against his back.

Noah turned around and faced her. One hand pushed aside her hair as he studied her face and noticed the thin lines of worry that dimmed her smile. He pressed a kiss to her forehead. "You're a very special woman, Sheila Lindstrom, and I love you." He traced the edge of her cheekbones with his finger. "It's times like these that I wonder how I managed to live this long without you."

Sheila warmed under his unguarded stare. "I guess you must have a will of iron," she teased.

"Or maybe it's because I'm a stubborn fool." He draped his arm possessively over her shoulder and guided her out of the kitchen. "Let's go check on Emily."

"In a minute…. You go look in on her, I'll be there shortly."

She moved out of his embrace and pushed him down the hall. "I've got to make a phone call."

Noah looked at his wristwatch. "Now? To whom?"

She was ready for his question. "I think I'd better call Jeff."

"You're ex-husband?" Noah was incredulous. "Why?"

"He has the right to know about the accident," Sheila attempted to explain. Before she could get any further, Noah cut her off and his mouth pulled into a contemptuous scowl. A thousand angry questions came to his mind.

"Do you think he would even care?"

"Noah, he's Emily's father. Of course he'll care."

"From what you've told me about him, he hasn't shown much fatherly concern for his daughter!"

"Keep your voice down!" Sheila warned in a harsh whisper. "Jeff has to know."

Noah's face contorted with disgust. The skin stretched tightly over the angled planes of his features. "Are you sure the accident isn't some handy excuse?"

Sheila's gray eyes snapped. "I don't need an excuse. He has to know and I can't have him hear it through the grapevine."

"Why not?"

"How would you feel if it were Sean?"

"That's different. I care about my son. I would have done anything to have him with me. It was a little different with your husband, I'd venture to guess."

"He's still her legal father. This is a rural community, but word travels quickly. I either have to call Jeff or his mother, and I'd prefer not to worry Marian. If I call her now, she'll be over here within a half hour."

"And what about Coleridge? Is that what he'll do—come racing over here to check on his daughter and his ex-wife. Is that what you're hoping for?"

"You're impossible!" Sheila accused. "But you're right about one thing, I would be thrilled to pieces if Jeff came over here."

"I thought so," he commented dryly as he crossed his arms over his chest and leaned against the wall, looking as if he were both judge and jury. She, of course, was the unconvincing defendant.

"But not for the reasons you think," she continued, trying to stem her boiling anger. "Jeff is Emily's father, for God's sake. She's just been through a very traumatic experience, and I think she could use a little support from Daddy."

"A little is all she'd get, at the very best," Noah pointed out in a calm voice. His blue eyes looked deadly. "Jeff Coleridge is no more Emily's father than Marilyn is Sean's mother! I can't believe that you're still hanging on to ideals that were shot down years ago when he walked out on you and your kid, Sheila. You don't have to paint the picture any rosier than it really is. It's not good for you, and it's not good for Emily."

"So look who's handing out free advice—*Father of the year!*" The minute her words were out, she wanted to call them back. She hadn't meant to be cruel.

Noah's hands clenched and then relaxed against his rib cage. "Once again, the sharp tongue cuts like a whip, Miss Lindstrom. I'm not trying to hurt you, I'm only attempting to suggest that genetics has nothing to do with being a parent. Oh, sure, Coleridge *sired* your child, but where was he when the chips were down? Or have you conveniently forgotten that he walked out on you and took up with another woman? A man like that doesn't deserve to know that his child was hurt. Face it, Sheila, he just doesn't give a damn."

Sheila's nerves were strung as tightly as a piano string, her voice emotionless. "Each summer Emily spends a few weeks with Jeff. He's expecting her by the end of next week."

"Does she want to see him?"

Sheila wavered. "She's confused about it."

Noah's lips twisted wryly. "What you're saying is that she knows he doesn't want her, and you're hoping that when he learned of the accident, he'll rush to her side and reestablish himself as a paragon of virtue in her eyes. Don't delude yourself, Sheila, and for Emily's sake, don't try to make your ex-husband something he's not. Let her make up her own mind."

"She will," Sheila said softly, "whether I call him or not. But I am going to call, you know. It's his right as a father."

"He has no rights—he gave them up about four years ago, wouldn't you say?"

For a moment they stared across the room at each other, trying to repair the damage their argument had caused, but it was impossible. "Excuse me," Sheila said shakily, "but this is my decision." She turned to the telephone and dialed the long-distance number to Spokane.

Noah turned on his heel, uttered a low oath, and headed down the hall toward Emily's room. Women! Would he ever live to understand them?

Chapter 11

Though never mentioned again, the argument hung over Noah and Sheila like a dark, foreboding cloud. Noah had decided to spend another week at the winery to double-check Anthony Simmons's conclusions concerning the fire. Sean was entrusted with Noah's car and sent back to Seattle to pick up a couple of changes of clothes and some documents from the office of Wilder Investments. The boy was back at Cascade Valley as he had promised, the car intact.

For his part, Noah was a whirlwind. He decided it was in the best interests of Wilder Investments to reopen the winery, and he began a full-scale cleanup of the estate. It took some fast talking, but even the local sheriff's department had reluctantly complied with his demands that the west wing be completely reconstructed. By late Friday afternoon D & M Construction, a subsidiary of Wilder Investments, had moved in, and the foreman was working with an architect to redesign the building.

Days at the winery were spent preparing for the autumn harvest; the nights making love. Noah didn't mention Jeff again, and Sheila hoped that the harsh words shouted in the heat of anger would soon be forgotten.

Noah began a furious study of viticulture, with Sheila and Dave Jansen as his tutors. Dave was a young man whose serious, plain face was offset by laughing brown eyes. He took Noah on a tour of the vineyards and explained, endlessly, the reasons that wine production was suited for the valley.

"Thirty years ago, few people thought that western Washington could hold a candle to California for wine production," he declared, proudly showing off a hillside covered with vinifera wine grapes.

"But you're changing their minds, right?" Noah asked.

"You got it. Everybody thinks it rains all the time in Washington, or that it's overcast, but that's because they haven't seen the eastern part of the state. Over here our summers are warm and dry with extremely low precipitation and cloud cover. This allows for a unique combination of moderate heat, high light intensity and long days that produce vinifera fruit with an excellent sugar-acid balance. All of our wines have a distinctive varietal character."

"But what about the winters? A couple of years ago the late snow just about wiped out the crop."

Dave nodded gravely. "That can happen," he admitted. "We try to select our vineyard sights as close as possible to the Columbia River. We use southern slopes above the valley floor to further decrease the risk of low temperatures. Recently we've been planting a hardier grape, a vinifera that can stand colder temperatures."

Noah's gaze ran skeptically over the vineyards.

"Really, this is a great place to produce wine," Dave stated firmly. "Look, Mr. Wilder—"

"Noah."

Dave smiled and inclined his head. "I know that Sheila's

had a run of bad luck here, but for my money, Cascade Valley will produce the best wine in the country."

"That's a pretty broad statement."

Dave pursed his lips and shook his balding head. "I don't think so." He held up his fingers to add emphasis to his point. "Eastern Washington has a good climate, the right amount of light, loamy soils and is relatively free of pests and disease. I don't think you can do better than that."

Noah squatted and ran his fingers through the soil. "So what's to prevent a competitor from building next to Cascade Valley?"

"Name familiarity and reputation," Dave replied quickly.

"A reputation that has been tarnished over the last few years."

"Yeah. I can't deny that, much as I'd like to," Dave conceded, opening the door to his pickup. "Want a lift back to the house? I'd like you to take a look at our latest investment, French oak barrels for aging instead of American white oak. They were Oliver's idea. He used a few of them several years ago and the end result is our reserve Cabernet Sauvignon, which we hope to market late this year."

"I think I'll walk back to the house," Noah decided. "I'll catch you tomorrow because I would like to see the reserve bottles."

"All right. See you then." The battered old pickup took off, leaving a plume of dust in its wake. Noah placed his hands, palms outward, in the back pockets of his jeans as he walked back to the house. He was lost in thought, considering all of the disasters that had struck Cascade Valley in the past few years. No one could be blamed for the volcanic eruption of Mount Saint Helens. The tonnage of ash and soot that had fallen on Cascade Valley and destroyed the harvest would have to be attributed to an act of God, or natural disaster. But the tampered bottles found in Montana were a different story. The contamination had been planned rather than accidental. Needle marks found in the corks of some of the damaged bottles proved that someone had to have been behind the sabotage.

Originally Noah had assumed that Oliver Lindstrom had executed the poisoning of the bottles; now he wasn't so sure. The image painted by people he had spoken with told him that Oliver Lindstrom wasn't the kind of man who would destroy all that he had worked so hard to build. If, as Sheila and the staff maintained, Cascade Valley Wines and the winery itself were Oliver Lindstrom's lifeblood, why would he want to tarnish a reputation it had taken years to establish?

Noah squinted against the setting sun and kicked a stone out of the rutted dirt road. It just didn't make sense. If a man needed money, he wouldn't consciously taint his product, thereby causing an expensive recall and losing consumer trust. Could Lindstrom really have been as desperate as Anthony Simmons wanted Noah to believe: desperate enough to take his own life in an arson attempt? The damned fire— always that damned fire—continued to plague Noah with doubts. As he walked up the final crest of the hill supporting the château, he stopped to look at the wreckage.

A disappearing sun cast red-gold rays over the charred timbers of the west wing. A yellow bulldozer was parked near the blackened building, waiting to raze the sagging skeleton. Noah ran his fingers through his hair as he studied the destruction. If only he didn't care about Sheila, it would be much easier.

Sheila was tearing the old wallpaper off the walls in the dining room when the doorbell rang.

"Emily," she called, pulling at an obstinate strip, "could you get that? Emily?" There was no immediate response, and Sheila remembered Emily mentioning something about going outside with Sean. Her ankle was much better and she was feeling more than a little cooped up in the house.

The doorbell rang again impatiently. "Coming," Sheila called as she wiped her hands on a nearby towel. Who could be calling today? she wondered. It was nearly the dinner hour, and she was a mess. Her jeans and blouse smelled like the sooty walls she had been cleaning, and her hair was piled in a bedraggled twist on the top of her head. She pulled out the pins and ran her fingers through it as she made her way to the door.

Before she could open it, the door swung open and Jeff Coleridge poked his head into the foyer. "So there is someone home after all," he remarked dryly, his eyes giving Sheila a quick head to heels appraisal.

Sheila managed a thin smile. "Sorry—I thought Emily would get the door."

"And I thought she was laid up," he replied with a smirk. "Or was this just one of your rather obvious attempts to see me?"

Sheila's gray eyes didn't waver. "That was a long time ago."

"Not that long."

Sheila stood in the entryway, not letting him pass. "I assume you came here to see Emily."

"Who else?" His smile was as devilish as ever, his dark eyes just as flirtatious. He was still handsome; living the good life seemed to suit him well. His lean torso reflected hours on the tennis courts, and his devil-may-care attitude added to his cunning charm. After all of these years, Sheila was immune to it.

"I hope no one. Emily's outside. I'll go and get her."

"Sheila, baby." He reached out a hand and touched her wrist. "What is our darling daughter doing out of bed—I thought she had some horrible ankle sprain. At least that's the story you gave me."

Trying desperately not to be baited, Sheila withdrew her

wrist and pasted a plastic copy of his saccharine smile on her face. "That was no story, and if you would have shown up a few days ago, you would have found her in bed. Fortunately she's young and heals quickly."

"Now, now," he cajoled, noting the sarcasm dripping from her words. "Your claws are showing, sweetheart. You know I couldn't come any sooner."

"You could have called."

"Is that what you wanted?"

"What I wanted was for you to show some interest in your child. She's not a baby anymore, Jeff, and she's beginning to understand how you feel about her."

"I'll just bet she does," he snapped, losing his calm veneer of self-assurance. "With you poisoning her mind against me."

"You know I don't do anything of the kind." Sheila's face was sincere, her gray eyes honest and pained. "You handle that part of it well enough on your own."

Jeff's frown turned to a pout. "I thought we were supposed to have a 'friendly divorce,' isn't that what you wanted?"

"When I was naive enough to believe it."

"I suppose you think that's my fault, too."

"Not really. We couldn't get along while we were married; I should never have expected that the divorce would change anything."

"You act as if it's carved in stone."

"I wish I thought it wasn't," Sheila sighed, leaning against the door.

"So what do you want now, Sheila?" His eyes narrowed suspiciously as he looked down upon her.

"I want you to be an interested father, Jeff. And I don't want it to be an act. Is that too much to ask?"

Jeff took in a deep breath, attempting to stem the rage that took hold of him every time he saw Sheila and was reminded of her quiet beauty. It unnerved him. Perhaps it was her fiery spirit coupled with her wide, understanding eyes. There had been a time in his life when he had been proud to show her off as *his* wife. But she wanted more—she wanted a child, for God's sake. Not that Emily wasn't a great kid…he just didn't like the idea of fatherhood. It made him feel so *old*. If only Sheila would have given a little more, seen things his way, maybe the two of them would have made it.

Even in dusty jeans and a sooty blouse, with a black smudge where her hands had touched her cheek, she looked undeniably beautiful. Her hair fell in a tangled mass around her face, the way he liked it, and she still carried herself with an elegance and grace he had never seen in another woman—even Judith. Whereas Judith's beauty was beginning to fade, Sheila's was just beginning to blossom.

Jeff cleared his throat and tried to ignore Sheila's intent stare. He coughed before answering her question. "You know I care about Emily," he said with a shrug of his shoulders. "It's just that I've never been comfortable with kids."

"You've never tried. Not even with your own."

Jeff shook his head, and he looked at the boards of the porch. "That's where you're wrong, Sheila. I did try, honestly…"

"But you couldn't find it in your heart to love her."

"I didn't say that." His eyes lifted to meet the disgust and rage simmering in hers.

"You have never loved anyone in your life, Jeff Coleridge, except yourself."

"That's what I've always liked about you, Sheila: your sweet, even-tempered disposition."

Sheila was shaking, but she attempted to regain her poise. If only she could look at Jeff indifferently. If only she didn't see a man who rejected his infant when she looked into his eyes. "This argument is getting us nowhere," she said through tight lips. The strain of trying to communicate with Jeff was getting to her. "Why don't you come into the kitchen and wait while I get Emily. She's just on the patio."

Jeff hesitated, as if he wanted to say something more, but decided against it. Sheila stepped backward, allowing him to pass, and tried to calm her anxious nerves. When she found Emily, she didn't want to infect the child with her worries about the disintegrating relationship between father and daughter.

She stepped onto the patio and drew in a steadying breath. Emily was watching Noah and Sean trying to outdo one another in a Frisbee throwing contest. Emily was giggling in excitement, Noah was concentrating on the returning Frisbee and Sean was smiling with satisfaction, sure that the plastic disc would elude his father. It was a tender scene, a family scene, and it pulled at Sheila's heartstrings knowing she had to destroy it.

"Emily," she called softly. "Someone's here to see you."

"Who?" Emily demanded, riveted to her spot and eyeing Noah's ungraceful catch. He flipped the Frisbee back at his son.

"Daddy's come to see you."

Emily's smile faded. "My daddy?"

Sheila's grin felt as phony as it was. "Isn't that great?"

"He's not going to take me with him to Spokane, is he?"

"Of course not, honey," Sheila said with unfelt enthusiasm. "He just came to see how you're doing with that ankle of yours." Pushing aside an errant curl around her daughter's face, Sheila continued. "Come on. He's waiting in the kitchen."

"No, I'm not," Jeff's cheery voice called as he walked out the door. He smiled down at his daughter. "It's been a long trip, and I couldn't wait any longer." It was then, when his eyes lifted from his daughter's serious gaze, that he noticed Noah and Sean. The game had ended and Noah was staring intently at the man who had once been Sheila's husband. "Pardon me," Jeff announced with a wary, well-practiced smile. "I don't believe we've met."

Noah strode slowly up to the patio, his blue eyes challenging Jeff's dark ones. Sheila could see that every muscle in Noah's body had become rigid, the skin drawn taut. "The name's Wilder," he stated. "Noah Wilder. This—" he cocked his head in the direction of the blond boy in cut-off jeans "—is my son, Sean." He extended his hand, took Jeff's and gave it a short, but firm, shake.

"Jeff Coleridge."

Noah's smile twisted as if smiling at a private irony. "I assumed as much."

"Wilder?" Jeff's eyes followed Noah's movements as he placed his body between those of ex-husband and wife. The move was subtle, but not lost on either Sheila or Jeff. "You're connected with Wilder Investments?"

"My father's company."

"Ben Wilder is *your* father?" A note of genuine respect and surprise entered Jeff's voice.

"That's right." Noah didn't return Jeff's growing smile.

"Oh…so you're here because of the winery…as a business partner to Sheila?" Jeff assumed. He seemed relieved.

"Partly."

"I don't understand."

"Noah is Mommy's friend," Emily interjected.

"Is that right?" Jeff's thin eyebrows raised, and his accusing dark eyes impaled Sheila.

There was an awkward silence while Sheila struggled with the proper words. Both men regarded her intently. From the corner of her eye, Sheila noticed that Sean was walking toward the orchard, away from the uncomfortable scene. An embarrassed flush crept up her neck, but her eyes never wavered, and her voice was surprisingly steady. "Yes, that's right. Noah is a friend of mine, a very good friend."

The nasty retort forming on Jeff's lips died under the power of Noah's stare and the innocent, wondering eyes of his child. He didn't want to appear the fool. "I see," he returned vaguely, as if he really didn't understand at all. Then, as if dismissing the entire conversation as something that should have been swept under the rug, he pulled at the crease in his pants and bent on one knee to talk to his daughter. He took one of Emily's little hands and pressed it between his own. He considered it a very fatherly gesture. "So tell me, Emmy, how're you feeling?"

"Fine." Emily was suddenly shy as she found herself the center of attention.

"You're sure now? How about that ankle?"

"It's okay."

"Good…that's good. Are you going to tell me all about your fall in the creek?"

"Do you really want to know?" Emily asked skeptically.

Jeff's thin smile wavered. "Of course I do, precious," he replied, patting the top of her hand nervously. He led her over to the chaise lounge and indicated that she should sit with him. "Why don't you tell me all about it?" He pressed the tip of his finger awkwardly against her nose.

Noah felt his stomach lurch at Coleridge's stumbling attempts at paternity. While the man turned all of his attention upon his child, Noah took his leave, heading in the direction of the west wing.

Sheila watched Noah stride angrily across the yard, and she had to suppress the urge to run after him. Until she was assured that Emily was comfortable with Jeff, Sheila felt her responsibility was to remain with her child.

Noah was soon out of sight and Sheila swung her eyes back

toward Jeff and Emily. Her gaze met the brittle dark stare of her ex-husband. "How long has *he* been here?" he sneered.

"About a week."

"Do you think that's such a good idea?"

"He's helping me reestablish the winery."

"I bet he is." The insinuation in Jeff's flat statement couldn't be ignored.

"Look, Jeff. I like Noah.... I like him a lot. Not that it's any concern of yours."

"He's an arrogant SOB, don't you think?"

Sheila's eyes flew to Emily's young face and then back to Jeff, silently warning him against any further derogatory remarks while Emily was close at hand.

"I think he's a very kind and considerate man."

"And I'm not?"

"I didn't say that." Sheila shot Jeff another threatening glance. "Would you like a cup of coffee?" Somehow she had to change the course of the conversation, for Emily's sake.

Jeff tried to relax and appear comfortable. "Got anything stronger?" he inquired, running a shaky hand through his neatly combed hair.

"I think so."

"Good." He let out his breath. "Make it a vodka martini."

"All right. It will take me a few minutes." He didn't argue. He, too, must have been looking for a way to avoid further disagreement. Sheila turned toward the house, her eyes still searching for Noah, when Jeff's voice reached her. "With a twist, okay?"

She nodded curtly without glancing back in his direction, muttering under her breath, "With a twist...with a twist." Sheila had forgotten how demanding Jeff could be—a real pain in the neck. Damn him for ruining the peaceful afternoon. Damn him for interrupting what she had hoped would be an intimate *family* meal.

That was the problem, wasn't it? She considered Noah and Sean as part of the family, while she looked upon Jeff as an outsider, an intruder who would only cause trouble.

Her chestnut hair swept across her shoulders as she shook her head at her own foolishness. What had she expected? she asked herself as she walked into the den.

She was startled to find Noah sitting at the desk, going over the original blueprints for the west wing of the château. A pencil was in his hand, its lead point tapping restlessly on the yellowed paper. He didn't move when he heard the sound of Sheila's sandaled feet enter the room, nor did he speak. Instead he stared broodingly at the blueprints, seemingly engrossed in the faded drawing. Sheila could feel the rift between them deepen, and she wondered if she had the courage to bridge it.

"I'm sorry you had to witness all of that," she began as she moved across the room to the bar to pull out a bottle of vodka. The pencil stopped its erratic tapping on the desk.

Noah's voice was controlled to the point of exasperation. "Don't apologize to me. It's none of my concern."

"But it is," she disagreed. "And I didn't mean for it to turn into a circus."

"Didn't you? Don't kid yourself, Sheila. You were the one who invited him here. How could you possibly expect things to turn out differently?"

"I had no choice. I had to tell him about Emily and invite him to visit her."

"Save it, Sheila. I've heard all this before."

She could read the anger in the crunch of his shoulders, feel his questions begging for answers, see the pride in the lift of his chin. "Please, Noah," she pleaded, setting the mixed drink aside. "Don't shut me out."

"Is that what I'm doing?" He tossed the pencil down on the desk and rubbed his hands wearily against the back of his neck.

"Aren't you?"

"No!" He got out of the chair and faced her for the first time since she entered the room. Ignoring the pain in her eyes, he wagged an accusing finger in her face. "I'll tell you what I'm doing," he stated hoarsely, "I'm sitting on the sidelines, hoping to hold on to my patience, which isn't exactly my long suit to begin with, while the woman I love clings to some faded, rose-colored memories of a past and a marriage that didn't exist."

"I'm not—"

"I'm trying *not* to throw out a conniving jerk whose fumbling attempts at being a father border on the pathetic, for the sake of holding up appearances!"

"Jeff's just trying to—"

"And," his voice increased in volume, "I'm attempting, Lord knows I'm not good at this sort of thing, but I'm trying damn it, to understand how a beautiful, sensitive woman like you could have ever gotten tangled up with a creep like Jeff Coleridge in the first place." The cords in Noah's neck were bulging, the muscles in his shoulders tight, the line of his mouth curled in distaste. He looked as if at any moment all of his simmering anger might explode.

Sheila picked up the martini with trembling hands. "I think that's enough," she whispered, her wide eyes unseeing. Her voice shook with the wounded tears of pride that had settled in her throat as she turned toward the door.

Noah was beside her in an instant, and his powerful arm reached out to impede her departure. He twisted her back to face him and the drink fell to the floor, breaking the glass and spilling the colorless liquid.

"No, Sheila," he stated through clenched teeth, "you're

wrong." He ignored the shattered glass and the pooling liquid. He gave her arm a shake to make sure she was giving him all of her attention. "I love you," he admitted, the hardness in his gaze beginning to soften. "I didn't want to fall in love with you. I fought it...I fought it like hell...but I lost." His grip loosened on her arm, but she didn't move as she was spellbound by the honesty in his eyes. "And I have no intention of letting you go—not to that snake you once called a husband. Not to anyone."

Sheila felt her anger beginning to wither. Her gray eyes were colored by her conflicting emotions. "Then, please... please try and understand that I'm only putting up with Jeff because of Emily."

"Do you think you're fooling that child?"

"I'm not trying to fool her. I'm just trying not to bias her opinion of her dad."

"By letting him intrude where he's not wanted?" His eyes left hers to stare at the spilled drink. "By jumping at his every whim?" He touched her cheek tenderly. "Or by covering up his mistakes and omissions?"

"By letting her make her own decision."

"Then let her see him as he really is."

The muscles in his jawline tensed. "How important to you is Jeff Coleridge?" he demanded.

"He's the father of my child."

"Nothing more?"

"He once was," she admitted. "I can't deny that, and I wouldn't try to. But that was a long time ago. Please believe me, Noah, I'm not in love with him. I don't know if I ever was."

Noah wrapped his arms tightly around her slim shoulders, and she could feel the warmth of his body where his arms touched her. Tenderly he brushed the smudge of soot from her cheek. "All right, Sheila," he said with a reluctant sigh. "I'll try and tolerate that jerk. But, believe me, if he gets obnoxious with you *or Emily,* I'm not going to apologize for throwing him out on his ear. Fair enough?"

Sheila's smile spread slowly over her lips, showing just a hint of her white teeth. "Fair enough," she agreed.

"Now, why don't you work on dinner, let Jeff and Emily alone, and I'll finish up with the blueprints."

"Only if you promise to clean up this mess," she suggested, flipping her open palm toward the spilled drink, "and pour Jeff another vodka martini."

"Not on your life, lady. Doting on that man is where I draw the line. If he wants a drink badly enough, he can damn well come in and mix his own."

Sheila laughed and clucked her tongue. "Not very hospitable, are you?" she teased.

Noah raised an inquiring eyebrow. "Can you blame me?"

"No," she admitted with a trace of wistfulness, "I really can't. But, do *try* to be civil."

"If that's what you want," he conceded. "But for the life of me, I don't understand why."

She wrapped her arms around his neck and stood on her toes. "It won't kill you," she pointed out.

"No, I suppose not. But watching him drool over you might."

"You're imagining things." She kissed him lightly on the lips.

The muscles in his body reached out to hers. She felt his thighs straining against hers, his chest flattening her breasts, his arms pressing against the small of her back. "The kinds of things I imagine with you are very private. They have nothing to do with your ex-husband." His lips brushed against hers and his tongue rimmed her lips. "Let's get rid of him and put the kids to bed early."

Sheila laughed against his mouth. "Somehow I don't think Sean would take kindly to going to bed at six-thirty."

"Spoilsport." Slowly he released her.

She started toward the door, but paused to look over her shoulder at him and give an exaggerated wink. "Later," she promised throatily.

The rest of the evening was uncomfortable but tolerable. Jeff stayed for dinner and looked stiff and ill at ease with Noah, Sean and Emily. His perfectly pressed suit had become wrinkled, his hair unruly and his eyes begged Sheila to find some excuse to get him away from Noah's intense, uncompromising stare. Noah was polite but quiet, and his blue eyes very rarely strayed from Sheila's ex-husband. It made Jeff uncomfortable; the man's stare bordered on the eerie.

Jeff made his excuses, begged off dessert and was back on his way to Spokane long before eight o'clock. Even Emily seemed relieved that she didn't have to go back to her father's sterile apartment and persnickety old wife, Judith, at least for a few more weeks.

For the first time in over a week the dark cloud of argument between Sheila and Noah had disappeared, and they made impassioned love without the shadow of Jeff Coleridge hanging over their heads.

Chapter 12

The end of Noah's stay came much too quickly for Sheila. The fact that he hadn't been clear about his decision concerning the status of the winery worried her. She knew that he wanted to rebuild the west wing—the construction crew that had been razing the old structure was proof enough of that—but still he was hesitant. It was as if he were keeping something from her. She could feel his reluctance whenever she would broach the subject of the fall harvest. As far as she could tell, it had to be something to do with the fire.

It was morning on Noah's final day at Cascade Valley when Sheila summoned the courage to bring up the fire and Anthony Simmons's report. Over the past week Noah had managed to dodge the issue, but this morning Sheila told herself she had to have answers—straight ones.

The first rays of dawn filtered through the terrace doors to bathe Sheila's room in a golden aura of dim morning light. Dewdrops clung to the underside of the green leaves of the clematis that grew against the glass doors, and the chill of the mountain night hadn't disappeared.

Noah was still asleep, his face pressed against the pillow. Sheila slowly extracted herself from his embrace, and while still lying near to him on the antique bed, stared at his sleeping form. The dark profile of his face, etched in relief against the ice blue sheets, seemed innocent in slumber. The powerful muscles were relaxed, the corners of his eyes soft. His near-black hair was unruly and would seem almost boyish if it hadn't been for the contrast of his shadowy beard.

Sheila felt her throat tighten at the sight of him sleeping, oblivious to any of the anxieties that aged his face. He seemed incredibly vulnerable, and it touched the deepest, most feminine part of her. She wanted to smooth back his hair and comfort him. *I love him,* she thought to herself. I love him too much. This is the kind of blind love that can be dangerous, the kind of self-sacrificing, unreturned love that can only cause pain. It's a love that causes dependency and inspires jealousy, like a drug addiction. More than anything else in the world, I want to be with this man, to be a part of him. I want my life to blend with his, my family to be one with his, my blood to run in his body.

She bent over and kissed him softly on the forehead. I know he cares for me—he says he loves me—but I know that he is hiding something from me. He won't let himself trust me.

She drew herself away from him and got out of the bed. After snuggling into the downy folds of a cream-colored velour bathrobe, she once again sat on the edge of the bed, content to watch the even rise and fall of Noah's chest as he lay entwined in the sheets. Why won't you tell me, she wondered. Why won't you tell me everything about the fire? What are you hiding from me?

Noah rolled over onto his back and raised an exploratory eyelid against the invading morning sunlight. His dimpled smile slowly emerged as his gaze focused on her. "God, you look incredible," he growled as he wrapped an arm around her waist and pulled her down beside him on the bed.

"Noah," she whispered, trying to ignore the deliciously warm feel of his lips against her throat. "We have to talk."

"Later." His fingers found the zipper on her bathrobe and slowly lowered it.

Against the yearnings of her body, she put her hand over his to impede the zipper's progress. "Now."

"Let's not waste time with talk," he grumbled as he kissed the exposed tops of her breasts. The zipper slid lower, and the downy robe parted. "This is my last morning here," he murmured against her bared skin. Sheila felt her pulse jump and the blood begin to heat in her veins.

She attempted to clutch the robe together. "Precisely why we have to talk now." She tossed her hair away from her face and looked him steadily in the eye as she disentangled herself from his persuasive grip. Her breath was uneven as she eased her body off the bed.

After somewhat shakily taking a seat in one of the chairs near the terrace, she nervously ran her fingers over the open neckline of her robe. Noah propped himself on one elbow, raked his fingers through his dark hair and stared at her with amused, but smoldering, blue eyes. The sheet was draped across his body, exposing the hard muscles of his chest and leaving his lower torso covered. "All right, Sheila, out with it."

"What?" She really didn't know where to begin.

"The inquisition."

"You're expecting one?" She was surprised.

"I'd have to be a fool not to know that before I went back to Seattle, you and I would have a showdown about the fire. That is what this is all about, isn't it?"

Sheila's eyes narrowed suspiciously, and her fingers stopped toying with the collar of her robe. "I just want to know why you've been avoiding the issue of the fire and the rebuilding of the west wing."

"Because I hadn't made a decision." His honest blue eyes begged her understanding and patience.

"But you have now?"

"I think so."

"*Well?*"

The corners of Noah's eyes twitched. "I'm going to transfer a quarter of a million dollars into an escrow account from Wilder Investments when I get back to Seattle. The money will be in escrow for the express purpose of rebuilding Cascade Valley."

Sheila's smile froze on her face as she read the hesitation in his gaze. "But what about the insurance company...and that report by Anthony Simmons?"

Noah waved off her questions as if they were bothersome insects. "Don't worry about that end of it; that's my problem."

Sheila held back a million questions, but the one nagging doubt in her mind refused to die. Her voice was hoarse. "But what about my father's name? Will you be able to clear it?" she asked cautiously. The look of sincere concern in her light gray eyes pierced him to the soul, and he found his deception entrapping him. He had decided not to tell her anything about the fire or Simmons's report, knowing full well that what he would have to disclose to her would only cause her more pain. In his mind she had borne more than her share. He couldn't add to it.

"I hope so," he whispered, damning himself for his duplicity.

She sighed with relief and closed her eyes.

"We do have another problem to consider."

She smiled wryly and opened her eyes to study him. "Only one?" she asked sarcastically.

He laughed aloud. How long had it been since he'd laughed in the dawn? The thought of leaving Sheila sobered him, and he realized it was an impossible task. She sat across the room from him, her toes peeking out from the folds of creamy fabric, her hair beautiful in its coppery disarray. And her eyes, a warm gray, the color of liquid silver, surrounded by thick, sexy black lashes, watched his every movement. "Maybe we have two problems," he acquiesced with a slow smile. "The first is simple. If construction of the west wing is incomplete by harvest time, I'll lease a facility nearby and we'll still bottle under the Cascade label. It will be expensive, but better than selling our crop to the competition."

Sheila thoughtfully nodded her silent agreement.

"So that brings us to our next dilemma."

"If you come up with another blockbuster solution, like you did for the first problem, I doubt that there will be any dilemma at all," she quipped, smiling radiantly. At last she knew for certain that the winery would reopen. She couldn't help but smile.

Noah rubbed the edge of his chin before he tossed off the sheet, stood up and strode over to the chair in which she was sitting. Positioning his hands on either arm of the chair, he imprisoned her against the peach-colored cushions. "The solution depends entirely on you."

The corners of her mouth twitched, and a light of interest danced in her eyes. She cocked her head coquettishly and let the chestnut sheen of her hair fall over one cheek. "On me? How?"

His voice was low and serious, his gaze intent as it probed her eyes. "Sheila, I want you to marry me. Will you?"

Her playful smile disappeared as the meaning of his words sunk in. An overwhelming sense of ecstasy overtook her as her heart flipped over. "You want to get married?" she repeated, her voice filled with raw emotion.

"As quickly as possible."

Her self-assurance wavered. "Of course…I mean, I'd love to…" She shook her head. "This is coming out all wrong. I guess I just don't understand what's going on here."

"What's to understand?" His lean muscles entrapped her, and his lips nuzzled softly behind her ear. When he spoke, she could feel his warm breath against her hair. "Because I love you, Sheila. Haven't you been listening to what I've been saying to you for the better part of the week?"

"But…married?" she stammered. Visions of her first marriage filled her mind. She remembered the hope and the love, a gorgeous ivory lace gown that had yellowed with the lies and the faded dreams. She had rushed into marriage once, and though she loved Noah with all her heart, she was wary of making the same mistake again. The thought of losing him was too agonizing to her. "I…I don't know," she said, and the confusion she felt was reflected in the gray depths of her eyes.

The muscles of his arms tensed as he gripped the chair more savagely. "Why not?"

There were probably more than a dozen reasons, but Sheila couldn't think of them. Memories of Jeff closing the door in her face kept closing in on her. "Have you thought about the kids? How is this going to affect them?" She was grasping at straws, and they both knew it. He provided the perfect response.

"Can you honestly think of any better arrangement for Sean or Emily?"

"But that's no reason to get married…to provide another parent for your child."

"Of course it isn't. Think of it as a fringe benefit," he suggested. His hand had been touching the collar of her robe, gently rubbing the delicate bones surrounding her neck. Suddenly he stopped touching her and took a step backward. "Are you trying to find a polite way of telling me no?" he challenged, his features growing hard.

Sheila shook he head, tears of happiness welling in her eyes. He misread them.

"Then what is it? Certainly you're not satisfied with a casual *affair?*"

"No, no, of course not."

He crossed his arms over his chest, his blue eyes intent on hers. "Has this got something to do with Coleridge? Damn it! I knew he was still in your blood."

"He isn't…. It's just that I'm overwhelmed, Noah. I didn't expect any of this…. I don't know what to say."

"A simple yes or no will do."

"If only it were simple." She wrapped her arms around herself as if protecting her body from a sudden chill. "I'd love to marry you…"

"But?"

"But I think it's all a little sudden." Why was she making up excuses? Why couldn't she just accept his vow of love?

As she looked into Noah's brooding eyes and honest, angular face, Sheila's doubts fled. If she knew nothing else, she realized that Noah Wilder wasn't the kind of man who would stoop to deceit. She shook her head as if shaking out the cobwebs of unclear thought that had confused her. "I'm sorry," she apologized shakily as she touched her fingertips to the solid wall of his chest. "It's just that you surprised me. The truth is that I love you and I can't think of anything I'd rather do than spend the rest of my life with you."

"Thank God," he declared prayerfully. He folded her into the strength of his arms and pressed his hungry lips to hers. A warm glow of happiness began to spread through her as her lips parted to accept the promise of his love. She closed her eyes and sighed against his mouth as she felt the robe slip off her shoulders and the chill of morning touch her skin when Noah guided her to the bed.

"Woman," he groaned against her skin, "I need you so desperately." She shivered in anticipation as she fell against the cool sheets and was warmed only by the gentle touch of the man she loved.

Sheila's life became a whirlwind. Between scanning blueprints submitted by architects, attempting to organize the interior designers sent by Wilder Investments and working with Dave Jansen on the fall harvest, Sheila had little time to dwell on the distance that kept her apart from Noah. She fell into bed exhausted each night and was up at the crack of dawn each morning. One hot summer day bled into another as June flowed into July.

Though Sheila was working herself to the bone, it was worth it. Everything seemed to be going her way. Jeff had called earlier in the week, and when Sheila had explained that Emily had reservations about visiting with him in Spokane, Jeff didn't press the issue. In fact, he had almost sounded *relieved* that he wouldn't have to entertain his child until later in the summer.

Emily missed Sean, but Sheila took that as a positive sign. She prayed that the two children would continue to get along after the marriage, whenever that was. Noah had been pressing Sheila for a date, even had gone so far as to suggest eloping. Sheila admitted to herself that running off to get married might be the best solution for all involved. She had once been married in an elaborate ceremony; it hadn't guaranteed success.

Perhaps this weekend, she mused to herself as she pressed her foot more heavily on the throttle of the car. The auto responded and climbed the Cascade Mountains more quickly. For the first time in four weeks, there had been a break in the work. The interior of the château was nearly completely restored to its original regal design. Only a few details remained unfinished. The fabric for the draperies was woven in Europe, hence the delay. But the walls had been resurfaced and painted, new wallpaper hung and the old stained burgundy carpet replaced by a new, elegant champagne-colored pile.

Emily was spending the weekend with her grandmother, and Sheila decided to visit Noah. He would be surprised, no doubt, as he hadn't expected to see her until all of the legal papers surrounding the refurbishing of the winery were complete, but when she hadn't been able to reach him by telephone, Sheila had thrown caution to the wind, packed a few clothes and jumped in her car.

It was a beautiful summer day, the mountain air fresh with the scent of wildflowers and pine trees, and Sheila had the confident feeling that nothing could ruin the feeling of exhilaration that claimed her. The prospect of spending a quiet weekend alone with Noah made her smile to herself and hum along to the pop music coming from the radio.

Nothing can possibly go wrong, she thought to herself as she turned up the circular drive of the Wilder estate. This weekend is going to be perfect. She smiled when she saw the familiar silver Volvo sitting hear the garage. At least she had caught Noah at home.

She knocked on the door and waited for it to be answered. The mysterious smile that had spread across her face froze in place when the door was opened by a well-mannered, gray-haired man of near fifty. He was dressed in formal livery and displayed not one shred of emotion as he inquired as to the nature of her call.

A butler, Sheila thought wildly, not really understanding.

Noah employed a butler? He hadn't mentioned hiring any servants in his telephone conversations. An uneasy feeling began to grip Sheila. Something was wrong.

"I'm here to see Mr. Wilder," Sheila explained to the outwardly skeptical butler.

"Is he expecting you?"

"No. You see, this is kind of a surprise."

The butler cocked a dubious gray eyebrow and his lips pressed into a thin, firm line. "You do know that Mr. Wilder isn't well. He isn't seeing visitors."

Sheila's eyes widened, and her heart leapt to her throat. What was this man saying? "What's wrong with him?" she demanded, fear claiming her emotions.

"Pardon me?"

Sheila forgot all sense of civility. "What's wrong with Noah? Was he hurt in an accident?" Her hands were shaking. "What happened?" How could this character out of *Upstairs Downstairs* take Noah's health so casually? She looked past the butler into the stone house, her eyes searching for some evidence that Noah was all right.

"Miss, if you will calm down! I wasn't speaking of Noah Wilder, but his father."

Sheila's eyes flew back to the butler. "Ben? Ben's here?"

The man in the doorway raised his nose a bit higher, but Sheila sensed kindliness in his sparkling hazel eyes. "Would you kindly state your name and business?"

"Oh, I'm sorry. I'm Sheila Lindstrom," she replied rapidly. Thank God Noah was safe. Her breath released slowly. "I'm…a friend of Noah's. Is…is he in?"

"Yes, of course, Miss Lindstrom. This way please." The butler seemed pleased that he had finally made sense of her appearance. He turned on a well-polished heel and escorted her into a formal living room.

It was a cold room, not at all like the warm den where she had met Noah. It was decorated in flat tones of silver and white, with only a sprinkling of blue pillows on the expensive, modern furniture. White walls, icy gray carpet and tall, unadorned windows. In the middle of it all, sitting near the unlit flagstone fireplace, was a man Sheila guessed to be Ben Wilder. He didn't bother to rise when she entered the room, and his smile looked forced, as cold as the early morning fog that settled upon Lake Washington.

"Miss Lindstrom," the butler announced quietly. "She's here to see your son."

At the mention of her name, Ben's interest surfaced. His faded eyes looked over her appraisingly, as if she were a thoroughbred at auction. Sheila felt an uncomfortable chill.

"Pleased to meet you, Miss Lindstrom. I'm Noah's father."

"I thought so. I think I met you once, years ago…"

Ben was thoughtful for a moment. "I suppose you did. I came to the winery to see Oliver—by the way, please accept my condolences."

"Thank you." Sheila anxiously fingered the clasp on her purse. Where was Noah? The man sitting in the snowy chair was not anything she had expected. When she had met Ben Wilder he was robust and bursting with energy. Though it had only been nine years, Ben Wilder had aged nearly thirty. The pallor of his skin was gray, and his hair had thinned. He still appeared tall, but there was a gauntness to his flesh that added years to his body. Ben Wilder was gravely ill.

"Did I hear someone at the door?" a female voice asked. Sheila turned to see a woman, younger than Ben by several years, walk into the room. She was graceful, and the smile that warmed her face seemed sincere.

"This is Sheila Lindstrom," Ben said. "My wife, Katharine."

Katharine's smile wavered slightly. "Noah's mentioned you," she stated vaguely. "Would you care to have a seat?"

"Thank you, but I really did come to see Noah."

"Of course you did. He was outside with Sean. I think George has gone to find him."

Thank God, Sheila thought to herself as she settled onto the uncomfortable white couch. Katharine attempted to make conversation. "I was sorry to hear about your father, Sheila." Sheila nodded a polite response. "But I hear from Noah that you've made marvelous strides toward rebuilding the entire operation."

"We're getting there," Sheila replied uncomfortably.

"A big job for a young woman," Ben observed dryly.

Sheila managed a brave smile and turned the course of the conversation away from Cascade Valley. "I didn't know that you had come back from Mexico," she explained. "I should have called and let Noah know that I was planning to visit him here."

The silence was awkward, and Katharine fidgeted with the circle of diamonds around her thin neck while she studied the young woman in whom her son had shown such an avid interest. An interest that had taken him away from his duties of managing the business. Sheila Lindstrom was pretty, she thought to herself with amusement, but beautiful women had held no interest for her only son. What was so special about this one? She heard herself responding hollowly to Sheila's vague apology. "Don't worry about that," Katharine stated with a dismissive wave of her slim, fine-boned hand. "Noah's fond of you. Therefore, you're welcome anytime. No invitation is necessary."

"Did Noah tell you all the details that Anthony Simmons dug up on the fire?" Ben asked, bored with social amenities.

It was time to get down to business. He reached for a cigar and rotated it gently in his fleshless hand.

Sheila felt her spine stiffen. "Only that the report was inconclusive," she replied, meeting his gaze squarely.

Ben smiled, still watching her over the cigar. He reached for a match, but was halted by his wife's warning glare. "I figured as much."

"Pardon me?" Sheila inquired, pressing the issue.

"I didn't think he told you everything...."

"Ben!" Katharine's smooth voice held a steely note of caution. She lowered it slightly. "Let's not bore Miss Lindstrom with all this talk about business. Sheila, would you like to stay for dinner? It really would be no imposition...."

Her voice faded as the sound of heavy, quick footsteps caught her attention. A wavering smile broadened her lips. "Noah, guess who dropped by?" she asked.

"What are you doing here?" Noah asked fiercely. Sheila turned to see if his question was intended for her. It was. His face was hard, set in rigid lines. A muscle near his jaw pulsed.

"I wanted to surprise you."

"You did!"

Sheila felt something wither inside her under his uncomfortable stare. He appeared more gaunt than the last time she had been with him. The circles under his blue eyes gave his face a harsh, angular appearance. His inflamed gaze moved from her face to that of his father's. Ben's old lips twisted with private irony. "What have you been telling her?" he demanded, advancing upon his father.

"Noah, please..." Katharine interjected.

"I asked you a simple question," Noah said through tightly clenched teeth. "If you won't answer it, then fine. I'd like to talk to her...alone." He looked away from his father to meet Sheila's confused gaze. For a moment his face softened, and the defeat in his eyes seemed to fade. "Let's go into the den and talk," he suggested softly.

Sheila understood. He had changed his mind about her and the winery and the marriage. He was going to tell her that all of her dreams had turned to dust. A sinking sensation of doom, like that of falling into a bottomless black hole, enveloped her. Noah's persuasive hand was on her shoulder, encouraging her to her feet. Slowly, she rose. She felt dizzy, sick.

"No reason to shuffle her out of here, son," Ben said with sarcastic familiarity. "One way or another, she's got to know."

"I'll handle it," Noah spat. The pressure on Sheila's back increased as he tried to guide her out of the sterile living room.

"I'm sure you will, my boy," Ben agreed with a mirthless laugh.

"What's he talking about?" Sheila asked impatiently.

"Tell her," Ben demanded.

"Ben…let Noah handle this his own way," his wife whispered.

The pressure in Sheila's head got to her. She stopped her exit from the long living room with the cold carpet and announced in a calm, hushed voice. "Don't talk as if I can't hear you, because I can. What's this all about?"

She had to know, had to hear his words of rejection, waited with head held high for the final blow. Noah's lips compressed into a thin, uncompromising line. "I'll tell you everything, but it will be best if we're alone."

"Oh, hell, boy! Stop pussyfootin' around, for God's sake." The old man rose shakily from his chair and rubbed his freckled scalp. "What Noah is trying to tell you, honey, is that your father started that damned fire and it cost the company one helluva lot of money, let me tell you. The insurance company hasn't paid us a dime; there's a doubt that they ever will!"

Sheila's face turned ashen, her stomach lurched and she

thought she might faint. She turned her eyes to Noah's and read the guilt and remorse in his look. He had known. From the time that Anthony Simmons had turned in his preliminary report Noah Wilder had known about her father and the fire.

"No!" she attempted to shout. But no sound escaped from her constricted throat. His deceit was too much for her to accept.

Ben enjoyed the scene. It was hard for an old man with a heart condition to get many thrills out of life. He enjoyed the intrigue of passions and deceit. It didn't matter that it was his own son. The sanctimonious heir had been looking down his nose at his father's morals for the last sixteen years—even to the point of refusing to work for the company, until he was forced to by Ben's most recent attack. It did old Ben's failing heart good to see the tables turned for once.

"Sheila," Noah said softly, touching her chin. She drew away, repelled by his touch. "Things aren't exactly what they seem."

"But you knew about Dad!" she accused.

"Yes," he admitted loudly.

"And you didn't tell me!"

"I thought I could prove the report wrong...I was convinced that with a little time, I could sort things out, and the results would be different."

"*But you knew!*" Her heart sank to the blackest depths of despair. "And you wouldn't tell me...."

"I didn't want to hurt you."

"So you *lied* to me?"

His response was quick. "I've never lied to you."

"Just omitted the facts, avoided the issues...."

"Tried to stop your pain."

"I don't want a man to *protect* me from the truth. I don't want anyone who can't trust me...." The ugliness of the situation became blindingly apparent to her, and another wave of nausea took all of the color from her pale face. *"You thought I was involved, didn't you?"*

"No."

"Didn't you?"

"No!" he screamed. He shook his head, and his blue eyes pleaded with her to understand him. "Not after I met you. I couldn't."

"Oh, Noah," she whispered, shaking her head, running her fingers through her long, chestnut hair. "What has happened to us?"

She had forgotten there were other people in the room. When she looked up, she met Katharine's sorrowed gaze. "I'm sorry," Katharine murmured. "Come on, Ben, let's leave them alone." She tried to help her husband out of the living room, but he refused.

Ben yanked his arm out of Katharine's grasp. "I think you should understand something, Miss Lindstrom." Sheila raised her head to meet his cool, laughing eyes. It was as if he were enjoying some private joke at her expense. "I'm a businessman, and I can't let you continue to operate the winery."

"What do you mean?"

"I mean that I'm not prepared to invest the money Noah promised you to rebuild the winery."

"Don't worry about it," Noah interjected. "I'll handle it."

Ben continued, unruffled by his son's visible anger. "The most prudent thing for you to do, Sheila, would be to sell out your portion of Cascade Valley to Wilder Investments."

"I can't do that.... I won't."

Ben's toothy smile slowly turned into a frown. "I don't think you'll have much of a choice, considering the information in Mr. Simmons's report—"

"Stop it!" Noah shouted, taking Sheila by the arm and

nearly dragging her out of the living room. "Don't listen to him...don't pay any attention to any of his suggestions."

She pulled what little shreds of dignity she could find and turned her cold eyes on Noah. "I won't," she assured him coolly, while extracting her arm out of his fingers. Her eyes burned, her throat ached, her heart bled, but she held her face as impassive as possible. "Nothing you or your father can say will convince me to sell my father's winery."

"I know that," he admitted softly.

"But you were the first one to suggest that I sell."

"At that time I thought it would be best."

The unhappy smile that twisted on her lips was filled with self-defeat. "And now you expect me to believe that you don't?"

"You know that, Sheila." His fingers reached out to cup her chin, and they trembled as he sought to rub his thumb along her jawline. She had to turn away from him; she was too numb to feel the tenderness in his caress.

"Leave me alone, Noah," she whispered tonelessly. "I'm tired."

"Don't go," he begged, his hand dropping impotently to his side. The pain in his eyes wasn't hidden as he watched her move slowly toward the door. "Don't let the old man get to you."

"The 'old man' isn't the one that got to me."

"Sheila!" He reached for the bend of her elbow, clutching at her arm and twisting her to him. He held her so savagely that she wondered for a moment if she could breathe...or if she really cared. The tears that had slid over her lips to warm them with drops of salt told her she was crying, but she couldn't feel them. She didn't feel *anything*. Empty. Hollow. It was as if the spirit she had once owned had been broken.

"Let go of me," she said through her sobs.

"You can't go. You don't understand...."

"I understand perfectly! You may have been able to get what you wanted from Marilyn by paying her off, but you can't buy me, Noah Wilder! No man can. I'll go bankrupt before I'll sell you one bottle of my cheapest wine!" She wrenched free of his hold on her and backed toward the door.

He watched her leave, not moving from the foyer where he had held her in his arms. They felt strangely empty as his eyes followed the path of her flight. The door slammed shut, closing her out of his life. He fought the vain urge to follow her and tried to convince himself that everything was for the best. If she trusted him so little, he was better off without her.

Chapter 13

For five long weeks Sheila tried futilely to get the image of Noah Wilder out of her mind. It had been an impossible task. Everywhere on the estate she was reminded of him and the bittersweet love they had shared. There wasn't a room in the château where she could hide from him or the memories of the nights of surrendered passion they had shared together. She couldn't even find solace in her own room, the sanctuary where they had held each other dear until the first stirrings of dawn. Now the room seemed pale and empty, and Sheila was alone. She attempted to convince herself that she never had really loved him, that what they had shared was only a passing fancy, an affair to forget. It was a bald-faced lie, and she couldn't deceive herself for a minute. She had loved Noah Wilder with a passion time and deceit couldn't erase. She loved him still.

The winery had become a ghost town. Reconstruction of the west wing had been halted by one fell stroke: an executive order from Ben Wilder himself. Gone was the whine of whirring saw blades consuming wood, vanished were the shouts and laughter from the construction crew. The air was untainted with the smell of burning diesel or the scent of freshly cut lumber. The west wing of the winery was as defeated as her dreams.

Sheila had tried, ineffectively, to tell Emily about Noah. As comfortingly as possible she had mentioned that Noah and Sean wouldn't be back to Cascade Valley as they had originally planned and that her marriage to Noah would probably never happen. If Sheila had hoped not to wound her child, she had failed miserably. Emily was heartbroken. When Sheila had explained that she doubted if Noah and Sean would return to the winery, Emily had burst into tears, screamed that it was all her mother's fault and raced from the dinner table to hide in her room. It had taken several hours for Sheila to get through to her and calm her down. The child had sobbed on her shoulder bitterly, and it was difficult for Sheila to hold back the tears stinging the backs of her eyes.

Part of Emily's reaction was due to incredibly bad timing. The girl had just returned from a dismal trip to visit her father, a vacation that was to have lasted a week and was cut down to five regretful days. It seemed as if Jeff and his wife, Judith, just didn't have the time or the inclination to take care of a busy eight-year-old. Emily felt rejected not only by her father but by Noah as well.

The final blow to Sheila's pride had come from a local banker she had dealt with for years. Regardless of the winery's past record, Mr. Stinson couldn't justify another loan to Cascade Valley. It had no reflection on Sheila, but the winery just didn't qualify. There was simply not enough collateral to back up a quarter of a million dollars of the bank's money. He was kind and told her that he would talk to his superiors, although he was sure that her request was next to impossible. There was a distinct note of inflexibility in his even voice.

Sheila found it increasingly difficult to sit idle. Time seemed to be slipping by without purpose or meaning. Within a few short weeks Emily would be enrolled in the fall semester of school and the autumn harvest of grapes would be ripe. Sheila had no alternative but to sell the crop despite Dave Jansen's protests. He was convinced that this was the best year Cascade Valley had seen in a decade. The yield per acre was ten percent better than the previous year's, and the grapes held the highest sugar and acid content he had seen in several years. All in all it looked like a bumper crop. But Sheila had no choice. She was backed into a corner by Ben Wilder and his son.

She sighed wearily and ran her fingers through her hair as she picked up the telephone and dialed the number of Mid-Columbia Bank. A cheery receptionist put Sheila through to Jim Stinson. Sheila could envision the perplexed look of dismay that must have crossed his features when he learned that she was calling. He probably wanted to avoid this conversation as much as she did.

"Good afternoon, Sheila," Jim greeted heartily. "How've you been? Busy, I'll bet."

Sheila was taken aback at his friendly response to her call. "It's about that time of the year," she agreed.

"How's the construction going?" Jim asked good-naturedly. "Are you going to get the west wing finished before harvest?"

Sheila choked on her response. Jim, better than most people, knew of her plight, and it wasn't like him to rub salt into a wound. He actually sounded as if he thought she were running the winery as she had planned. "I can't do that, Jim, because construction has stopped on the west wing."

There was a moment's hesitation before Jim laughed. "Is this some kind of a joke? Haven't you begun to rebuild yet?"

"As a matter of fact, no. I was hoping that Mid-Columbia would give me a loan, remember?"

"But that was before you got your other loan."

Once again silence.

"Other loan?" What the devil was Jim talking about? He wasn't usually one to talk in circles.

He acted as if she were incredibly dense. "You know, the quarter of a mil."

"The loan I requested from you."

She heard an exasperated sigh. "Just a minute." She was put on hold for a minute and then he was on the phone again. "Is there some mistake?"

Before she could ask what in the world he was muttering about, he spoke again. "No…no, everything looks right. You do know that a deposit of two hundred and fifty thousand dollars was made to the winery's account on the thirtieth of August, don't you?"

Sheila's mind was reeling, her voice faint. "What deposit?" she asked.

"Let's see…it was a cashier's check drawn on Consolidated Bank of Seattle. Didn't you get a loan from them…Sheila?"

Sheila felt as if she were melting into the kitchen floor. Noah! Noah had deposited the money. From somewhere in her conscious mind, she was able to respond to Jim Stinson. "Of course I did…I just wasn't aware that they had transferred the money so quickly. My statement hasn't come yet."

"But didn't they call you?" Stinson asked.

"I've been out a lot lately…down in the vineyards." She lied, trying to find a way to get off the phone politely. "Thank you very much."

"No trouble, but you might think about putting some of that money into savings or another account. Deposits aren't insured for that large a sum."

"You're right. I will. Thanks, Jim."

She hung up the phone and leaned against the wall. Hot

beads of perspiration dampened the back of her neck. "That bastard!" she muttered between her teeth. Why couldn't he leave her alone? He must have deposited the money out of a guilty conscience from the coffers of Wilder Investments, perhaps as incentive for her to sell. But that didn't explain everything. Why would she have to sell anything? The money was hers, or so it appeared.

Her anger grew white hot. Ben Wilder might have bought Marilyn Summers sixteen years ago, but no man, not even Noah, could purchase her or her father's dream. She balled a small fist and slammed it into the wall. "Emily," she called as she raced to the back door.

Emily was playing distractedly with a fluffy white kitten. She turned her head to watch her mother nearly run out of the back door. "What?"

Sheila tried to hold her fury in control. "Get your overnight case and pack your pajamas and a change of clothes. We're going to Seattle."

"Seattle?" The girl's dark eyes glittered with expectations. "To see Noah and Sean?" she asked hopefully.

"I...I don't know if we'll see Noah, honey." The trembling in her voice belied her calm. "And I really doubt that Sean will be where we're going."

The smile on Emily's face fell. "Then why are we going to Seattle?"

"I have some business to discuss with Noah and his father."

Emily's brows drew together, and her rosy cheeks flushed. "Then why can't we see Sean? Won't he be with Noah?" She was genuinely concerned...and expectant.

"Another time. But we're going to Noah's office. Sean's probably at home."

Emily's lower lip stuck out in a pouty frown. "Can't we go see him? We don't go to Seattle very often."

Sheila shook her head but muttered a quick "We'll see," hoping to change the subject. "Hurry up and get your things." She left Emily in her room, packing, and did the same herself. She was out the door before she remembered the checkbook. Cascade Valley's checkbook. The one with a balance of over a quarter of a million dollars in it.

She tried to smile as she imagined herself self-righteously scribbling out a check for two hundred and fifty thousand dollars and dropping it theatrically on Noah's desk. Her smile faded as she visualized the scenario. Where was the justice she would feel? Where the triumph? And why, dear God, why wouldn't this ache leave her heart?

It was nearly five o'clock when they arrived in Seattle. The drive had been tedious due to the combination of roadwork on the winding mountain roads and Sheila's thinly stretched nerves. Her palms were damp on the steering wheel, her lips tight over her teeth. Emily had been quiet for most of the trip, but as they got closer to the heart of the city and she caught a few glimpses of Puget Sound, she began to chatter, asking Sheila questions about Seattle. The questions were intended to be innocent. Each one wounded Sheila anew.

"Where does Sean live?"

"Not down here. His house is near Lake Washington."

"Have you been there?"

"A couple of times."

"Can we go to Sean's house together?"

A pause. The lump in Sheila's throat made speech impossible. She tried to concentrate on shifting down as the car dipped along the hillside streets.

"Can we? Will you take me?" Emily repeated, looking at her mother with the wide-eyed innocence of only eight years.

"Maybe someday."

The water of Puget Sound shimmered in the brightness of the warm summer sun. Seagulls dipped and dived over the salty water; huge, white-hulled ferries with broad green stripes down their sides plowed through the water, churning up a frothy wake and breaking the stillness with the sound of their rumbling engines.

Sheila parked the car across from the waterfront and stared out at the open water. Perhaps when all of this business with Wilder Investments was over, she would be able to take Emily out to dinner on one of the piers. Perhaps...

"Come on, Em," she stated with renewed determination. "Let's go."

The Wilder Building was an imposing structure. A concrete and steel skyscraper that towered over the neighboring turn-of-the-century buildings, it proudly boasted smooth modern lines and large, reflective windows. Sheila's stomach began to wind into tight, uncomfortable knots as she and Emily rode the elevator to the thirtieth floor.

The elevator doors parted, and they stepped into a reception area. A plump woman of about a sixty greeted Sheila and Emily with a cool but efficient smile.

"Good afternoon. May I help you?"

Sheila gathered in her breath. "I'm looking for Mr. Wilder... *Noah* Wilder. Is he in?"

The secretary, whose nameplate indicated that her name was Margaret Trent, shook her perfectly coiffed red tresses. "I'm sorry Miss..."

"Lindstrom," Sheila supplied hastily. "I'm Sheila Lindstrom, and this is my daughter, Emily." The daughter smiled frailly.

Maggie showed just the hint of a dimple. So this was the Lindstrom woman all the fuss was about. "I'm Maggie Trent," she said warmly. Then, remembering Sheila's request, continued, "I'm sorry, Miss Lindstrom, but Noah doesn't work here any longer." Her reddish brows drew together behind her glasses. "Didn't you know? Things haven't…" Maggie quickly held her tongue. She had been on the verge of divulging some of the secrets of Wilder Investments to this slender young woman with the intense gray eyes, but she quickly thought better of it. She hadn't gotten to be Ben Wilder's personal secretary by idly wagging her tongue at anyone who walked through the door. Quite the opposite. Maggie was a good judge of character and could tell from the looks of the determined woman in the soft blue dress and the well-mannered child that she could trust them, but prudence held her tongue.

The look of disappointment in Sheila's eyes did, however, give her pause. "I think that Noah was planning to go back to Portland," she offered, leaving the rest of the sad story unsaid. It wouldn't do to gossip.

Sheila had to swallow back a dozen questions that were determined to spring to her lips. Intuitively she knew that Maggie was privy to the workings of the Wilder household. The thought that Noah was actually leaving staggered her, and the blood drained from her face. She had to know more. Suddenly it was incredibly important that she see him. "Is it possible to speak with Noah's father?" she asked, tonelessly.

The secretary looked as if Sheila had hit her. "Ben?" she repeated, regaining her composure. "No…Mr. Wilder isn't in." The warmth in the woman's eyes faded as she turned back to her typewriter. She looked at Sheila over the top of her glasses. "Was there anything else? Would you like to leave your name and number?"

"No," Sheila said, her voice beginning to quiver. "Thank you."

Together she led Emily to the elevator, and they began the descent. "Mom, are you okay?" Emily asked as they walked back to the car.

"Sure I am."

"You don't look so good."

Sheila forced a smile and gave her daughter a playful pat on the shoulders. "Is that any way to talk to your mother?"

They slid into the car simultaneously, and Sheila turned the key to start the engine. Emily looked out the passenger window, but Sheila saw the trace of a tear in the corner of her daughter's eye. "Emily?" she asked, letting the engine die.

"What?" Emily sniffed.

"What's wrong?"

Emily turned liquid eyes to her mother and her small face crumpled into a mask of despair. "He's gone, really gone, isn't he?"

"Honey...what?"

"Noah!" Emily nearly shouted, beginning to lose all control. "I heard that lady at his office. She said he's gone, and I know that he took Sean, too! He left, Mommy, just like Daddy did. He doesn't love me either..." Her small voice broke, and her shoulders began to heave with her sobs.

Sheila reached out for her child and wrapped comforting arms around the limp form. "Hey, Em, shhh...don't cry." Her own voice threatened to break. "It's not like that, you know. Noah loves you very much."

"No, he doesn't. He doesn't call. He doesn't come see us. Just like Daddy!"

"Honey, no. Noah's not like Daddy at all." Sheila kissed her daughter on the forehead and wiped the tears from the round, dark eyes.

"Then why doesn't he call?"

Sheila closed her eyes and faced the truth, the damning truth. "Because I asked him not to."

Emily's body stiffened in Sheila's arms. "Why, Mommy, I thought you liked him."

"I did...I do."

"Then why?"

"Oh, Em, I wish I knew.... We had a fight. A very big fight and...I doubt that we'll ever get it straightened out."

Sheila attempted to comfort Emily as she guided the car out of the heart of the city. Emily's accusations reinforced her own fears, and her mind was swimming by the time she reached the stone pillars flanking the long driveway of the Wilder estate. She drove without hesitation, knowing that she had to speak to Ben. Surely he would know how to get in touch with his son. Her purpose had shifted. Though her checkbook was still in her purse, its significance diminished and the only thoughts in her mind centered on Noah and the cruel insinuations she had cast upon him the last time they were together. No matter what had happened in the past, Sheila was now face-to-face with the fact that she still loved him as desperately as ever. She also realized that her love wasn't strong enough to bring them together again—nothing was. Too much mistrust held them away from each other. Too much deceit had blackened their lives.

Sheila pulled on the emergency brake, and Emily eyed the massive stone house suspiciously. "Who's house is that—it's creepy." Her voice steady, she was once again composed. Her young eyes traveled up the cornerstones of the house and the brick walk that led to the large double doors.

"It's not creepy," Sheila countered, and added, "Ben Wilder lives here."

"Sean's grandpa?" Emily asked, not hiding her enthusiasm.

"That's right."

"Maybe Sean will be here!" Emily was out of the car in a flash, and Sheila had to hurry to catch up with her.

"I don't think so, honey," she said as they both stood on the arched porch. Emily ignored her mother's doubts and pressed the doorbell, which chimed inside the house. Sheila prepared herself to meet George the butler's disapproving glare.

Hurried footsteps echoed in the house, and the door was thrust open to expose Sean on the other side. He wore a sneer, but it quickly faded into a brilliant smile of clean, white teeth. He was dressed, as usual, in cut-off jeans and a well-worn football jersey that had once been blue.

"Hi ya, pip-squeak," he greeted Emily. "How're ya?" His grin widened as he pretended to punch her in the arm.

"Good...real good," Emily piped back delightedly. An 'I told you so' expression covered her face as she turned to look at Sheila. "See, Mom, Sean *is* here, just like I thought," she declared with a triumphant gleam in her eyes.

Sean's face sobered slightly as he looked at Sheila. She thought he seemed older—more mature—than he had when they were all living at the winery. She couldn't help but notice how similarly featured he was to his father. The sadness and maturity that had entered his gaze reminded her of Noah, and her throat became dry. "Hi, Sheila. You lookin' for Dad?"

Sheila's heart leapt to her throat. "Is he here?"

Sean nodded silently.

"I expected to find your grandfather."

Sean's eyes darted from Sheila to Emily and back again. He bit at his lower lip, scratched his neck and seemed to ponder what he was about to say. It was as if he were hesitant to trust her, and Sheila felt a knife of doubt twist in her heart. What had Noah told his son about their breakup? "Ben isn't here now," Sean explained. "He's...at the hospital. I'm not supposed to say anything about it, you know, in case some reporters come nosin' around here, but I suppose it's all right to tell you about it." He didn't seem sure of his last statement.

"Is it serious?" Sheila asked quietly.

Sean shrugged indifferently, but worried lines scarred his

flawless forehead. He pushed his hands into the pockets of his ragged shorts. "I think so. Dad doesn't talk about it much."

Sheila felt a deep pang of sadness steal into her heart. "Where is your father, Sean?"

Sean cocked his head toward the back of the house. "He's down at the lake, just walkin' and thinkin', I guess." His blue eyes met the sober expression in Emily's. "Hey, pip-squeak, don't look so down.... Maybe you and I can walk down to the park and grab an ice-cream cone. What do ya say?"

Sheila recognized and appreciated Sean's rather obvious way of giving her some time alone with Noah.

"Can I go, Mom, *please?*" The look of expectation on Emily's face couldn't be denied.

"Sure you can, but come back in a couple of hours, okay?"

Sheila doubted if Emily heard her. The child was already racing across the wooded lawn, her dark curls escaping from the neat barrettes over her ears. Sean was loping along beside her, seemingly as excited as Emily.

When the dangerous duo was out of sight, Sheila took in a deep breath of air, hoping to fortify herself against the upcoming confrontation with Noah. As she closed the door behind her and headed through the elegant main hallway of the manor, she wondered if Noah would listen to what she had to say. He had lied to her, it was true, but her reaction had been vicious and cold, entirely without reason. If only she had trusted him a little.

She walked through the den and a pang of remorse touched her heart as she remembered her first night with Noah, the dying fire and the heated love they had shared. Tears burned the back of her eyes as she opened the French doors and stood upon the veranda from which she had attempted to make her escape into the night several months before.

As she leaned against the railing she looked down the rocky

cliff on which the veranda was perched. Nearly a hundred feet below her, standing at the edge of the water, was Noah. He stared out at the gray blue water as if entranced by the distant sailboats skimming across the lake. Sheila's throat became dry at the sight of him; her love tore her soul in two.

Without thinking about how she would approach him, she half ran across the flagstones, her fingers slipping upon the railing, her eyes glued to Noah's unmoving form. The old cable car had seen better years, and it groaned when Sheila pressed the call button. It shuddered and then steadily climbed the cliff to dock at the end of the deck. Sheila climbed inside the cab and pressed against the lever that released the brakes and slowly took the old car back to its original position at the base of the cliff. Noah didn't seem to notice; he didn't glance toward her, but continued to stare out at the cold lapping water.

He seemed to have aged since she last saw him. Deep lines outlined his eyes; his jaw was more defined, his face more sharply angled. Either he hadn't been eating properly or he wasn't able to sleep. Perhaps both. Her heart bled silently for the man she loved and the guilt he bore so proudly. How could she have accused him of everything she had? How could she have been so cruel as to add to his torment? A man who had given up everything to claim his unborn son; a man who had bucked tradition and raised that son alone; a man who had grieved when he thought he had failed with that same precious son.

The wind off the lake blew his hair away from his face, displaying the long lines of anxiety etching his brow. It was cool as it pushed the soft fabric of her dress against her legs and touched her cheeks to chill the unbidden tears that slid from her eyes.

He stood with his feet apart, his hands pressed palms out in the back pockets of his jeans. At the sound of her footsteps in the gravel, he cocked his head in her direction, and when his blue gaze clashed with hers, the expression of mockery froze on his face.

What was there to say to her? Why was she here? And why did she look more beautiful in person than she had in the sleepless nights he had lain awake and imagined her?

Tentatively she reached up and pushed a wayward lock of black hair from his forehead and stood upon her toes to kiss him lightly on the lips. He didn't move.

She lowered herself but continued to rest her fingertips on his shoulders.

"You must have come here because of the money," he said, his voice breaking the thin stillness.

Sheila's voice was firm. "I just found out that you deposited the money in my account, and I decided to come and throw it back in your face."

His smile was still distrustful. "I knew you would."

"You expected me to give it back to you?"

He shook his head at his own folly. "I hoped that you would come and see me face-to-face. If you hadn't, I had decided to come back to Cascade Valley and try and talk some sense into you. I only waited because I thought we both needed time to cool off."

"You knew we could work things out…after all that's happened?"

He looked away from her and out at the lowering sun. "I didn't know anything," he admitted, "except that I couldn't live without you."

"But why didn't you tell me about the fire? Why did you lie?"

"I didn't lie to you, and I just needed more time to look into the cause of the fire. You have to believe that I would never intentionally hurt you, nor would I deceive you."

"Only when you thought it was for my own good."

"Only *until* I had all the answers," he replied quietly.

"And do you?"

He closed his eyes and sighed. "Oh, woman, if only I did!"

When he opened his eyes to look at her again, some of his hostility seemed to have melted. His gaze traveled from her windswept chestnut hair, down the column of her throat and past the swell of her breasts, draped loosely in a soft blue dress.

"Then why did you want to see me?"

"A few things have changed around here," he responded cryptically.

"Because of Ben's illness?"

Noah nodded and his eyes grew dark. "He's in the hospital again, and the doctors are concerned that he won't get out."

"I'm sorry...."

Noah waved her condolences aside. "Maybe it's better this way." His dark expression didn't falter.

"What do you mean?"

"It's a long story. Basically, the doctor in charge of my father, Dr. Carson, has ordered Ben to give up working. Not only must he step down as president of Wilder Investments, but Ben's got to give up even going into the office."

"And that would kill your father?" she asked, trying to follow Noah's line of reasoning.

"Ben's not the kind of man to sit idle."

"I suppose not."

"He likes to be in the middle of things. Anyway," he continued with an expression of indifference, "the old man asked me to take over as head of the business, sell out my operation in Portland to Betty Averill and move to Seattle. I wasn't too hot for the idea."

Sheila tried to hide her disappointment. "Then you are moving back to Portland," she surmised.

"I thought so, but things have changed." Sheila's heart turned over, and her throat went dry. "Anthony Simmons's report was invalid."

"*What?*"

Sheila didn't know that she was shaking until Noah placed a steadying hand on her shoulder. "What are you saying?" she asked in a hoarse whisper.

"Pac-West Insurance Company continued with its investigation on the fire." Sheila held her breath. "You were right about your father, Sheila; there is no evidence that he started the fire."

"How do you know this?' Tears once again began to slide down her cheeks.

"Because the insurance company found out that Ben hired Simmons to start the fire. Ben's confirmed all this and he's cleared your father's name. Therefore the insurance company is refusing to pay the claim."

"But the money...in my account."

"I took it from Wilder Investments to rebuild the winery, as I'd promised. And as far as I'm concerned, the note against the winery has been satisfied. Within a few weeks you should get the legal papers that will acknowledge and guarantee that you are sole owner of the winery."

"Oh, Noah," she whispered hoarsely, her emotions strangling her.

"It's all right, Sheila," he said, wrapping his arms around her and kissing the top of her head. "I'm just sorry that my family had anything to do with your father's death or his financial worries." His voice had lowered. "Ben even admitted that he had been behind the tampered bottles in Montana, in a move to force your father out of business. It looks as if he will be prosecuted for the arson and involuntary manslaughter."

"Oh, God, Noah...but he's ill...."

"That's no excuse for the things he's done."

"What are you going to do?" Her tears were running freely.

"I've agreed to run the company since Ben's given me sole authority, and I'm going to try and right my father's mistakes." His mouth twisted into a line of disgust. "I don't know if it's possible. That's why I started with you. Ben tried to cheat you out of the winery rather than just continue to share the profits with you. It's all yours now. Wilder Investments is out of it."

He watched her reaction, gauged her response. "You don't understand, do you?" she whispered. "Nothing...not the winery...not my father's reputation...none of it means anything unless you're with me."

"You were the one who left."

"But only because I didn't understand." His arms tightened around her.

His voice caught. "Dear God, Sheila, if only you knew how much I love you...if only you could feel the emptiness I've had to deal with."

"I do," she vowed, "every night that I'm alone."

"Never again," he promised, "you'll never be alone again. Promise me that you'll marry me."

Sobs of joy racked her body. "Oh, Noah, I've been such a fool. I love you so dearly and I tried to convince myself that I could forget you.... I thought I wanted to."

"Shhh...it's all right. We're together now, and we will be forever. And we're going to have our own family—Sean, Emily and as many more children as you want."

"Do you mean it?"

"Of course I do, love. More than anything I've ever said. Will you marry me?"

"Do you have to ask?" she sighed, tipping her head to look at him through the shimmer of unshed tears. A slow, satisfied smile curved his lips, and his eyes caressed hers.

"I love you, Sheila," he vowed. "I promised that I always will."

"But what about the winery?"

"We'll work that out later. If you want, I'll move the headquarters of Wilder Investments to Cascade Valley. It doesn't matter where we live, just as long as we're together."

"Noah…"

"Shhh…don't worry about anything. Just love me."

"Forever," she vowed against his chest before his lips claimed hers in a kiss filled with the promise of a blissful future they would share.

★ ★ ★ ★ ★

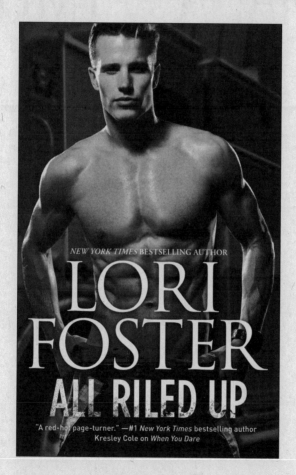

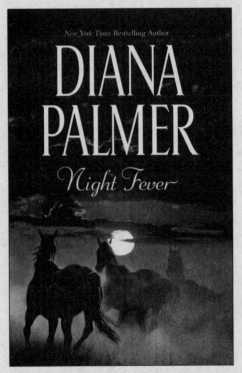

USA TODAY bestselling author

CHRISTIE RIDGWAY

introduces a sizzling new series set in Crescent Cove, California, where the magic of summer can last forever....

When book doctor Jane Pearson arrives at Griffin Lowell's beach house, she expects a brooding loner. After all, his agent hired her to help the reclusive war journalist write his stalled memoir. Instead, Jane finds a tanned, ocean-blue-eyed man in a Hawaiian shirt, hosting a beach party and surrounded by beauties. Faster than he can untie a bikini top, Griffin lets Jane know he doesn't want her. But she desperately needs this job and digs her toes in the sand.

Griffin intends to spend the coming weeks at Beach House No. 9 taking refuge from his painful memories—and from the primly sexy Jane, who wants to bare his soul. But warm nights, moonlit walks and sultry kisses just may unlock both their guarded hearts....

Available wherever books are sold!

www.Harlequin.com

PHCR740TR

Revisit the enchanting Donovan clan from
#1 *New York Times* bestselling author

NORA ROBERTS

**These fascinating cousins share a secret that's
been handed down through generations—a
secret that sets them apart....**

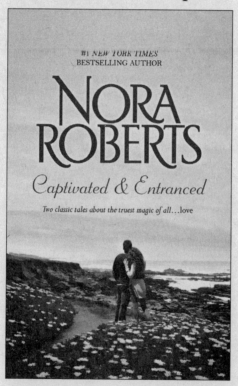

Available wherever books are sold!